Ink

Praise for Damien Walters Grintalis

"Damien Walters Grintalis writes with a distinct voice, yet one which contains whispers of Sturgeon, Bradbury and Ellison."

—Jamie Todd Rubin, author of *In the Cloud* and *SF Signal* contributor

"As soon as I read this one, I immediately wished that I thought of the idea — but if I had, I doubt I could have executed it half so well."

—Matthew Bennardo, co-editor of *Machine of Death* on "Like Origami in Water"

Ink

Damien Walters Grintalis

SAMHAIN
PUBLISHING

Samhain Publishing, Ltd.
11821 Mason Montgomery Rd., 4B
Cincinnati, OH 45249
www.samhainpublishing.com

Ink
Copyright © 2012 by Damien Walters Grintalis
Print ISBN: 978-1-61921-072-1
Digital ISBN: 978-1-61921-079-0

Editing by Don D'Auria
Cover by Scott Carpenter

First Samhain Publishing, Ltd. electronic publication: December 2012
First Samhain Publishing, Ltd. print publication: December 2012

Dedication

For Taylore and Ashton

(They know why.)

Acknowledgements

Although the act of writing is a solitary art, turning that writing into something other than pages of chaos is not. First of all, thank you to Don D'Auria and Samhain for liking *Ink* enough to want to publish it, and to the art department, for creating a gorgeous cover that made me shriek in delight.

To Linda Epstein, for plucking *Ink* from the slush pile, and to Mark McVeigh, for helping me add flesh on the right pages. To my beta readers: Ellen Collins, David McAfee, Jennifer Payne, and Sean Connell. To the Hellions and the Horror Hounds at Absolute Write. While the names might sound frightful, the people are anything but. To all my friends who've offered encouragement along the way. There are far too many of you to list, and I would never forgive myself if I forgot a name or two. You know who you are.

To my father, for gifting me with a love of books, and for taking me to see *Alien* one and a half times in the theater. To my mother, who I wish were here to see this happen. To Stephen King and Peter Straub, for scaring me to pieces when I was a child. To Christian and Hunter and the rest of the staff at Saints and Sinners in Fells Point.

To my children, the best kids a mom could have. To the babies, Jeremiah and Chloe, for making me smile. To my favorite brother (would that I had more than one so they could ponder over which one I meant), my sister-in-law and niece, and the rest of my family. And to my husband, for his endless support, encouragement, and love. Always and ever, babe. Always and ever.

And last but not least, to you, the reader. Thank you for taking this journey with me. I have, in the name of artistic license, made some alterations to places and such within Baltimore.

Chapter One

Topside

At first glance, nothing made the man in the tailored suit memorable—no cleft chin, no razor-sharp cheekbones, no scars. An ordinary face, an unremarkable man, albeit dressed in an expensive suit and a silk tie—the second-best part of being William, in his opinion. He doubted the previous owner, the real William, felt the same.

He moved with a hitching stride, a sort of low-slung walk as if unaccustomed to the fit of the pants. A far from ordinary gait. The city buzzed and hummed around him, but he paid it no mind; he had things to do.

Baltimore smelled of overflowing trashcans, stagnant water and dog excrement. Old, familiar smells, although it had been a long time since his last visit. He walked until he came to a row of brick buildings with darkened windows and a door with faded paint, a door a hundred passersby would never notice.

He did not bother to lock it behind him. Anyone who wandered in would find nothing at all if they were lucky, a bit of darkness and pain if they weren't. A narrow staircase with old, scuffed wooden stairs led up and up and up, and at the very top, another door swung open with a long, high-pitched creak.

"Had a girl and she sure was fine," he sang out in a deep, gravelly voice. "She was fine, fine, fine."

Once inside the room, his words echoed away. The floorboards were warped and stained, the wallpaper hung in tattered shreds and a smell lingered in the air, faint but somehow liquid. The stink of rot and ruin, of old dreams, broken screams and wicked, dirty little things.

With a sigh, he peeled off his suit and smiled a terrible smile. He was ash and cinder, pain and sorrow, and he was always clever.

Chapter Two

Ships in the Night

1

"Bitch." Jason whispered the word and took a drink from his beer. Beer, not a fancy "let's pretend we're literary thinkers" drink, not a Shelley-approved drink at all. He looked down at his left hand, smiling at the little stripe of fish-belly pale flesh across his finger. "Bitch," he repeated, and the word rolled off his tongue with unexpected, but welcome, ease.

He finished his beer, belched, and for one quick instant the words *I'm sorry* crept up, but he caught them before they came out. He caught them hard and shoved them down. No more sorry, no more "you can't buy that book" (complete with *the look*, all turned-up nose and narrowed eyes, because heaven forbid any husband of hers might be interested in a creepy tale or two), no more twelve dollar martinis, and the most important no of all?

No more Shelley.

Jason was the only customer in the bar. The bartender, a bored-looking twenty-something, wore a black T-shirt that displayed the slogan *Real Women Swallow*. A real class act, definitely not Shelley-approved. After giving Jason his beer, he sat back down on a stool behind the bar and opened up a paperback. A horror novel.

A television hung in the corner, its screen silent and dark. Not many people with a reason to drink at one in the afternoon on a

Tuesday, Jason guessed, but he didn't care. He had no interest in conversation or company; he wanted to consume copious amounts of impolite beer, stagger home and maybe puke on Shelley's side of the bed.

Jason had his third beer in hand when the sailor walked into the bar. Probably in his mid-fifties, with a fluffy gray halo of hair and several multi-colored tattoos on his long, muscular arms, but neither the hair nor the tattoos made Jason think sailor. The walk did. He moved with a strange rolling step more suited to a cartoon character. If Jason had been drunk, he would've laughed.

He used the big mirror hanging behind the bar to watch the sailor's progress; as he walked—rolled—closer, the lines on his face popped into view. Deep lines, as if someone had taken the dull edge of a knife to damp clay. The sailor rolled up to the bar, climbed up onto a stool four away from Jason's and with a thick, gravelly voice, a smoker's voice, asked for a beer. The bartender handed him the drink and went back to his book. After a few minutes, the sailor turned watery, pale green eyes toward Jason and raised his bottle. Jason did the same, very glad he'd held in the laugh. Those watery eyes weren't right somehow. The sailor gave Jason a long look before he turned back to his beer. Jason finished his third and ordered a fourth.

"I will take another one as well, and pay for them both," Sailor said.

"Thanks, man," Jason said.

Sailor replied with a nod.

Halfway through the fourth beer, Jason took a trip to the bathroom. On his way back, with a loose, swimmy feeling in his head, he noticed Sailor had moved over to the stool next to Jason's. A cold finger of dread traced its way down Jason's spine. He shook it off, blamed it on the alcohol and took his seat. This close, Sailor's eyes weren't the only thing off. He smelled...odd. Sort of a gray, ashy smell. Jason shook his head.

It must be the beer.

"You do not mind, do you?" Sailor asked.

"No."

"You look like a man who has had a rough day."

Sailor looked like a guy whose higher education had consisted of ropes and pulleys, but despite the growl in his voice, he didn't sound like one. His words came out formal and clipped, like a college professor. English, maybe, minus the tweed jacket and wire-rim glasses. The funny, off feeling disappeared. Jason smiled and took a swig from his bottle.

"My wife left me today."

"Let me guess, your best friend?"

Make that psychology.

"No," Jason said with a shake of his head. "Her best friend."

"Well, I am sorry."

"Don't be. Shelley was a—"

"Bitch?"

"You got it." Jason drained the last inch of beer in his bottle. It was quite funny when he thought long and hard about it, even if he didn't feel much like laughing. He didn't feel much of anything.

"Bartender, may we have two more?"

"Thanks again. I owe you one—well, two now."

"Do not worry about it. You can pay me later. So your wife left you and you are here. Celebrating?"

"Something like that."

Several beers later, Jason was riding a happy train wreck of intoxication. He couldn't quite follow the conversation anymore, and his words were well past the point of slurring into nonsense, but it didn't seem to matter. All was right in his world. No more Shelley.

"Well my friend, I must be going," Sailor said after he finished his beer. He climbed off the bar stool, his watery eyes sober. "Have you ever considered getting a tattoo?"

Jason blinked. Where had that come from? He thought they were talking about football, unless he'd missed a sentence or two, which, given the way his eyes couldn't focus on Sailor's face, wasn't really a surprise.

Sailor sighed, a deep, wet sigh that pushed out a small wave of smoke-scented breath. "A tattoo. Ink and skin?"

"No," Jason said, turning away from the lingering smell. They didn't allow smoking in bars anymore, a stupid law, but he didn't remember Sailor stepping outside.

"That is a shame. If you happen to change your mind, call me."

Sailor handed him a business card. When Jason tried to read it, the letters blurred together into one large, illegible smear of ink.

"It was a pleasure to meet you, Jason."

"Yeah, you too."

Sailor tapped Jason's upper arm twice, tipped his head forward in a nod, and rolled out of the bar.

2

Jason woke up with a headache the size of Texas and a sour taste in his mouth. When he tried to pick up his head to look at the clock, his brain said yes, but his body ignored the command. It wanted to sleep. He took a few deep breaths and tried again.

Liftoff.

He couldn't see the clock. That was bad. He couldn't see the clock because he was curled up on the bathroom floor next to the toilet. Even worse. And he was naked. That wasn't so bad, just odd. He pulled himself up with a groan, and his head screamed in some alien language filled with squeaks, screeches and weird little hitches in between the chaos. Why had he thought drowning his sorrow was a good thing?

He should be with Shelley on a beach in Cancun, a drink in his hand, on a nice little Wednesday through Sunday vacation getaway, and he would have been if not for her little announcement. But her announcement had changed his plans and his plans only. She and Nicole got the warm sand and clear water; he got the cold tile and the sour smell of vomit.

Great.

Using the edge of the sink for leverage, he managed to pull himself upright. Once his legs steadied, he splashed cold water on his face, avoiding the bleary-eyed reflection in the mirror, and dry swallowed several aspirin. The alien voices still chattered away, but a long shower turned their noise into something more manageable. He popped another aspirin, pulled on sweats and a T-shirt, and when the headache backed down to the size of Maryland, he realized it wasn't going to get any smaller, not without food and coffee.

The clock on his nightstand said 2:00 p.m. He couldn't remember the last time he'd slept that late or the last time he drank (or was allowed to drink) half as much as he did.

He found his jeans, underwear and one sock in the hallway and his polo shirt on the stairs. The stumble up the stairs was a half memory, but the final trip into the bathroom was lost to the drunk gods of fortune. On his way into the kitchen, he passed by his shoes, discarded in the dining room like old thoughts or unneeded husbands. His wallet and keys were on the kitchen table along with his other sock, which made no sense at all.

He vaguely recalled the taxi ride home. The driver ran half a dozen red lights, afraid Jason would throw up in his car. The struggle to get the key in the lock was a little blurry around the edges. He'd leaned up against the dining room wall next to the door into the kitchen to kick off his shoes, but how in the hell did his sock get back in the kitchen? Even if he took it off and pitched it over his shoulder, it would've landed on the floor. He'd have to be a magician to get his sock to veer over to the table. All things considered, the sock's placement was incidental, but it bugged him nonetheless.

He pushed it out of his mind, made coffee and opened the refrigerator. The contents were a dietician's wet dream—all organic, all healthy, all from a grocery store with high prices and employees with nose rings and tie-dyed shirts. Shelley insisted. He could eat whatever he wanted for lunch at work, but at home? Not a chance. Jason wanted something greasy and un-organic, like pizza. He grabbed his wallet to check for cash, and a white business card fell out face down onto the floor. When he bent down to pick it up, he almost fell on his face.

"Shit."

Okay, so he was more hung over than he wanted to admit. He grabbed the card and stood up, closing his eyes against a wave of dizziness. When it passed, he held up the card and frowned. It read *John S. Iblis, Tattoo Artist* in simple black lettering with no logo, no address, just the name and a local phone number. He tapped the card against his chin, and the memory of the sailor with the funny walk came back in a rush. He'd given him the card on his way out, when Jason was already deep into his drunk. Sailor had asked him if he'd ever thought of getting a tattoo. He'd said no.

He'd lied.

Not sure why. Maybe just the beer, or maybe because he hadn't thought about a tattoo in a long time. He'd wanted one when he was twenty, something big and dramatic like a skull or a snake. And then he met Shelley. She thought they were tacky, so he nixed the idea: she was cute and sophisticated, and he wanted to get in her pants. When he mentioned it again a few years later, Shelley gave him *the look*—her way of saying not on your life, buddy. They were married then, for better or worse, which meant Shelley made the rules and Jason followed them.

After that, the desire to get a tattoo got pushed back in the corner with all the other things he wanted but didn't get because Shelley said no. He flipped the card over and over in his hand. He *would* get a tattoo; Shelley couldn't bitch about it anymore. Maybe he'd get a motorcycle, too, and anything else on the Shelley list of nos. In fact, he'd make a list and check it twice, like the jolly fat man. Jason

18

grinned. He didn't have to go back to the office until Monday. He had five days of total freedom, and his headache didn't seem so important anymore. Five days to do whatever the hell he wanted, to do whatever Shelley would hate.

A little ink on the skin would be a perfect way to celebrate. Perfect and safe. A little money, a little blood and one hell of a boost to the ego. A fair exchange in Jason's mind. It wasn't like a tattoo carried the risk of death or mutilation.

What was the worst that could happen?

3

The phone rang three times, then an unmistakable voice kicked in with an apology for not being able to take his call. How early would someone have to start smoking to get a voice like that? Eleven? Ten? Maybe instead of a pacifier, his mother gave him a Marlboro.

Jason hung up without leaving a message. Despite the growl, Sailor spoke like a man of the world, a definite Alpha male. The voice made Jason feel small.

And a little afraid.

He turned on the television and propped his feet up on the coffee table. The headache poked and prodded, then slid down a little more, small enough to be ignored. Jason watched television until the sun started to fade from the sky, put his head back and fell asleep.

The shrill ring of his cell phone startled him out of a dream involving the new receptionist at the office. While he slept, the sun had disappeared, and the living room was dark except for the glow of the television. The display screen on his phone showed neither name nor number, only the words *Unknown Caller*. Jason wasn't on call this week, but old habits were just that, and he hit the answer button.

"Hello?"

"Who is this?" a familiar voice asked.

Goosebumps broke out on Jason's arms and for half a second, he contemplated hanging up the phone. "This is Jason. I met you at the bar last night."

"Yes, Jason of the newly departed wife. How may I help you?"

"I was thinking about the tattoo."

Sailor chuckled. "Just thinking?"

"No, I want one."

"Are you certain?"

Maybe.

"Yes."

"Sure this is not just a little get back at the wifey?" Sailor's voice was amused. A little mocking. A little Alpha.

"Yes, I'm sure. More than sure, actually," he said. And he knew exactly what he wanted. Not a skull or a snake, nothing quite so prosaic.

"Since you are more than sure, when would you like to come to the shop?"

"What about tomorrow?"

Before he changed his mind, before he listened to the Shelley-voice in his head and chickened out.

"Let me check my appointments."

Jason rubbed the sleep from his eyes while he waited.

"How about 6:00 p.m.?"

"Okay."

"Have you a pen?"

"A pen?"

"Yes, for the address." His voice held the mocking tone again.

"Hold on," Jason said. He went into the kitchen and grabbed a magnetized notepad and pen from the refrigerator. "Got one."

"Good. 1303 Shakespeare Street. In Fells Point."

"Okay, cool."

"I will see you at six tomorrow evening. Please do not be late."

"Okay."

Jason waited for a reply, but the phone pushed out a heavy silence. No breathing, no background noise, nothing. He was ready to press the *end call* button when he heard an odd muffled sound, an inexplicable wet sound that reminded him of sheets flapping on a clothesline on a windy day. Finally it slid away with a serpentine hiss, followed by a low chuckle, then a tiny, tinny click as Sailor disconnected the call.

4

The sky was a vivid blue streaked with pale clouds. A warm spring night perfect for long walks along the harbor, soft whispers in tangled sheets, and definitely perfect for a little ink on the skin. For Jason, anyway.

Jason drove past the space where the tattoo shop should be three times. Three-story buildings with gently sloping roofs lined both sides of the narrow street. Old brick, tall windows with grimy glass, doors that led out directly onto the sidewalk instead of the typical Baltimore marble stoop. 1301 Shakespeare Street was a café with a colorful sign above the door, 1305 an empty space with a *For Rent* sign in the front window. At first he thought he'd missed the shop and turned the car around in the middle of the street. He slowed down but still saw nothing. A white car came up fast behind him, and the owner tapped its horn once. Jason turned around again, stopping with the back half of his car in front of the café and the front half in front of the empty building.

1303 Shakespeare Street did not exist.

"What the hell?"

I know I wrote the address down correctly. It has to be here somewhere.

A car pulled out three cars up, and Jason took the spot. He got out and walked down to where 1303 should be, his footsteps echoing on the pavement. A soft wind, carrying the scent of pizza, beer and cheap perfume, pushed his hair back from his forehead.

1305 didn't look like it had been empty for long—the front window was clean and the *For Rent* sign new. The café was closed. The two buildings were right next to each other, snug as two cigarettes in a pack and in between? Nothing.

Oh come on, my eyes are playing tricks somehow. Unless...

Jason shoved his hands in his pockets and walked back to his car with slow steps. Sailor didn't seem like the kind of guy who would pull someone's leg for the hell of it. Another breeze lifted his hair; this time it held a trace of cigarette smoke and rotting garbage.

"You are early."

Jason jumped. Sailor stood a few feet away, dressed in dark pants and a long-sleeved shirt with his fluffy hair slicked back neatly and a black briefcase in one hand, looking more like a door-to-door salesman than a sailor.

"Well, nothing to be done about that now," he said.

"I'm sorry, I can wait in my car."

Sailor removed a handkerchief and dabbed at his eyes. "No need for that. Come."

The shirt concealed his tattoos, but Sailor couldn't hide the walk. It was even more noticeable when Jason fell in step beside him. The gait wasn't uneven but odd, as if his hips rolled forward first and his legs followed along for the ride. Maybe an old injury or hip replacement surgery. Sailor said nothing as they walked, just hummed a song under his breath until they stopped in front of the two buildings.

"Are you sure you are ready?" he asked, and his voice had that mocking lilt again.

Jason nodded.

"Well then, shall we go in?" He walked between the buildings and

Jason blinked. A plain wooden door with faded paint and a brass handle darkened with age swam into view. The door, set back several feet from the brick front of the buildings, might have been black at one time, but the paint had faded to a dusty gray. A weathered sign on the side read 1303. All but the last number hung with a crooked slant.

Sailor tucked the handkerchief into his shirt pocket and pushed the door open. "Follow me."

Jason did.

5

Jason stepped through the door and swallowed hard. Dim yellow lighting revealed a narrow staircase with well-worn steps and water-stained walls of pale gray. The sour smell of mold hung heavy in the air, a thick, wet smell that clung to the back of his throat. The faded wallpaper held traces of odd swirling designs like faces—screaming faces. Jason traced his fingertips across the surface, pulling his hand away as one of the swirls appeared to shift closer into view.

He turned his eyes forward and focused on Sailor's back as they walked the rest of the way up. He wondered what would happen if he touched the wall again. Would he feel firm wall and wallpaper, or would his hand slip beneath the surface to touch the cold skin of those trapped inside? Jason kept his hands down, as far away from the walls as possible. Sailor, looking over his shoulder, chuckled, then hummed his tune and rolled his walk.

They came to a narrow landing and another door, the paint little more than a washed-out stain of reddish-brown. When Sailor turned the knob, the door swung open with a high-pitched creak to reveal a dark room. The tiny hairs on the back of Jason's neck stood up. Not just dark, but black—the light from the hallway stopped at the doorframe. Jason's hands clenched into twin fists.

"Hold on, let me turn on the light before we go in. I do not want you to trip and fall. You would sue me, then I would be done for."

Sailor disappeared into the darkness.

Jason's heart beat heavy in his chest as he looked into the darkness and saw nothing—no shadowy movements, no suggestion of shapes. He should at least hear Sailor moving around, especially with his walk, but the room kept its silence well, leaving him with only the smell of dust, old walls and neglect for company while he waited.

Shelley would hate this entire scenario. She wouldn't find it eerie. She'd find it offensive. The old hallway, the faded paint and the smell whispered words like dirty needles, hepatitis and abandoned hope. Jason thought maybe he should reconsider his hasty decision. He forced his fingers to uncurl from his palms. Hellish nightmares did not exist, and if they did, he was quite sure they didn't live in Baltimore.

Still, when the light turned on, he jumped.

"Well, do not stand out there all night. Come in."

6

The room was bright white and antiseptic with the bite of alcohol lingering in the air. A shock compared to the tired, drab staircase. Jason blinked a few times, and all thoughts of nightmares disappeared. "Wow," he said.

Spotless white walls picked up and magnified the overhead lighting. He could almost see his reflection in the gleam of the dark wood floor. A long table with metal legs stood in the center of the room, next to a smaller table covered with plastic bottles, rolls of paper towels, a tattoo gun and small pots of ink; a chair with a padded seat and a stool sat on the opposite side. Sailor put his briefcase on the floor and bent over the small table.

Jason looked at a series of framed prints on the far wall. "Is that your work?"

"Yes, a few of my original designs. Look closer if you want. They will not bite."

Jason let out a low whistle when he got close to the first. Inside the old wood frame, a red-eyed dragon with scaly, pebbled skin reached up and out. Jason smiled and leaned closer. Sailor's work was extraordinary. He was an artist in every sense of the word, despite his chosen medium of needles and flesh.

Jason walked with slow steps past the second framed image, a fairy with green wings and a long sword, then to the third, a long-legged pinup girl in a sexy pink nightgown with something hidden behind her back, both in scarred, chipped frames.

"How do you come up with your ideas?"

"My customers tell me what they want, and I use my imagination to create something that fits."

The next frames, also old, held images of a sleek black cat with claws extended, a grizzly bear with its mouth opened in a snarl, its teeth and muzzle dripping with blood, and a serpent coiled around a bleeding cross.

"What if someone doesn't know what they want?"

"People always know what they want," Sailor said. "Even if they do not think they do. I have helped many make their decisions. Customers are never disappointed when they leave this room."

The last frame, an empty one with the remnants of sticky adhesive from a price tag marring the top corner, hung on the wall next to a tall, narrow doorway covered with a dark cloth. No light peeked around the curtain, and a faint trace of dust speckled the bottom edge—the only evidence of dust in the room at all. As Jason turned away, the sound of small feet pattered across the floor. He paused, waiting for a mouse to emerge, but the curtain remained still, and the sound ceased.

Sailor finished setting up and sat on the stool with his hands on his upper thighs. "Sit here," he said, indicating the chair beside him. "Have you given any thought to what you want?"

Jason sat down with a small smile on his face. "A griffin."

An easy decision, once he'd thought about it. Easy and perfect. Six months ago, Shelley went away for a girl's weekend with Nicole. Not long after she left, he went to the bookstore and bought a paperback.

He couldn't remember the title or the author or even the story, but he remembered the cover and the creature on it—a griffin with gold wings and green eyes. He read the book in one sitting, and the image of the griffin stayed with him for weeks, long after the story faded from his mind.

He'd tucked the book away on a shelf; a few weeks later, he'd found an empty spot in its place. When he asked Shelley if she'd seen it, she'd given him a cruel smile that said what he'd already known. Shelley wouldn't be able to throw this one away, and the tattoo would serve as a promise to himself—never again would he give up control over his own self.

"Ah, a griffin. One of my favorite things. Powerful creatures," Sailor said.

"Good thing they're not real, right?"

"Yes, quite a good thing. I imagine they would cause considerable trouble."

Jason laughed. "And I'd like it to have green eyes and golden wings, please."

Sailor lifted the briefcase, balancing it on his legs, started to hum the same unfamiliar tune and pulled out a sketchpad and pencil. "Where do you want the griffin?"

"My upper arm. The left one," Jason said.

"Good choice. Would you like the wings outstretched or back?"

"Outstretched, definitely."

"Black and gray or color?"

The cadence of Sailor's speech was soothing, completely at odds with its rough smoker's growl. This close, the lines on his face resembled crevices or vast bottomless canyons that spoke of many years, but more than the lines, his very skin pushed out an innate sense of old age. For the first time, Jason realized that the odd, ashy smell did not come from a cigarette, but something darker and thicker—strange, yet not repugnant.

"Color."

Sailor's pencil made short, scraping noises on the paper. "Menacing or simply imposing?"

"Um, imposing."

"Anything in your griffin's talons?"

"My ex? Just kidding."

Sailor laughed softly, but his watery eyes were serious as his hand moved across the paper. He finally lifted the pencil, nodded once and flipped the sketchpad around. "Is this the sort of griffin you had in mind?"

Jason's voice vanished as he marveled at the intricacy of the design. The griffin appeared ready to step out of the page. Ten times— no, a hundred times better than the cover of the book. Its wings were outstretched, each individual feather drawn with precision. From the razor-sharp points of the talons and beak to the tuft of fur at the end of its tail, it was perfect. He wouldn't have believed anyone capable of drawing that much detail in such a short time if he hadn't seen it himself.

Jason swallowed and found his words. "Wow. It's beautiful."

"Well, if you are going to have something permanently etched into your skin, it should be a damn good something." Sailor pulled the handkerchief from his pocket and wiped his eyes. "Allergies," he said, tucking it back in.

"Will the tattoo have that much detail?"

"No, it will have far more. This is just a rough sketch, after all. My skill with the needle and ink far surpasses that with pencil and paper. I believe you will be quite surprised with the end result."

"I'm almost afraid to ask. How much will this cost?"

"Ah, the price. Yes, there is always a price." Sailor turned his eyes down to the sketch and hummed his tune again. "I am quite sure we will be able to do this in one sitting, so I will give you a small discount. Say, four hundred dollars."

Jason blinked in surprise. The price was far less than he'd anticipated once he'd seen the sketch, and he'd been worried he hadn't pulled enough cash from the bank machine. He had a credit card but hadn't thought to ask Sailor if he even accepted them. "Sounds good," he said, and fished the money from his wallet.

Sailor pocketed the cash without glancing at the bills. "I almost forgot." He opened his briefcase again and rummaged through its contents. "I need your signed permission. The city frowns upon tattoo artists proceeding without permission."

He pulled a sheet of paper from the briefcase and handed it over. Jason didn't know what a standard tattoo consent form looked like, but this one had Sailor's name and address at the top center. After that, a bunch of legalese stated he was older than eighteen, any and all risks were assumed by him, not the tattoo shop, and he granted permission for Sailor to use the image created for marketing purposes. Jason lowered the pen and stopped just before the tip touched the paper. A faint shadow of writing, spidery and ornate, appeared underneath the typeface. Odd. He looked up to find Sailor watching with an anticipatory light in his watery eyes.

Jason looked back down at the paper but saw nothing strange. It must have been a trick of the light. Or something.

After he signed the form and handed it back, Sailor smiled. "If you ever change your mind about the tattoo, come back and see me. Tattoo removal is also one of my specialties."

"Removal?"

"Yes. You would be surprised. Sometimes people change their minds. Sometimes they decide a tattoo was not the smartest decision to make. Especially a tattoo with this kind of detail. The devil is all in the details. You are warned—the removal is painful, and it leaves one hell of a scar." He gave Jason a quick wink. "So," he said as he put the paper back into his briefcase. "Shall we begin?"

7

An hour later, Jason sat white-knuckled with beads of sweat on his forehead. He'd overheard one of his co-workers say a tattoo felt like a cat scratch, but at the moment, he was only inclined to agree if said cat was a tiger.

"Still with me?"

"Yes," Jason managed between clenched teeth.

"Not so good with pain, are you?"

"Guess not."

"The pain will not last forever," Sailor said. From time to time, he stopped to take out his handkerchief and wipe his eyes, a quick little lift and dab. "I think this might be my best work ever."

Each time the needle touched Jason's skin, it left a red-hot jolt behind. Jason looked down, surprised that Sailor almost had the outline complete. The tattoo gun buzzed and hummed, the sound echoing in the air when Sailor paused to dip the needles in the ink. The smells of ash, blood and ink mixed together and hovered in the air—a dark perfume of art in progress. Jason swayed in the chair as bright spots of light danced chaos in front of his eyes.

Sailor pulled the gun away. "I suggest we get you something to eat before you pass out."

The pain in Jason's arm receded to a tiny throb of irritated flesh. Before he could speak, Sailor rolled his way to the back of the room, pushed through the dark cloth, and returned a few moments later, humming under his breath, with a bottle of soda in one hand and a chocolate bar in the other.

"Here. When you finish these, we shall start again."

"Okay."

Sailor wiped at his eyes as Jason took the first bite of chocolate. "So what will be your next act of newfound independence? A motorcycle perhaps?"

The chocolate lodged in Jason's throat, and he took a drink from the bottle. "I'm not sure yet."

"Perhaps a girl? Get yourself laid well and proper? Perhaps visit a strip club and bestow single dollar bills upon women with plastic breasts and artificial smiles?" He nodded as Jason blushed.

"I thought so. You look like a man who has been deprived." He winked, and a tear ran from the corner of one eye to his cheek.

Lift. Dab.

Jason swallowed another bite of chocolate. "Shelley, my wi—my ex, hates tattoos and motorcycles and thinks strip clubs are practically the devil's den."

Sailor chuckled. "Doubtful, although many a young man has gotten into trouble within their walls. How long were you married?"

"Seven years—well, almost eight."

"That long? You must have married young."

"Yeah, we did."

"Ah, the folly of youth. How unfortunate, or perhaps not, since Shelley's misdeeds led you to me."

"Have you ever been married?"

A deep peal of laughter rang through the room. "No, no. Never. I am not the marrying kind, as they say. Since you are finished, shall we begin again?" He plucked the empty wrapper from Jason's hand.

"Sure."

When Jason felt the bite of the tattoo gun again, his arm sang out in protest; he half expected to look down and see his skin hanging in ribbons of raw flesh. The coppery smell of blood rose up, strong enough to taste.

"I assume the change in your marital status was quite unexpected?"

"Yes."

"Well, not to worry. A young man like yourself will find a new friend soon enough, and your wife will become a distant memory."

"Maybe."

"Oh, I am certain of it."

He whispered the last so low, Jason could barely hear the words over the steady hum of the tattoo gun.

Just a little pain.

It wasn't the end of the world, and the tattoo was going to be unbelievable when Sailor finished. The needle bit, then lifted, and Sailor wiped away blood.

"Yes, I think this will be one of my masterpieces."

He started to hum, and his hand moved faster across Jason's skin. The scratch no longer belonged to a tiger but to a creature with razor-tipped claws. Jason closed his eyes, breathed in and out, counting to five each time, and listened to Sailor's wordless tune. When Sailor lifted the tattoo gun away from his skin for the last time, Jason shook out his cramped fingers, unsure how much time had passed.

"See, that was not so bad, was it?" Sailor took out his handkerchief.

Lift. Dab.

"Let me clean it up a bit, then you can take a look."

Sailor ran a moistened cloth across the tattoo, and Jason held his breath as his skin shrieked. Sweat ran in a cold trail down the center of his spine.

"Almost done," Sailor said.

Jason didn't exhale until Sailor took the cloth, now tinged pink with his blood, away and held up a small mirror.

"What do you think?"

"Holy shit."

It was more than unbelievable, so much more. The creature, its feathers and fur done in shades of amber, gold and tawny brown, looked ready to spring up from his skin. Its beak and claws were pale but tipped with dark, its eyes a piercing green, and the massive chest leaned forward and up—regal, haughty, and proud.

"Judging by your expression, you are pleased?"

"Very."

"I told you it would be even better than the sketch."

"Yeah, you did."

"Good. Now, I am going to put a bandage over it—"

"Can you wait a minute?"

Sailor narrowed his eyes. "Yes?"

"I want to take a picture of it first, before you put the bandage on." Jason pulled out his cell phone and took a quick picture while Sailor watched with an amused expression. When he slid the phone back into his pocket, Sailor gave him a crisp nod and covered the tattoo with a gauze pad.

"Leave the bandage on tonight as it may bleed for a few hours. I have an ointment for you to use three times a day for a week, which will aid in the healing process. It should take two weeks, at most, to heal completely, and during that time no hot tubs, swimming pools, or soaking in the tub. Itching and peeling, especially with this amount of detail, is quite normal, but it will pass. Have you any other questions?"

"I don't think so."

"Then I think we are finished," Sailor said, reaching out, oddly enough, with his left hand.

Jason shook it, and an odd tingle raced up his arm, all the way up to the tattoo, then disappeared. Sailor smiled, wiped his eyes again and handed Jason a white, unlabeled tube.

"Thank you. I mean really, thanks a lot. This is amazing," Jason said.

"I am sure you will be the envy of all your friends. Now if you do not mind, I have another client who will be arriving soon, and he is a very private sort of person." Sailor walked in his odd way and opened the door.

"Oh, okay. Sorry. Thanks, I mean it." He turned to say thank you one last time, but Sailor had already shut the door. Jason walked down the staircase, ignoring the strange wallpaper. His arm burned under the bandage, but he didn't care. It wasn't just a tattoo.

It was a work of art.

8

Behind the door, John S. Iblis smiled, raising the handkerchief to his leaking eyes. He had not lied to Jason. The tattoo was indeed one of his best.

9

Sitting in his car, Jason sent the picture to his co-worker and friend, Brian. The response came only minutes later.

"That's fucking awesome. Where did you find a tattoo guy in Cancun?"

Jason replied with a short message. "Not in Cancun."

"Why not?"

Jason laughed while he typed his response. "Shelley and I split up." *Split up* was far better than *Shelley left me*, even though it came down to the same damn thing. She'd finally gathered up all her pretensions and carried them out the door.

And I think I'm okay with it. A lot better than okay.

He flexed his left arm. The bandage crinkled, but the tape held. His skin gave a small twinge of protest, not horrible, yet enough to make its presence known.

If he wanted to be truthful, he wondered why Shelley stayed with him for as long as she did. In theory, he could have left her, but theory wasn't always realistic. Maybe the tattooed Jason could have left her.

But the Jason before, could he have left? He pushed the uncomfortable thought way down.

Brian wrote back. "Sorry, dude. I'm at McAfee's. Want to join me?"

"Sure."

I can't believe I did it.

He smiled and looked down at his arm once more before he drove away.

10

Jason walked into McAfee's, a bar and restaurant at the opposite end of Fells Point, and found Brian at a table in the back, along with Vic, the newest employee on the team. Jason and Vic were friendly but not exactly friends; he and Brian, on the other hand, had known each other since college.

Hidden speakers pumped classic rock into the air. The passage of twenty years' worth of customers had walked the shine off the wood floor, the tables were scuffed and scratched, and the bar top was marked with old cigarette burns and water stains. Tourists often passed the place by, in favor of the flashier places right off the water, but McAfee's served some of the best burgers in the city and the prices were cheap.

"So what the fuck happened?" Brian asked. The body spray he used, to "attract the ladies", lingered in the air, though only a ghost of its usual potency.

Jason shook his head and pushed a plate of half-eaten nachos out of the way. "I was getting ready to pack, and she said she wanted to talk."

A cute blonde with a tiny tank top and low-rise jeans passed by, smiling at Jason, and he smiled back.

"Just like that?"

Jason nodded and ordered a beer, a burger and fries from their waitress. "Just like that."

He had known by the look in Shelley's eyes she wanted more than a quick little talk and once she started, her words sped up until they were an incomprehensible blur. After the words, she left with her suitcases in hand, without a look back over her shoulder. For once, she didn't want to stay and watch him bleed. Or maybe she feared there wouldn't be any blood at all. Maybe she knew that last stick of the knife might not have been as painful as she hoped.

"You're better off," Brian said. "She was a bitch. She's had your balls in a sling for years, man."

"Yeah, I know."

Brian had no idea. It had been more than a sling. She'd had them in a set of vise grips and whenever he stepped a little out of his expected Jason-place, she squeezed them tight.

The waitress brought Jason's beer; he winced at the quick sting of skin against bandage as he took the bottle from her hand.

Vic pushed his glasses up on his nose. "So, are you going to show it to us or what?"

"It's still all bloody. You probably won't be able to see the detail."

"Big deal, come on." Brian said.

Jason grinned. "The picture wasn't enough, huh?"

"No fucking way, man. Stop being a tease. I want to see it in person."

With the edge of his fingernail, Jason loosened the surgical tape holding the bandage in place and peeled it back. Blood speckled the bottom of the white gauze, but the tattoo itself emerged clean.

"That's fucking amazing," Brian said.

"Holy shit," Vic said at the same time. "How long did that take?"

"About two and a half hours."

"Bullshit," Brian said.

"No bullshit."

"Are you serious?" Vic asked, his eyes wide.

"Dead serious. The guy worked fast."

"No way," Vic said. "My brother got one with half the detail. It took four hours in two sittings."

"I'm serious."

"Was it flash or a custom design?" Brian asked.

"I told him what I wanted, and he sketched it on paper first, then he started with the gun. The picture looked good, but not half as good as it turned out."

"Damn," Brian said. "Hold your arm up. I want to see it better."

Jason held his arm over the table.

Brian whistled. "That's crazy good. It looks like it's alive. Where'd you get it done?"

"Over on Shakespeare Street. I met him Tuesday night at Schaefer's Pub and—"

"Wait." Vic leaned forward. "You just met the guy Tuesday, and you let him do your tattoo?"

"Yeah, but I saw examples of his work at the shop before I let him start."

"When you got there?"

"Yes."

Vic shook his head. "You hadn't even seen his work when you went to the shop?"

"No. I mean, I saw his tattoos—"

"That doesn't mean *he* did them," Vic said.

Brian frowned. "Jason, are you crazy? Since when did you want a tattoo anyway?"

"I wanted one a long time ago."

When I was Jason, not just Shelley's husband.

Understanding flashed in Brian's eyes; he clinked the neck of his beer bottle against Jason's. "To freedom, man."

36

"That's a great tattoo."

Jason turned. The blonde in the tank top stood next to their table, looking down at his arm with a smile on her face. "Thank you. I just had it done," he said.

"Can I take a closer look?"

"Sure. Go ahead."

"Wow, the detail is really impressive. My ex-boyfriend is a tattoo artist, but his work doesn't even come close. I love the shading in the wings and the way your guy gave him eagle's talons on his forelegs. I've seen a lot of designs with just lion's paws. They don't look as good that way, in my opinion. I kind of have a thing for griffins." She straightened up and lifted the hem of her shirt. "My ex did this one." The griffin tattooed on her side paled in comparison to Sailor's work. She gave Jason an even bigger smile and pushed her shirt back down. "I'm Mitch."

"Jason."

Mitch sat down in the empty chair. "Who did your work?"

"His name is John. He has a shop on Shakespeare Street," Jason said, folding the bandage back down over the tattoo. "Do you want a drink?"

"Sure. Shakespeare Street? Is it a new shop?"

"I don't think so, but it might be." Jason waved the waitress over and smiled when Mitch ordered a beer, not a candy-colored drink with a stupid name. When the waitress came back with his food and her beer, Mitch took the bottle and moved her chair close enough so the ends of her hair brushed against his forearm. She smelled like coconut, but not perfume, maybe shampoo. Shelley had worn enough perfume for two women, but Mitch's coconut smell didn't make his eyes water or his throat itch like Shelley's had. And she was cute, definitely cuter than Shelley. Not Hollywood starlet beautiful but girl next door pretty, with blue eyes, a slight gap between her front teeth, and an old scar over one eyebrow, like a comma tilted on its side.

She helped him finish his fries, and the four of them talked about nothing and everything in between. Mitch worked in a hair salon and told stories about some of her clients, Brian did his best impersonation of their boss but kept it going too long as usual and Vic told bad jokes that resulted in a lot of frowns and much less laughter.

A little after eleven, Vic and Brian said their goodbyes. On his way out, Brian leaned close enough for Jason to smell the beer on his breath. "She's hot and she likes you. Call me tomorrow."

Not long after that, Mitch hid a yawn behind her hand. "Well, I should head out. I had a long day, and I didn't plan on staying out so late."

"Are you okay to drive?"

"I walked. My place is close. How about you? Are you okay?"

Silence stretched out between them. Jason looked into her blue eyes and thought about lying. He'd had three beers and food. He was fine to drive, but he liked the way she smiled. He liked it a lot. "Maybe I should walk you home," he said.

She smiled and put her hand on top of his. "I'd like that."

They left the bar, and halfway down the block she stepped a little closer so their arms were almost touching.

"Do you have to work in the morning?" she asked.

"No, I'm off the rest of the week."

"My first appointment isn't until ten tomorrow."

Jason feared reading anything into her words. Maybe she was just making conversation. "I plan to sleep until noon."

"Lucky you."

Mitch stopped in front of a narrow rowhouse with shuttered windows and a marble stoop. "This is my place."

"We—"

She cut off his words with a quick kiss, her mouth soft against his. "I don't normally do this kind of thing, but do you want to come in?"

He did. He wanted to go in, kiss her again, and strip off all her clothes. Instead, he lifted her hand and kissed the back of it even while a voice in his head called him a stupid fool. "I'll be honest. I'd like to, but I'd rather wait."

Mitch smiled. "Okay." She rummaged in her purse and pulled out a business card. "My number is on here."

Jason pulled out his wallet and did the same. She leaned forward and kissed the corner of his mouth. He breathed in her coconut smell, his body protesting his decision.

"I like you, Jason. I hope you call me."

"I will," Jason said, and he meant it.

After she went inside, a quick click let him know she'd locked the door. He turned around and walked back in the direction of his car. He would call and ask her out. Dinner, maybe, but someplace nicer than McAfee's.

11

Jason awoke in shadowy darkness, confused by the sound of scratching. The red letters of his clock glowed like ghosts in the room—3:35 a.m. He rolled over on his back, raised his arms above his head and listened, but the house replied only with silence. He closed his eyes, almost asleep when the sound came again.

Scrrrrtch.

A small, insistent sound. The sound a cat made when it pawed at the door to be let in or out, if said cat had its claws extended. Jason sat up and pushed his hair off his forehead. He'd forgotten to close the blinds, and the streetlamps outside cast a dim light into his room.

Scrrrrtch.

This time it sounded close and angry. He didn't have a cat, and his bedroom was on the second floor. It didn't make sense. Only half awake, he pushed back the blanket, swung his legs over the side and walked across the room, the wood floor cool beneath his feet. He looked out the window at the empty street. No people, no cats. He looked under the bed. Nothing there either, just the long expanse of dark wood floor and a few dust bunnies that had escaped the vacuum cleaner.

Jason sat back down on the bed. The half-asleep part of his mind beckoned; the half-awake part said find the damn cat and chase him away.

Scrrrrtch. Scrrrrtch.

Jason looked down at the bandage on his arm. Dried blood had turned the fabric stiff. He should take it off, use the ointment and put on a fresh bandage, but—

Scrrrrtch.

Jason froze. It sounded as if the scratching noise came from underneath the bandage.

Impossible.

He shook his arm, waited a few minutes, then shook it again, but the scratching noise did not return. Writing it off as a trick of the night, house-noise made too vivid in the shadows, he went back to bed. It had been a stupid thought, anyway. The only thing underneath the bandage was the tattoo.

12

The next morning, Jason took the bandage off and covered the tattoo with ointment, wincing when his fingers touched the still-tender skin. He spent almost ten minutes staring at the detail. The griffin's talons looked sharp enough to scratch and tear open flesh, the beak hooked and ready to strike. Each feather of its wings, Jason's favorite part, ended in a golden brown the color of wet sand. They appeared soft enough to touch; real enough to spread wide and take off at a moment's notice.

After coffee, he thought about calling his parents to break the news about his marriage. His dad would be fine. He'd never been fond of Shelley. But his mom? A different story. She loved Shelley, and love made it easy to turn a blind eye to a person's faults. He knew that all too well. His parents were retired and liked to go on day trips, so they might not even be home, but he called anyway, happy when his dad answered the phone.

"Jason, I didn't expect to hear from you until you got back."

"Well..."

"How is Mexico?"

"I'm not in Mexico. Shelley went without me."

His father cleared his throat. "Why would she do that?"

Jason didn't bother to lie. "She left me." He walked into the living room and sat down on the sofa.

"She what?" His dad's voice turned hard.

"Yeah, she left me and not just for a separation or anything like that. We're done."

He wouldn't tell them about Nicole. He didn't want his parents to hate Shelley, not really, but he had a small, niggling fear they might take her side.

"You okay, son?"

Jason smiled. No, his dad would never take Shelley's side. Not unless he did something terrible like hit her, and his dad knew he wouldn't. His mom ran the ship, but his dad always knew how Jason was on the inside. After he told his parents he'd asked Shelley to marry him, his dad pulled him aside and asked if he was sure he wanted to get married. Jason said yes, but he thought his dad knew something was a little off about Shelley. Something a little too controlling. He didn't push, though. He'd just nodded and said "Okay, son."

"Yeah, I'm fine. It wasn't really a surprise. Things have been kind of...rough for a while. I didn't want to say anything and get you both upset. It's not like you could do anything about it."

"No, these things happen. Have you talked to a lawyer yet?"

"Not yet. I have to find one."

"Make sure you find one soon. I don't want to see you get screwed over. Thank God you didn't have any kids."

His dad needn't have worried about that; Shelley refused to even think about having children. Ever.

"I know."

A small silence, then his dad sighed. "Oh Christ, your mother."

"Yeah, I know. I'm not looking forward to telling her, that's for sure. She's not going to take the news like you. I guess I can't bribe you to tell her for me, can I?"

"Don't think so, son. I'll go get her—she's in the other room sewing or something like that. No matter what, remember, I'm here for you, okay?"

"I appreciate it, Dad."

"And don't worry. Things will just get better for you from here on out."

The phone made a soft thud. Jason heard muted voices, then his mom's raised in alarm.

"Jason?"

"Hi, Mom."

"What's wrong? Why aren't you in Cancun? Where is Shelley? Is one of you hurt?"

Jason knew she had her hand up, waving it around as if pushing smoke away from her face. She did it whenever she got upset.

"Mom, calm down. Nobody's hurt. It's just—"

"What? What's wrong?"

"Well—"

"What did you do?"

Jason tapped his fingers on the coffee table. "Nothing, okay? Shelley and I split up."

"Did you say what I think you said?"

"Ye—"

"This isn't funny, Jason."

He knew she'd moved her waving hand to her hip. Pretty soon she'd exhale through pursed lips and shake her head.

"It's not a joke. Really, it isn't. We split up. Things have been rough—"

"What did you do?"

The same question again. Great. Of course his mom assumed he'd done something. He knew she would. He didn't do anything. He did *everything*. Everything Shelley wanted and then some, but in the end, none of it mattered. She'd wanted something more, and he wasn't convinced it had anything to do with Nicole at all.

Shelley grew up in an area of town known for its unkempt yards, alcoholism and teenage mothers. A place where dental hygiene was a foreign word and education a necessary evil until the legal dropout age. Her mother had worked odd jobs when sober, and not at all when she fell into the bottle. They'd relied on the support of her endless string of boyfriends, each one a bigger loser than the last. Shelley's own dad split when she and her older brother were still in diapers, and her mother had three more kids after that, all with different fathers.

When Shelley turned eighteen, she left home, cut her family out of her life and reinvented herself from top to tail. And she never stopped. She piled on one pretension after another until she ended up nothing more than a caricature of everything she wanted to be. The happiness she thought she'd find always hovered one step away and it turned her bitter, spiteful and cruel. Oddly enough, despite her distrust of mothers in general, she loved Jason's, but she treated his dad as if he were an afterthought.

"I'm telling you the truth. I didn't do anything," he said.

"Is Shelley there? Let me talk to her."

"No, she isn't here, she went to Mexico."

"Without you?"

"Yes, without me."

"When she gets back, you need to talk to her. You need to work it out."

"She left me," Jason said. "There's nothing to work out. It's over."

His mom exhaled heavily into the phone. He could almost hear her head shake.

"Jason, this doesn't make sense. She loves you."

No, she doesn't. And I don't love her, either. Not real love anyway.

"Mom—"

"I'll talk to her when she gets back. It has to be a mistake. Maybe she just needs a little time away. Your brother and Eve split up for a few weeks, and they got back together. Their marriage is stronger than ever."

"This isn't like that. This is for good." And Ryan's marriage wasn't stronger than ever; he and Eve still had problems, big ones. His mother just refused to see them.

"You can't say that, Jason."

"Yes, I can. It really is over. It's not a bad thing, okay? Things have been horrible."

His mom fell silent, but it didn't last long. "Come for dinner Sunday night. We want to see you. I'll make lasagna."

And she would try to make him see the error of his ways. It was pointless to argue with her, though.

"Okay, I'll come over on Sunday."

"I love you, Jason, and everything will be fine. I know it will."

He had a new tattoo and a date on Saturday night with Mitch; things couldn't get much better.

13

On Saturday at seven o'clock, Jason pulled up in front of Mitch's house and knew his sweaty palms had nothing to do with the warm weather. She opened her front door before he had the chance to knock and for a long moment he couldn't speak, just stare. She wore a simple black dress, which covered more than it revealed, but his voice ran away and hid in awe.

"Hi," she said finally, her mouth curved up into a smile.

"You look beautiful," he said.

"Thank you. You said to dress nice, I hope this is okay."

So much better than okay.

"It's perfect."

She smiled when he opened the car door for her. "So, are you going to tell me where we're going?"

"And ruin the surprise? Nope."

"So how do I know if I'm overdressed?"

"You're not. Not at all."

"Can you give me at least a hint?"

"I hope you're hungry."

She gave his arm a gentle poke. "That's not a hint at all."

"What can I say? It's all I got."

"Tease."

When they pulled up to the restaurant on East Franklin Street, a place well known for its steak, pine-nut cake, and impeccable service, her eyebrows raised and she twisted her hands together.

"You're kidding, right?"

"I wouldn't joke about a place like this," Jason said.

Once inside, they sat on a cushioned bench to wait for their table. Dark red glass lamps hung down from the low ceiling, casting a warm glow. Beneath the voices of the wait staff and the patrons, a hint of music could be heard. Something soft with mandolins and guitars.

Mitch sat close enough to him so the length of her thigh pressed against his. Even with her hair pulled back from her face, she still smelled like coconut. Jason fought the urge to press his lips to the little sideways comma scar above her eyebrow. A couple walked in, dressed in formal dinner wear, and she leaned even closer. "I think I might be underdressed. I should've worn my pearls."

"Yeah, my Rolex is in the shop."

She turned her face toward his shoulder and giggled. "The limo, too?"

"Didn't I mention it before? I sold it to pay for dinner."

"The food better be good, then."

"You've never eaten here before?"

"No. Have you?"

"A couple times, but only on special occasions." Like his fifth anniversary.

"Does this count as a special occasion?"

Jason smiled and touched her hand. "Yes, I think it does."

"So what were you humming in the car?"

"What do you mean?"

"On the way here, you were humming something. I couldn't place the song, though."

"I don't know. Just nothing, I guess," Jason said. He didn't remember humming at all and yet an unfamiliar tune tickled the back of his mind. Something odd, something old, then the maître d' beckoned them to follow him, and the song vanished.

Halfway through dinner, the tattoo started to itch; he rubbed the bandage through his shirt, but it didn't help. He wasn't sure if he was supposed to keep a bandage on it, but he couldn't remember Sailor telling him not to, and without it, the ointment left oily traces on his shirts.

Mitch saw the gesture and smiled. "It itches?"

"Just a little."

"I hate that part. It's worse than getting it done. Just ignore it. It'll stop. I made the mistake of scratching with my first one and had to get part of it touched up later."

He took a drink of sangria, trying to ignore the itch, but it pleaded for his attention, annoying and persistent.

"So, you said you work in IT, but what do you do?" Mitch asked.

"I handle all the mobile devices for the company. Cell phones, PDAs, wireless cards, that sort of stuff."

She smiled. "Sounds interesting."

"It can be, especially when the CEO is out of town and drops his PDA into a puddle, but most of the time, it's just mindless work." His hand twitched toward the bandage, but he grabbed his fork instead.

"Like mine sometimes. Every time a Hollywood star gets a new, groundbreaking hairstyle, all my customers come in, wanting to look exactly like her. It gets old."

"Sounds fun."

"Right. Until the next star does something like"—Mitch lowered her voice to a whisper—"add highlights. Then the whole process starts again."

Jason tried to laugh, but the itch, like many-legged insects crawling back and forth across his skin, made it hard. The waiter stopped by their table and filled his empty glass. As soon as he stepped away, Jason drank half the glass and tried to ignore his arm, half expecting to hear the buzz of a hundred insects as they took flight.

The restaurant noise wrapped around them like a glove. The music, hushed conversations, muted laughter and silverware tapping against plates. Mitch reached across the table to touch his hand, and the jolt it sent through him pulled him away from the itch. She traced his knuckles with the tip of one finger, then drew circles in the skin above. One lock of her hair had come loose, and it hung against the pale of her cheek in an S-shaped wave. Then the itch took hold again; he jerked his hand back, and Mitch pulled hers away fast.

"Sorry," Jason said. "It's just my arm."

"It's okay. Is it like a mosquito bite? That's what mine felt like."

A mosquito bite? Maybe if the bug had a proboscis as large as

D.C.'s Washington monument.

"Something like that," he said and took a bite of steak. It tasted like nothing in his mouth; his brain would only process the itch. The poison ivy bush he'd fallen into on his tenth birthday had nothing on this. His skin begged him to scratch the bugs away, to send them scattering out into the restaurant in search of fresh prey.

Mitch said something in reply, but her words were nothing more than background noise. The itch was the main instrument in the orchestra pit, and it played big. Without the bandage covering the tattoo, the temptation would be too great to scratch and scratch and scratch until his skin bled.

Jason lifted his fork and ran his fingers over the tines. Yes, they would do the trick nicely. Never mind the gouges left in his skin. Never mind the damage to the tattoo. He could take the fork into the bathroom, strip off the bandage and rake the tines over his skin. A hundred times, a thousand. The pull to make the trip made his heart race. How would he explain it to Mitch?

He could pretend to drop it on the floor and slide it in his pocket when he reached down. Tuck it away, then excuse himself for a few minutes. He could bandage it back up when he was done and keep his shirt clean. He could—

Stop it. It's just an itch.

Ignore it, it will stop, Mitch had said. Mitch's mouth moved, and he tried to focus on the conversation, but he was only half there. The other half? Under the bandage, screaming for the itch to stop. It was like the orchestra from hell, and every single damn insect in the state of Maryland got an invitation to perform.

Five minutes in the bathroom. All it would take. It would hurt like a bitch, but then he wouldn't have to worry about the itch anymore. And the four hundred dollars and Sailor's artwork? Not important. Not important at all. Three minutes, if he had to. Just a few quick swipes with the fork. Just enough to make—

It stopped. One minute his arm sang out in a symphony of poison ivy and insects; the next, the musicians gave their final bow. He looked up in surprise.

"Did it stop?"

"Yes," Jason said. The insects had marched on without an encore. They hadn't even left their sheet music behind.

"I told you it would."

He tapped the fork on the edge of his plate, then impaled another piece of steak.

14

Jason's arm stayed quiet on the ride back to Mitch's house. He helped her out of the car, and she kept her hand in his as they walked to her door.

"I think that was the best meal I've ever eaten," she said. "And the company wasn't so bad, either."

Before he could respond, she leaned close and pressed her lips against his. Heat spread through his body as he brought his hands up around her. She wound her fingers in his hair, and when she broke the kiss, she didn't step away. Jason kept one hand on the small of her back, and the soft ends of her hair brushed the edge of his fingers. He reached out with his other hand, tracing the pad of his thumb across the scar above her eyebrow. She shivered.

"Do you want to come in?" she said.

The same words she'd used Thursday night, but this time the question held serious intent. He shouldn't, but when he opened his mouth, he couldn't say no.

Chapter Three

Into the Wind

1

Jason woke up in an unfamiliar bed, with his body curled around a now very familiar body. Mitch slept, her breathing soft and even, with one hand tucked under her cheek, like a child. He kissed the back of her head and climbed out of the bed, careful not to wake her up. Should he leave? Would she want him to stay? Last night, after falling back on the bed, exhausted, she asked him to stay the night. Now, with the harsh glare of sun shining in the windows, doubt crept in.

Déjà vu hit when he walked from the bedroom and saw the clothes scattered in the hallway and on the stairs. He found one of his shirt buttons halfway down the staircase. The memory of her hands tugging at his belt sent a shiver down his spine. He didn't want to leave yet; it would feel like sneaking out. They'd had coffee with dessert, so he knew she liked it. He'd make some and wake her up with a cup. Sugar, no cream. That's what she'd told the waiter.

When he reached the bottom landing and turned to walk into the living room, he stopped, frozen in place. The griffin, huge and menacing, stared at him with its beak raised. Sunlight danced across its feathers and turned them gold. The eyes bored into his with grim intelligence.

So real.

He took two steps closer. The talons were weathered, as if it had been on a long journey. The muscles of the back legs, the lion legs, rippled through its fur, and the claws extended just enough to reveal curved tips as sharp as the talons. Jason knew it was a male—an Alpha male. The chest puffed forward, haughty and superior. It had every right to be smug.

"I told you I loved griffins," Mitch whispered behind him.

"Jesus." Jason whirled around.

Mitch folded herself into his arms, laughing against his chest. "I didn't mean to scare you."

"Did you...?"

"No, my brother painted it one year and gave it to me for Christmas."

"It's beautiful."

The griffin looked ready to jump out of the canvas, which was at least three feet wide and almost as tall. This close, he could see the brush strokes and the way the colors blended into each other. It did look a lot like his tattoo, even down to the vivid green eyes.

Mitch pulled away from him and took his hand. "Come on, let's make coffee. I'm grumpy when I'm not caffeinated."

She kept her hand in his as they walked through her dining room. He stopped in front of a bookshelf, one of many that lined the walls, and ran his fingers over the spines. Shakespeare, science fiction, poetry, books about Henry VIII, horror novels...

"You like to read horror?"

Mitch nodded. "They're my favorite. I love reading them when I'm curled up on the sofa with only one light on. I especially love it when I get so scared I'm afraid to go upstairs without turning on all the lights."

"I haven't read a good one in a while. My ex thinks they're all crap. She used to throw them out when I wasn't looking."

"Ouch, that's low. If someone tried to throw away my books, they'd have a serious fight on their hands. So this ex of yours, how does she feel about tattoos?"

She pushed him into the bright sunshine yellow kitchen, down into a chair, and ran her fingers through his hair. Her tank top was thin enough to show off the rose-pink of her nipples, and her boxer shorts—not baggy men's boxer shorts, but short and clingy—were sexier than the most expensive silk and lace, in his opinion, but he looked away. A black-and-white cat clock with a hanging tail and moving eyes ticked away the seconds with tiny, audible clicks.

"She thinks they're trash, but she thinks most everything is, unless it's something she likes."

Mitch moved away from him and pulled coffee from one of the cabinets. As she reached, the edge of the boxer shorts lifted a little; the curve it revealed left Jason tongue-tied. The memory of her body under his filled his mind with vivid images, almost too much to take.

"How much of an ex is she?"

Jason ran his fingers along the edge of the kitchen table, unable to meet her eyes. "A new one."

"Should I be scared? Is she going to come here, kicking and screaming and demanding that I give you back?"

Jason shook his head. "No, it was a long time coming. I guess neither of us wanted to admit it. I should be glad she decided to leave." Because he didn't think he would have, no matter how miserable it made him. The damn vise grips hurt like hell, but they were a comfortable—and familiar—hurt.

She turned around. "She left you?"

"Yes, for her best friend."

"Oh. Oh." Mitch giggled, then clamped her hand over her mouth. "I'm sorry," she said between her fingers.

"Don't be. I'm glad," he said, then he, too, laughed. Once he started, he couldn't stop. Mr. Good Guy Jason, who always did as he was told, got dumped for his wife's best friend. Such a bad movie cliché. They'd been friends for years and he hadn't suspected a thing.

Soon enough, both he and Mitch had tears in their eyes. She kept one hand on the counter and clutched her stomach with the other. He almost fell out of the chair.

When the laughter subsided, she finished making the coffee and brought two mugs over to the table. "Do you like scary movies?"

"Sometimes. If they're good movies, not just hack, slash and gore."

"Ugh, I don't like those either. I'm not against gross stuff, but at least dress it up inside a real story. Anyway, there's a new movie out now," she said. "A remake of a Japanese film about a haunted house, and it looks incredibly creepy. Want to go with me to see it?" She lifted the mug to her lips but kept her eyes on his.

"Yes, I would, and I promise to hold your hand when you get scared."

"Nope, I'll hold your hand when *you* get scared." She refilled his mug and touched the edge of the bandage on his arm. "Can I see it again?"

"Sure."

She pursed her lips together when he took off the bandage. "Just amazing. It looks as real as my brother's painting. I don't think I've seen a tattoo like this one. The detail. Was it expensive?" She shook her head. "I'm sorry, that was rude."

"I don't mind you asking. It wasn't too bad. Four hundred bucks."

"That's it? For something like this? How long did it take?"

"About two and a half hours."

"You're joking."

Jason shook his head. Vic had said the same thing. Mitch's eyes widened, very blue in the bright kitchen.

"Two and a half hours for this detail? The guy is brilliant. I *so* want his name. Maybe he can redo mine."

"I have his card."

Jason checked his wallet but couldn't find the card. "Sorry, I guess it's at home."

"It doesn't matter. I can get it later." She ran her finger down his arm, next to the tattoo. "Does it still itch?"

"Not now. It feels sort of like a sunburn."

"What's his name?"

"What?"

"The griffin. He has to have a name. One like this definitely has to."

"Okay, now you're joking."

"Nope. Mine is Maxwell."

"Maxwell?"

"Yes. Maxwell the Great."

Jason laughed, and she pushed his shoulder with her hand. "Okay, I know it's silly."

A name floated into his thoughts, like a ribbon of smoke in candle flame. "Geryon."

"Geryon? Interesting. I think I've heard the name before, but I can't remember where."

"I have no idea where it came from, it just popped into my head."

"Griffins guard treasure, you know."

"That's what I read."

"So what's he guarding? What's your treasure?"

"I don't know," he said.

Myself. So I don't do anything stupid like Shelley, ever again.

"Maxwell guards my heart."

"Against?"

"Nefarious men."

Her grave eyes belied the tone of her voice. He reached out and touched her shoulder. "I'm not nefarious. I promise."

"I know. I can tell."

2

On Sunday, he arrived at his parents' house a little after five-thirty. The air held a promise of rain, and faint clouds hovered in the distance. His parents still lived in the same neighborhood, the same house, he grew up in, a neighborhood with well-kept lawns, towering trees, and canvas awnings over the windows and porches. Jason's dad had handled the paperwork for a construction firm for thirty-five years before he retired. His mom worked at a bank until she got pregnant in her thirties with his older brother, Chris. The pregnancy and the two that followed were surprises. They'd married young and resigned themselves to being childless when children didn't arrive right away. Jason followed two years after Chris and Ryan, two more after that.

His dad met him at the door and smiled at the flowers in Jason's hand. Daisies, his mom's favorite. His mouth watered as soon as he stepped into the kitchen and smelled his mother's lasagna, hands down the best he'd ever had. The Italian restaurants in town couldn't come close, even the oldest, most established ones. She made the sauce from scratch and refused to tell anyone exactly what spices she used; as a kid, Jason used to eat the sauce by the bowlful, with a slice of white bread to wipe the bowl clean.

His mom stood next to the oven with a floral apron covering her clothes and a wooden spoon in one hand. She smiled at the flowers and gave him a kiss on the cheek. Her perfume, the same one she'd worn for the past twenty-five years, made him smile. Neither expensive nor designer, but it held childhood memories in its scent, memories of ice cream after school on Friday afternoons, of Sunday matinee movies and holiday cookies covered in sprinkles.

She took the flowers and smiled a small, tight smile. "Go talk to your father while I take care of this," she said, pushing him out of the kitchen. "I'll call you both in when the lasagna is finished. Since it's just the three of us, we're going to eat in here."

Jason sat down at one end of the sofa; his father sat on the other with his feet propped up on the edge of the coffee table and the television on, scrolling through channels at the speed of light. He finally stopped at a news channel and put the remote down. "How are you doing, son?"

"I'm good."

"You sure?"

"Yeah. Everything is okay, it really is."

"You're warned. Your mom is pretty upset."

"I know," Jason said. "I have a feeling she will be for a while."

"She still thinks you and Shelley are going to work it out. Are you?"

Not for all the money in the world.

Jason shook his head, and his dad gave a small nod. "Well, it is what it is."

His dad's stock answer for everything. Had a bad day at work? Car accident? Your wife left you? It is what it is. The phrase always irritated the hell out of Jason. Such is life, another Dadism. These statements were always delivered with the little nod and the implacable feeling the matter was settled, at least in his dad's opinion.

Except he's right. It is exactly *what it is. Mom might not see it, but Dad does. Just like always.*

"Did you get a lawyer yet?"

Jason shook his head. "It's only been a couple of days. A few more won't hurt."

"What are you waiting for? Christmas?"

Jason laughed. Another Dadism.

"Don't wait too long." His father dropped his voice low. "I could see Shelley making things hard for you. Don't let her. You file for divorce first. It's better that way. Is it someone else?"

Jason thought of lying, not to protect Shelley, but to protect that little nagging doubt inside. He'd been a good husband. He knew he had. Shelley leaving him for a woman didn't mean he lacked anything other than the wrong shape, but a small, quiet place inside wondered. The memory of Mitch's face after they made love swam up unbidden, and his face grew warm. If he lacked anything in that department, she hadn't noticed. No, Shelley's leaving had everything to do with herself and nothing to do with him.

"Yeah, it is."

"I figured as much. She had no other reason to leave you. I guess she found someone else to take her crap better than you did."

"Dad, she—"

His dad lifted one hand in the air. "Nope, sell it to someone else. She did give you crap, son. You can't lie to me about that. Maybe your mom has some idea that things were grand and wonderful, but I saw the way she talked to you. It wasn't that she wanted to be the boss. Any man knows a woman wants that, and a smart man lets his woman think she is, but Shelley had a mean side to her that had nothing to do with being boss. I think her upbringing made her hard. You deserve better than that. And that is what it is." Jason's dad reached over and patted his shoulder. "You'll be okay. You're strong on the inside, where it counts."

A lump formed in Jason's throat.

"Ryan's tough, but he's not strong, like you are, and Chris? He was born with a horseshoe up his ass. He's never had to handle any hot water. All three of you have been good sons, in your own ways, but you're stronger than you think you are. I'm glad Shelley left. Now you can be who you are, not who you think you need to be."

Jason turned his head to the side, blinking back a sting of tears.

Strong? He thinks I'm strong?

He knew his dad wouldn't think less of him if he saw the tears. At his grandmother's funeral, he'd said, *"Let it out, son. Tears are nothing to be ashamed of when they fall for the right reason."* Still, he kept his face turned away.

"You know we're here for you, if you need anything. Once all this blows over, your mom will be fine too. She's your mom, not Shelley's.

58

Once she remembers that, she'll be fine."

His dad picked up the remote and changed the channel. Jason settled back on the sofa, watched the television through blurred eyes and waited for his mom to call them to dinner.

He was on his third bite of lasagna when she spoke up.

"I left Shelley a message on her phone, I want you to know," she said.

"Okay, that's fine with me."

"I'm sure it's some kind of misunderstanding you two can work out."

"It really isn't that simple."

She gave him the look—the one he used to get when he snuck in the house after curfew or when she found the stack of men's magazines in the back of his closet. Disapproval and disappointment all wrapped up in one. Her *I am your mother* look.

"Nonsense. Of course it's simple. The two of you will get back together and work it out. It might not be easy, but you'll manage. You can even go to counseling if you need to."

"Mom—"

"No, Jason. You and Shelley have been together for nine years. You don't just throw that away."

Jason tossed his fork down on his plate. "It was her decision to leave, not mine," he said.

"Well, I'm sure she had a reason."

How could he tell his mother the end of his marriage made him happy? How could he explain the sense of relief underneath the surprise and the anger? His mother wouldn't understand. And sometimes you did just throw it away; sometimes it was better that way.

"All marriages have problems, Jason. They all come with good years and bad years. You don't just throw it away when things get tough. That's not what marriage is about, Jason."

"Shelley and I have had a lot of bad years, Mom. A lot. It's done. I'm sorry, I know you like her, and you can still have a relationship with her if you want, but it's really over between us."

"I don't believe that."

He should just tell them about Shelley and Nicole, but he couldn't. Despite the memory of Mitch's parted lips and flushed cheeks, he couldn't go there with his parents. His father would laugh, maybe interject one of the familiar Dad phrases, but his mother had antiquated and incorrect thoughts about sexuality. She thought lesbians just hadn't found the right man, so what would that make him in her eyes? And bisexual? He didn't think she even knew what the word meant.

"I don't understand. You don't even seem upset," she said.

He wanted to say "I'm not," but the words ran away when he looked at her face. Under the anger, she had tears in her eyes, but she blinked several times and they disappeared.

"Jack, tell him please. Tell him how ridiculous he's being."

Jason's dad looked up from his plate. "Maggie, if Jason says it's over, maybe it is. Come on, let the boy eat."

His mother tossed her napkin down. "I can't believe this."

Jason rubbed his arm, wincing as his shirt slid against the skin.

"What's wrong with your arm?" his mother asked.

"Nothing."

"Jason."

The only thing worse than his mother's look—the voice. A by-product of childbirth, maybe. The last time he went to the mall, a little kid of about six threw a temper tantrum until his mother used the deadly duo together. The kid's tears vanished in a heartbeat, like magic.

Fine.

"I got a tattoo, and the skin's a little sore still."

His dad looked up again and couldn't hide the surprise on his face.

60

The corner of his mouth lifted up in a quick smile, but his mother folded her arms across her chest.

"You got a what?"

"A tattoo."

Her eyes narrowed into slits. "You and Shelley are having problems, and you went and got a tattoo? What were you thinking?"

Freedom. Nothing but freedom.

"Mom, it's no big deal. Lots of people have them."

"If lots of people jumped off a bridge, would you follow? Bikers and trailer trash get tattoos. I raised you better than that."

"Maggie, you're overreacting. It's just a tattoo," his dad said. "And lots of people get them, not just bikers."

The chair legs dragged across the tile when she stood up. "Our son is separated from his wife, and he went out and got a tattoo. I am not overreacting. What would you like me to do? Throw a party?" She pushed the chair in, gave them both the look, and left the kitchen without another word.

Jason's father rolled his eyes at her back. "What did you get, son?"

"A griffin," Jason said as he pushed up his shirtsleeve.

"I'm not a big fan of tattoos either, but that's pretty decent. The damn thing looks real. How much did that set you back?"

Jason shrugged. "Not too much."

And worth every penny.

3

When Jason got home from work Monday night, the smell of Shelley's perfume hung in the air like rotting, overripe fruit. She'd taken all the books on the first floor, a lamp she bought a few months ago and the fleece throw from the end of the sofa—a fleece throw she never used. She'd left a note on the coffee table, but he didn't pick it up. What else could she possibly need to say? It was a bit late for origami heartbreak.

The stink of perfume was even stronger on the second floor. Her closet door stood open, with nothing left except a few wire hangers. She'd taken all her makeup from the bathroom. Ditto for her shampoo and the expensive face creams from the medicine cabinet.

When he walked back downstairs, a faded rectangle of pale gray on the wall at the bottom of the steps caught his eye. He stood in front of the empty space for a long time, but he could not remember what had been in the spot. He walked by it every day more than once, and yet he had no idea. Maybe a bit of artwork that Shelley picked up? Maybe a gift? It must not have been important. He stared at the blank spot, trying to conjure up the image in his head. His mind said absolutely nothing in return and called him a fool for standing there so long. He finally gave up and went over to the coffee table.

If you find anything else of mine, let me know. I'll have my lawyer contact you soon. I hope you don't plan on making this difficult.

He folded the letter back in half, his mother's words echoing in his head. "*You don't even seem upset.*"

Jason took the letter into the kitchen, pulled out a beer and tossed the cap onto the counter where it rolled a few times before landing with a soft clink. The refrigerator hummed, and the ceiling fan overhead whirred as it spun in lazy circles. The palpable absence of Shelley's presence and her voice and the knowledge of its permanency were finer than his mother's cooking.

"Cheers," Jason said to the empty room, lifting his beer. "To freedom."

His freedom, like the beer, tasted sweet. He took a long drink and washed the taste of Shelley's perfume down. Had she walked around the house with the bottle, spraying everything? He could imagine it— her eyes narrowed, her lips held together in a tight line as she pushed down on the perfume bottle's nozzle to leave behind a little mist of floral memory, a little bit of *don't you dare forget.*

Jason opened the trashcan, and a whiff of perfume rose up. He waved his hand in front of his face, pushing the scent out but not away. A mass of broken glass and splintered wood lay in the trashcan like a macabre game of pickup sticks. The glass gave a tiny rattle when he tossed Shelley's letter in.

Scraps of paper littered one corner of the counter. Previous letter attempts? Doubtful. Their surfaces slipped and slid against his fingertips. Not pieces of paper at all but the remnants of a photo ripped to shreds. Nicole must have been with her; Shelley's anger was cold, not destructive. Jason flipped a few of the pieces over. A scrap of white, a bit of black, and then his face and Shelley's. Their heads close to each other, their mouths wide with smiles—genuine, happy smiles. It clicked into place. The wedding photo. The blank space on the wall.

Nicole saw it and it pissed her off. I bet she smiled when she ripped it up. I bet Shelley didn't say a word, just let loose with another toxic spray of perfume.

Nicole had always been cool toward him, but he'd never given it much thought. It made perfect sense now. Jason picked up the rest of the pieces, carried them over to the trashcan and smiled when he dropped them in.

4

By ten-thirty, the smell of perfume had faded, and the itch in his arm returned. Not the maddening symphony from the restaurant, just a few musicians playing a soft, mournful tune under the skin, almost low enough to ignore. Jason went into the bathroom and pulled out the tube of ointment. It didn't cure the itch, but it helped. It smelled of petroleum jelly and something else, something spicy like cinnamon but not. The unlabeled tube, as plain as the white tiles in his shower, had no name, no ingredients, nothing. Sailor's special blend?

Jason squeezed out a dime-sized bit and rubbed the slippery substance into his skin. The itch backed down another notch. One lone musician winding down for the night. The tattoo's detail stood out sharply in the bright glare of the bathroom light, every line, every curve, even those thinner than the edge of a fingernail, dark and well defined. The ointment made the vivid green of the griffin's eyes shimmer like twin emeralds. His father hadn't lied. It did look real enough to spring off his arm, real enough to jump up and out and take off, flying into the night with curved talons extended and ready to strike.

Jason smiled and flexed his bicep. The griffin shifted. He washed his hands, shook the water from his fingers, then curled his arm up again while his laughter bounced off the tiles. When he straightened his arm and turned it from side to side, the eyes gleamed. He moved his arm, imagining the griffin's flight. The play of sunlight on its wings as it circled in the sky. The loud push of air as its wings moved up and down, gliding over a mythical city filled with people watching its passage. Its sleek silhouette as it dove down. Intent, focused, strong—

Strong on the inside, where it counts.

His father's voice rang in his head. Unexpected tears blurred his vision and pushed away thoughts of the imaginary flight. The tattoo was the best damn decision he'd made in a long time. He'd never let anyone pull any Shelley-crap on him again. He had a griffin for protect—

The eyes moved.

"Shit."

Jason jumped back from the sink. The backs of his calves hit the edge of the bathtub, and he grabbed the shower curtain. The metal rings shimmied across the bar with a sound like wind-up plastic chatterteeth. The fabric—stupid, satiny fabric Shelley had to have— slipped in his hands. In slow motion, his left heel rose up as his body twisted, the shower curtain slid through his palm, and he fell into the tub. His head met the tile wall with a dull thud, his tailbone hit the bottom of the tub and his elbow banged into the spigot. Once he caught his breath, he laughed until his stomach hurt. He was half-stuck in the bathtub because he thought the eyes of his new tattoo had moved.

Ridiculous.

No, more than ridiculous. Stupid and absurd, all wrapped up in one. When he pulled himself out of the tub, his funny bone screamed in a very unfunny way, and both his tailbone and the back of his head joined in the pain chorus.

They didn't move. It was the light. The eyes didn't move. They can't. It's just ink on skin. Nothing more than that. That's what I get for having an overactive imagination.

Despite the pain, he laughed again.

I sound like a nutcase, but I don't care. Right, Mr. Whatever-the-Hell-Your-Name-is Griffin?

A long streak of ointment remained on the shiny fabric when he tugged the shower curtain closed, but he didn't care. He hated the damn thing anyway.

5

"Man, you look like shit."

Jason glared at Brian, poured a cup of coffee and leaned back against the counter. The bright lights of the office kitchen sent a dozen sharp-tipped needles into his brain. He raked his hand through his hair and took a sip of coffee that burned, hot and bitter, all the way down. "Thanks for stating the obvious. I feel like shit, too."

"You should go home, take some drugs, and get in bed," Brian said. "Keep your germs to yourself."

"I'm not sick. I just didn't sleep well last night."

A polite understatement, but he wasn't about to discuss the nightmare with Brian. He wouldn't be able to anyway, not in any worthwhile detail. The hodgepodge of images so vivid upon waking, sweat-soaked in tangled sheets, had faded before he finished his shower. The only things left behind were hazy memories of white walls and flapping wings.

As far as he could remember, the last nightmare bad enough to wake him up happened over five years ago, when his dad had a heart attack. For almost a week, he'd woken up every night, his head filled with vague images of doctors and nurses with dark gleams in their eyes. They'd left him with a great deal of unease but didn't make him feel as if he'd been tossed and turned like a madman.

His body ached and his arm throbbed under the tattoo as if the griffin had dug into the soft parts of his skin with those long, sharp talons—dug in and pulled.

"Didn't sleep, huh? How much did you drink last night?" Brian asked.

"Not a drop."

"Sure, whatever you say. With a face like that, if you aren't sick or hung over, you should be."

Jason raised his middle finger in reply.

"How's the tat?" Brian asked as he poured his own coffee.

"Still sore. It's started itching, too."

"Fun stuff."

"Yeah, the other night at dinner, I wanted to rip my skin off, it itched so much. It would have made a memorable first date."

Brian put the coffee pot down hard and stared at him with wide eyes. He smelled like he'd taken a bath in cologne, then added more on the way out the door. Or maybe not having Shelley and her perfume around made Jason more sensitive to the smell.

"First date? Look at you. You're not wasting any time. Do I know her?"

"Remember the girl from the bar?"

Brian smiled, wide enough to show teeth. "The hot little blonde? Yeah, I remember."

"She and I went out to dinner."

"Dinner, huh. That's all? Did you—"

"None of your damn business."

Brian patted him on the right shoulder. "You don't have to say a word. It's plain on your face. Good going. That's the best way to forget about Shelley."

"Whatever."

"So who's next?"

"No one. We're going out again this week."

"No, no, no. You just split up with your wife, man. Don't jump into anything. There are lots of women out there for you to hang out with. Don't limit yourself. Remember Emily, the redhead with the big—"

"Yeah, I remember her."

"I figured you did. She's kind of hard to forget. She's got a friend who just got dumped by her boyfriend. How about if I hook the two of you up? She's hot. I mean, not like Emily-hot, but I'd do her."

"That's not really a compliment," Jason said. "You'd do just about anything that walks."

"You're killing me. I do have standards."

"Like what? A pulse? Seriously, I really like Mitch, what can I say? We're going out on a second date, not getting engaged."

Brian snorted. "Yeah, well, have your fun and move on. You're single now. Enjoy it."

"Like you?"

"Hey, watch it. I'm having fun, and you'll never guess who I hooked up with last night."

"Is that why you smell like that? No time to shower?"

"Screw you. You're just jealous of my appeal to the ladies."

"If that's what you want to call it, be my guest," Jason said, refilling his coffee cup. An image flashed in his mind, a dark shadow rising up against brilliant white, then Brian started comparing the merits of redheads to brunettes, and he pushed it away.

6

Jason and Mitch sat in the middle of the back row at the movie theater, surrounded by the buttery smell of popcorn and the noise from dozens of teenagers. The kids sitting on Mitch's right were holding a conversation with another group seated six rows away while those on Jason's left engaged in a half-hearted popcorn fight.

"I think we're the oldest ones here," he whispered in her ear.

She grabbed a handful of popcorn from the tub on his lap and looked around the theater. "Nope, look down there. Second row."

"The guy with the dreadlocks?"

"No, that's a girl, I think. Look two seats over."

"All I see is someone with dark hair."

"Yes, but I saw his face before he sat down. He's older than we are."

"So we're *almost* the oldest ones here. Maybe that guy's taking his kid to the movies. There are a lot of them here, in case you hadn't noticed."

"Ha! These aren't kids, they're teenagers. A totally different species." She popped another piece of popcorn in her mouth. "Don't you remember being a teenager? I would've killed someone for calling me a kid."

"I've pushed the memories out of my head, sorry. Either that or I'm just old, and my mind is already starting to go."

A stray kernel of popcorn sailed through the air and landed on Jason's lap. Mitch grinned and brushed it onto the floor, but not before she gave his thigh a quick squeeze.

"I meant to ask at dinner, but I forgot. How'd you get the scar on your forehead?"

"A haunted house."

He tossed a piece of popcorn in her direction. "Right. Come on, tell me the truth."

"I am," she said. Her lips curved in a small smile, but her eyes were serious. "I got it in a haunted house. A real one, not a Halloween thing."

"A real haunted house?"

She grabbed another handful of popcorn. "Yep, Scout's honor."

"Okay, so what happened?"

Another piece of popcorn flew by, and she batted it away. "A lot, but if I tell you, you'll think I'm crazy."

"No, I won't."

She grinned. "Trust me, you would. Do you believe in ghosts and paranormal stuff?"

"Not really. I mean, I think people *think* things happen, but I think it's all in the imagination."

"See, I told you. You think I'm crazy. It doesn't matter, anyway. It was a long time ago, and I was just a kid. A kid-kid, not a teenager, and who knows? Maybe I did imagine it," she said, but she looked down at her hands. "I think it's the reason I love scary books and movies, though. Now you have to tell me something. Was the name a joke?"

"What name?"

"The griffin's name. Geryon."

"No, it wasn't a joke. It just popped into my head, like I said. I guess I heard it somewhere, and it just stuck."

"Hmm. I was curious, so I looked it up."

"And?"

She rubbed her hands on her thighs. "According to Dante, it's a giant who guards Hell."

"Nice."

"Hey, you picked it," she said with a smile.

"Okay, I changed my mind. His name is Frank."

"Frank?"

"Yes, Frank."

She laughed. "That's not very griffin-like."

"Better than the name of a guardian from Hell."

"Point taken." She reached over and patted his left arm. "Nice to meet you, Frank."

When the lights dimmed, she slipped her hand into his. The upcoming movie trailers started, and he tried to remember the last time he held Shelley's hand anywhere. Maybe at a family function. They always put on a good show for his family even though the sterile way their hands met held no warmth. He and Shelley had kept their disintegration private, which, no doubt, explained his mother's mindset. Mitch shifted in her seat and leaned closer, and all thoughts of his soon-to-be ex-wife vanished.

The movie involved a ghost stalking a group of people spending a weekend in the house, and half the teenagers shrieked the first time the ghost appeared. The second time, he and Mitch both jumped in their seats, but she kept her hand in his, and the rightness of her touch put a smile on his lips.

The poke on his arm, a tiny bit of feather-light pressure, caught him off guard. Jason turned his head to the left, but the teenager next to him, a girl with heavy smears of black makeup, sat facing forward, her eyes wide with rapt fascination, so he brushed it off as an accident.

The heroine of the movie walked through a long hallway unaware of the ghost right behind her. The background music, dark and ominous, could not hide the squeals and shouts of "turn around" that filled the theater. Mitch whispered "idiot" under her breath, but she gripped Jason's hand tight. The heroine finally turned, and more than half the people in the theater echoed her scream. Mitch didn't scream, but she pressed her hand against her mouth. He smiled, and she pushed at his right arm with her hand at the same time the girl touched him again. He looked over, not surprised she'd poked him this time because her hands were flailing in front of her like living things while the boy next to her laughed and slapped his hands on his thighs.

The heroine got away, barely, and the next ten minutes of the film offered a quiet lull as she tried to convince her friends that something was wrong. Mitch moved even closer and put her head on Jason's shoulder. Her hair didn't smell like coconut tonight. It smelled flowery but sweet. Impulsively, he kissed the spot where her hair met her forehead.

When the heroine and her friends started exploring the house room by room, the gentle pressure on his arm returned. Jason looked over at the girl and swallowed hard. Her hands were wrapped around the boy, their mouths mashed together in oblivious abandon.

Not her? Impossible.

Something happened onscreen that caused several people to burst out in nervous laughter, but the kids paid no attention.

No, it had to be her.

The ghost appeared onscreen again, and the room broke out in a deafening scream, multiple voices blending together in one long howl of terror. Mitch's shoulders shook as she laughed, but the sound disappeared into the chaotic roar.

Someone nudged his arm again. The teenagers' lips had finally parted, but the girl sat halfway in the boy's lap. Jason's mouth went dry.

I am not imagining things. I know what I felt. But if she didn't touch me, who did?

Another round of screams rose up around him; this time Mitch let out a quick, loud yelp of shock, and her hand tightened around his. The movie screen turned into a blur of ghostly images and running feet as the music built up to a fevered pitch. The girl untangled herself from her boyfriend, but sat with her knees pulled up and her hands over her eyes.

The girl onscreen screamed as the ghost approached with arms outstretched. Mitch's grip tightened even more, and the unseen finger touched his arm again, pressing hard. He whipped his head around to the left and glared at the girl. "Stop it," he mouthed. She frowned. He pointed to his arm, and she looked away.

Of course it's her. Who else could it be?

The ghost reached forward to wrap its long arms around the heroine. Mitch yelped again and pulled her hand from Jason's. She covered her eyes but kept them spread enough to peek through. The ghost threw its head back and howled. The heroine's scream, impossibly high and shrill, went on for several long minutes, then the screen went black and the theater burst into nervous applause as the credits started to roll and the lights came on. Mitch touched his shoulder, and he jumped.

"Gotcha." She laughed, tucking her hair behind her ears, then looked over his shoulder with a frown.

He turned to find the girl staring at him. "What's your problem?" she asked.

"You kept hitting my arm."

"I didn't touch you."

Her boyfriend leaned over. "Is he bothering you?"

"No." She got up and gave Jason one last dark look before walking away. "But he thought I hit his arm and he…"

"What was that about?" Mitch asked.

"Nothing, really. She bumped into my arm a couple of times, and I told her to stop."

"Don't worry about it. The guy next to me did it, too. You sort of expect it to happen when the theater is this crowded. Come on, let's get out of here," she said as linked her hand in his and tugged him up out of his seat.

7

On their way out of theater, the hairs on the back of Jason's neck rose.

Someone watching?

A quiet hush filled the lobby. An employee with heavily pierced ears swept crumbs and discarded candy wrappers from the floor with an almost vacant expression on her face. Another employee with even more piercings wiped the surface of the counter with long, lazy strokes. A teenage girl in a short skirt and heavy makeup waited by the door. Someone hummed, low and under their breath, but the odd tune trailed off before Jason could figure out which direction it came from. A plain-faced man in what appeared to be an expensive suit stood near a small doorway on the right side of the lobby. He watched them with an odd gleam in his eyes. Jason reached out and took Mitch's hand.

You're with a pretty girl, he's just looking at her.

But he wasn't. His eyes, pale and green, were on Jason, not Mitch. He took a step forward, and Jason slowed his pace.

The walk.

The man tipped his head in Jason's direction, shifted his eyes to Mitch, then back to Jason and winked. Jason had seen him before but where? Like the name of someone met at a long-ago holiday party, the answer hovered out of reach; the more he tried to grab it, the further away it slid. The man's face held nothing special in its features. Nothing. A wallpaper face—Shelley's term for a person neither attractive nor ugly. In the case of the suited man, the term fit like a well-cut glove. He could be a schoolteacher or a Wall Street executive, although the suit pushed him closer to the latter category.

Mitch gave his hand a squeeze, and Jason pulled his eyes away from the man.

"They just opened a gelato place not too far away. Do you want to stop by and see if they're still open?"

"It sounds like a plan to me," Jason said, leading her out of the lobby. He paused to look back over his shoulder, but the man in the suit was gone.

8

When Jason's alarm started its insistent chirp, he wanted to throw it across the room. Instead, he turned it off and rolled over to find the other side of the bed empty. He touched the still-warm sheet; Mitch hadn't been awake long. The faint smell of fresh coffee made him smile.

After a quick shower, he headed downstairs. The scrape of a kitchen chair across the floor let him know Mitch heard him coming. He hummed under his breath and quickened his step, his head filled with thoughts of the soft skin above her hipbones and the way her back arched up when his lips—

"So who's the blonde?"

Shit. Mitch wasn't in the kitchen after all. He could smell Shelley's perfume from across the room, a heavy cloud of musk and flowers.

"What are you doing here?"

"Who is the blonde?" She stood up and put her hands on her hips in her best *you will do what I want* stance. Her *are we going to fight about this when you know I will win* pose. She'd left him, moved her stuff, and now she stood in his kitchen asking questions she had no business asking, stinking up the room with perfume that tasted like poison in his mouth.

"Jason."

He grabbed a mug from the cabinet and turned around to meet Shelley's eyes. Her face, a stranger's face that left him with a hollow sense of nothing inside, twisted into a grimace.

"Who is she?"

Jason poured coffee into his cup and smiled. "She's none of your business."

Her eyes narrowed. "Very funny. Were you seeing her before I told you about Nicole?"

"Shelley, I said it's none of your business."

Her eyes flashed with surprise, and her resolve slipped just a little. The smile on his face grew wider.

It's almost funny.

"You had her here, in our house, in our bed?"

He couldn't believe it. She and Nicole snuck around behind his back for who knew how long and she was pissed at him. It wasn't because he'd been with another woman. It went deeper than that. Much deeper. She was angry because he was neither miserable nor pining for her.

It's not almost funny at all. It's pretty goddamn hysterical. She expected me to find me crying in the corner like a kid whose favorite toy fell apart.

"No offense, but you left this house. And since it was a gift to me from my grandmother, it's my house, not yours. You left the marriage first, remember? You have no right to ask me anything about who I see or don't see."

Damn, that felt good.

Shelley glared at him, but the index finger on her right hand rubbed back and forth across her thumbnail. She only did that when nervous or afraid. She hid it well, but the little gesture gave it away. Nervous or afraid of him? No, Jason didn't think so. The unexpected response? Most likely. She gathered her emotions back up, and the Shelley he knew best came back.

"So you fuck some little chicky and think it makes you more of a man?"

She always had a way with words, but this was a new low. Something had touched a nerve. No, not something, someone.

His smile stretched out even farther. "Maybe."

She winced, a quick, tiny chip in the façade. He wanted her to be hurt by his words. All the times she ridiculed the things he expressed an interest in because she didn't think them worthy. All the things she said and didn't say. Every last look in her eye. He enjoyed the wince. He enjoyed the tiny break in her artificial sense of self.

"Well," she said. "I only came by to pick up some things I left in the basement."

Jason took a sip of coffee. "Did you get them already?"

"Yes, while you were in the shower."

"Fine." He held out his hand. "The key, please."

Spots of color bloomed on her cheeks, but she dropped the keys on the table and left without another word, leaving behind silence and the stink of her perfume.

Brian had said she had his balls in a sling, but not anymore. His balls were firmly in his own hands now, and it felt better than good.

It felt fucking grand.

9

He called Mitch when he got to the office, but the call went straight to voice mail. As the hours passed with no reply he convinced himself Shelley's appearance had chased her away and when she called him back that night, he hesitated, almost afraid to answer.

"I'm sorry," he said, before she had a chance to speak. "I had no idea she would stop by like that. I completely forgot she still had a key."

"That was your ex, right?"

"Yes, it was. I promise, it won't happen again. I took the key back."

Mitch sighed and his grip on the phone loosened.

"A little warning would have been nice. She scared the crap out of me when she came in," she said. "And the worst part? She said nothing. She came in and stood there with her hands on her hips and just stared at me."

Jason couldn't help it. He laughed. "She did the same thing to me when I came downstairs."

"I tried to say hello, but it didn't work out so well. I wanted to come up and warn you she was there, but I wasn't sure. I figured the best thing to do was leave. She reminds me a lot of my ex, unfortunately. They have the same glare. And that perfume she was wearing? Let me tell you, it stinks."

"I know. Believe me, I know. I can still smell it in the kitchen even with the window open."

A comfortable silence hung in the air, then they both spoke.

"I thought—"

"Do you like—"

"You go first," Jason said.

"Okay. This might sound weird, but do you like carousels?"

"I did when I was a kid. I don't think I've been on one since then. Why?"

"You know they have one at the Inner Harbor, right?"

"Yes?"

"Sometimes I go there and ride it. I know it's a little weird, but it would be nice to have some company the next time. If you're free, I was thinking maybe Saturday night. It's supposed to be warm. We could ride the carousel and sit on a bench and people watch," she said in a soft voice. "Maybe pick up some French fries."

"Only if you like them with vinegar. Lots of vinegar."

"Of course. How else could you possibly eat French fries? So, it's a date then?"

Jason smiled so wide his face hurt. "Definitely."

"How about if I pick you up around seven-thirty? I did ask you so I should drive."

"Okay. Seven-thirty it is. But the fries are on me."

"Deal."

French fries, people watching, and a carousel ride. It would be an interesting date. The more he got to know Mitch, the more he liked her, even if she did believe in ghosts.

10

The tattoo started to peel the next morning. As he spread the ointment on his skin, thin flakes sloughed off, and the colors appeared even more vibrant and defined. He would not have believed a human hand capable of such precision if he hadn't seen it himself.

Jason liked the tattoo a lot more than he thought he would, but even more than the ink itself, he liked the way it made him feel. Before his trip to Sailor's shop, he never would have gotten the last word in with Shelley or asked someone like Mitch out on a date. And now? Everything and anything at all was possible.

He flexed his muscle and grinned at his reflection in the mirror. The griffin's eyes caught and held the light, shimmering as if in agreement with his thoughts.

11

Jason, Brian and a few other guys from work were meeting at nine for what Shelley always called a beer and bullshit night, and on that, she was right. They drank, griped about work and Brian flirted with any woman who had the misfortune to sit nearby. Inevitably, someone would drink too much, and they'd send him home in a cab.

Brian had asked for Sailor's contact information. Since the number didn't show up on his phone, Jason figured he would just give him the card, but when he looked in his wallet, it was nowhere to be found.

He checked the trashcans in both the bedroom and the bathroom. No luck. The pockets of every pair of pants he'd worn since he got the tattoo were next. No luck there, either. When he went downstairs, he looked behind the sofa cushions and found plenty of crumbs and spare change, but no card. He checked the kitchen table, the kitchen counter, even the top of the microwave. Nothing.

He remembered putting the card in his wallet, but he didn't remember taking it out. After he went through the contents of his wallet again, discovering an old picture of Shelley and an even older insurance card, both of which went into the trash, he gave up. No card.

His best guess? The card must have been on the kitchen table when Shelley came over for her things, and she tossed it out. He imagined the expression on Shelley's face, wrinkled nose and all, when she picked it up, and the glint in her eyes when she decided it was unimportant to her, therefore unimportant to him. She probably smiled when she dropped it in the kitchen trashcan, then sprayed a little more perfume. *"Here, have a little stink to remember me by."*

After that, he threw it away when he took out the trash. Simple. He'd give Brian the address, and if he really wanted one of Sailor's tattoos, he could stop by and talk to him there.

12

Mitch picked him up as planned on Saturday night, but she was quiet on the drive to the Inner Harbor. Jason didn't want to pry so he held his tongue. Once they parked, bought fries and sat down on an empty bench she opened up.

"I'm sorry, I've had a rough day. My ex-boyfriend called me today," she said. "His mom has lung cancer and it's bad. They've given her six months at most." She spoke the last few words in little more than a whisper, almost swallowed up by the noise of a half-dozen teenagers shouting nonsense to each other as they walked by. Beyond the wide brick walkway tracing the harbor's edge, sunlight danced on the water. Crowds of tourists and locals moved in and out of the two pavilions that held restaurants and retail shops. In between the two pavilions, more people had gathered to watch a street performer juggling a set of bowling pins while riding on a unicycle, and the sounds of laughter and clapping drifted through the air.

Jason reached over and squeezed her hand. "I'm sorry."

"I think I'm going to go and visit her in a few weeks. Adam, my ex, is an ass, but she was always nice to me, so I feel like I should. I haven't talked to her in a really long time. She lives in Colorado now, but when she used to live here, we talked a lot. After I broke up with Adam, it just got weird because he'd pump her for information about me and use her to relay messages to me, so I stopped calling. Eventually, she stopped calling me, too." Mitch rested her head on his shoulder. "And now she's dying, and I feel like shit."

Jason kissed the top of her head. She'd switched back to the coconut shampoo. An older couple walked by holding hands, and the woman looked over with a smile.

"It's the cancer part that makes it so tough, though. Adam's mom smoked two packs a day, so it's not a big surprise that she has lung cancer, but my brother died of cancer," Mitch said.

"I'm sorry."

She remained silent for several minutes, then her words came out in a rush. "Zack was only twenty-two. He had an aggressive form of lymphoma and at first the chemo seemed to work, but after a while..." She shook her head. "It was horrible. He was so sick from all the medicine in the beginning, then when they stopped the treatments because they realized they weren't working, he was in so much pain.

"I thought I'd forgotten about all of that, but when I talked to Adam today it all came rushing back—the way Zack looked, the way he smelled, like chemicals and rot, the way he used to smile in spite of it all, in spite of everything. I almost cancelled our date, then I remembered something he told me near the end. He said he had the easy part of it. Dying, he meant. It would be harder for us, but he made me promise I wouldn't let his death take over my life." Mitch took one of the paper napkins and twisted it in her hands. "And then he was just gone."

80

She crumpled the napkin in one fist and shifted on the bench so she faced him, her eyes shimmering with unshed tears. She opened her mouth to speak, then shook her head, leaned into his arms and kissed him. When the kiss broke, she smiled. "Thank you."

"For what?"

"For being here. For listening. I know it isn't exactly great date conversation."

He linked his fingers with hers. "I don't mind at all. I'm sorry your brother died, but I'm not sorry you told me about him."

She ran the fingers of her free hand through his hair. "Zack would have liked you. And he would've loved your tattoo. He had a thing for griffins. That's why I got my tattoo. Remember the painting in my living room? Zack painted it when he was eighteen."

"Eighteen?"

"Eighteen. He was an amazing artist. Gifted, really. I think he would've been famous." She smiled, but tears glistened in her eyes again. "Come on, enough of my doom and gloom. Let's eat the fries and go ride the carousel."

13

The carousel was either very old or a very good replica. The horses were all brightly colored, and the underside of the canopy looked like the night sky in a fairy tale. Painted stars formed imaginary constellations, and the moon had craters shaded in the suggestion of eyes and a smile.

Jason and Mitch waited in line behind a large group of noisy children. The kids tossed kindergarten insults back and forth—"poopy breath," "stinky" and "no, you're the fart-mouth." Mitch hid a smile behind her hand, but they both laughed out loud when one little girl with pigtails and serious eyes said, "Boys are stinkier than girls because they have penises in their pants."

The man operating the ride pulled back a chain and let them

enter, glaring at the children as they rushed past him in a whirl of sticky hands and open mouths. When Mitch stepped through, the glare vanished, and his gaze moved up and down and back again until he caught them both watching, then he shrugged one shoulder and grinned, revealing chipped, yellow teeth.

Tinny music, sad, yet vaguely eerie, played from unseen speakers. The tune reminded him of a song he heard...somewhere. Jason thought it a rule—all amusement rides, even one as innocuous as a carousel, had to be a little frightening. Something to make the kids squirm and shriek.

He doubted any of the kids would notice the horses' eyes. At first glance they were happy, smiling, *safe* eyes, but a closer look revealed a sort of abject terror, as if they knew they could run and run and run but, caught in an endless prison of up and down and around and around, they would never truly be free.

Jason and Mitch linked hands as the carousel began to spin, and the children's laughter rose and fell like the horses. Mitch smiled and held his hand tight, the light in her eyes warm and childlike. Parents stood on the grass beyond the ride, clapping their hands, waving and taking pictures.

Then Jason's eyes met familiar green. Sailor stood, with a straw hat tipped back on his head, at the edge of the crowd, a few feet away from everyone else. Jason raised a hand in greeting, but the carousel moved and Sailor fell out of view. The tinny music played on, the same mournful notes over and over.

On the next pass, Sailor had moved closer to the carousel yet still removed from the crowd. One little girl stared up at him, and a sneer appeared on Sailor's face when he looked down. The little girl's mother whipped her head around and stared at Sailor without saying a word, then took the child's hand and drew her several feet away.

Jason leaned over and whispered in Mitch's ear, but she shook her head as the music, the children's laughter, and the squeak of the machinery swallowed up his words. He raised his voice higher. "Do you see the guy out there with the hat?"

The carousel made another pass, and for a moment, Jason thought Sailor had left, then he spotted the hat. Sailor had moved again, back another foot or so. The carousel continued around, and she leaned in closer.

"No, I don't. Who is it?"

"He's standing to the right of everyone else. That's the guy that did my tattoo."

They circled around again, and Sailor tipped his head in a slow nod.

"I don't see him," Mitch said. "I thought I saw a hat, but I'm not sure."

Jason's left arm grew warm and his fingertips tingled. The music echoed off the platform and the canopy, with one note slightly off-key, barely noticeable unless you really listened, but once Jason heard it, he couldn't *not* hear it. It conjured up images of abandoned buildings with dust in the corners, damp basements, spider webs and old boxes. The heat in his arm pulled in, pushed out, then vanished. The carousel took one more spin, and Jason shook his fingers; the tingle drifted away like the voices in the crowd.

"I think I saw him," Mitch said after they circled around again.

"When the ride stops, I'll introduce you. Wait until you hear his voice."

Mitch laughed. "Okay."

The carousel started to slow its pace, and all the children groaned in protest. Sailor turned his back to the carousel and stepped farther away from the crowd; his odd gait made the hat bob like a buoy in the ocean.

"So what's up with his voice?"

"He sounds like a heavy smoker. It's all gravelly and rough, but he talks like a teacher and he's got a weird walk, too. You'll see. I nicknamed him Sailor the first time I met him."

When the carousel slid to a shuddering halt, their horses faced away from the crowd. Jason tried to look over his shoulder, but the edge of the crowd fell beyond his line of sight. It took a few minutes to dodge the children and leave the carousel. The music with the single odd note played on, and Jason wanted to be away from the noise.

Mitch grabbed his hand in surprise when a young boy with a smear of dirt on his forehead ran in front of them, almost knocking them over. They walked hand in hand toward the grassy patch. This far away, the music sounded even more unpleasant, and the disembodied notes hung in the night air like stale perfume.

Sailor's hat bobbed behind the crowd and Jason frowned. "Damn." He tried to walk faster, but a group of kids ran circles in front of them, halting their progress. Jason looked over the crowd but didn't see the hat anywhere. Impossible. Sailor couldn't have gotten that far away, not the way he walked. Jason looked again, farther out just in case. A tiny flash of pale, maybe a straw hat, maybe someone's hair, but too far away to be Sailor.

"What's wrong?" Mitch asked.

"I think he left. I know he saw me on the carousel. He stood there the whole time. I don't know why he didn't wait," he said, and pressed a light kiss on her lips.

When they walked far enough away from the carousel to leave the music behind, she laughed.

"What?"

"You're still looking for him, aren't you?"

"Maybe a little."

Why wouldn't he wait? He watched us on the carousel. He could have waited a few more minutes. Didn't he want to see how the tattoo looked?

"Maybe he didn't want to disturb our date or maybe he had someplace else to go. If you really want to see him again, you can just go to his shop, right?" She squeezed his hand. "Is it really that important?"

84

"No, not really."

And it wasn't. It wasn't important at all.

14

John S. Iblis walked along the harbor's edge, humming under his breath. The crowds had dispersed, but he did not mind the solitude. In the water, a few fish swam in erratic circles, then disappeared like ghosts into the murky gloom.

He walked away with a smile on his face, tapping the paper tucked inside his pocket. For safekeeping, of course.

15

By Tuesday evening, the skin on Jason's arm stopped peeling.

Chapter Four

A Storm's a-Brewin'

1

Jason hired a lawyer and found out that Shelley's infidelity made it possible for their divorce to be finalized in months instead of the usual year's wait. No children, the house in Jason's name, and Shelley's income, higher than Jason's by a significant amount, made it an easy divorce according to Michael K. Dillon, Esquire. Easy translated to not too expensive in Jason's mind, and he swore he saw a flash of disappointment in the lawyer's eyes.

His mother still refused to talk about it, but her angry silence told him communication with Shelley was either nonexistent or discouraging.

The job had the same ebb and flow as always. Some days he walked into the office to panicked phone calls from users who dropped and broke their cell phones or left them behind in a taxi on a business trip, and on others, the hours passed without a crisis in sight.

Mitch left to visit her ex-boyfriend's mother on a rainy Thursday afternoon. That same day, he received a letter from his lawyer that stated that Shelley's lawyer agreed to all the terms, and they'd have a court date soon.

His freedom was well worth every penny the lawyer asked for. A piece of paper may have bound them together, but a new piece of paper would render that null and void. A little bit of ink, like a tattoo.

It only hurts for a little while.

It didn't hurt, though. In fact, just the thought of that paper made him grin like an unmedicated asylum lunatic. No more Mr. & Mrs. Jason Harford.

When that piece of paper arrived in the mail, he planned to take his wedding band and flush it down the toilet, the perfect farewell to the disaster he'd signed up for, then he might frame the divorce decree and hang it on the wall where the wedding photo used to be.

His father's words echoed in his head when he folded the letter back up.

It is what it is.

And it was all good.

2

On Saturday morning, halfway through his second cup of coffee, Jason heard a knock at the front door. When he opened the door, one of the neighbor's kids looked up at him with very wide, very dark eyes, a girl somewhere between elementary and middle-school age who he recognized, but not well enough to remember her name.

"Hi, have you seen a gray cat?"

Her words were low and polite, but she shook hair out of her eyes with a gesture that spoke of the insolence right around the corner. Give her a few years, and she'd have a nose ring and a bad attitude and wouldn't be caught dead knocking on her neighbor's door. Jason stayed on friendly terms with most of his neighbors but didn't consider any of them friends. Sure, he'd wave while he mowed the lawn or took out the trash, but Shelley had never been interested in hanging out with any of them. If they'd lived in a high-rise penthouse surrounded by money and class, it would have been a different story.

"I'm sorry, I haven't seen your cat."

No reason to tell her he just woke up and hadn't been outside yet;

she was still a few years away from sleeping until noon on the weekends. He thought he knew the cat she asked about, a big, gray tomcat who preferred one of two things—sleeping or hissing. The cat liked to curl up in their backyard near the birdbath Shelley picked out last summer and lay in wait for unsuspecting birds. Twice, Jason found traces of the cat's spoils near the end of the yard.

"Okay, our cat, Shiny, didn't come home today. So if you see him, could you call my dad? We live three doors down, in the brick house." She handed Jason a phone number scrawled on small scrap of paper.

"If I see him, I'll be sure to call."

"Thanks, Mister."

She walked away and joined up with a younger boy whose hopeful expression she dashed away with a shake of her head. Jason shut the door. Shiny? What a name for a cat. Maybe good old Shiny ran away in search of owners with a better imagination or a yard with a bigger birdbath and more victims.

3

That night, Jason went to Brian's house, drank too much and stumbled into Brian's spare bedroom a few minutes past 2:00 a.m., collapsing on the bed fully clothed. Brian's dog, a huge golden retriever named Mac, climbed up on the bed, and Jason passed out with the room spinning circles in his head and Mac snoring in his ear.

When Mac's barking pulled him awake, the room no longer spun, but it slanted one way, then jolted in the other direction. "Knock it off," Jason said, but Mac raised his muzzle and barked louder. Jason groaned, covering his ears with his hands. The dog whined, jumped off the bed, paced in a circle, his nails clicking on the wood floor, then moved close enough so Jason could feel his breath as he let loose with a series of short, clipped barks.

"Come on, Mac, quit it." He rolled over and buried his face in the sheets.

Brian liked to joke that if someone broke in the house, Mac would let him walk out the front door with anything as long as the intruder scratched behind his ears and gave him a dog biscuit. Mac nudged Jason's shoulder with his snout, gave another string of barks and growled in his ear, his fur pushing out a low, musky scent.

Jason pushed himself up, but the room slid to the right, his stomach twisted and he fell back on the bed. Mac's growl deepened, then he retreated to the other side of the room, near the door. "Okay, boy. Give me a second. I'll get up and check it out." He sat up, closing his eyes as the room tilted to the left. Brian was going to owe him for this one, big time. Jason swung his legs to the side of the bed, and Mac advanced with his ears back and his tail high, stopping a few feet away.

"Mac, stop it."

When Jason stood up, Mac took another step forward, baring his teeth. The room twisted, he sank back down on the edge of the mattress and the dog moved back with another growl. Jason held out his hand. The growl deepened.

"Mac?" he said, his voice whisper-soft and liquor-heavy. What little moisture he had in his mouth vanished.

The dog crouched low, his liquid eyes focused on Jason's as his lips pulled back farther from his teeth, a posture suggesting violence, suggesting all the dog biscuits in the world wouldn't help Jason now.

No way, not Mac.

"Come on, boy. Good dog."

Mac growled once in reply. Jason stood up again, holding on to the edge of the nightstand, and Mac sprang to his feet. Forgetting about his pounding head and his racing heart, Jason staggered forward. The room filled with high-pitched barking, loud enough to echo off the walls, and the thick scent of fur as Mac approached.

Jason backed up with his hands raised until the mattress pressed against the back of his legs. "Mac, knock it off right now." He tumbled back, pulling his legs up and away only seconds before Mac's jaws snapped in the air where his right ankle had been.

"What the fuck is wrong with you?" Jason said.

Mac withdrew, his paws heavy on the floor, until he reached the doorway. He bobbed his head up and down twice, whined long and low, then ran out. Jason had only a moment to wonder before the room shifted in front of his eyes. Everything turned gray and blurry, and he spiraled down into the dark hole of drunk nothingness with the echo of Mac's barking still ringing in his ears.

4

When Jason walked into the kitchen the next afternoon, he found Brian hunched low over a cup of coffee. Mac sat on the other side of the room with his head on his paws and his eyes closed, but Jason caught the twitch of his ears from the corner of his eye when he sank down into one of the scuffed chairs.

"Is Mac okay?"

Brian glanced over his shoulder. "Yeah, he's fine. Why?"

"Didn't you hear him last night?"

"I didn't hear a damn thing. What happened?"

"He woke me up in the middle of the night, barking like crazy, and when I got up, he snapped at me."

"Mac? He wouldn't snap at you. He's known you since he was a puppy. Maybe you were dreaming."

"I'm telling you, it wasn't a dream. If I hadn't moved my leg away, he would've bitten me."

Brian shrugged. "I don't know, maybe he heard something that spooked him. It's happened once or twice, but I'm guessing you just imagined the snapping. You were pretty tanked after all."

"Maybe. Maybe I did. All right, I'm heading out. I need a long shower, a handful of aspirin, and a nap." He picked up his car keys and walked past Mac to the door. The dog instantly reared up, pulled his head back and gave a low whine. Jason looked back at Brian. "Do you see that?"

Brian swung around in the chair and patted his leg. "Mac, come here."

Mac gave Jason a wide birth as he padded across the room to sit at Brian's feet. "He's fine. Maybe he doesn't like the way you smell this morning."

"Right. After living with you all these years? Just keep an eye on him, in case he's sick or something."

"Sure, sure I will." Brian patted Mac's head. "That's my good boy, yes." The dog swung his head around fast and gave a low growl. "Silly dog, it's Jason." Brian looked up and smiled. "Sorry, man. You do smell pretty ripe."

Jason kept his eyes on Mac's and didn't smile back.

5

Thanks to copious amounts of water and aspirin, Jason woke up from his nap hangover-free. He listened to his voice mail—two messages, one from Mitch saying hello, another from his mom asking him to call her back—tucked the phone in his pocket and walked outside.

The sun hung low in the sky, but the day still held enough light for a quick pass through the backyard with the lawn mower. As he pushed the mower back and forth, the grass brushing against his ankles, he thought about Mitch and couldn't help the stupid grin that rose to the surface. Contrary to Brian's belief, he wasn't ready to ask her to move in or marry him, but he liked her a lot. Maybe a little more than a lot.

The mower gave a small lurch in his hands and he turned it off, breathing in the scent of freshly cut grass, and flipped it on its side. It never failed. The neighbor's maple tree dropped branches into his yard all the time, and he always forgot to check before he started. One of the blades had a smear of something dark and red. He walked back over the patch of grass he'd just cut, looking for a rabbit hole or maybe the remains of a bird, courtesy of Shiny.

Something gray and white, about four inches long, lay partially concealed in the grass. Jason bent down to look closer. "Shit." The bright, sickly-sweet smell of rot rose up, strong enough to taste. He gagged and stood up, backing away. The gray was perfectly still, but the white moved in a macabre dance like a shore-bound wave.

Oh God.

He hated maggots. Give him spiders, slugs, or even roaches, but maggots? He shuddered, walked back and forth across his lawn and took several deep breaths to clear the foul smell from his lungs. He found a large rock that would have either dulled or chipped the mower blade, a small tree branch, a scrap of white paper, but no more evidence of a cat, living or dead.

Shiny wasn't in his yard, well, most of him anyway. The cat had either messed with the wrong dog or raccoon or fell victim to a neighborhood kid playing a sadistic game of vivisection. Nice. Wasn't that one of the early signs of a serial killer? Come to think of it, the boy across the street did seem strange, but strange enough to play Dr. Vet from Hell? Jason didn't know and didn't care.

He went back in the house for a plastic bag, not sure if he should call the neighbors or not. "I found a piece of your cat, I think," wasn't exactly good news, but maybe they should know Shiny was...wounded.

A cat could live without part of its tail, right?

6

Jason's boss held up his watch and gave it a shake when Jason walked past his office on Monday morning.

Asshole.

Jason had called him when he woke up at nine, he'd told him he overslept, and it wasn't a lie. He didn't tell him he overslept because he had a nightmare and refused to go back to sleep for several hours until the nightmare faded. He fell back to sleep with the mad chittering of waking birds in his ears, then turned off the alarm clock when it beeped its cheerful good morning at six-thirty.

He'd contemplated calling in sick, but in the end decided going in late was better than not going in at all. When he finally got to his desk, he regretted the decision. The company had a use-it-or-lose-it policy for vacation and sick days; last year, Jason called out sick twice and forfeited the remaining five sick days.

I should've stayed home.

The three cups of coffee he drank at home only pricked the surface of his sleep-deprived mind. He read through his email, and when he got to the end he had no idea what he'd read. He stared at the time display on his phone, wondering how he'd manage until five o'clock. The caffeine had made him jittery, but far from awake. Maybe he should just claim illness and leave early, but if he fell asleep and had the nightmare again...

He'd dreamed of a white room littered with the corpses of small animals, some without heads, others without tails, in pools of congealed blood turned a shocking red against the white of the floor. Maggots squirmed and danced on the rotted flesh, and the breeze blew its foul stink down Jason's throat. When a feathery rustle filled the room, he knew, with the surety that only comes in dreams, that soon his body, broken and battered, would lie on the floor, his blood would mingle with the animals', the maggots would cover his flesh then eat and eat and eat until he existed no more.

And somewhere, hidden in the horrible white room, someone had laughed and screamed and called his name. He'd woken up shouting incoherencies, and in the darkness the flapping of wings sounded real.

When his desk phone rang, he jumped and pushed the nightmare away. It was going to be a long day.

7

He picked Mitch up from the airport on Tuesday night, and she folded into his arms with a warm smile and an even warmer kiss. After he loaded her suitcase into the trunk of his car and pulled away from the airport, she slipped her hand into his.

Maybe it's not the right time, but she feels like the right girl.

"Did everything go okay?" he asked.

"It went a lot better than okay. I'm glad I went. Adam was a pain in the ass, but I just ignored him. His mom was really happy to see me, and that made it all worthwhile. Except at the end, when she told me I should go see my mom. Ugh."

"Why is that bad? Don't you two get along?"

"I haven't seen her in years," she said. "We talk on the phone sometimes, but that's it, and we don't really talk, just exchange words, if that makes any sense."

"It makes perfect sense. You just described the last few years of my marriage."

"What about you? Are you close with your parents?"

"We're pretty close, but lately, it's been weird. My mom is taking the whole split-up pretty hard. She liked my ex, and she blames me for the split. It's my fault, really. I should've said something earlier about the problems, but I just didn't want to look that close. I'm really good at looking the other way."

"It's not your fault," Mitch said and paused to give his hand a light squeeze. "It's human nature. You know what they say about hindsight being 20/20. And sometimes it's easier not to say anything, because then families feel like they have to get involved and help fix things."

"My mother definitely would have. My dad is a different story." Jason tapped the fingers of his left hand on the steering wheel. "There's no love lost there. He tolerated her, but never really liked her."

"A man after my own heart."

They both laughed.

"Yeah, he's a good guy. He's one of those quiet types."

And strong on the inside, where it counts.

Jason smiled.

"What?" Mitch asked.

"Oh, sorry. I just thought about something he said to me."

"Do you want to share?"

Jason shook his head. "Really, it's nothing."

"With a smile like that, it's more than nothing," Mitch said.

"When I told him about Shelley, he said I'd be fine because I was strong on the inside, where it counts. It surprised me."

"Why?"

"I've never thought of myself as strong."

"Of course you are. You lived with your ex, didn't you? I could tell what kind of person she was the minute she walked in your kitchen. You'd have to be strong to put up with that."

"But I wasn't. She jumped, and I asked how high." The minute he spoke the words, he wanted to take them back. His cheeks flooded with shame.

"Maybe you just forgot how to be strong for a while. Adam used to push me around, too. It took a long time before I realized if I stayed with him, I'd lose myself completely."

"But you left."

"You would have, too. I'm sure of it."

"I did get your message, by the way, but I didn't want to intrude or call at a bad time. I figured it was better to wait and talk to you when you got home."

She gave his hand another squeeze. "I just wanted you to know I was thinking about you."

When he stopped at a red light, he looked over. She'd kicked off

96

her shoes and sat with her legs tucked up and her cheek resting on one knee. "You look tired."

"You look tired, too."

"Yeah, I haven't been sleeping all that well. Just work stress," he lied.

He'd not had a nightmare since Sunday night, but he'd woken up on Monday at 4:00 a.m., sure he'd heard a bird in his house, but after checking every room including the attic, he went back to sleep, convinced he'd been mistaken. Last night, he'd woken up with the distinct feeling of being watched, and even after he'd turned on all the lights, the sensation had remained. He'd ended up late again for work, but luckily his boss wasn't there.

When he double-parked in front of Mitch's house, she frowned. "Aren't you going to park and come in?"

"Well, I didn't want to be presumptuous."

She laughed. "The perfect gentleman. Okay, then. Would you like to come in?"

"Yes."

"See, it's settled. No presumption necessary. You have to come in anyway, I have something for you, and it's buried in my suitcase. On Monday, I took a couple of hours for myself, found this neat little shop and saw something that made me think of you."

Once inside, she pawed through her suitcase and handed him a small, heavy object wrapped in brown paper. He unfolded the paper to find a stone griffin about five inches high, almost an exact replica of his tattoo.

"I thought it was perfect, so I had to buy it."

"It is perfect. Thank you."

"I missed you," she said in a low whisper.

"I missed you, too."

She smiled, took the griffin from his hand and put it on the coffee table, and when they kissed, all thoughts of griffins, ink or stone, vanished.

8

On Friday, when Jason got home from work, a flyer for a missing black-and-white cat named Percy hung on the light post next to his driveway. In his opinion, the name belonged to an English prep school student or a man who favored smoking jackets and cigars, not a fat tuxedo cat, but he hoped it came home soon, before the raccoon or something—or someone—worse found it.

The strange kid who lived across the street rode his bike in aimless circles in the middle of the street with a sullen expression on his face. When Jason got out of his car, the kid, maybe fourteen or fifteen, stopped the bike near the curb, staring in Jason's direction with dark, dull eyes. Jason lifted one hand in greeting. The kid's jaw moved, he blew a large, bright pink bubble, sucked the gum back in and rode off.

"Nice," Jason said and went inside.

He'd invited Mitch over for Chinese food and a game of chess. Although he hadn't played in years, when she told him she loved the game, he rummaged around in the attic until he found his old set, buried beneath a box of Shelley's winter clothes.

Mitch arrived, carrying a bottle of wine, five minutes after the deliveryman, and *he'd* shown up thirty seconds after Jason finished shoving dishes into the dishwasher, gathering up dirty laundry and setting out candles on the coffee table.

While he unpacked the bag, she poured the wine; together they carried everything into the living room and curled up next to each other on the sofa.

She pointed toward the empty bookcase. "So what happened to all your books?"

"Take a guess."

"I sort of figured."

"Yeah, but they were mostly hers, anyway, not that she read much. She just liked having them around. Those are mine, though." Jason waved his chopsticks at a small pile of paperbacks stacked on the corner of the coffee table, next to the stone griffin. "I picked them up last week. They just haven't made it to the shelf yet."

"We should go to the bookstore. I think you need more than four books. Those shelves look lonely." She speared a chunk of sweet and sour chicken. "Maybe we should go tomorrow. Unless you have other plans?"

"Well, I do know this sexy blonde, and I was going to—"

A plastic-wrapped fortune cookie hit him square in the chest. "Sexy, huh?"

"Very," he said.

She leaned over and pressed her lips, soft and sticky from the food, against his. When she broke the kiss, the corners of her mouth lifted. "I am going to kick your ass in chess."

"You think so, huh?"

"Oh, I know so. My father taught me when I was eight."

"I have you beat. My grandfather taught me when I was six. I beat him the first time when I was ten."

"Lightweight. I beat my dad at nine. He was better at teaching than playing, but he never let me win. He said it was good for my character to learn how to lose. Not that I lost that much, but..."

After they finished the food and dumped the empty containers, Jason lit the candles and turned off the lamps, plunging the room into a golden glow that made Mitch's hair shimmer.

"Kind of cheesy, I know," he said.

She shrugged. "I don't think so. I like it."

She clapped her hands together when he pulled out the box containing the chess set.

"Wow," she said, picking up one of the pieces. "These are all hand-carved, aren't they?"

He nodded, placing the board on the table. "It belonged to my grandfather. My grandmother bought it for him when they were first married. He used to sit on the front porch and chain smoke while he explained strategies to me and my brothers, but I'm the only one who could beat him. He used to curse under his breath when I won, then my grandmother would come out and yell at him. He was like every movie version of the typical grumpy old man. He'd yell at the neighborhood kids for running across his lawn, grumble when it rained the day after he washed his car and gripe about whatever president served in office. All bark and no bite, though. A real softie at heart."

Mitch set the piece down in its spot. "Like you. Oh, wait, before we play, we need to read our fortunes." She unwrapped a cookie, cracked it open, and grinned. "'*Man should be like turtle. Slow, steady, and with a thick shell.*' I think this means it's going to be a long game."

Jason broke his in half. "'*A man without dreams is a man without vision.*'" he read, and a chill raced down his spine. One of the candles sputtered out with a soft hiss, leaving behind a thin trail of curling smoke.

When he put the cookie aside, Mitch shook her head. "Nope, you have to eat it, otherwise you'll have bad luck."

He refilled their wine glasses, and they played chess in silence. A tiny crease between her brows appeared and disappeared as she contemplated each move. Flames from the candles reflected in her eyes, turning them into dark sapphire pools. Every so often, she'd shake her hair out of her eyes. Each time, Jason caught a hint of her shampoo—neither coconut nor the flowery sweet smell, but vanilla. Halfway through the match, Jason knew he'd lost the game, but they played on anyway. He liked watching her fingers touch the pieces with something close to reverence and the way she nibbled on her lower lip right before she lifted her hand away.

After several more moves, she looked up and smiled. "Do you want to keep playing?"

Without a word, he pulled her into his arms, tasting wine and fortune cookie when their lips met. His breath turned ragged and hungry as she traced long, lazy strokes up and down his back and gently tugged the back of his hair. He lifted off her shirt, ran his fingers across her collarbones, then down to her nipples, hard beneath the dark blue lace of her bra. When she pressed her lips against his neck, a shiver of anticipation raced up his spine. After he unhooked her bra, he bent his head down to her breasts, sliding his tongue around first one nipple, then the other.

She stiffened in his arms. "Shit, stop." She pushed him away, grabbed her shirt and pulled it over her chest.

"What's wrong?"

"I just saw someone looking in the window," she said, breathing hard.

Jason stalked over to the front window, his hands clenched into fists. He'd shut the blinds, but two of the slats hung askew, leaving just enough room for someone to peek out. Or in. The neighbor boy's bike sat on its side on the curb, one tire spinning in lazy circles, but there was no sign of the neighbor boy himself. Great. The psycho kid moonlit as a peeping Tom; wasn't that behavior part of the serial killer's handbook, too? Jason turned the rod to close the blinds and turned back to Mitch. "I'm sorry, I think it was the neighbor's kid. I don't know what the hell his problem is. Give me a second, okay?"

But by the time he opened the front door and stepped out onto the porch, the kid had fled, his bike disappearing into the shadows as he pedaled down the street.

9

"On three?"

"You know we're going to get soaked."

Mitch grinned. "But it'll be fun, and we can dry off later."

On the way to the bookstore, the light drizzle that started in the morning had turned into a full-fledged storm. They sat in the car, parked at the far end of the lot (the only available space Jason could find) with rain bouncing off the roof—a steady drone that swallowed up the ticking of the cooling engine. The streaks of water dripping down the windows coupled with the condensation on the inside made everything beyond the glass a blur of color and indeterminate shape.

"One."

"We could just give it another five minutes," Jason said.

"Two."

"I should mention that I used to run track in school."

"Oooh, so it'll be a challenge then. Three!"

They opened their doors at the same time and sprinted across the lot, linking hands halfway. When they burst through the entrance with hair plastered to their heads and jeans soaked at the cuffs, a customer standing by the door shook his head. "You're both crazy," he said, but he wore a smile that reached all the way up to his eyes.

Mitch peeled off her jacket, pushed her hair back and shook the rain from her fingertips before she grabbed a shopping basket. "It was his idea," she said over her shoulder as they passed the customer. "He's the crazy one."

Dodging bright-faced children and suburban housewives, they made their way through the aisles until they reached a section in the back. She stopped in front of one of the shelves, handed him the basket and rubbed her hands together. "Okay, where do we start?"

"I am at your mercy," Jason said.

"Are you sure about that? Give me a half hour in this place, and I could empty your bank account."

"I trust your judgment. Pick your favorites, and if I don't like them, I'll bring them over to your place, or you can read them when you're at mine."

She turned her face toward the shelf but not before he saw her smile.

"It's a deal." She tucked her hair behind her ears and ran her fingers across the spines. "Here, you have to read this one," she said, holding out a paperback. "It gave me nightmares."

The book had a black cat with glowing yellow eyes on the cover.

Come hang out in my neighborhood, and I bet that kid will wipe the snarl off your face.

Someone bumped into his hip, and he moved aside. When the bump came again, he turned with an admonition under his breath but stopped before it came out. An old man with a stooped back and a cane in one hand shuffled past, stopped to grab a book from the shelf, and sighed as it slipped out of his hand onto the floor. He leaned on his cane and started to reach down.

Jason bent down and picked it up, catching a glimpse of wrinkled cheeks, sagging jowls and wet, pale eyes before the old man took the book from his hand. The sleeve of his shirt slid up, revealing a tattoo of a snarling bear, oddly bright against his aged skin. Their fingertips touched, and Jason pulled his hand back fast, resisting the urge to wipe his hand on his pants to rid the loose, slippery feel of the man's skin from his own.

"Thanks, sonny," the old man said, with a voice as gnarled as his hands. "It is a rough thing, growing old. Enjoy your youth while you can."

He gave Jason a wet, rheumy wink and shuffled out of the aisle, leaving behind a stale smell, a mix of cigarette smoke and something else, a sickly nursing home smell—a nursing home where all the patients had terminal illnesses, and the stink of their diseases leaked out of their pores. As he stepped out of sight, a raspy, singsong whisper emerged from his lips. "Had a girl and she sure was fine."

It was, perhaps, a snippet from an old song, but his grizzled voice turned it obscene. The words trailed off into a hum as he limped out of sight, and Jason's arms broke out in gooseflesh. Something about the song danced in the back of his head. He fought the urge to go after him and ask—

What? He's just an old man who can barely walk.

Mitch wrinkled her nose and waved her hand in front of her face. "Poor thing," she whispered, then pulled another book from the shelf. When she turned the cover in his direction, he put the old man out of his mind. "You've read this one, right?"

"No. I've heard of it, but I never had a chance to read it. You saw my entire, pathetic collection of books the other night."

"Well, it's one of the scariest books ever. Um, you're not afraid of clowns, are you?"

"Not at all, at least I wasn't until I saw that cover."

"He's great, isn't he? Let's see..." She scanned the shelves and added two more to the basket. "Oh, definitely this one. It's more fantasy than horror, but the story's great. And the other one is fabulous. Two boys, a crazy magician, a girl that is really a—" She laughed. "Nope. I'm not going to spoil it. You'll have to read it to find out."

Jason shifted the basket to his other hand. "If you keep this up, we're going to need another basket."

"I warned you," she said, leaning close.

He moved forward, bridging the gap between them, and kissed her.

"Imagine this."

The voice rang out, too loud and too dramatic, accompanied by a whiff of perfume, and he and Mitch both jumped.

Just perfect.

"Hello, Shelley," he said, turning around. "Nicole."

Nicole's face remained blank as she sized Mitch up with a long, lazy look, but Shelley kept her eyes on Jason's, her lips pressed together in a tight, thin line. The ring finger on her left hand was bare, but on her right, a new ring with a dark blue stone sparkled in the store lighting, not quite large enough to cover the tiny, dark mole near her little finger. She caught Jason's glance and raised one eyebrow, daring him to make a comment.

On impulse, he reached up with his right hand to idly scratch his left arm. The fabric at the edge of the sleeve bunched up, revealing the bottom of the tattoo. A flash of anger twisted her features, turning them hard.

See that, Frank? Aren't you glad you don't live with her?

He dropped his hand and waited, but she held her tongue, and an uneasy silence stretched out between them.

"So who's your friend, Jason?" Nicole asked.

"This is Mitch. Mitch, Nicole, and you remember Shelley, don't you?"

Mitch smiled. "Of course. It's nice to meet you, Nicole."

Nicole gave her a curt nod in reply.

Shelley looked down at the basket in Jason's hand and finally spoke. "A little light reading?"

"Just refilling my bookshelves," he said.

She tossed her hair over her shoulder. "Yes, well, it's obvious you're not interested in filling them with anything worthwhile," she said, her eyes on Mitch.

Mitch just smiled and slid her hand in Jason's.

"I think that depends on your point of view," Jason said.

"Well, we'll let you two get back to your shopping," Nicole said and tugged Shelley's hand. Shelley opened her mouth as if to let loose with a parting barb, then shook her head and spun on her heels.

"My, my," Mitch said after they raced out of the aisle. "I don't think they like me very much."

"Don't worry. They don't like me much either," Jason said.

Mitch laughed and gave his hand a squeeze.

10

Jason rushed into the office on Tuesday morning, his hair still damp from the shower, holding tight to the backpack slung over his shoulder as he passed his boss in the hallway. He held his breath, but received nothing more than a raised eyebrow.

He'd screamed himself awake in the middle of the night and sat in bed shaking while the nightmare faded, grateful Mitch hadn't spent the night. When he fell back to sleep, it returned; he woke the second time thrashing in twisted sheets, with nothing left behind of the dream but a sense of sorrow and pain and an odd stiffness in his left arm. His phone rang as he pulled out his laptop, and he sank down in his chair before answering.

"I'm sorry to bother you at work," his father said, "but your mother is convinced you're mad at her and asked me to call you."

"It's okay," Jason said, rotating his shoulder. "I'm not mad at her. I've just been busy."

Frank, are you doing flips in there or something?

"That's what I told her, but you know your mother. Shelley hasn't returned any of her calls, either."

"I'm not surprised. I didn't think she would."

"I didn't either and honestly, I think it's better that way. I told your mother that, too, but she doesn't want to hear it. She always thinks she can fix things. She means well, you know that, but sometimes she only sees what she wants to." His father cleared his throat. "Like with Ryan and Eve. Ryan keeps telling me they're fine when I ask, but I know he's lying. There's no shame in calling it quits sometimes. Life is way too short to spend it miserable. Anyway, enough of that. How are you doing, son?"

The phone slid out of Jason's hand, but he caught it before it landed on the desk. An innocuous question his father had asked many times before, but he'd forgotten one word this time.

How are you doing, son, really?

Jason had always brushed it off as nothing more than the words themselves, but the real meaning was hidden in the last word. He'd asked the same thing when Jason had a problem with a bully in fifth grade, but then it meant "did that little punk give you any grief today?" When Jason's answers went from "okay" to "I don't want to talk about it," his father went to the school. Although Jason overheard his dad tell his mom that trained monkeys could operate the school better than the morons who worked there, the bully left Jason alone after that, and the word—really—disappeared from his dad's question.

How are you doing, son, really?

How many years had his father been asking the question since he got involved with Shelley? Jason traced the edge of his desk with his fingertips. Since the beginning, the very beginning, right after he introduced her to them.

He's been my father for almost thirty years, and I'm just now figuring it out.

At the last family gathering he'd asked Jason and Ryan the same question, but to Chris, he'd simply asked, "How are you doing," because Chris was doing fine, and he knew it. If Chris and Lisa's marriage was any sweeter, they'd both have a mouthful of cavities.

Jason dropped his voice low. "How long, Dad. How long did you know?"

"What? About Ryan and Eve, or you and Shelley?"

"Me and Shelley."

"Jason, you know I'm not one to meddle. I leave that to your mother. I believe everyone has to make their own way and along the way, make their own mistakes. I always figured if you wanted to talk about it you would have."

"I didn't know how bad things were," Jason said. "I mean, I knew I was unhappy, but..."

"Sometimes it's like fine print. You know it's there, but it's too blurry to read. You can't see it when you're in it, but you're out of it now, so that's all that matters. The rest? It is what it is."

Despite the lump in the back of his throat, Jason smiled.

"Your mom is out right now, she'll be home later tonight. Maybe you should give her a call, but only if you want to, okay? And I know she'll remind you, too, but don't forget that we're having a birthday party for your brother here on Saturday."

Shit. He'd made plans with Mitch.

"You are coming, right?"

"Yeah, of course I'll be there."

A throat cleared; Jason's boss stood in the doorway with a stack of paper in his hands.

"Okay, Dad. I have to go. I'll give Mom a call tonight."

11

"Oh, come on," Jason said, slamming on his brakes to avoid the front bumper of the car in front of him. He'd left the office later than usual, thanks to a new, time-sensitive project his boss had dumped on his lap, but not late enough to avoid the rush hour traffic. He sighed, glaring at the string of brake lights in front of him, and picked up his phone, regretting the decision as soon as his mother picked up the phone.

"Have you talked to Shelley? She won't return my calls." Her voice was hard, her words clipped.

"Mom, please. No, I haven't talked to her. We are not getting back together."

"Jason—"

"I know you keep thinking this is just some type of separation or argument but it isn't. We're done. It's really over. We've been having problems for years. Years. I'm glad it's over because it's been miserable. I've been miserable."

Sometimes she only sees what she wants to see.

"But—"

"I'm serious. This is not a bad thing, okay? And she's already involved with someone else."

"What? Please tell me you're joking."

"No, I'm not. She's been seeing this person for a long time."

His mother fell silent for so long he thought she hung up. As he passed a three-car accident, the drivers' yells mingled with the smell of exhaust and gasoline, and traffic slowed even more.

"I don't know what to say," she finally said, the hard edge gone. "Why didn't you tell me?"

"I didn't want to say anything because I thought you and Shelley might stay in touch, and this person isn't the real reason we split anyway. I wasn't lying about the problems. This split has been a long time coming."

He inched his way to the far right lane as his exit approached.

"I'm sorry, I wish you would have told me. No wonder she hasn't called me back. And what about you? Did you have someone else, too?"

"No, I didn't," he said, as he pulled onto the exit.

"Good. I raised you better than that."

"I know you did. Before I forget to ask, what time is everyone getting there on Saturday?"

"Two o'clock. Will you bring a bag of ice? I asked Ryan, but I'm afraid he might forget. He always does. And Jason? I'm sorry I blamed you. I really am."

Jason pulled into his driveway a few minutes after they said their goodbyes. He grabbed his backpack, humming under his breath as he stepped up onto the back porch, but a cloud of foul-smelling air turned the hum into a strangled gasp.

"Oh, shit."

A long black tail, with dark streaks of blood matting the white tip, lay curled in a neat spiral in the center of the doormat.

Did I walk right past it this morning?

He replayed the morning in his head: the frantic leap from the bed, the five minute shave and shower, the rush downstairs, the quick grab of his backpack, keys, and cell phone, the bleary-eyed run to his car, not thinking about anything but getting to the office. Yes, it could've been there. He must have stepped right over it, because if he'd stepped on it, the squish of flesh and fur and the crack of tiny bones would've stopped him in his tracks.

And were there maggots? Oh yes, plenty of them, squirming and twisting on the ragged end, partially obscuring the gore. A soft breeze pushed the sick-sweet smell of rot in his face and down his throat, and his stomach lurched. He shoved the key in the lock, thrust the door open and stumbled into the kitchen, the stench following close behind.

Once inside, he turned on the faucet and splashed cold water on his face, then drank from his cupped palms, washing away the slick taste of roadkill in his mouth. He wiped his hands dry on his pants and grabbed a trash bag before heading back outside.

Suppressing a shudder, he rolled up the mat and slid it into the trash bag. His stomach twisted as he knotted the bag. Two cat tails? No coincidence there. And why were they left in his yard? He held the bag away from his body as he carried it to the trashcan at the end of the yard and took several deep breaths once he slammed the lid shut.

He'd never seen a cat and a raccoon fight, but raccoons were tough; a cat wouldn't stand a chance. After a fight, bits and pieces might be left over. As he approached the porch, his breath caught in his throat. A wad of bubble gum was nestled in the crack at the base of the bottom step—bright pink bubble gum.

12

Another storm rolled in Thursday night, carrying a heavy veil of humidity. Jason sat in his living room with the windows open and his laptop on his lap, pretending to work. A distant rumble of thunder sent a neighbor's dog into a fit of barking, then a voice called out and a door slammed shut, cutting off the sound. He stared at the long columns of price plans and minute usage until his eyes blurred, giving up once the first raindrops landed on the roof.

He closed the windows, grabbed a beer and went out to sit on the back porch. Dark, oily clouds roiled across the hazy sky, brightened at the edges by flashes of intermittent lightning. Rain bounced off the tin roof with small echoing ticks; the sound held a peaceful, hypnotic rhythm.

Many years before, Shelley had wanted to change the tin for a regular shingled roof, but Jason had refused—one of the few battles he'd won. The tin roof reminded him of summer nights spent at the house during his childhood. Whenever it rained, his grandfather would grab a beer and sit out on the porch. He told Jason there was music in the rain, if he listened hard enough.

Wind blew through the trees, rattling the branches, and the leaves made slapping noises as they shook. A light spray of rain misted his face. He'd not said a word to anyone about the cat tail and the gum, although he'd come close to telling Mitch when he called to change their Saturday plans. He was sure the neighbor boy was responsible, but how could he tell the parents? He *should* tell them, but they weren't friends. They weren't even acquaintances. In fact, he couldn't remember the last time he saw the mother, and the father was just a vague, suited blur who emerged from the house in the morning at the same time as Jason. His car, a sleek, dark thing with tinted windows, was never in the driveway when Jason got home. There was an older sister, a red-haired girl with long, coltish legs and a perpetual frown on her pale face, and although she didn't seem as strange as her brother, she wasn't friendly.

The family never attended the annual block party; they were quiet and kept to themselves. And wasn't that what Jeffrey Dahmer's neighbors said? The old stereotype—he seemed like such a nice kid. The bicycle-riding, gum-chewing kid didn't fit that bill, though. He was odd, yet odd didn't mean he was into magic tricks.

Poof, watch the kitty disappear.

Jason could imagine it, if he summoned up the courage to pay them a visit. "Hello, I live across the street and I think your son is playing doctor with the neighborhood animals. Oh yeah, he also likes to peek in windows." They'd slam the door in his face. And wouldn't he in the same situation? Watching crime dramas on television didn't make him an expert in anything but a Hollywood construct of crime scenes and lab work.

He took a sip of beer and shifted in the chair, wincing at the pain in his left arm. He'd woken up with it tucked under his body, and until the pins and needles started, it hung at his side, nothing more than a lump of dead flesh, as if Dr. Frankenstein had snuck in during the night, removed his real arm and replaced it with the inanimate limb of a corpse.

The wind picked up, blowing rain across the porch. He finished his beer and went inside.

13

Jason woke up at 3:30 a.m. with a shout caught in his throat. He sat up in bed, beads of sweat cooling on his brow and trailing down his spine. His mind tried to shake off the hands of sleep, but the dream didn't want to let him go. A vague sense of chaotic movement hovered in the back of his mind, a remembrance of being dragged him by his arm to an unknown, hostile place of heat and stone, some unpleasant place where his struggles meant nothing.

The dream lingered, beckoning him back down into the deep. He fought against it, but his eyelids slid shut, his chin dropped down, once, twice and—

The horrible smell of smoke, ash and cinder. Distant, pain-filled screams. His feet burned as they scraped across rocky ground. Sweat from the heat stung his eyes. A voice. A scream. His own? Heat. Fire. Wind. Angry, flapping wings. And so much—

Jason's eyes snapped open. No. He was not going back. He stood up on shaky legs and stumbled to the bathroom. His hand missed the light switch but found the cold, porcelain edge of the sink, then the curved faucet. He ran the cold water for several long minutes and splashed his face until the dream retreated.

As the water bubbled out of the sink, he turned on the light. Dark purple smudges shadowed the skin underneath his eyes. The left side of his neck hurt, stiff where it curved into the shoulder, and he rubbed it hard. His fingertips found a hard little knot under the skin, and he pushed it, gritting his teeth when discomfort turned to pain. When the knot finally released, his shoulder sagged in relief.

Heading out of the bathroom, he flipped the switch with his left hand and stopped. He took a step back and turned the light on again, walking backward until his body reappeared in the mirror over the sink, with eyes as wide as a carousel horse.

Several dots of dried blood marred the skin on his left arm only an inch above the crease of his elbow. Small specks so dark they appeared almost black. They weren't horrible. A bug bite, or scratches made by the edge of sharp fingernails in the midst of a dark dream. No, they weren't horrible at all, but his skin... His skin was horribly wrong. No gaping wounds or torn flesh. No signs of violence but wrong nonetheless. He made a sound in the back of his throat. The beginning of a what? A yell? A scream? Maybe the dream still held him tight. That would make sense. Asleep and dreaming. And maybe in his dream world he didn't have a tattoo because the skin on his arm was as ink-free as it had been the night he met Sailor in the bar.

No tattoo. Geryon, Frank, or otherwise.

Jason couldn't tear his eyes away from the mirror. He grabbed the edge of the sink with both hands, holding tight to the porcelain as if it were a talisman or a totem of good luck and reappearing tattoos. He closed his eyes and counted to ten.

Tattoos don't disappear. It's just my eyes playing tricks.

No matter what, he wouldn't say a word, and he definitely would not yell. He held onto the sink hard enough to make his fingertips ache while the exhaust fan whirred overhead. A faint, metallic smell wafted up from the drain. The smell of coins piled up at the bottom of a fountain filled with scummy water. The smell of a man killing time.

Jason opened his eyes.

He looked in the mirror first, then down at his arm. His heart gave a heavy thud. No trace, no suggestion, of ink at all. His right hand lifted. Stopped. Lifted. Stopped. He raised his hand again and turned off the light. His fingers itched to turn it back on and check again, but his mind refused. Tattoos, nothing more than ink drawings, did not get up and walk away. A very loud voice in the back of his mind shouted in protest. It called him a wimp, an idiot, a fool.

He wasn't going to turn on the light again, not for all the money in the world. The bathroom rug felt warm under his feet, too warm to be anything but real. He could accept the fact he wasn't dreaming, but he would not accept an ink-free arm. It didn't work like that.

It's there. It has to be.

He walked back into the bedroom, his steps slow and heavy. He'd left the light on, and it bathed his room in a soft bluish glow, low lighting but bright enough to see the socks he'd tossed on the floor. Bright enough to see a tattoo or a lack of one.

The compulsion to look down at his arm felt like a strong hand on the back of his head, pushing it down. *Look. Look.* The kid in the back room at the party with a joint in his extended hand. *You know you want to. Come on, it won't hurt.*

No. Not for a second, not for a half second; it was better to be a fool than a madman. If he looked and saw bare un-inked skin he might not be able to hold in a yell. He might scream out loud. If he saw its absence again how could he convince himself of a dream, a daydream, a hallucination? It wasn't worth the risk.

And anyway, there's nothing to see. Move along, nothing here.

A smell lingered in the room, an odd, musky scent like an animal's fur—a feral, hungry smell—and the voice in his head shouted things that did not (and could not) make sense. He shoved back at the voice until it choked on its own words and gave up.

Dream trickery, that and nothing more.

He climbed into bed, burying his face in the pillow, and the smell of Mitch's coconut shampoo kept him company. He thought of her face, her smile, the soft noise she made in the back of her throat when he kissed her neck. He did not think about ink or skin.

14

When Jason woke up, his eyes protested the sun's invasion of his bedroom. The curtains were wide open, and the overcast sky had gone on holiday. He moved on autopilot into the bathroom. The sun turned the walls into panels of luminosity so bright they sent a searing pain through his temples.

He gripped the edges of the sink, the porcelain cold on his palms. The metal smell drifted up again, and he fought the urge to go back in his room and grab a coin. Heads, he looked. Tails, he didn't. Near the very bottom of the sink, a single hair curled into a small, backwards C. Too short to be Mitch's and anyway, it was dark, not light and—

Stop being a coward and just look up.

White-knuckled, he did. His hair stood up from his scalp in crazy, porcupine spikes, bruise-colored shadows marred the skin under his red-rimmed, bleary eyes and his arm... He sagged against the sink in relief.

"Hi, Frank." His voice, ragged at the edges, came out in little more than a whisper.

The tattoo, with all its intricate lines and shading, did not answer back.

A dream. All of it. The illusion of unmarked skin, the panicked flutter of his heart, the strange smell. Nothing more than a late-night subconscious trick, no matter how real his imagination made it.

Of course it was a trick. Tattoos don't disappear.

15

John S. Iblis stood before the wrought-iron gate surrounding the Washington Monument, staring up at the structure—178 feet of white marble with a standing figure of good old George Washington himself on top. The monument had been built in Baltimore's Mount Vernon area more than fifty years before the one in Washington D.C., and such a fuss it had created. Rumors of portents in the shape of shooting stars and an eagle landing atop the monument. Or so John had heard.

With a sigh, he gave the sturdy padlock barring his entrance one last tug, then walked away. Such a shame, really. He had always been fond of the view from the top.

Chapter Five

Below the Waterline

1

The bag of ice slapped against Jason's thigh as he carried it into his parents' house. His sister-in-law's distinct laugh, high-pitched with an odd lilt at the end, rang out from the kitchen and, a moment later, his mother's followed. Ryan slouched on the sofa next to their dad, his lips pressed in a tight line and his eyes shadowed. Problems with Eve, no doubt. The two spent more time arguing, although in quiet, clipped tones, at family functions than not. They did their best to hide it, especially from his mom, but the tension was always palpable.

But Mom just sees what she wants to.

Judging from Ryan's expression, the argument had already started. Jason knew the rules, though; the problems between he and Eve were off-limits.

"The cooler is on the back porch, as always," his dad said, after giving Jason a hug. "Can you take the ice out?"

Ryan followed him out the sliding glass door to the porch and lit a cigarette while Jason dumped the ice in the cooler. "I heard the big news about you and Shelley splitting up. Mom told me when she called me the other day. You really shook her up with that one. Maybe you should've waited a while, you know, gave her a few hints first before dropping the bomb."

"Believe me, it would've been worse if I'd waited, especially if she'd called Shelley, thinking everything was okay. Did she tell you about my tattoo, too? I think that freaked her out more than the split."

"You got a tattoo? You?"

"Check it out," Jason lifted his sleeve, wincing at the ache.

"That's wicked cool. Damn. I can't believe you of all people got a tat."

"What's that supposed to mean?"

Ryan shrugged. "No offense, but you just never seemed like the type, that's all. So what really happened with you and Shelley?"

"The short version? She was seeing someone else."

Ryan's eyes grew wide. "The ice queen had an affair?"

"Yeah, but it's not a big deal, things were bad long before that."

"No shit, Sherlock. Anyone could see that. You look a hell of a lot happier, that's for sure."

"It's hard not to. We should've split up a long time ago."

"You lucky son of a bitch." Ryan took a long drag from his cigarette. "I wish I could say the same thing. I fucking hate being married some days, and today is one of those days." He dropped his voice low. "Eve is pregnant. We found out this week. We haven't told Mom and Dad yet, so whatever you do, don't say anything."

"No, I wo—"

"There you are." Their mom stepped out on the porch and gave Jason a hug, holding onto him a little longer than usual. A flare of pain raced up his arm, from elbow to shoulder. "Put that out and both of you come inside," she said to Ryan. "I thought you were going to quit."

"Mom, please."

Voices drifted out through the open sliding door, and her face brightened. "Your brother and the girls. Well, are you two going to stand out here all day or are you going to come in and be sociable?"

Jason followed her in; Ryan followed suit a few minutes later. By that time, Jason had already said happy birthday to Chris and hello to his wife. Chris and Lisa both wore bright smiles, a strong contrast to the strained one on Ryan's face. He bent down to say hello to his nieces, both toddling over on chubby legs, and Mia tugged on his ear. A heartbeat later, Allison grabbed his nose.

Mia, the elder by three minutes, grabbed his left arm, then pulled her hand away with a frown, her face twisting into the expression his dad called the monkey look—eyebrows drawn close together, chin lowered, mouth turned down—and everyone laughed. The old family photo albums contained many pictures of all three boys with the same look when they were kids.

Allison reached forward and touched his arm, too, and soon enough, her face matched Mia's. She didn't pull her hand away, though. She pushed up the sleeve of his shirt and stared at the tattoo, then poked it with one finger. She looked Jason in the eye and shook her head. "Bad," she said.

Chris and Lisa both laughed.

"Yes, you keep thinking that way, baby girl," Chris said. "No ink for you."

Ryan rolled his eyes. "Your kids have no taste, that's all I can say."

When Mia reached over and pulled Allison's hand away, Allison tipped her face up to Jason, her lower lip trembling and tears shining in the corners of her eyes.

Great. My nieces are scared of my tattoo. Nice job, Frank.

"Bad birdie," Mia said.

"Bad birdie," Allison echoed.

"I'm glad I'm not the only one who thinks it was a silly idea," Jason's mother said, and everyone laughed except Jason and the twins.

2

Jason arrived at Mitch's house a little after six, and she asked him what was wrong as soon as she closed the front door.

"Nothing, why?"

She touched his cheek. "I don't know, you just look like something's bothering you."

He put his arms around her, held her close and kissed away her frown. When they parted, the question remained in her eyes. "It's not a big thing, and it's probably going to sound really stupid..." He rubbed the skin under his jaw.

"I don't think it'd bother you so much if it was something stupid, but if you don't want to tell me, that's okay, too."

"No, I just, I don't know, it was weird. My nieces saw my tattoo and after that, they avoided me all afternoon, then they refused to give me a hug goodbye when I left. My mom thought it was cute, but they were acting like they were afraid of me because I have a tattoo. See? I told you it was stupid."

"It's not stupid. How old are they?"

"My nieces? Two and a half."

"So they're babies."

"Yeah."

She touched his cheek again. "And does anyone else in your family have a tattoo?"

"My brother, Ryan, does."

"Have they seen it?"

"No, I don't think so. It's on his back."

"Well, then, there you go. Kids are funny sometimes, that's all it is." She kissed his forehead. "You shouldn't take it so personally. Now, close your eyes," she said, taking his hand to lead him through the living room into the kitchen. "Keep them closed, and no peeking."

120

She'd turned the lighting in the kitchen low; he could tell even with his eyes closed. Her feet made soft, slippery sounds on the floor, and the scent of spices and roasting meat wafted through the room. Then he heard the clink of glass, the scraping of something, maybe a spoon, against the side of a pot, the quick snick of a zipper. Opening or closing? He resisted the urge to peek, drumming his fingers on the edge of the table instead.

"Okay, open your eyes."

The candlelight turned her eyes dark. She'd changed out of her jeans into a shimmering dress that flared out loose around her hips and hung down to her ankles. Her skin gleamed pale against the dark fabric.

He reached out and pulled her over. "What's the occasion?" he said, sliding his arms around her hips.

"No occasion at all. I just thought it would be a nice surprise. Do you want to have dinner first or dessert?"

"Dessert. Definitely dessert."

3

When Jason pulled onto his street on Sunday afternoon, he found the annual neighborhood block party in full swing. Music, loud and bass heavy, pushed up into the air. Several neighbors had pulled their grills out onto the sidewalk and stood by in flip-flops and khaki shorts, flipping burgers and drinking bottles of beer concealed inside foam cozies. Kids ran in erratic circles in the middle of the street, enjoying the warm weather. The sky was a perfect shade of spring blue dotted with fluffy clouds in crazy popcorn shapes.

Maybe he'd grab a few bottles of beer from his refrigerator and be sociable for an hour or two before he settled down to work; he didn't want to spend his entire Sunday stuck behind his laptop. He turned into his driveway, and his hands tightened on the steering wheel. A bike leaned against the side of his house, half hidden behind an azalea bush, far enough back so it wasn't visible from the street, but the kid was nowhere in sight.

So where was he? Crouched by a window, trying to have a little look-see? And if so? The kid, old enough to have racing hormones, probably hoped to catch a glimpse of Mitch. In the summer of Jason's fourteenth year, a very young nurse housesat for the family next door when they went on vacation. She worked at night and spent the hot afternoons stretched out on a towel in the backyard. The sight of her cleavage spilling out of her bikini top was enough to make Jason forget his name, and he'd discovered he could see her if he climbed halfway up one of the trees in his own yard. For two weeks, he'd spent hours up in the tree, hidden from view, watching her. After that, she became the object of many a fantasy and many sticky midnight dreams.

But since the kid's bike was parked—hidden—near the end of the house, the absence of Jason's car would be obvious. Which meant he knew no one was home. So what was he doing?

The music swallowed up the sound of his car door opening and closing. Jason crept around to the back of the house and peeked around the corner. No one lurked by any of the windows or stood on his porch. He rubbed his forehead. The kid could be crouched down on the other side of the porch, but for what reason?

Jason had good deadbolt locks on his doors, and he knew all the windows were locked up tight; the kid had to be somewhere outside the house. Plus, if there'd been thefts in the neighborhood, the community association would've added it to their monthly bulletin. If, in fact, the kid *was* breaking into houses, he couldn't be stealing anything worth value. Of course, he could be stealing dirty magazines or women's underwear, something to make his own midnight dreams a little sweeter. What man would admit that his secret stash of porn had disappeared? A wife might notice her favorite blue panties were gone, but she'd probably blame the dryer or maybe the dog.

At the far edge of the porch, a small black mound rose up, then disappeared, a small black mound that looked suspiciously like the top of a baseball cap. "I got you," Jason whispered. The mound made another quick up-down bob, and he crept forward, keeping his feet on the grassy patch between the sidewalk and the house. His heart rate sped up as he closed the distance. When he reached the porch, he quickened his steps and rounded the corner. The kid, indeed wearing a baseball cap, looked up, his mouth dropping open.

"What do you think you're doing?" Jason said, reaching out.

His fingers brushed the edge of the kid's sleeve, but the fabric slipped out of his hand when the kid crab-walked backward several feet away. Then he scrambled to his feet, thrust his hand forward, and something flew through the air toward Jason's chest. Jason stepped back and waved his hand, knocking it out of the air. The kid took off running, back down along the side of the house, toward the front, and Jason started forward, then skidded to a halt. The kid had already made it to the front lawn. He'd never catch him, and if his neighbors saw him giving chase, what would they think?

He stalked back and nudged the grass with the toe of his shoe, revealing a foot-long stick the width of his finger. A small scrap of bark clung to the front of his shirt; he brushed it away and bent down. The kid had dug several long grooves in the empty flowerbed next to the porch. Jason used his foot to fill them in.

Then a loud thump came from the end of the yard, and Jason whirled around, his mouth dry. The door to the shed hung halfway open. The latch didn't close properly, and if the door wasn't given an extra push when closed, it popped back open, swinging back to thump against the corner.

What had the kid expected to find in the shed? A small stretch of the imagination provided an answer, not a nice answer but an answer nonetheless. Maybe he wanted hedge trimmers; they would do some serious damage to soft kitty flesh.

Jason crossed the yard and swung the door all the way open. The rake, the lawn mower and the hedge trimmers were all in their places, neat and tidy. He shut the door, making sure to give it the extra push, promising himself to buy a lock. The kid had been empty-handed, but it didn't mean he wouldn't come back.

4

When the sun began its descent in the sky on Monday night, Jason slipped on his shoes and left the house, locking the door tight behind him. The early evening air, cool with only a hint of a breeze, made the perfect excuse for a walk.

The kid's bike sat out on his front lawn (Jason had left it propped up against his own house; the kid had come back to reclaim it sometime during the night), but the house itself loomed dark and lifeless, the driveway empty. Jason strolled down to the end of the street. A few teenagers sat on the curb in front of a big white house, doing a lot of nothing, but the neighbor kid wasn't one of them. He crossed the street and walked back up.

I just want to know why he's nosing around my house, that's all.

He'd stopped after work to buy a new doormat, wondering, when he'd set it down on the porch, if the kid would leave him another present. Maybe he'd be nice enough to leave it on the step the next time.

Two steps away from the kid's still-dark house, a collie dashed up the sidewalk, trailing a leash behind it, and stopped right in front of him. It lifted its nose to sniff the air, then backed up. An old man with thinning hair and a paunch came jogging up the walk a few seconds later.

"I'm sorry, Jasper pulled the leash right out of my hand, then he ran away from me. He thinks it's a game. I don't run as well as I used to, but he doesn't realize that."

Jason put out his hand; the collie cocked his head, then bared his teeth. No growl, just very visible, very long teeth.

"Come on, Jasper, say hello to our neighbor."

Jasper flattened his ears and settled back on his haunches. Jason pulled his hand back and introduced himself.

124

"Don't mind Jasper. I guess he's just not himself tonight. He usually loves people. I'm Martin," the man said. "Martin Cooper. I live in the brick house down at the corner."

"The one with the big flagpole, right?"

"You got it. That one's yours, right?" Martin pointed.

"No, the one next to it."

Jasper lifted his lips, revealing more teeth. Martin didn't notice, but Jason did. He wouldn't want to be alone with the dog, collie or not.

"Well, Jason, I'd love to stay and talk, but I need to get home. I turn in early these days. If you ever want to come down for a cup of coffee, you know where I live. My door's always open, except when it's shut."

"That sounds good. Hey, do you know the name of the kid who's always out here riding his bike?"

"Which one?" Martin said with a shake of his head. "They all have bikes these days. Always riding around in the middle of street like they own the damn thing."

"He lives in the gray house."

"Oh, the Marshall's kid. Alex. He's a weird one, if you ask me."

You have no idea.

"Thanks. I was going to ask him if he'd cut my lawn."

Martin laughed, and Jasper echoed the sound with a bark. "I doubt it. The kid is aimless. The Marshalls have a lawn service. I know because they tried to sell their service to me, too. The day I can't take care of my own lawn is the day I need to sell my house."

"Okay, thanks. Maybe I'll ask them for their number."

Martin made a face that let Jason know exactly what he thought of that idea.

"Don't bother with any of the kids in this neighborhood. Not a one of them mow lawns or wash cars or anything. That's the damn problem with kids these days. They're lazy and want everything handed to them. They don't know the meaning of work."

125

Martin shook his head and gave him a wave as he turned to walk back down the street, still mumbling about kids. Jasper followed suit, but not before he gave a very low, unfriendly woof.

5

The high-pitched ring of his cell phone woke Jason up an hour after he'd climbed into bed, and his stomach dropped when he saw the name and number on his phone's display: Towson General Hospital.

"Jason, it's Mom." Her words came out in a husky whisper.

"What's wrong?"

"It's your father. We're at the hospital. He had another heart attack, but they said it wasn't a major one. The doctors think he's going to be okay."

"I'm on my way." Jason got out of bed and started grabbing clothes.

"Jason that's not—"

He heard a voice, then his mother's in reply, then everything muffled. Thirty seconds later, the phone disconnected with a small, definitive click.

6

When Jason arrived at the hospital, he went straight to the emergency room, but neither his mother nor father was there. He spent ten minutes at the front desk, shifting his weight from foot to foot and drumming his fingers on the desk; they didn't have his father's name in their system yet, so he had no idea where to go. The receptionist finally called the Cardiac Care Unit and nodded to Jason.

Please don't let me be too late.

The hospital had recently finished a huge renovation, and as he raced down a long, unfamiliar hallway, wrapped up in the smell of antiseptic and illness, his heart raced, and his palms turned sticky with sweat. He came to the end of a hallway, but the sign in front of him said nothing about the CCU.

Shit.

His father's last heart attack was minor, but his mother's voice, that strange whispery tone, made him think this one might be much worse, and the click as she hung up on him did not bode well at all. Jason backtracked down the hallway until he came to an opening that he'd missed. The sign pointing him to the CCU was small; no wonder he'd missed it.

As he walked down another long hall, identical to the first, he realized he hadn't passed a soul.

Like I'm the only person here.

He came to another opening, another small sign, and still there was no sign of anyone else. Sweat ran in a cold trail down his spine as he took the hallway to the right.

Like one of those movies where the hero wakes up and finds he's the last man left alive. And at first, he thinks he's the lucky one. He thinks something horrible happened to everyone else. Until he realizes that something horrible has happened, but he isn't lucky at all.

Another sign. Another turn. As he rounded the corner, he almost collided with an orderly in a tan uniform. Jason stepped aside to avoid him, and his left arm hit the wall hard enough to send a flare of pain down to his fingertips.

"Shit, I'm sorry," Jason said.

The orderly, a tall man with a bald head, dark skin, and deep-set eyes glared at Jason. A tattoo on his arm caught Jason's eye—a pinup girl in a sexy pink nightgown with something hidden behind her back. She wore a very naughty expression on her face, and not naughty in a nice way.

"You should be careful," the orderly said in a low, cigarette-rough voice.

"I will."

The orderly scratched his head, and his scalp rippled with the movement. A stink like an old ashtray filled to overflowing rose up and out as the orderly turned, waving him away with one hand. "Go on now."

Jason's mouth went desert dry. He couldn't move. The orderly laughed, a quick humorless sound, and stared at him with pale green eyes nearly swallowed up by his heavy lids.

"You lost?"

Jason shook his head.

"Better get moving then."

Jason turned his face away from the strange eyes, but his legs would not cooperate. The orderly's feet shuffled on the tile, and his uniform made a whispery noise.

He's coming toward me.

Jason's slowly turned around, his hands curled into fists. The orderly was gone. The hospital swallowed up the noise of his slow, uneven footsteps. No music played, no voices crept out from behind the closed doors, no equipment beeped. From where he stood, the hallway looked like it went on forever.

Maybe I'm stuck in some horrible place. And no matter how far I walk, no matter how long I walk, there will always be another turn. Another hallway.

His stomach gave a sickening lurch, and he leaned back against the wall, breathing hard. This was stupid. It was a hospital. Not a movie. No zombies, no demented orderlies waited around the corner. He was tired and worried, that was all.

He pushed off the wall. The hallway did have an end, and when he made another right turn he breathed a sigh of relief to find a set of double doors, clearly marked Cardiac Care with an intercom panel set to the right of the doors. He pressed the button and a scratchy, tired voice came out; after he gave his name, the intercom went silent, and the doors opened with a mechanical hiss.

The strange silence followed him in. His shoes made small, slapping noises on the tile floor as he approached the nurses' station. A short, round woman behind the desk wore scrubs patterned with cartoon characters and spoke to Jason in a voice made only a little less scratchy without the intercom. She sounded like Sailor's sister. Did everyone in the hospital smoke? That orderly... No, best not to think about him. He was wrong.

Instead of pointing him in the right direction, she grabbed a clipboard and guided him down a quiet hallway with half-open doors on each side. The doors were painted dark blue, the walls a pale shade of grayish-tan. Her shoes made no sound at all as she walked with quick, purposeful steps. Nothing like Sailor's rolling walk. He didn't think he'd ever seen *anyone* walk like that.

Something dug into his memory and he shuddered. The CCU was quiet but not silent. Jason heard muted voices from one room, the steady beep of unseen equipment from another, and a quiet sobbing from yet another. Each door had a small brass nameplate in the center, with the patient's last name handwritten on a white card.

And when they're done, they slide those little cards out and throw them away. Then they slide in the next patient, the next name.

They passed another nurse in less colorful scrubs, and the two women simply nodded to each other.

The whole wing feels like a tomb. Everyone here is waiting for their ride to come along. Their last ride.

She stopped at the last door on the right, a fully closed door with an empty nameplate. Why wasn't his father's name written on a little white card?

"Go on in," she said.

Before Jason could move, she walked across the hallway into the opposite room. He stared at the blank nameplate and balled his hands into fists. He didn't want to go in. A hard but simple truth. If he stood out in the hallway he could pretend everything was fine. No, he

129

couldn't deny he was in the CCU, but maybe the room belonged to someone else. Not his father. A neighbor maybe or a nameless stranger. Maybe this whole thing was just a mistake. The door held the answer. He simply had to put out his hand and push it open.

But that empty nameplate...

Maybe they forgot to add the little card. People forget things all the time.

Jason took a deep breath and went inside.

7

His father was a still shape beneath the white sheets; Jason paused in the doorway until he saw the rise and fall of his chest. His mother got up, moving slow, and when he hugged her she slumped forward, sighing against his shoulder. She let go first, stepping back to wrap her arms around herself like a butterfly chrysalis, with growing wings made of nightgown and old sweater instead of kaleidoscopic chitin. The shadows beneath her eyes added several unkind years to her face.

"He's sleeping," she whispered.

"Is he going to be okay?"

"Yes."

"Maggie, you don't have to whisper, I'm awake," his father said in a thin, papery voice.

But he was alive. That was the most important thing. Jason walked over to the bed and squeezed his hand, ignoring both the cool, clammy skin and the smell of sickness and stale hope radiating from the walls. The steady beep of a heart monitor kept time, punctuated with a drip-drip-drip from an IV bag of clear fluid.

"How are you feeling?"

"Like I just had a heart attack. Next stupid question." Despite the gruff words, his dad smiled. "Sit down, both of you. You're making me nervous standing around. I got enough of that from the doctors and nurses."

"Jack, you're supposed to be resting," his mother said, perching on the edge of the chair closest to the bed.

"I'm in a hospital bed, hooked up to who knows what. What else can I do but rest? I can talk and rest at the same time. And why did you wake Jason up? He has to work in the morning."

Jason hid a smile behind his hand and sat down, the vinyl seat pushing up a puff of cool air around his thighs. "Dad, it's okay. I'm glad Mom called me, okay?" He turned to his mom. "Are Ryan and Chris coming?"

"I called Ryan, but he didn't answer. Chris is on his way, and he's going to keep trying to reach Ryan. Chris said the traffic won't be so bad this time of night."

"I don't know why the damn fool had to move to Virginia in the first place," his father said. "And Ryan probably turns off his cell phone at night. Jason, you should go home. I'm fine," he said in that papery, unfine voice. "Don't give me that look. It wasn't that bad. They're going to do a stress test tomorrow and some other things..."

"Jack, please rest."

Jason's dad lifted one hand from the bed and dropped it back down. "It is what it is, Maggie," he said, but closed his eyes, and soon enough, his soft snores drifted up from the bed.

"Mom, what happened?" Jason kept his voice low.

"He didn't feel well after dinner, so he took a nap and woke up about an hour later with chest pain. He didn't want me to call 911, of course, but I did anyway because he could hardly breathe from the pain."

"I wish you would've called me earlier."

She reached over and patted his hand. "I called you as soon as they got him settled in this room. What could you have done? Stand around in the waiting room? Your father didn't want me to call you at all."

The door swung open, and the nurse with the less colorful scrubs came in. She checked the monitor and the IV, jotted something down on a clipboard, and nodded at Jason and his mother before she left the room, leaving the door partially open.

"You should just go home," his mother said. "There's nothing you can do here. He's just going to sleep. You can come back in the morning, or you can wait and come over when he gets home. They won't keep him here for more than a couple of days."

"I want to stay, okay?"

She nodded in reply, and tears glimmered in her eyes.

"Try not to worry. He'll be okay, he's strong. You know that."

She nodded again.

"Do you need anything? Want me to get you some coffee or something?"

"No, I'm fine. They'll probably end up kicking you out, you know. It's past visiting hours."

"I'll stay until they do, but I think it's okay. The nurse would've kicked me out before if it wasn't."

Leaning back in the chair, she rubbed her eyes. "If you're going to stay, I think I'll rest my eyes for a few minutes, but if I fall asleep, make sure you wake me up if the nurse or the doctor comes back in."

It didn't take long for her breathing to become slow and even. Jason shifted in the uncomfortable chair, but he didn't want to leave the room, not with both of them asleep. Even in sleep, his father's face wore shadows and gray. A bruise bloomed on the back of his hand around the IV needle, and beneath the thin blanket, his legs weren't limbs, but twigs. Tubes and wires snaked out from underneath the covers like alien appendages.

His mother's face glowed ghostly pale in the dim lighting, her lips totally devoid of color. Inside the too-big sweater, she appeared shapeless. She twitched in her sleep, and her nightgown's ruffled hem rose up a few inches, revealing dry, flaky skin crisscrossed with spidery blue veins, sensible shoes with rubberized soles and mismatched white socks. His eyes were drawn back again and again to the blue veins on her legs.

When did they get so old?

A memory, sharp and strong, raced in. A trip to the ocean when Jason was eight, his brothers six and ten. The sun had set over the water, turning everything gold and red. His parents stood up on the beach, holding hands, while the boys ran in and out of the surf, then his dad whispered something in her ear, and her laughter rang out over the water. Bright laughter. Good laughter.

Another nurse poked her head in the door and smiled at Jason, but she didn't tell him to leave. Instead she pulled the door closed behind her. He rested his head back against the chair and stared up at the tiled ceiling. Underneath the electronic chirp, the heart monitor gave off a steady hum, and he listened to the chirp and the hum and stared at the ceiling and thought about the ocean and the way the waves had swirled icy cold around his ankles as the sun slipped behind the horizon, the shells glistening on the beach, pearly white against the dark sand.

8

Jason dreamed of the white room again. Seashells, not dead animals, covered the floor, and his father stood off to the side in a hospital gown. Heart monitors filled the room, all of them beeping in a chaotic frenzy. Jason knew his father shouldn't be in the room, but his face wore no fear. His legs were pale below the edge of the blue-and-white-checked gown. As he turned his face toward Jason, he shook his head.

"Son, this isn't right. Didn't you read the fine print?"

Jason wanted to tell him he didn't understand, but a gust of wind blew through the room, hot and fetid, and he choked on his words. The seashells rattled against each other with a thin, bony sound. The wind sucked back out of the room, leaving behind the smell of small dead things with an antiseptic bite. Somewhere, a bird circled overhead, its wings flapping in a deadly arc.

Just a seagull circling over the ocean.

Yes, even the ocean surf was here. He couldn't see it, but he could hear its steady rush and roar as it gathered up and crashed down.

But it's only a dream wave. Not real at all. That sunset happened so long ago. The waves came up and washed away our footprints. Washed them all away.

His father shook his head again. "What did you do?"

What did he do? Nothing.

This room wasn't his making, his design. His father turned around and shuffled away through the seashells, dragging an IV pole behind him, the bag filled with a thick and viscous fluid. *Things* swam in the fluid, white worms chuckling as they took their turn down the spiral of tubing into his father's arm.

The rush of the ocean wasn't an ocean anymore, but the steady hum of voices, many voices, all of them whispering, humming. The voices of the mad and depraved.

Jason wanted to yell, to tell his father to stop, but his own voice didn't work. It wouldn't. He wasn't allowed to speak here. He raised his hands, and as his father moved farther away, the heart monitors sped up to a shriek as they joined together, growing louder and louder. Jason's father walked on with slumped shoulders. The seagull flapped its wings overhead, and the heart monitors screamed...

"Jason."

Dad, come back. Don't stay in that white room.

"Jason."

This time, the word was little more than a gasping breath.

Jason's eyes snapped open. The heart monitor beeped chaos, and his father's hand clutched his chest. His eyes rolled wildly in his sockets, his feet danced under the sheet, and he held out one hand toward Jason. His eyes were

scared, he's scared

cloudy and filled with pain. A strange huffing noise emerged from his throat, a strangled cry for help. His mouth moved as if he wanted to speak, then his eyes *stopped*. They fixed on Jason's, and a growl spilled out of his mouth, a growl with words underneath, but they were unintelligible and even more horrible because of it.

"Oh, God, Dad." Jason jumped up from the chair and moved to the bed.

His father reached out one hand, grabbed Jason's arm, his left arm, and squeezed. His fingers dug in like claws. "I saw," he forced out with a thick voice as if he spoke around a mouthful of sand and shells.

He's speaking through the sunset, Jason thought and knew the words made no sense, yet they were true. Then his father's eyes rolled up until only the whites were visible, his mouth opening in a silent circle of pain.

No more words, no more sunsets.

Several people rushed into the room, and Jason stepped back from the bed. He had a chance to see his mother's empty chair before a nurse propelled him out into the hallway. Short, clipped voices followed him out, a strange, controlled routine that sent dread into his heart as he stood against the wall, rubbing the sleep from his eyes.

This isn't a sunset dream anymore. This is real, and my father is dying in that room. That white room. And they don't know. They don't know about the things in that room.

A sensible voice piped up in his head. *Shut up and wake up. There is no white room. This is the hospital, and your father is having another heart attack.*

A nurse raced by, pushing a cart into the room—an evil-looking thing, with knobs and paddles and plastic-wrapped syringes. Jason wanted to walk away; fear held him immobile. The heart monitor stopped its frantic chirp, and the sound became one long tone. Flatline.

It meant his father was—

Lost in the white room.

"Clear."

A male voice, gruff and practiced. An odd, jumping noise. The smell of static heat. The monitor droned on without pause.

Lost and gone.

"Clear."

What did you do?

His father's question. Like an accusation. The monitor went on and on. Muffled voices, then the same male voice.

"One more time. Clear."

Come on, Dad. You can do this.

Tears burned in Jason's eyes. His father's traitorous heart had abandoned ship. The double doors swung open at the end of the hallway, and his mother walked through with two cups of coffee in hand. She stopped five feet away, locked eyes with Jason, then her mouth dropped open in a silent O. The coffee cups in her hand tipped forward in slow motion, landing on the floor with a liquid thud. Coffee sprayed out in all directions; the smell cut through the antiseptic hospital stink.

The heart monitor droned on, still that steady

flatline

single tone.

His mother looked down at the coffee puddled around her feet and stepped over it as her mouth closed. Her chest rose and fell as she took a deep breath.

She knows. She's steeling herself for the news. It's that sad, sure knowledge when the phone rings in the middle of the night. Nothing you can do but hold yourself tight and wait for it all to be over.

Someone turned off the heart monitor. Hushed, matter-of-fact voices filled the ominous silence. His mother stepped forward again.

Once, then twice, and when a nurse came back out of the room with a grim expression on her face, a low wail emerged from her lips. Jason rushed over and grabbed her before she sagged to the floor.

"No," she said and shook her head. "No, oh, no."

The nurse walked over to them, and his mother held her hands out in front of her as if she could push the nurse away, push away the news, and pretend for just a little while longer. Her hands dropped, her shoulders shaking as she cried silent tears in his arms. Jason held her close, trying to forget the look in his father's wild eyes before the chaos started.

Didn't you read the fine print?

9

Jason didn't like the funeral director, a prim, dour-faced man named Edward Vaughn, on sight. He didn't like his prissy way of speaking or the way he rubbed his right earlobe from time to time. Mr. Vaughn ushered Jason, his mother and brothers into a room with thick, dark carpet and pale walls. The dark coffin at the far end of the room gleamed under the lights. The scent of several large floral arrangements masked the stink of the funeral home, but it lingered underneath—the sharp, chemical smell of suppressed decay.

His mother, her eyes red-rimmed but dry, held onto his right arm as they walked in. This was their private goodbye. Soon enough, the room would fill with people paying their respects, but for now, it was theirs alone. Soft music, meant to be soothing, drifted down from speakers set into the ceiling, but it wasn't soothing at all. The hair on the back of Jason's neck stood up and screamed as the high-pitched notes trickled down.

My father's de—

He couldn't even think the word.

Who's going to ask me if I'm really doing okay now?

Prissy Mr. Vaughn said a few words to his mother, then slipped out of the room, walking like he had a rod of iron in place of a spine. They walked up to the coffin together: he on the left, Ryan on their mother's right, holding her arm, and Chris halfway behind them both, with his hand on the center of her back. At first, only the dark wood of the coffin's side and the white satin lining of the opened lid were visible. Then the edge of the fabric inside the coffin. Another step revealed the top of his father's head, yet another, the dark blue shoulder of his suit.

His only suit. The one he wore to funerals and weddings. Such is life, but it isn't. It's not fair. He wasn't old enough to d—

That word again. That awful, ugly word.

He wasn't old enough to go away.

His mother stopped, turned her face into Jason's arm and sighed heavily.

"Okay," she said, straightening herself up. She tugged her arms from both Jason and Ryan. "Give me a minute, boys, okay? I'd like to spend a little time with him alone."

They stayed back while she took the last few steps to the coffin by herself. She didn't make a sound, but her shoulders shook as her head bent down. The minutes passed long and hard while Jason resisted the urge to go to her. Chris took a half step forward, then back. Ryan kept his head down with his fists curled up tightly at his sides.

A lump, horrible in its finality, grew in Jason's throat.

We shouldn't be here. He *shouldn't be here.*

Jason tried, but he couldn't hold in the tears. They fell down his cheeks, far too cool for the twisting pain inside his chest. It wasn't right. His father was too young. The words echoed in his head and drowned out the music.

Dad, I still need you. Everything isn't okay now. I need you to ask me the question because I'm not okay. Not now. Not really.

Their mother finally motioned them forward, and Jason closed the distance with heavy feet. The flowers pushed out their cloying scent, making the back of his throat itch. Up close, they were as strong as Shelley's perfume. His father's face appeared calm, restive, as if he was asleep, not dead.

But he was. It wasn't a bad joke or a nightmare. He was gone.

Jason reached out and touched the casket, the wood slick under his fingers. Reaching forward, he touched his father's stiff, unyielding arm, and the coldness of his skin pressed through the fabric to Jason's fingertips and shattered the illusion of sleep. The tears ran down. Blurred his vision. Jason put his hand atop his father's. For one quick instant, Jason had an image of his father rising up to pat him on the head, and he wanted to roll back the years, capture the feel of his father's hand when it was warm and alive and tuck it in his pocket so he would never forget.

I won't ever forget him, but I can't remember how his hand felt. Now it's just cold—cold and gone.

He was vaguely aware of his brothers next to him, of his mother not so far away, yet he didn't reach out for any of them. The sound of a sob cut through the music. His mother's? His brothers'? His own? He didn't know. Jason pulled his hand away from his father's and gripped the edge of the casket, holding on until his fingertips ached, with an ache in his heart a thousand times worse.

I didn't tell him I loved him. I thought he would be okay and I forgot to say it. Why didn't I tell him? I was there with him, and I didn't say I loved him.

10

An endless stream of well-wishers filed into the funeral home. Family, some Jason hadn't seen in years, and friends, all whispering "I'm sorry" and "let us know if there's anything we can do." He knew the words were spoken with sincerity, but by eight o'clock his head pounded with a steady throb, and he wished the night were over.

His mother's face showed the strain of the day, and Ryan took a smoke break every fifteen minutes. Chris's replies were little more than monosyllabic murmurs. Jason kept his eyes away from the coffin. It was safer that way. If he didn't see his father, he could almost convince himself it was all a dark dream. Almost.

When Shelley walked in the viewing room, Jason stifled a groan. He hadn't been expecting her to show up. She'd sent flowers, wasn't that enough?

I can deal with her presence for a little bit. For the sake of my mom. And my dad.

Shelley went to his mother first. At first she stiffened when Shelley put her arms around her, then she smiled and leaned into the embrace. They spoke in soft tones, too low for Jason to hear, then Shelley said a few words to Ryan and Chris but embraced neither. As she walked away from them, toward Jason, Ryan rolled his eyes, and Chris shook his head. She gave Jason a brief hug, and the smell of her perfume made his head throb anew. When she pulled back, she smiled and the ring on her right hand gleamed very blue in the overhead lighting.

"I'm very sorry," she said.

Maybe it wouldn't be so bad, after all.

"Thank you."

She looked around the room and gave him another smile, one he knew too well. His hands tightened into fists, tight enough so the edges of his fingernails dug into the skin of his palms.

"I'm surprised your new friend isn't here."

His nails pressed in harder.

Why would she do this? Why here?

To a casual observer, the question wasn't cruel. A simple query. But he knew Shelley, and he knew what the smile meant. At the bookstore, he'd made her feel small. She hated that. This was her way of getting even, of getting in a last, little dig. She wouldn't stick the knife in too deep, just enough to sting. Even here.

"Or hasn't she met the family yet?"

She made a face of disdain that turned her face ugly.

"Thank you for coming," he finally said through clenched teeth and walked away.

11

When Jason stepped out of the limousine, the impossibly green color of the cemetery grass gave him pause, even through the lenses of his sunglasses.

Of course it's green. Good fertilizer here.

Jason shuddered and helped his mother step out. In the five days since his father's death, he thought she'd lost at least as many pounds. Always thin, she now verged on skinny, the sharp ends of her collarbones jutting out from beneath a veil of flesh. Jason and his brothers took her out to eat after the funeral home viewings, and she'd simply picked at her food. After a while, she stopped pretending and set her fork down. Maybe when the funeral was finished, she'd eat. There was plenty of food at her house.

Jason understood the corollary between death and food, making sure the loved ones left behind didn't have to worry about something as mundane as cooking. When he'd opened his mother's refrigerator this morning, it was crammed full of casserole dishes, pies, cakes and a large tray of deviled eggs. Neighbors and friends, she said when Jason asked. The eggs were from her sister, Betty, for after the funeral. Out of curiosity, he'd peeked in the freezer and found more dishes there. The handful of people coming to her house after the funeral would not even put a dent in the food.

And why are you thinking about food right now?

They walked over to the gravesite in silence.

Because it's easier.

The low quack of ducks startled him out of his thoughts. A pond not far away shimmered in the sunlight. Who put a duck pond in a cemetery? That took the whole *let's make the death of your loved one as nice as possible* thing too far. A loose, rubbery sensation raced through his abdomen as they moved closer to the gravesite.

Dad, I'm really not okay. Not this time.

The coffin rested atop a metal frame and underneath, the waiting hole gaped mouth-like, waiting to swallow his father whole. In front of the coffin, a portable awning covered several rows of folding chairs. Jason guided his mother to one of the chairs in the front, and she sank down without a word. He tugged at his collar but didn't sit. He couldn't. It was too warm for a suit, even underneath the awning. Another duck quacked, and Jason sighed. He didn't care how many ducks there were; it was still a cemetery, and his dad was still gone.

The minister, an old man with thick, white hair, bent down and spoke to his mother in a hushed voice. He'd married Chris and Lisa, but Jason didn't know his name. He'd stopped going to church in high school, when he decided he didn't believe in either God or the devil. It had upset his mother, but after her initial protestations she didn't nag. His father's doing, no doubt. Jason knew his dad went with her on Sundays to make her happy, not for any great spiritual reasons of his own. A memory returned, as vivid as the grass—the day he walked downstairs and told his father he was an atheist.

Of course I told Dad first. I told him everything first.

His father had put down his newspaper, gave him a small smile, and said, "Son, I believe every man has the right to make his own decision about politics and religion. You might not legally be a man yet, in the eyes of the law, but I think you're old enough to know what's in your mind and your heart."

Jason could hear his father's words as clearly as if he stood next to him right now, and he brushed tears away with the back of his hand. After a few minutes, the minister rose, smiling when his knees creaked in protest.

"How are you holding up?"

My father's dead. How do you think I'm holding up?

"I'm okay."

"Good," the minister said. He reached out his hand, patted Jason's left arm, then drew it back with a low hiss.

What the hell?

A wave of bright pain exploded in Jason's arm, and he rocked back on his heels. It was like a million needles digging into his skin all at once, or a dozen razors scraping down deep. His breath rushed out with a small sound; the minister stepped back and looked down at his own hand with an odd look, then he looked back up at Jason and rubbed his palm on the leg of his pants.

The sharp pain subsided slowly, leaving a dull ache in its place. Jason tasted blood in his mouth, sharp and metallic, and fought the urge to spit. Soreness on the side of his tongue confirmed the source of the blood.

Good one. The minister was trying to be nice, now he's looking at me like I'm the Antichrist.

Jason squirmed under the weight of the minister's stare, but he turned the movement into a small stretch. He didn't like the way the minister's eyebrows had drawn together or the questions in his eyes.

What happened when he touched me?

Lisa walked over and put her hand on the minister's shoulder, and Jason took that moment to turn his head away. He reached up and touched his arm. Heat pressed against his palm.

Of course it's warm. You're standing out in the sun.

No unexpected shock of pain, no screaming knives, only an odd ache. Jason sat down next to his mother. She had her head down and her eyes closed. Whatever had happened, she'd missed it, and Jason sighed in relief.

Just a muscle cramp. Nothing to worry about. Nothing to explain.

The minister finished talking to with Lisa, and when she sat down he began to speak. When his mother raised her head, her cheeks damp with tears, Jason reached into his pocket and handed her a small packet of tissues. He stared at the coffin as the minister droned on and on. When he started to read a passage from the Bible, Jason tuned out the words. They weren't important, anyway.

12

The minister cornered him in the kitchen at his mother's house. When he approached, Jason's mouth went dry and he stepped back.

"I wonder if I could speak with you a few minutes, son."

No.

"Sure."

"I felt something very odd when I touched you at the cemetery."

Jason bet it was nothing like he felt.

"I just got a tattoo," Jason said. Neither a total lie, nor the total truth. "You happened to touch the spot where it is. The skin is still tender."

"Oh," the minister said, his features twisting in confusion. "I could have sworn, well it may sound odd, but your arm felt warm, son, almost hot. It was a little...strange."

If you call me son one more time, I might yell. You're not my father. He's dead and in the ground. Remember?

And maybe Frank just doesn't like you.

Jason smiled at the ridiculous thought. "Not really, sir. We were out in the sun."

"Yes, that could be the explanation. That could be it exactly." The lines on his forehead smoothed out, then he smiled. "Please forgive this old man's fancies. I shouldn't have troubled you on this, of all days. I'm not sure what I was thinking."

Jason just nodded. What else could he say?

Yes, I felt it too. It felt like my arm was on fire.

The minister opened his mouth as if he had more to say, then closed it and shook his head. He offered a small smile. "In the days to come, if you need someone to talk to, to help you cope with your loss, my door is always open. I know you're not a member of our church, but your parents have been for many years."

Sure, right. Just please go away.

"Thank you," Jason said, breathing a sigh of relief when the minister finally walked out of the kitchen.

13

Jason called Mitch as soon as he left his mother's house; when she answered the phone, tears burned his throat, trapping his voice inside his chest.

"Are you okay?"

He forced out a sound, his tears turning the streetlights into streaks of white light.

"Come over, please," she said.

Jason found his voice. "Okay. I'd like that."

She opened her front door before he had a chance to knock, and without a word she wrapped her arms around him and held him close. Her soft, coconut smell brought fresh tears to his eyes.

Later, in the dark, he whispered, "I love you," and she said the words back.

14

Jason's shoulders slumped as soon as he unlocked his kitchen door Sunday night. He pushed the door open, stumbled into the kitchen, and tossed his keys toward the table. They spiraled down and landed with a clink on the floor. He didn't bother to pick them up. The twilight outside turned the corners of his living room into dark, secretive places, banished once he turned on a lamp and the television.

Dad is dead.

The words played over and over in his head and he flipped through the channels without thought, the actors' faces passing in a blur. With a sigh, he turned it off, tossed the remote on the coffee table and put his head in his hands. His dad had been fine when he got to the hospital. Pale, tired, but fine. The damn heart monitor had chirped away, pronouncing everything well and good, but it lied, nothing more than a pretty illusion of happy ever after, like a seemingly perfect beach hiding poison shells in quicksand.

Jason swallowed, tasting tears. He cried into his hands until his palms were slippery. He cried until his throat hurt and he couldn't see through the tears. It wasn't right and it wasn't fair.

It is what it is.

His father's voice. He'd give anything to hear his dad say the words for real. Not this false ghost voice. When the tears stopped and his vision cleared, he stared at the darkened screen, catching a glimpse of his own reflection.

He rubbed his upper arms and winced, then pushed up the sleeve of his shirt. Bruises, five of them, marred the skin on his left arm, fingertip shaped and pale purple, almost concealed by the tattoo's ink.

He grabbed me, right before he said his last words.

The look on his father's face, the horrible, scared look was burned into his memory. And his words. "*I saw.*" What had he seen? Death coming for him in a gilded carriage? Jason's mother living out the rest of her days alone? The knowledge that he wouldn't see his grandchildren grow up?

Jason rubbed his arm again, and pain rippled just underneath the skin, reminding him of the sensation when the minister touched him.

No, I am not going to think about that. No way. Not tonight.

15

Jason was sitting at the kitchen table when his father, in a dirt-encrusted suit, knocked at his back door. He whispered his name with a wet voice (a wrong voice), the S nothing more than a gentle hiss of exhaled air, but Jason made no move to get up and unlock the door. It would be a mistake.

Because they can't hurt you until you let them in.

Then his father walked *through* the door and came to a stop in the middle of the room, holding out his hands with something inhuman and awful in his eyes, something that shifted, liquid and loose, behind the irises. "Daddy's home now, son."

Jason tried to speak, tried to tell him he was dead and needed to go back, but as his father walked toward him with pale hands outstretched, the words fled. He ran upstairs, slamming his bedroom shut behind him and flipping the puny lock meant only for privacy, not protection.

His father's steps on the staircase, each one heavier than the last, carried dark promise in each weighty thump, and when his hands scraped the door, Jason pressed his back against it to keep him out.

When he comes in, he's going to tear me apart with those hands.

The slippery whisper of his name again.

It's not my father, no matter how much he looks like him. My dad is dead. He's nothing but worm food and this is just a dream. A dream.

A terrible pulling sensation ripped through his chest as his not-father walked *through him.* A foot and leg emerged first, between his own, then a shoulder and arm. One final pull, and the rest came through, reeking of grave dirt and rot, flesh turned foul and rancid. The not-father took two steps forward, turned around, and his features changed.

The cheekbones melted and reformed, high and sharp. The chin widened, exposing a gaping maw with hot, fetid breath. The nose stretched, elongating into a razor-sharp protuberance that dripped saliva and blackened red gore. The unrecognizable thing let out a high-pitched shriek and the dark suit ripped in two and fell to the floor as the rest of its bones shifted. A terrible creature rose from the ruins of the suit, something so terrible, Jason's mind shrieked in protest. A dadmonster, all claws and fur and furious anger.

It opened its mouth, and his father's voice screamed, "It is what it is! It is what it is!"

The dadmonster rose with the frenzied flapping of wings, pushing foul air into Jason's face, circling over his head, higher, then back down again, moving close, then pulling back, spinning and screaming. Jason fell to the floor, covering his head with his hands as the not-father, the dadmonster, the thing, spiraled and descended again and again and again until finally, his mind rolled over and sent him elsewhere.

16

John S. Iblis reread the paper he held in his hands and smiled. He wondered how Jason was sleeping as of late. Not well, he presumed. Perhaps Jason even had strange pain in his arm. He wondered if Jason suspected anything at all. In his mind, good old Sailor (a clever nickname, he would admit) was nothing more than a tattoo artist.

John S. Iblis traced his fingers over Jason's signature, then rubbed his palms together in anticipation. The weak-minded were such easy prey.

The game itself was just for fun.

17

Jason was late for work on Monday. Again.

Chapter Six

Red Sky at Night

1

On Thursday morning, Jason opened his back door and froze in place. The tail draped across the doormat in a comma of bloodstained brown and white fur did not belong to a cat.

That little piece of shit.

The morning air held a chill, enough to prevent the stench from rising up in the air, though not enough to dissuade the flies. They circled what remained of Jasper, or some other unfortunate collie, landing, then flying off, only to buzz around and take up residence elsewhere amid the fur, as if testing to find the sweetest spot. Or the most vulnerable.

His arms broke out in gooseflesh. Rubbing them briskly, he stomped into the kitchen and grabbed a trash bag. He guessed cats weren't good enough for the kid now. What in the hell had he done to attract the kid's attention? Why was his doormat the unlucky recipient of his psychosis? When he got home from work, he planned to walk across the street and have a little chat with Alex Marshall's father. He thought it was time someone let him know what a sick little shit he had for a son.

2

By the time Jason got home, all thoughts of the kid across the street had vanished. His boss held a project status meeting at the end of the day; the look of irritation he wore lingered in Jason's mind. Yes, he knew that Jason's dad died, yes, he knew that things were tough, but he needed Jason to "stay on the ball" and "stay focused".

Asshole.

He grabbed his mail and went inside, but after tossing the mail on the table, he paced back and forth in his kitchen, jingling his keys in his hand.

"Fuck it," he said, and walked back out, slamming the door shut behind him. His car door was half open when a distant voice carried up from the end of the street.

"Jaaasper."

A few minutes of silence.

"Jaaaaaaaaaasper."

Martin, I hate to tell you, but Jasper isn't coming home any time soon. Maybe you should ask Alex if he had any last woofs.

He slammed the car door shut, too. His hands shook when he pulled out of his driveway, and with no destination in mind, just a feeling of helplessness deep in his bones, he drove. Familiar and unfamiliar streets turned to a blur. Time slowed to a crawl. The sun dropped low in the sky, and the streetlights turned on with a low metallic buzz. Jason drove and drove and drove.

Dead dog. Dead Dad.

The words popped up, unbidden—a sharp little hurt of severed hope. Pins and needles struck when he arrived in Fells Point, racing from the top of his left arm all the way down to his fingertips, then back up again. He shook his arm, but two minutes later, they returned, down, up, down, up. Extending his arm out the window, he flexed his fingers once, twice. His entire arm exploded with the sensation, his right hand slid on the steering wheel, and the car swerved to the left. He turned the wheel to the right, overcorrecting, and slid by a parked car with only inches to spare.

Shaking, he pulled into an empty parking spot on a side street and sat, breathing hard, with his left arm curled against his chest. "Dammit," he said and punched the door panel with the side of his fist. The prickling flared, exploding into white-hot pain. He grunted out loud and got out of his car; when he let his arm drop to his side, the pain subsided. Standing with his back against the car, he stared out at nothing but rubble. He'd parked next to a fenced lot with the piled remnants of dilapidated buildings, all part of the Fells Point rebuilding progress. Many of the old buildings were being torn down to make way for new buildings—houses, offices, shops, all designed to bring more money to the city. To bring life to the dead parts of town.

Can't resurrect the dogs or the dads, though, not with all the concrete in the world.

Jason walked away from the parking lot, ignoring his arm. The purple of twilight turned the pavement gray and shadowy, and a breeze picked up, sending discarded cigarette butts and scraps of paper spinning through the gutters.

He passed a homeless man wrapped in the stink of his miserable existence. The man held out a grimy hand. "Got any spare change, mister?" he asked, his voice raspy.

Averting his eyes, Jason caught only a glimpse of dirty, gray hair, soiled clothes and sunken cheeks. The man chuckled, a wet, cheerful laugh. Jason shoved his hands in his pockets and kept walking. Behind him, the homeless man broke out into a wordless song, more than a hum but not quite singing. Chanting? Jason shuddered, walking faster. Not just homeless. Crazy, too.

Jason took a right turn at the end of the street and passed several old row houses already dressed up in their renovation best with new windows and doors. The front windows of one house revealed a gleaming, dark wood staircase and freshly painted walls. They'd salvaged the old brick exterior and gutted the inside instead of total demolition. A few years ago, only rats and the homeless made these houses their homes; now they sold for ridiculous sums of money. Some of them, like Mitch's house, were only fifteen feet wide—tiny, yet charming.

The tingle in his arm faded as he crossed another street. More narrow houses with brightly painted front doors, more marble stoops. A white cat curled up in a window raised its head when he walked by and yawned, exposing a tongue the color of cotton candy.

Or bubble gum. Be glad you don't live in my neighborhood, puss.

Jason turned another corner, but the buildings on the new street did not have the shine of renovated bliss. A *For Rent* sign sat in one dark window, the red letters beginning to show signs of sun fade. The window, with the first traces of dust at the corners, shimmered in the pale light of a far streetlamp. The streetlamp closest to the building was dark, the curve of the bulb smoky gray.

Dead bulb. Dead dog. Dead Dad. These buildings are close to dead. Even the café with its colorful sign.

Jason stopped and stared into the darkness as a wave of déjà vu raced over him. He'd been here before, oh yes, he had. The empty building was number 1305. On Shakespeare Street. Home of emptiness, closed cafes and tattoo shops, but not just any tattoo shop—Sailor's shop.

Drove to get away from everything, and somehow I've ended up here. Maybe he can tell me why my arm hurts? It has to be a coincidence, but I don't remember having this pain before the tattoo. Only after.

Once again he could not see the entrance for 1303 Shakespeare Street.

It's a trick entrance, remember?

Jason stared at the spot where the entrance should be until his vision blurred and his eyes stung. Still nothing but a faded brick wall.

Oh, come on. The door is there. It's set back, just a little bit.

He stepped back to the edge of the sidewalk and tried again. When his eyes started to burn, he blinked several times, willing his mind to see the door, and still, nothing. No door, no weathered sign, no entrance at all. It didn't make sense.

Jason walked up to the building and pressed his hands, palms flat, against the brick. It was cool and rough to the touch.

Wrong. There should be a door here. A door with faded gray paint. Not just brick.

He ran his hands down the brick, feeling for a break, a seam, a doorframe.

No door. But of course there's a door. I went through it. Through the door and up the stairs with the weird, face-like wallpaper and into the shop.

"Find everything you're looking for, mister?"

Jason whirled around. The homeless man stood a few feet away, leaning up against the dark streetlamp. The wind shifted and carried a rich, high smell of stale urine, spilled liquor, unwashed flesh and the ashy stink of bummed cigarettes. He rummaged under his tattered coat, and Jason stepped back.

What if he has a knife or a gun? The guy is crazy. It's easy to see. Those eyes, all faded and watery, like he's leaking.

The man pulled out a bottle but didn't brandish it over his head. Didn't threaten or yell. Instead, he unscrewed the cap. His fingernails were long and ragged and stained a bilious yellow-brown; the creases of his fingers were caked with filth. After a quick nod of his head in Jason's direction, he took a large swallow. The amber liquid disappeared in a rush.

Yo-ho-ho and all that.

The bottle vanished back under his coat, and he walked away. No, he didn't walk. He *rolled.* Sailor?

"Hey," Jason called out, but the man kept moving, his steps fast, despite the hitch in his stride.

The homeless man sang out the horrible, familiar song without words again. He'd almost reached the end of the block when Jason took his first step, his feet making quick taps on the pavement as he tried to catch up. With the tattered coat billowing out behind him, Mr. Walks Like Sailor spun around the corner. Jason jogged to catch up, and when he approached the corner, he had a sudden fear that the homeless man wanted to lure him somewhere, perhaps to smash him over the head with the bottle of rum and take his wallet.

And maybe he was just paranoid.

Sure, the shipwalk was sort of the same, and they both had that strange rasp in their voice, but the face wasn't the same. Even under the dirt, it wasn't Sailor. So why was he following him? Jason slowed his steps, and the pins and needles in his arm danced under the skin.

Why, indeed? He should turn around and forget about the homeless drunk, but then he might stop to think a little harder about the disappearing tattoo shop, or dead dogs and dead dads, and he thought there'd been quite enough of that already.

The corner of the last building loomed ahead. He'd made it this close, he might as well look. What harm could it do? He took a deep breath, held it in and turned the corner.

The homeless man was gone.

3

Jason pulled into his driveway, his headlights carving out a bright arc in the darkness. Someone stood on the sidewalk with his head down. Jason's heart rate doubled. The homeless man?

It wasn't the homeless man of course. He was thirty minutes away, in Fells Point, and unless he grew wings the possibility of said man in front of his house was slim to none. He'd been nothing more than a crazy drunk anyway. No, Martin Cooper stood outside, his thinning hair hanging over his forehead and something in his hand.

He found the tail. He went in my garbage can and found the tail and thinks I did it. Oh, shit.

Jason got out of his car as slow as possible and walked around to the front. It wasn't the tail. Martin held a leash—Jasper's leash. Relief flooded Jason's veins, followed by a wave of guilt. Martin turned his face toward Jason, his mouth downturned. The dark shadows under his eyes turned his skin gray.

"Have you seen Jasper around by any chance?" Martin said in a paper-thin voice.

Dead dog. Dead Dad.

"No," Jason said, and his stomach twisted. It wasn't completely a lie. The tail could've belonged to another dog. There were other collies in the neighborhood, weren't there? The end of the leash trailed over Martin's hand and dangled in the air, like Jason's lie.

I didn't lie. If I tell him what I found, the anguish will turn to outright horror. I can't do that to him. And I don't know for sure it was his dog. I don't know for sure his dog is dead.

A warm wind blew by, carrying the smell of freshly cut grass, and the leash swung gently in the breeze.

Sure, tell yourself another lie. Do you think someone would cut off a dog's tail and leave the rest of him intact? Do you?

"We have a doggie door. He went out the other night and didn't come home. But he has a collar and a tag, so if someone found him they'd call, right?"

"Of course they would. I mean, they will. He's probably out running around, enjoying his freedom." Jason forced a smile. He couldn't tell him. He just couldn't.

"Yeah, sure," Martin said and turned to go. Then he turned back and gave a small shake of his head. "Except I keep the gate locked, and Jasper can't jump the fence."

Jason opened his mouth, but nothing came out. What could he say? Not the truth, that was certain. When Martin walked away, the hair on the back of Jason's neck rose. He glanced around and a shadow across the street moved. The kid, Alex, standing near his own house, with a baseball cap, red this time, not black, pulled low over his eyes. Watching him.

You little son of a bitch. You did it, didn't you? And I bet you like seeing the old man crushed at the edges. It probably helps you sleep at night. Most kids think about what they want to be when they grow up. I bet you think about what you'll kill when you grow up.

Or maybe who.

A chill raced up Jason's arms as he turned away. Maybe it was all just a strange coincidence. Maybe the kid had done nothing wrong.

Maybe, but the weight of his gaze followed Jason into the house.

4

That night, Jason double-checked all the locks in the house before he went upstairs. He turned off the light and climbed in bed, but the wind pushed tree branches against his window, a sound far too much like tapping.

Let me in, son.

The dark shadows in his room shifted, and he fought the urge to call Mitch. Sure, he'd call her and tell her he was having trouble sleeping and could he come over because a tree was knocking on his window? She would love that.

He rolled over, and the shadow in the corner of the room moved.

Dad? Is that you again?

It moved again. Jason's mouth went dry.

Something in my room. With me.

He waited for a sensible voice to pop up in his head and call him a fool; the voice didn't come. The wind rose in a high-pitched wail. Jason stared at the corner shadow. His stomach twisted.

Here. With. Me.

156

Moving fast, he turned on the lamp on the nightstand, but it threw off more shadows than it chased. It did, however, illuminate the corner of his room enough to make out a pile of folded laundry on the corner of the dresser.

No one here. Just me.

He got up and flipped on the overhead light. Once back in bed, he folded his arms behind his head and frowned up at the ceiling. With the light on, the tiny tap of the tree branches was just that. A trick of the wind. The racing heart in his chest didn't care, though. No, it thought the sound was horrible, like a skeletal hand knocking softly.

Keep on knocking, you can't come in.

Jason closed his eyes and, after several long minutes, fell asleep.

5

His father stood in the corner of his room, wrapped in shadows. Jason didn't want to see him; the smell was enough—sweet and sickly, the kind of smell that climbed inside and stuck to the back of the throat. It wasn't the not-father—the dadmonster—this time. Jason sat up, unafraid. His dad didn't want to hurt him. He just wanted to talk, to stay on this side for a little longer. Once he crossed the line, he wouldn't come back. He couldn't.

"Son, what did you do?"

"Nothing, Dad. I didn't do anything."

"It's bad, Jason. I think you know it is. You should've read the fine print."

"I don't understand."

His dad shook his head. "It doesn't matter. It is what it is." The words echoed off the bedroom walls. "I can't stay long, but you have to find a way."

"What do you mean?"

"I know you're smart, but he's tricky. Don't forget that."

How could he forget what he didn't know? And who? Who was tricky?

"I'm sorry, son. I have to go now." His flesh made a wet and sticky, slithery sound as he stood up, gripping the wall with his right hand.

"Wait, don't go. Please." Jason crossed the room and reached out. When his fingertips brushed against his dad's hand, the smell of rot grew stronger. Thicker. He gagged and stumbled back.

His father began to spin in the corner, moving in a tight circle, and as he spun, he faded. The dark blue of his suit turned transparent, then his father turned into a spiraling column of ashy gray. It lifted from the floor like a tornado. Jason smelled burning flesh. His father's voice twisted and turned inside the column, then a scream, high-pitched and inhuman, exploded from within. Jason stumbled back, covering his ears. A horrible nightmare of pain and rage moved inside the spiral. Something not—

Not-father! Not-father! He's back and he wants me.

Jason scrambled back on the bed until his back pressed hard against the headboard. The scream came again and again and again and its eyes... Green, gleaming eyes, filled with a liquid hate. They bored into Jason's, and the venom behind the gaze burned into his mind. The swirling mass lifted and moved toward the bed, toward him. The end stretched out into a long, needle-sharp point and stabbed into his left arm. The pain of a thousand needles, tipped with poison, tipped with fire, burning their way inside him. The column spun faster and faster around him, engulfing him in rushing wind and screaming fire.

Just a dream. I need to wake up. I need to wake up right now!

Caught inside the spiral, he couldn't scream. Heat scored his cheeks. The eyes found his and screamed their fury.

Jason woke up with his hands pressed to his ears and a ragged whisper in his throat, and sat up, staring out the window at the lightening sky while his heartbeat slowly returned to normal. He pulled off his sweat-soaked T-shirt, wincing as the left sleeve stuck to his arm. After he tossed the shirt onto the floor, he looked at his arm. Smears of blood streaked the skin and oozed from a scratch, three inches long, right below the tattoo, a curved and bleeding wound that wasn't deep, but stung when he touched it.

And he had blood underneath the fingernails of his right hand.

6

Jason picked Mitch up at eight on Friday night and took her to a small restaurant not far from her house. The spare key to his house, Shelley's old key, rested heavy in his pocket. He hoped it would be okay. Maybe it was crazy—he and Mitch had not been dating that long—yet it felt right.

Once they'd ordered their food, he took her hand and kissed the top of it. "I meant what I said the other night," he said against her skin.

"I know."

"I just didn't want you to th—"

She pressed her fingertips to his lips, cutting off his words. "I didn't, and I meant what I said, too. I wouldn't say something like that if I didn't." She took her hand away from his mouth. "You have huge circles under your eyes. You're not sleeping well, are you?"

Jason shook his head. "No, between dad and the weird kid, I'm not."

And the nightmares, he couldn't forget those, but he kept them to himself.

Mitch frowned. "What weird kid?"

"The kid who lives across the street from me. The one who looked in the window that night."

"Oh, *that* kid. Has he been peeking in the window again?"

The kid's dull eyes hung in Jason's memory. Why hadn't anyone noticed just how far from normal those eyes were? "No, but I caught him in my backyard, and he's been watching me," Jason said, dropping his voice to a whisper. "And some neighborhood animals have gone missing. I think he might be responsible."

"Responsible?" Mitch asked. "In what way?"

Jason looked into her eyes. "In a serial killer-in-training way."

The waitress brought their appetizers over, then a busboy refilled Jason's almost empty water glass, a glass he didn't remember drinking from.

This is not a good dinner conversation at all.

"What was he doing in your backya—"

It was his turn to press fingers to lips. "No, I'm sorry I brought it up. We can talk about it some other time. I don't want to ruin dinner, okay?"

She kissed his fingertips and smiled when he took them away. "Okay."

"Close your eyes," he said when they were finished with the appetizers. "And hold out your hand." Mitch giggled, but she did both. With a shaking hand, Jason placed the key in her palm. "Okay, you can open them now."

She looked down at the key, frowned, then smiled.

"I thought it might come in handy sometime," Jason said. "It doesn't mean we're married or anything."

Mitch laughed and curled her fingers tightly around the key.

7

After dinner they took a walk in Fells Point. Music drifted in the air from the bars around the center square and groups of patrons stood outside on the sidewalks, smoking. Five motorcycles roared by, filling the night with exhaust and engine noise.

Mitch kept her hand in his as they walked. "So tell me about this kid. He was in your backyard?"

"I found him there the other day, crouched down by my porch. He ran away before I could ask him what he was doing. I thought at first he might be looking for you, but the driveway was empty, so he knew I wasn't home."

"Did you call the police?"

"No, he wasn't really doing anything. I figured I'd talk to the parents first. I just have to figure out what I'm going to say."

They sidestepped a girl who tottered by on high heels, trailing the sour smell of vomit.

Mitch leaned up against him. "How about 'your kid's been looking in my windows and I found him in my backyard'?"

Jason pulled her into his arms and kissed her. Several shouts of approval rang out and when they parted, a group of guys standing on the corner raised and shook their fists, grinning. Mitch's cheeks turned pink.

"What was that for?"

"No reason at all."

They crossed a street still lined with cobblestones from an earlier era, passing by the same drunk girl. She stood, swaying, in the middle of the street, trying to pull off her heels, ignoring the blare of a car horn. They stepped up onto a curb and Jason stopped, looking up at the street sign—green with white lettering, like every other sign in the city: Shakespeare Street.

"Do you mind if we walk down here?"

Mitch scratched the back of her neck and peered down the street. "Is there anything down there? It just looks like old buildings."

"Maybe," he said, forcing his lips up into a smile.

Their shoes made little noise on the pavement, and the bar noise disappeared into a muffled hush behind them. The darkened windows of the buildings loomed like giant, unseeing eyes, and Jason fought a wave of unease, but if Mitch felt anything, it didn't show.

And what was he going to say when they get there and saw that blank brick wall? What was he going to tell her? He got his tattoo in a shop that didn't exist? Impossible. He didn't see it the other night because he was upset, then the homeless man showed up, and things got weird.

The light from the streetlamps didn't illuminate the street; they filled it with shadows. Farther down, the glow from the streetlamps vanished into gray as if the street just stopped.

"Why so quiet?" Mitch asked.

He kept his voice low. "I don't know. Just thinking, I guess."

She pressed her shoulder up against his. "The buildings are different on this street. I don't think I've ever come this way. See the arches above the windows?"

Jason tipped his head back. "Yes."

"I know my street doesn't have them. I don't know, it makes them a little...creepy. They all look empty, too."

Another wave of unease slipped under his skin.

Maybe the buildings are different because this street is different. Maybe we're not in Fells Point anymore. Maybe this is one of those streets in between the real streets, just like Sailor's shop is between the real buildings.

He laughed at the absurdity of his own thoughts.

"Okay, what's so funny?"

"I was just thinking this is kind of stupid. There isn't anything down here, after—"

1301.

The café. The closed café. He didn't think it was ever open. It was an illusion, like the fake western towns in the theme parks. Maybe none of the buildings were real.

"Jason?"

He'd stopped right in front of the café. If he took another step, he'd be in front of 1305.

But there's nothing in between. Just a space where the door should be.

162

"Jason, is everything okay?" A crease marred the skin between her brows.

Just take the step. Just one step.

His right foot lifted, as if in slow motion, swung forward, and came back down, then the left foot—up, over, down. A thin trail of laughter slipped from his lips. A door with faded gray paint. The old brass handle. The weathered sign. The numbers. 1303. No need to step back and stare. No need to touch palms to brick. The entrance sat exactly where it should be, because doors didn't disappear.

Mitch had a half smile on her face, but the crease remained—a tiny frown of worry. "What?"

"This is the tattoo shop. Where I got mine done."

"Here?"

"Yes." Jason looked over his shoulder. Shadows lined the street, but no people, homeless or otherwise. His arm gave a tiny throb of pain and he rubbed it, hard.

"It looks abandoned."

"That's what I thought, too."

Mitch stepped back, close to the curb, and looked up. "It's weird. I can't tell which windows belong with what door. It's like they're all part of the same building. They're all dark, too. The shop must be closed."

Jason stepped closer and stretched out his hand. For one split second, his hand passed through the air where the handle should be, and the hairs on his arm stood on end, then his hand touched the brass, the metal warm under his hand. His arm throbbed again. It would be locked, but it was okay because now he knew the shop was really there. He pushed. The door swung open with a low creak, and Jason jumped.

Mitch giggled. "I guess it's open after all."

The hallway appeared exactly as Jason remembered. Pale gray walls, worn steps, narrow stairs and the sickly yellow lighting. Dim lighting. Shadows concealed the top of the stairs. All the hairs on the back of his neck stood at attention.

"So, are we going to go up?"

"Do you want to?"

"Sure. I want to meet this guy," she said, but her voice held hesitation.

She doesn't want to go. If I just tell her we should go, she'd say okay. And I should, but I want to. I think.

Jason crossed the threshold first. As he stepped up onto the first step, Mitch slid her hand into his. The yellow light turned her eyes green; something about the color struck him as oddly familiar, but he brushed it away. Another jolt of pain, small and sharp, burned in his arm.

"Ewww, mold," she said, wrinkling her nose. "You really had your tattoo done here?"

"Yes," Jason said. "But the shop doesn't look like this at all."

The steps creaked and groaned as they went up. With each step, Mitch's grip grew tighter. Jason kept his eyes forward, refusing to look at the swirling wallpaper; the faces could move all they wanted.

"Ugh," Mitch said in a whisper. "My grandmother had wallpaper like this in her bathroom. I hated taking a bath at her house. The paper always looked like faces watching me. It was creepy as hell."

Jason didn't know how many steps they climbed when Mitch stopped. She pushed a strand of hair behind her ears and frowned. "It's weird. Doesn't it feel like we've been walking up a long time? What floor is the shop on?"

"I don't remember," Jason said. He didn't remember the staircase being so tall or so narrow. He and Mitch's shoulders touched, even though he stood one step ahead of her.

This isn't a good idea. We should just turn—

They reached the landing before the little voice in his head could finish. Mitch bumped into him and giggled. His arm ached, a short pulse of pain. As he gave it a rub, he looked over his shoulder; the

164

stairway down stretched past the light. When he raised his right hand to knock, she gave him a small tug.

"Do you smell that?" she asked.

"What?"

"Like something burning."

Jason sniffed. "I smell something, but not like burning exactly."

He wasn't sure what he smelled, but he had a sudden image of billowing clouds of oily smoke and a huge fire. Mouths open in silent screams. Fresh pain bloomed in his arm.

Mitch leaned over and whispered in his ear. "I think someone is in there. Listen."

He did.

A muffled step.

"Let's go," she said in a husky voice.

A soft thump.

"Please." She tugged on his hand again, harder.

"Okay."

Mitch went down the staircase first. Her hand held his in a grip strong enough to make his fingertips tingle. When they got to the bottom, Jason thought he heard the creak of a door.

Behind us, he's behind us.

Mitch pushed on the door.

But I didn't close it.

"Jason, it won't open," she said in a high, thin voice.

He grabbed the handle and pushed. It didn't budge.

Won't open.

A strange sigh drifted down from the top of the stairs. A sigh of anticipation? He pushed the door with his shoulder.

We're locked in here.

Another sigh, low and *wet*. He pushed the door again and another voice, his father's voice, piped up.

You're not locked in. The door swings in, not out. You can push it all you want. You need to pull, son.

"Mitch, step back, okay?"

She turned her eyes to his. Her breath came in quick little gasps.

"The door, it opens in," he said.

Comprehension dawned in her eyes, and she stepped up onto the first step. He pulled on the handle, but the door didn't open.

Maybe we are locked in.

A chuckle, deep and throaty.

"Hurry," Mitch said.

He pulled again, and the door opened with a shriek. They spilled out of the doorway, and as he yanked the door shut behind them, the pain in his arm retreated.

Mitch burst into laughter. "That was crazy. I swear I heard someone in the hallway."

Jason wiped his palms on his jeans. "Yeah, crazy."

For a minute, we were locked in. The door didn't swing in or out. And that laugh. I know I heard it.

"Was it that creepy before, when you got your tattoo?"

"Not like that."

"They say there are lots of ghosts in Fells Point. Maybe one hangs out here. The ghost of tattoos past." She smiled, then dropped her voice to a low whisper. "Maybe someone died while getting a tattoo, and his spirit lingers on, to warn away the living. Of course, there *is* another explanation."

"What's that?"

"I don't know. You might not be able to handle it."

"Try me."

"It's an old building, and we heard a mouse or a rat."

But rats don't laugh.

"Anyway, things always seem creepier at night," she said and grabbed his hand. "Come on, let's get out of here."

But halfway down the street, Jason couldn't resist the urge to look back. Nothing moved, human, mouse, or otherwise.

8

Later, naked beneath the sheets in her bed, Mitch touched his arm. "What happened?"

"What?"

"The scratch on your arm."

Jason pulled her closer and kissed her cheek. "I had a nightmare about my dad and scratched myself in my sleep."

"Mmmm."

"Did you have nightmares after..."

"My brother? Yes, I had some, but mostly I just couldn't sleep. It's funny, sometimes I dream about him now and when I do, the dreams are so vivid I wake up thinking he's still alive. Dreams are powerful things." She ran her fingertips over the tattoo, then hissed through her teeth and pulled her hand away.

Jason half sat up. "What's wrong?"

Her eyes were wide. "I don't know. It felt like your skin moved."

Frank?

Their eyes met and held, then she laughed and pushed him back down. "I'm being silly. I guess I still have the creeps from the hallway. Tattoos don't move. It was probably a muscle spasm. Did you feel anything?"

"No, just your hand."

She pressed her lips to his and put her hand back on the tattoo. "Nope, nothing in there but you."

Later still, with Mitch fast asleep beside him, he placed his palm flat against his upper arm for a long time. Finally, he rolled over on his left side and closed his eyes. Tattoos didn't move; they were just ink. Right before he fell asleep, his father's voice drifted in, faint and whispery.

Didn't you read the fine print?

Dreams were powerful things, Mitch had said, but what about nightmares?

9

Jason sat on his front porch early Saturday evening and watched the gray house across the street. The windows were dark and the driveway empty. His laptop sat on the other lawn chair, forgotten for now. A young girl with hair the color of coffee laced with cream walked up the sidewalk, handed Jason a folded sheet of paper with a shy smile and raced back down to her waiting parents. They lifted their hands in greeting, then walked down to the next house.

Please tell me it's not another missing cat.

It wasn't. The monthly neighborhood newsletter contained the customary reminders of recycling pickup day and recommendations for lawn services, but when he flipped the paper over, his breath caught in his throat at the note at the very bottom.

"Several animals have gone missing from our neighborhood. We don't know what's happened, but urge everyone to keep their animals inside at night. Make sure to block any pet entrances as well. If you have any information regarding the disappearances, please contact Joseph Murphy, the president of the neighborhood association."

Well, Mr. Murphy, maybe you should check with Alex Marshall. I bet he has more information.

Jason put the newsletter down and picked up his laptop. So far, his searches for allergic reactions to tattoo ink were unsatisfactory. Rashes, redness, and in rare cases, anaphylactic shock. One site reported it more common for allergies to appear years after getting the tattoo. Nothing about pain or pins and needles, but he wasn't imagining the pain. He knew he wasn't. His imagination wasn't that good.

It came and went, worse at night before bed. Despite what the websites said, an allergic reaction was the only explanation. He could either deal with it or have it removed (and hadn't Sailor said tattoo removal was one of his specialties? A strange side-job for a tattoo artist), but neither option held much appeal. One website stated that the allergic reactions in some people disappeared after a time; Jason hoped he'd be one of them.

Mitch came out of the house with two bottles of beer. "I thought you might want one."

He shut the laptop as she sat down in the lawn chair. Her hair, still damp from a shower, clung to her shoulders. A car drove slowly up the street and pulled into the Marshall's driveway. As soon as it stopped, the passenger door flew open and a woman got out. She yelled something unintelligible into the car, slammed the door, and stomped around to the back of the house. A minute later, Mr. Marshall got out, slammed *his* door, and stalked toward the front door.

"Well now," Mitch said. "What a happy family."

"Yeah, I don't think tonight is the right night to tell them about their son," Jason said.

"No, I don't think so, either."

The daughter emerged from the car, tossing her coppery hair over her shoulder after she pushed the door shut. She leaned up against the car, pulled out a cell phone and made a call. The kid, Alex, got out of the car last. He shoved his hands deep into his pockets and kicked the door with his foot.

"God. It's like a soap opera or something," Mitch said. "Tales of the Suburban and Dysfunctional."

Serial killers always had family problems, didn't they, and the family looked like it was full of issues—big ones.

The girl closed her cell phone and stalked away from the house,

169

turning her head to say something to Alex. He shook his head, and she gave him the finger.

"Freak."

The word rang out very clear. After she said it, she sat down on the curb and picked at a fingernail. Alex's head whipped around, but he looked past his sister. His eyes met Jason's. Even from across the street, he had a palpable sense of strangeness. A defiant smirk flashed on his face, then he looked away and walked toward the back of the house.

Mitch shook her head when he disappeared out of sight. "Is that normal?"

"I have no idea. I think that's the first time I've seen them all together."

"Well, if that's normal, no wonder the kid is messed up."

No wonder.

10

The narrow stairs held barely enough room for one person. Jason ascended, and although he knew Mitch climbed behind him, she remained silent. The wallpaper twisted and screamed in silent symphony on either side. They went up and up and up, and still there were more steps. Shadows and smoke obscured the top—thick, roiling smoke that smelled of dead flesh and utter hopelessness. He didn't want to climb the stairs, but they couldn't stop now. With each step they took, the stair below dropped away into a chasm of hot air and muffled cries for help. The place was desolation.

Mitch's breath was warm on his neck. Excitement, not fear, rose from her pores. She didn't understand this wasn't a safe place. She would, though, and soon.

The hallway narrowed even more, and the walls skimmed his shoulders. Tiny hands, wallpaper hands, grabbed at his shirt and his hair. And still, they went up. A distant, inhuman roar rose from the

170

chaos below. Something angry. Something *hungry*.

He wanted to run, yet his feet would not cooperate. They didn't want to reach the top. There were worse things waiting ahead, hidden in the gray swirls. The roar again, louder. And the furious flapping of wings.

Closer.

Left foot, right foot, each step slow and careful. The walls pressed in even more. Jason turned his shoulders sideways, and the wallpaper hands ran their nails down his back. If he wouldn't help them get free

yes, because they're as trapped as I am

then they wanted blood. His blood. With the sting of a needle, they dug through his shirt. The roar turned to a shriek, and he and Mitch tried to run, but the walls closed in, tighter and tighter. The floorboards groaned and wind whipped around them, carrying the stench of ash and a heat so intense it ripped the breath from his lungs.

Jason stumbled and banged his leg against the wood. He opened his mouth to scream, but the taste of death erased the sound. The walls pressed against his chest, and he couldn't move any more. They were

trapped, we're trapped

stuck, and the creature rose into the space behind them. The wings rushed like an angry wind. It shrieked, its breath hot and reeking. Mitch screamed; he reached for her, but the wallpaper hands reached out and held him captive. Laughter behind the paper. Yes, they were happy. They wanted this. They'd gone mad in their glue and paper prison, and they wanted to see pain and bloodshed. Wanted to taste the bitter spice of fear.

He looked into the creature's eyes. Venomous green hatred looked back. It didn't want pain and bloodshed. It wanted to destroy him.

Mitch screamed again, and the creature answered with an ear-splitting roar. Its wings pushed hot air into their faces. It opened its mouth, revealing a gaping pit blacker than the darkest night. It sunk its talons into her flesh and pulled her away. He reached out his hand,

and for a brief moment, their fingertips touched, then it carried her away, down into the waiting fires.

Nononononononono!

Her cries drifted and spiraled, the walls pressed in tighter, and as the hands dug in, tears poured from his eyes.

Not Mitch, not her.

Jason woke up and reached out. His chest throbbed with a steady ache, and his skin burned, as if a million fire ants had feasted upon his flesh. His hand touched first empty air, then cool sheet; she wasn't beside him.

No, because it took her away. It carried her down, and I couldn't save her.

And on the pillowcase, three perfect drops of blood gleamed scarlet in the waking light of almost sunrise.

11

And in his room of trickery and screams, John S. Iblis laughed and laughed and laughed.

Chapter Seven

Shiver Me Timbers

1

Jason stared at the blood on the pillow for a long time. The pillow itself still held the indentation of Mitch's head, and with a lump in his throat, he sat up and touched the spots. His fingertips came away wet.

The toilet flushed in the bathroom, and Jason's heart jumped. A few minutes later, Mitch walked into the bedroom, her hair sleep tousled, with a long scratch, speckled with dots of fresh blood, running from the top of her collarbone across her shoulder.

She jumped; he drew in a sharp breath.

"Good morning," she said with a small smile.

Jason examined his hands and nails as she dropped down on the bed next to him, half her face veiled in shadow, half in pale, almost-morning light, then touched the end of the scratch. "I'm—"

"Hush. You didn't do it." She took his hand away and linked her fingers with his. "I scratched myself."

The talons. In my dream, Frank grabbed you with his talons.

He forced his voice calm. "I saw blood on the pillow and got worried."

She laughed. "I was dreaming about a giant bird. It was kind of silly, honestly. It flew by my face, so I tried to smack it away, and it scratched me. It's long and ugly, but it's not deep."

The sound of flapping wings pushed its way into his mind; he shoved them away.

But it was my nightmare. How could she have been in my nightmare?

"It just feels like a cat scratch, it's not really a big deal. It must be a silly couple thing, though."

"What do you mean?"

"You scratched yourself in your sleep, and now I've done it. Pretty soon we'll be finishing each other's sentences and answering each other's questions before we ask them." She smiled, slid off the bed and pulled the pillowcase off the pillow. "Come on, you might as well get out of bed. I'll rinse this out if you make coffee."

She wasn't in my nightmare. That's crazy. She just had a dream, a stupid dream about a bird, and dreams are powerful sometimes.

Jason groaned. "Look outside. The sun isn't even up yet. It's way too early, and it's a Sunday. Let's go back to bed." He reached for her, and she slid past his hand with a laugh.

"Aren't you taking your mom out for lunch?"

He groaned and threw his head back on the pillow, covering his eyes with one hand. "Yes, but not until one. It's too early for coffee."

"If I don't rinse this out, it will stain."

"I don't care. I'll buy a new one." He rolled over and reached out again; this time, she moved into his embrace, and he kissed the skin between her breasts. "I'll buy a new bed, too. You can help me pick one out."

A new bed, free from the ghosts of a bad marriage and bad memories. New pillows, new sheets. A fresh start. And then he could sleep at night.

Preferably without nightmares.

2

"Mom, are you sure you're eating enough?"

Her cheekbones belonged to an anorexic Hollywood starlet, not a mother of three, and her voice held a whispery, thin edge, as if she didn't have enough breath in her lungs to give the words strength.

She reached across the table and patted his hand. "Yes, I'm eating. I just don't have much of an appetite, and I'm still learning how to cook for one. Most of the time, it's just easier to heat up a can of soup."

"I'm worried about you. Are you getting out of the house? You know, seeing your friends?"

His mother waved her hand. "Yes, I am. And Ellen next door comes over and we play cards. I'm not very good, but it's helping. I'm taking each day as it comes." She traced her fingers on the edge of the table, then brought both hands up underneath her chin and pursed her lips together. "But I am worried about you. You look terrible."

"Yeah, I'm not sleeping all that well, and I have a big project at work. It's been a little tough."

Oh, and Dad keeps visiting me. He's not looking so good these days, and he rambles on and on.

"Your father wouldn't want that, you know."

Jason pushed his water glass in circles. "I know."

And the fine print. He wouldn't want that, either.

"I forgot to tell you. Shelley called me."

His fingers clenched around the glass. "What did she say?"

"Oh, I didn't get to the phone in time. She left a message, but I didn't call her back." She pressed her lips together in a small smile.

"You can call her if you want. It doesn't matter to me."

"I don't want to. I've nothing to say to her. She made the decision to not be a part of our family anymore. It would be different if the two of you had children, I think, or if you had left her, but as it stands now, there's no reason at all for she and I to stay in contact with each other. I think it's better that way, don't you agree?"

He nodded.

"Speaking of kids, Chris brought the girls over yesterday, and Ryan and Eve are coming over tonight for dinner." She picked up her glass, took a quick swallow, and set it down. "I should've stayed in the room with you, with your father. I shouldn't have left. I'm sorry."

Jason shoved the memory of his father's eyes and his grasping hand down hard.

It felt like he was trying to tell me something, but what?

"Mom, don't apologize."

"If I'd known—"

"How could you have known?"

She waved her hand in front of her face again. "The house is so quiet now. Sometimes I turn on the television just for the noise and every time, I put on one of his favorite shows." Her mouth quirked up into a half smile. "It's silly, but it helps. And I've been thinking of donating his clothes. It seems a shame to leave it sitting there unused. Maybe you can come over one day and help me box it up?"

"Okay, just tell me when, and I'll be there."

She gave a quick, sharp laugh. "Maybe I should get a dog."

"A dog?"

"Yes, you know your father had allergies, but it might be nice to have some company in the house."

Good thing she didn't live in his neighborhood.

"I really don't like those dark circles under your eyes."

It was his turn to wave his hand. "You don't have to worry. I'll be fine once the project is done. Really I will."

His mother's lips pressed into a thin line and she shook her head. "If you say so. Oh, at church this morning the minister asked how you were doing."

176

"Why would he do that?"

"Well, I know you don't share the same beliefs, but the minister is a good man. He's just concerned for all of us."

Jason shuddered at the memory of the strange heat in his arm at the minister's touch.

"Are you okay?" his mom asked, her eyes narrowed.

"I'm fine. I caught a chill, that's all."

"If you wanted to talk to him, I can give you his number."

The waitress set their plates down, and when she walked away, Jason said, "No thanks, Mom, but I appreciate the offer." He didn't want the minister anywhere near him.

"It might help to talk to someone," she said.

"I'm okay, really, and I don't want to talk to the minister. You need to eat before it gets cold. Please."

She picked up her fork. "See, I'm eating. Now, tell me about your new girlfriend. You *are* still seeing her, right? When are you going to introduce me?"

Jason dropped his fork.

"Your father is dead, but we're not. We have to keep living our lives. Your father would want that. Just like he always says, I mean *said*, it is what it is, right?"

She smiled, but her eyes shimmered with unshed tears.

3

When Jason arrived home late on Monday night, he tossed his mail on the kitchen table, and ten seconds later, a week's worth of unopened bills and junk advertisements cascaded in a rain of paper down onto the floor. "Shit," he said, bending down. Envelopes and flyers slipped and slid in his hands as he gathered them up into a pile. He dropped it back on the table and picked up the envelope on top, his latest electric bill. Underneath that, a credit card offer, then a flyer for a new pizza place, and next a white card—smooth, shiny, and blank on one side.

He flipped it over. Neither postage mark nor return address appeared on the other side, only two words written in inch-high letters: *I Know.*

The refrigerator clicked on with a soft hum as he stared down at the card, frowning at the slashes of black against the white. He lifted the card and breathed in the faint chemical bite still imbedded in the paper, then wet his thumb and traced it across the letters; his thumb came away clean.

Mitch knocked on the kitchen door with three quick raps of her knuckles, and he shoved the card back under the pile of mail before answering. It didn't take a stretch of the imagination to figure out who'd put it in his mailbox, but the meaning behind the words?

He could wager a few guesses, none of them pleasant.

4

Jason worked from home on Thursday, while waiting for the new bed to arrive. Not long after he sat on the sofa with the laptop balanced on his knees, pins and needles filled his arm. A half hour later, he pulled up a browser and typed in tattoo ink allergy symptoms. He didn't think he'd discover anything new, but what the hell. He'd already visited every link shown on the first page of search results, so he flipped to the second page, clicked on a link, and stretched out his arm, flexing his fist.

The pins and needles ran down to his fingertips, then scrambled back to his upper arm, under the tattoo. When all the photos on the page loaded, he gave them a quick scan, but the swollen, blistered flesh pictured bore no resemblance to his arm.

Flex.

His fingers twitched.

The hair stood up on his forearm. Maybe Sailor had jammed the needle in too far, striking a nerve. Except if he had, Jason would've known right away.

Flex.

A twinge flared in his upper arm.

He clicked on an ad that said *Search for Licensed Tattoo Artists in your Area* in bright yellow letters. The new site gave the option to search via shop name or artist name. He started to type Sailor and stopped. His real name wasn't Sailor. It was...

Shit. What was it?

He grabbed for his wallet, then stopped. He'd lost the card. "Shit." What was his name? John something.

Flex.

Heat spread out under the tattoo.

Jason shook out his fingers; the heat dissipated. The name lingered on the tip of his tongue. It had been short and easy to spell, but not common. Ives? Maybe. He typed it in and found several links for that name, none in Baltimore.

No, that's not it. It's not Ives. It's close, but—

Voices rose outside, then a series of heavy knocks. Jason showed the deliverymen the bedroom, then stood out of the way while they hauled the old bed away and brought in the new. After they left, Jason opened the new set of sheets and frowned.

An hour later, he had sweat running down his forehead into his eyes and a smile on his face. Although it had taken three tries to find the perfect spot, the new bed, dark wood instead of cold wrought iron, sat at an angle against one corner of the room, diagonal to the door, with one of the dressers at an angle against another corner. Shelley always insisted everything had to be flush against the walls or otherwise lined up in a straight fashion to be "aesthetically pleasing".

The pins and needles in his arm vanished underneath an ache from the exertion. He ran his hands along the edge of the footboard, imagining Mitch's pale hair spread across the dark blue of the sheets.

Iblis.

He raced downstairs and typed John Iblis into the search bar. The site returned one result—Iblis Designs in Maine, not Baltimore, but he clicked on the result anyway. A graphics-heavy page opened up with the name Iblis Designs in ornate script the color of Pinot noir. The menu bar on the left side gave him the option he wanted—Tattoo Artists. The new page had six photographs—five men and one woman, all young and heavily inked.

"Damn."

He went back to the main page and found the phone number and shop hours at the bottom. Although they closed at 6:00 p.m. and his watch read 6:04, he dialed the number anyway. It rang four times before a machine picked up, but he hung up without leaving a message.

5

Jason waited until lunchtime on Friday to call Iblis Designs again; after six rings, a male voice, too young to belong to Sailor, answered. Loud music thumped in the background, something angry and filled with the squeal of guitars.

"Hi, I'm looking for a tattoo artist named John Iblis."

"Sorry, dude, no one works here with that name."

He tapped his fingers on his desk. "I met this guy a few nights ago, and he said he owned the shop."

"He may have said so, but he lied. I own the shop and my name is Carl, not John."

"This is the shop on Merritt Avenue, right?"

"Yeah, but I promise you, there's nobody named Iblis here. It's just the name of the shop. Sort of my idea of a joke."

"A joke?"

"Yeah, my father's a preacher. Different religion and all, but whatever. It's still funny. Do you want to make an appointment with one of the other artists?"

"Let me think about it, and I'll call you back."

The phone disconnected with a soft click. The name was a religious joke? He opened up a search window, typed in the word Iblis, and clicked the first link. He frowned.

Iblis was the name for the devil in the Quran. He closed the window and rubbed his upper arm, still frowning.

It wasn't a very funny joke.

6

Jason woke from a deep, dreamless sleep clutching his left arm and holding in a groan. The pain—liquid and hot—centered just under the tattoo. The hallway light bathed the room in pale shades of gray; Mitch slept on her side with one hand tucked under her cheek and a lock of hair curled across her face. His fingers trembled as he tucked it behind her ear, then he rolled over on his back when another sharp pain struck. It faded into a sensation similar to an itch deep under the skin.

He pressed his palm flat against the skin, covering everything but the tips of the wings and the top of the griffin's head, and a strange, pulsing heat radiated up through his hand. Despite the heat, he didn't take his hand away. The promise of sleep tugged at the corners of his mind. He shifted his head on the pillow and closed his eyes, listening to Mitch's shallow, even breaths.

When the skin moved under his hand, Jason started. Opened his eyes wide.

No, that's not right.

The skin rippled against his palm, like a tide pool after a rock met its surface or a plastic bag caught in the wind, then it moved again, the wave of an ocean, rushing in and rushing out. Definitely not a muscle spasm. He sat up and pulled his hand away, breathing hard. The skin undulated, a roll starting at the top of his arm, near his shoulder, moving down to just above his elbow, the movement mesmerizing, almost hypnotic, but wrong, so wrong.

The pain pulsed and throbbed. He clamped his jaw shut tight. His heart raced when he touched his arm again. The skin, rough and soft and slippery at the same time, like feathers rubbed first the right way, then the wrong, rose under his touch, a hard pebble of skin rising up under the griffin's head, pushing his hand away.

No, oh no. Not real, not real, not real.

The pain in his arm turned brittle as it shifted and turned, then lifted. Pain like the edge of a dull knife tearing into his skin from the inside out. A thin moan locked in the back of his throat. His heart sped up, thudding hard against his chest.

As the skin rose higher, the ink of the tattoo blurred and changed, the one-dimensional image shifting into more. Under the skin, the griffin's head pushed and pushed, an implacable beast bent on escape. And under that, deep down, a sensation of weight, flexing and moving, coiling to strike. Then a trembling, like fluttering wings.

Inside? Inside me?

Ice cold sweat ran down his back.

Frank?

Jason tried to pull away, but he couldn't get away from his own arm. His own skin.

I'm not seeing this. I'm not seeing—feeling—this at all.

With a quick, wasplike sting, the griffin broke free, pulling apart from his skin like a blister, joined together in flesh, but not of the same. A smell spread out into the room—a hot, feral stink. The ears, gently furred, emerged first, then the rounded curve of the top of the head, all bronze and gold. A doll-sized living nightmare, warm and alive. The eyes opened, the green gaze fixed on Jason as the beak slid razor-sharp from its prison of flesh. He bit his lip to keep in a scream, and the sweet-sick taste of blood filled his mouth. The green eyes bored into his with grim intelligence. Staring at him. Seeing him.

It's just ink on skin.

The tip of one taloned limb rose up and rested its sharp edges on his skin. Tiny spots of blood bloomed like dark petals under the talons. The griffin turned its head in a slow arc to look at Mitch. She slept on, peaceful and still. It opened its beak, revealing a dark cavern

Just ink on skin. Not real. NOT REAL!

and turned back to Jason, its eyes narrowing. Fetid warmth spread across his skin as it hissed—a quiet, terrible whispering sound that held a dark promise of bitterness and pain. A fresh flare of agony raced through his arm as it moved inside, against his bone, and he shuddered. With one last hiss, the griffin sank back under, *into*, his skin, the talons digging fresh little gouges, the fur brushing with a silky wisp, the beak opening and closing, the head, its eyes like spots of green fire, and last, the ears, disappearing like tiny periscopes retreating back into the depths of an ocean, the whole turning back to ink on a flesh canvas. His skin quivered, gave one last ripple and stilled. Jason jumped up from bed, his heart screaming madness in his chest. Mitch sighed but didn't open her eyes.

He fled from the bedroom into the harsh light of the bathroom, bile rising in his throat. Hot tears streamed down his face as he staggered to the toilet, lifted the lid and threw up until his stomach ached with emptiness. His mind screaming twisted knots, he slipped to the bathroom floor, the tile cool against his cheek, then he slipped down into the dark.

7

A cold cloth on his forehead. The warmth of a blanket on his shoulders. A hand, rubbing his arm. Pain digging into his stomach. Heat. The world swirling around his head.

Then the darkness returned.

8

The cemetery on the corner of Fayette and Greene Street, once known as the Old Western Burying Grounds, smelled faintly of cigarette smoke and old sex. John S. Iblis made his way through the gloom to one headstone and sat down on the ground. To a passerby, he would look as if he were paying his respects. In truth, he bent his head to hide his smile.

The man honored on the tombstone died inexplicably in Baltimore on October 7, 1849. The ghost of the dead man was said to haunt the grounds. A lie, but a good tale nonetheless. "Lord help my poor soul," were his last words, or so it was said. His exact cause of death remained a mystery. To most, anyway.

John S. Iblis had offered him a way out. Regrettably, Mr. Poe had not taken him up on the offer.

9

Jason opened his eyes and blinked at the sun streaming in the bedroom windows.

"Hey," Mitch said, touching the back of her hand to his forehead. "I think your fever broke."

He shifted in the bed and started to rise, but she pushed him back down. "Nope, you stay in bed. Doctor's orders. You got sick last night. I woke up and found you on the bathroom floor."

"What time is it?" he said, his throat raw.

"It's about four."

"Four?" He started to rise again.

"Uh-uh." She pressed him down, her hand warm on his chest. "Stay put. I mean it. You were really sick. Chills, fever, the whole ball of wax. You don't remember any of it?"

He shook his head.

"That's probably a good thing. I had a hell of a time getting you back in bed. I dropped you on your head a few times." She smiled and pushed her hair back behind her ears. "You kept telling me to go away, it wasn't safe. How do you feel now?"

"I feel okay, just tired and sore. You should go home. I don't want you to catch this."

"It's probably too late for that but don't worry, if I get sick, you can take care of me." His stomach rumbled, and Mitch laughed.

"I went out and got tea and chicken soup. Do you want to try and eat something?"

"Maybe in a little bit. Not just yet."

"Okay." She climbed up on the bed and curled her legs up underneath her. "What does 'I know' mean?"

"What?"

"I found the card on the kitchen table. I tried to straighten up a little bit and it fell out, the index card, I mean. The one that says 'I know'."

"I don't know," he said.

Mitch lifted one eyebrow. "Is this a 'who's on first' thing?"

"No, I really don't know. Someone left it in my mailbox."

"That's weird."

"I..."

"Know," she said with a laugh.

"My guess is it's from the kid across the street."

"So he knows you know he was looking in the window? That doesn't make sense."

"Right, but remember I told you about the missing animals? Maybe he meant he knows I know."

"Okay, but you just suspect it, right? You don't really know, do you? He definitely looks like he's weird, and the whole hiding in your backyard is strange—"

"Don't forget looking in the windows."

"Yeah, but even that doesn't mean he's responsible for the animals," she said. "Pets run away all the time, and if they get out and get hit by a car..."

The words pushed at his lips, and he twisted the sheets in one hand. "But I found something in my yard a few weeks ago. It was, um, a cat's tail. Only the tail. The rest of it wasn't there. I thought maybe another animal did it, you know? Like a raccoon."

She wrinkled her nose. "Ugh. That's horrible and gross. Maybe a possum did it. They're pretty fierce."

He rolled over on his side. "But then I found another one on my doormat, and there was a piece of gum stuck on one of the steps. I don't chew gum, you don't chew gum, and no one else has been on my back porch."

He opened his mouth to mention the other tail but clamped it shut before a word could escape. The dog's tail pushed the whole thing way past possum territory. If the tail had belonged to a Chihuahua, maybe he could believe it, but he didn't think a possum could kill a large dog unless it was some sort of mutant.

"Okay, but that still doesn't make sense. If he did cut off a cat's tail on purpose, and that's disgusting and creepy as hell, and then left it in your yard, isn't that sort of daring you to find out? So his 'I know' note is just stupid. Maybe he's just trying to get a reaction."

He groaned and put his hands over his eyes. "I have no idea. I just wish he'd picked someone else. I've never done anything to him. Hell, I barely noticed him until he started poking around. Unless..."

"What?"

"Maybe he found the tails before I did and thinks I did it."

"That's ridiculous." Mitch traced her fingers on his upper arm. "You? Why would you cut off a cat's tail?" She shuddered.

"But he doesn't know me, and if he didn't do it, who did?"

186

She shook her head. "It's all too weird. There has to be some logical, normal, explanation. Maybe a fox? They can get pretty big, I think. Either way, I think you should still talk to his parents."

His stomach growled again, low and insistent.

"Okay, enough of this. It's time for you to eat," Mitch said, sliding off the bed. "No arguments." She leaned forward and kissed his cheek. "I'll be back up in a few minutes."

She slipped from the room, her footsteps soft on the stairs. Jason closed his eyes, and an image of the griffin hissing as it pushed itself out of his skin swam up in his mind.

"Shit," he said, opening his eyes to look at his arm.

I might have been sick, but sick enough to imagine that?

10

Later, after Mitch left, Jason stripped off his shirt and stood under the glare of the bathroom light, staring at his arm. The lines of the griffin were still, the green eyes immobile. He ran his fingertips over the skin. No heat, no pulsing flesh, no strange texture. Just...skin. "Frank?" He rubbed the skin hard, then pushed his finger in, distorting the ink. Nothing. Nothing but skin, nothing but *him*. "Frank, are you in there?"

He pawed through the medicine cabinet and found a jar of face cream Shelley had left behind.

Do you really think this is a good idea?

No, maybe not, but it was worth a shot.

Here comes your wake up call, Frank.

He curled his fingers around the heavy glass and swung it down. Pain flared up and out, and the griffin's colors darkened underneath a reddened circle of flesh.

Good thing you didn't do this when Mitch was here because do you know what this looks like?

"Shut up."

No movement. No Frank. Maybe he wouldn't come out during the day. Jason tried to laugh, but the dry, papery sound caught in the back of his throat.

11

At midnight, Jason sat on the sofa, his shirt in a fabric lump on the edge of the coffee table. His fingers drummed on the cover of the book in his hands, and he flipped page after page, seeing the words but not comprehending the text. He put the book down. Lifted his coffee cup. Took a long swallow. In the quiet gloom of closed curtains and dim lights, the hiss of the coffeemaker crept out of the kitchen, sputtering as it brewed a second pot.

He tossed the book aside and turned on the television, mindlessly switching from one channel to another as he waited. He'd already sent his boss an email informing him he wouldn't be in on Monday. At the moment, he didn't care about the repercussions. What he wanted, what he feared, was the griffin tattoo.

Mitch felt it.

Jason dropped the remote on the cushion and ran his hands through his hair. Tattoos didn't move, even if they had a name like Frank. And they didn't come out and hiss. They were just ink. Not real. The coffeemaker gave up its last drop of water (and didn't that last hiss sound vaguely familiar? Oh yes, he thought it did), and he went into the kitchen for another cup.

Maybe not, but I know what I saw. It looked at me. It was real. And I smelled it.

He shuddered and carried his mug back into the living room. What choice did he have? He had to see it. He had to know. And what would he do if it was real, if it stuck out its head, or worse? What could be worse? His hand shook as he lifted the coffee mug again. Too much caffeine or the fear that had wormed its way into his gut? He picked up the remote and flipped through the channels again.

An hour later, his heart beat heavy in his chest. His thoughts flickered from one thing to the next, and his fingers played piano on the edge of the coffee table, but it was a mad concert with an insane conductor. He got up and turned on every light in the house, even the small lamp on his nightstand. When he finished, tiny beads of sweat dotted his forehead. He contemplated a shower, but the thought of the griffin's head emerging from a veil of soap bubbles made him toss the idea out the window. Jason flopped back down on the sofa and picked up the book, but the words didn't even resemble English anymore.

Come on, Frank, I'm waiting.

His skin tingled but the tattoo was only ink on skin. Nothing more.

Just caffeine jitters. How much coffee have you had? Two pots? Three? Good one. You'll be up for days.

And what would he do if he did see the griffin? Grab it? Push it back in? He went back into the kitchen, humming under his breath. Shelley had taken the good knives, and he hadn't replaced them yet, but he thought he had a set of metal skewers. He dug around in the drawer.

And what are you going to do?

"I don't know," he said.

Poke it in the eye maybe?

"Shut up."

Shake its hand and say nice to meet you?

"Shut. Up," he said between clenched teeth.

Come on, seriously. Your tattoo is alive, and you're looking for a skewer? Going to have a little barbecue. A little griffin kabob? With a side of what? Madness?

"Shut the hell up," he shouted.

He slammed the drawer shut and opened another. It stuck halfway. He pulled. Nothing. He pulled it again. "You son of a bitch." He wrenched the drawer open. It flew out and fell to the floor, in a crash of serving spoons and spatulas. Metallic rain. No skewers though. He barked a short, hoarse laugh and went back to the other drawer. It slid out with one quick pull. He turned it over, dumped the contents on the floor, and tossed the empty drawer to the side.

"I know they're here somewhere."

Two more drawers, including the little drawer that held nothing but junk. He wiped sweat from his brow and yanked the larger one out first. He flipped it over and when the last spoon clattered to the floor, he threw the drawer across the room, wincing when it landed with a loud, wooden crack.

Crazy, this is cra—

"Shut up."

The junk drawer, the last drawer, came out with a sharp squeal. "I should fix that," he said. After one good shake, takeout menus rained down on the floor, along with rolls of tape, pens and several small screwdrivers. He laughed and picked up a handful of menus.

Pizza, Chinese, Indian, but where in the hell are the skewers?

He ripped the menus into pieces and knelt down on the floor, in the middle of the mess. Plastic and metal bounced and bumped together with a dull rattle. He pawed through the pile, sending utensils and pens scattering across the floor. A rubber-handled ladle spun in crazy circles, bounced off one of the legs of the kitchen table, and came to rest near the trashcan. Finally, he gave a sharp cry of triumph. There, in the mess of silver and paper shreds, standing out like an exclamation point—a skewer.

I knew I had them.

He curled his fingers around it, brandishing it like a sword, and grinned. "Come on out now, Frank." As he walked out of the kitchen with skewer in hand, he cast a look over his shoulder to the chaos strewn across the floor.

What were you thinking?

"I'm fine. The drawer was stuck. That's all."

12

At two o'clock, his hands still shook, and his blood pressure protested every sip of coffee, but the griffin was still just ink. He muted the television and played twenty-five games of Solitaire on his laptop. An hour after that, he threw in a load of laundry, carrying the skewer with him. At four-thirty, he felt like a fool.

A bird chirped outside his window and he jumped, sloshing lukewarm coffee over the back of his hand. Another bird answered, and he laughed, the sound high-pitched and alien. He rubbed his arm. Nothing happened. Then he picked up the skewer, running his finger over the sharp point.

What if I—

A crazy thought. Crazier than the kitchen mess, if he wanted to be perfectly honest. If he wanted to be perfectly *frank*. He brought the skewer closer to his arm and tapped the side on his skin.

"Come out, come out, wherever you are."

He knew where it was—under his skin, hiding. If he stuck the skewer in just a little, maybe it would come out. But for what? To play hide and seek?

Jason's heart thumped and thudded, and he gripped the skewer tight in his hand. Could he do it? He pressed the point in atop one of the griffin's eyes, not quite hard enough to break the skin. When he pulled the skewer away, a tiny, red indentation remained. He shifted the skewer over to the other eye, pushed it in a second time, then waited.

Nothing.

He moved the skewer over to the tip of the tail, pressed again, and hissed under his breath as he broke the skin. A thin trail of red trickled out, nothing more than blood—his own blood. Five more strikes with the skewer in rapid succession, along the edge of one wing, five more tiny holes, grunting under his breath at each sharp sting of pain.

"Come on out, Frank," he said, tapping his arm with the side of the skewer again, smearing blood across the amber and gold.

And again. And again. And again. Hard enough to leave red welts on his flesh that distorted the tattoo's edges.

"Come. On. Out."

He gripped the skewer tight in his fist and raised it high.

"I'll make you come out."

Jason caught a ghost of his reflection in the television screen and froze. What the hell was he doing? He dropped the skewer on the coffee table and put his head in his hands. Maybe he was going nuts.

The blood dried in dark streaks as he sat on the sofa, staring out at nothing. At five-thirty, with the edges of the sky lightening with the sunrise and birdsong chattering in the air, he went upstairs and took the skewer with him.

Just in case.

13

Jason drove down to Fells Point on Thursday after work, stumbled into McAfee's, and ordered a beer before he sat down.

Brian frowned. "You look worse than you did at the office. Are you okay, man?"

"Yeah, I just have a headache," Jason lied. His head didn't hurt, but the ache in his arm had popped back in to say hello. A steady throb under the skin, almost in perfect time with the music playing in the background. Jason downed half his beer in one gulp and ignored the look Brian gave him. Inside, a disjointed sensation turned his limbs heavy, as if his body no longer belonged to him, as if everything right had turned wrong. And that everything started with the tattoo. With Frank.

Jason took another swallow. No, everything started with Sailor. At the bar. A chill raced down his spine; he shook it away and ordered another beer. Brian spoke to him, but his voice floated in the air, vague and formless. Jason nodded in the right places and smiled when needed, but his own thoughts claimed center stage.

The bar near his house. The night Shelley left.

The chill again. He turned to look out at the bar. Waitresses walked with trays in their hands, girls in tight tank tops sat in groups of four or five and guys crowded around tables with beer bottles— empty and full—glittering in the overhead lights. Nothing strange or abnormal, but a prickling on the back of his neck said someone watched him. A thick, growling laugh pierced the air, radiating out in an overhanging, mirthless cloud.

Sailor.

Jason whipped his head around. No gray halo of hair, no rolling walk, no Sailor, but the laugh, that unmistakable sound, belonged to no one else. The chill turned to a finger of ice, teasing, tickling. A waitress put another beer in front of him, and his hand shook when he picked it up.

It's just a bad case of the creeps. That's all.

Jason set the bottle on the table, hard enough to send beer splashing out onto the table.

"What's wrong?" Brian asked.

Nothing. Everything. I didn't read the fine print, you know. That was my mistake. My dad said so.

"My head is killing me. I'm heading out."

"Are you okay to drive? You really don't look good."

"Yeah, I'll be fine." Jason threw money down on the table and headed for the door. The laugh drifted up again, softer, and the finger of ice stabbed and twisted. As he passed a table of guys in tan uniforms, one nodded and looked up with pale green eyes. Moist eyes. *Sailor's* eyes. Except it wasn't Sailor at all but the orderly from the hospital. Even seated, he looked big enough to break Jason in two without breaking a sweat. The hanging light over the table reflected in his bald head and his skin, darker than Jason remembered, gleamed like polished ebony, in stark contrast to the pale

Sailor's

eyes.

No, it's just the lighting.

When one of the other orderlies said something and the not-Sailor laughed again, the taste of beer burned in Jason's throat, and a slice of pain dug into his stomach. The bite of stale cigarettes clung to their uniforms. The orderly lifted a beer bottle and tipped the mouth in Jason's direction. He tilted his head back and drank, and Jason's vision blurred into an image of the homeless man on Shakespeare Street with his bottle of rum, then it was just the orderly again. The pink nightgown on the pinup girl tattoo was bright, even against his dark skin. Her lips were the same vibrant shade of pink, parted suggestively. He'd seen it before and not in the hospital.

He couldn't take his eyes from the tattoo. She was a work of art—perfect. She wore a smile that promised sin, but her hidden hand promised hurt and pain. Her breasts were full, straining against the nightgown, her waist tiny, and her hips wide. Long legs peeked out from the nightgown, one drawn up high. Dancer's legs. Perfume, soft and sweet, like rain and roses, drifted up. A woman like that would make you forget about everything. She would wrap those legs around yours and her hand—

"Find everything you're looking for, mister?"

Jason shook his head, the thoughts of dancer's legs and full lips drifting away.

The voice.

The orderly grinned and gave a short whistle. Part of a song? Jason's stomach clenched again. Another orderly turned around in his chair. Eyes dulled with too much beer peered out from a broad, not unkind, face.

"You need something, man?" he asked.

Jason's tongue pressed against the back of his teeth, a fat worm looking for the way out.

No way out of this one, buddy.

"Hello? Need something?" The same broad–faced orderly.

Jason pulled his voice up and out. "No, sorry." He stepped away from the table with heavy feet. He needed to get out.

Behind him, the orderly broke into a snippet of song. "Had a girl and she sure was fine."

The colors of the room swirled brighter; the words of the song wavered and stretched out like the discordant tune from a carousel. The other men burst out laughing, and Jason fled from the bar with the gravelly voice and the whistle echoing in his ears.

14

Jason drove home, his thoughts chaos, the city blurring past his windows as sweat seeped from every pore. The orderly had Sailor's voice and his eyes. It didn't make sense, but it was the truth. And the laughter. All the same. Sailor without his sailor suit.

Jason shuddered. And the song. Had he heard it before? He thought he had.

What did he say?

"Find everything you're looking for?" Jason said. His hands clenched on the steering wheel. The homeless man had said the exact same thing. When he stood in front of the tattoo shop, where the door should've been. He'd said those same words.

Doors didn't disappear. They were either there or they weren't.

Tattoos don't either.

His cell phone rang, high-pitched and shrill, and he yelled out, unable to keep the sound inside. He looked at the display, and another shudder sent a ripple through his spine—*Unknown Caller.*

It's Sailor.

The ring again.

Get a grip, Jason. It could be a telemarketer.

But he couldn't get a grip. Not on anything at all.

Again.

Because he knew it was Sailor.

And again.

Maybe he was calling to see how Jason liked the tattoo now.

The fifth ring cut off midway, and the steering wheel, sticky with sweat, slipped in his hands, sending his car into the next lane. He spun the wheel too far in the other direction and for one sick, long minute, he thought he'd lost control. The tires slid and slid, then caught and held the road like a lover. A lover in a pink nightgown with long, long legs.

I need to go home. Go home and...what? Wait up all night, loaded with caffeine? For what?

For Frank. Jason exhaled, a long sigh, one step away from a groan. So he could see it with his own eyes.

So I know.

He wiped first one hand then the other on his pants.

Know what? Know nothing. I was sick and thought I saw something, that's it. The orderly was just a guy, a heavy smoker, and his eyes? Lots of people have green eyes. He might have been wearing contacts for all I know.

When he finally turned into his driveway, the back of his shirt was wet against his skin. He got out of the car, the windows of his house looming dark and watchful. The faint sound of rubber on concrete pulled his eyes away from his house. The kid, Alex, rode his bike, circling in the street in front. He slowed down, the arc of his circle smaller and smaller with each pass until finally he stopped. If Jason's doormat held another present, he was going to take it over and give it to the kid's parents.

"You sick piece of shit. I know what you did."

Their eyes met, and anger bubbled up inside Jason, furious and *red*. Alex stood motionless, his lank dishwater hair falling past his brows. Jason took one step toward him and in a flash, Alex's feet turned the pedals, and he flew down the street. With a heavy sigh, Jason walked to his back door; as he drew closer, something on the mat flashed in the moonlight. The anger faded and his steps slowed.

I hope your parents are home, kid. If not, they're going to have a nice little surprise waiting for them.

He stepped up onto the first step and stopped. Nothing. Nothing but the doormat. The flash of something? Only his imagination. A lot of that going around lately.

Once inside, he locked the door and stood in the middle of his kitchen.

I should call Mitch. Maybe I could go over and we could watch a movie. It's not too late. But not a horror movie. Definitely not. Something lighthearted, a nonsensical comedy.

The girl. The pinup girl on

Sailor's

the orderly's arm. Long legs and pink lips.

His original designs. That's what he said.

One of the framed pictures on the wall at Sailor's shop. He remembered the grizzly bear and the girl. Look closer, Sailor said.

They will not bite.

15

The girl in the pink nightgown felt as good as she looked. Jason ran his fingers up her thigh, reveling in her soft skin. Underneath the nightgown, she wore nothing but her own skin, and her lips tasted like bubble gum. She kept her right hand tucked behind her back, ran the fingers of her left hand down his back, and dug her nails in, making him wince.

"You can call me whatever you want," she said.

He whispered her name—Marianne—and pulled her hips closer. She moaned low in her throat, the sound of beautiful danger, but he didn't care, not tonight. She was beautiful, warm and curved in every spot a woman could curve, her nipples hard against his palms even through the silk of her gown. Her laugh, low and husky, rippled out into the room. He couldn't take her home to meet his mother, but he could take her to bed. He'd be a fool not to.

She brought her right hand out from behind her back, and he pulled his hands away from her hips. Her lips curved up in a smile. Naughty girl, the smile said. *I'm a very naughty girl.* The edge of the straight razor shimmered in the moonlight. She smiled with her perfect pink lips and raised her hand. Jason tried to back up, to get away, but he froze in place. Another laugh slipped from her lips, and she brought the razor closer and closer and—

Jason woke up with the echoes of his scream still in the room and a sharp pain in his left arm. He sat up and put his hands in his head, his nose filled with the stink of his own sweat. The voices in his head didn't scream. They whispered dark thoughts of terrible beauty. With a groan, he pulled off his sodden T-shirt and threw it on the floor. His heartbeat thudded with a painful rhythm in his chest, and a slick taste—rotten apples washed down with bitter medicine—coated his tongue.

Was he going crazy?

He flipped on the nightstand light and held out his hands. Nothing strange about them. The same hands. The same skin.

So why do I feel like a stranger? Why do I feel like these aren't my hands?

Jason shook his head. A dull ache thudded in the center of his chest. He wanted to call Mitch, but it was two o'clock in the morning. What would he tell her? His tattoo stuck its head out the night he was sick, and he was afraid to be alone? Afraid it might come back? And as if that weren't enough, what about the guy at McAfee's who sounded like Sailor, had green eyes like Sailor and laughed like Sailor, who spoke the same words a homeless man had when he went to Sailor's shop? Only that night, neither door nor shop existed.

He barked out a harsh laugh. "What the hell is going on?"

Then his arm rippled, long and lazy, like a mud-thick river after a hurricane's devastation. Or an animal stretching after a long nap. His mouth dropped open as the skin on his arm rolled and twisted.

No, no, no. Not again. It wasn't real. It was—

"My imagination, that's all."

The tattoo shifted, the lines of the griffin blurred and focused. "This is not real. This can't happen." He put his hands over his eyes and counted to five, thinking of Mitch and her smile, the way her hair held tight to the scent of her shampoo. He opened his eyes. The flesh began to rise, stretching up. "No, no. It can't. It can't."

Yes, it can happen. It is happening because it is real. It's not ink. What the fuck did Sailor do to me?

The skin rose another inch, then another. Heat spread out, licking tiny, unseen flames down to his fingertips. A fluttering tingle moved deep inside, the soft press of fur and feathers against bone and muscle.

Didn't you read the fine print?!?!

His father's voice, not a sorrowful whisper but a scream of panic. Higher and higher, the skin of his arm bubbled up, stretching like taffy until the ears and head emerged. In and of his flesh, yet not Jason. Not him at all, but something living and breathing within. Like a botfly burrowed deep inside. Its limbs shifted; its muscles flexed, pushing up to the surface.

The griffin blinked eyes filled with malevolence. Once. Twice. Madness and death lay deep inside the green. It breathed a foul stench of rotten meat, warm against his arm. Jason climbed, *slid*, off the bed. Bright, needle-sharp pain screamed in his arm as unseen talons dug into the soft parts inside. He didn't care about the pain. It could rip off his arm if it wanted to. He just wanted it to go away.

He stumbled back away from the bed, and a harsh sound emerged from his throat. And from the griffin: a quiver of constricted wings, heat from its body, the *whisk-whisk* of a powerful tail swaying in an arc. Not out, but in.

Inside, inside, inside.

The taste in his mouth exploded into something noxious and foul. The taste of a thousand dark nightmares or a million lunatic screams. He needed to run, get away. Far away. He clenched his teeth together to hold in the scream pushing to be free, turning it into a terrible sound of chaos and lunacy. He stepped back again, with the sound of rushing blood loud in his ears.

I can't get away because it's in me. It's inside me!

One foreleg rose and flexed, the talons sharp. The leg lifted and dropped back down against his skin, and tiny spots of blood

my blood

beaded up like crimson pearls around the talons.

Alive. Not just ink. It's real. It's alive. And it's hungry.

Jason scrambled back, his feet pounding heavy on the floor. His ankle twisted and he reached out his

good arm, the griffin-free

arm. His fingers hit the wall hard; he moaned as the pinkie finger bent back, not far enough to break, but far enough to scream out in protest.

Can't get away. Can't get away.

The griffin's other foreleg raised, stepping up-out of his skin like a cartoon character lifting from the pages, except this wasn't a harmless mouse or cat about to wreak one-dimensional havoc. The legs swelled, grew, taking shape and substance. It leaned forward, breathing its heat, using its legs to pull its body up and out, its weight nothing more than a kitten's, its size much the same, straining like a conjoined twin twisting away to break free from the skin binding them together. Jason sank down to his knees.

I don't want to see this anymore. Make it stop. Just make it go away.

His neck ached, but he couldn't tear his eyes away. A smell of smoke, ash and animal musk filled the room, heavy and thick; it stung Jason's eyes and burned the back of his throat. The chest, proud and majestic, slipped free.

"You're. Not. Real. Not real. This is a dream. A bad dream."

It tuned its head and gave Jason a long, considering look, then lowered its beak and pulled again.

Dad, is this what you saw?

The wings unfolded and kissed warmth against Jason's skin. A harsh laugh, high-pitched and jittery, broke free from his lips at the touch. He scrubbed at his eyes with the back of his hand, and it came away wet.

My own feather pillow. My own griffin. Come on, Frankie-boy, I'll get your leash and collar and we can walk through the neighborhood.

The griffin ignored him, intent on breaking free.

Frank is alive. He is alive, and he's not friendly at all.

Small rivulets of blood dripped down Jason's arm as the griffin's talons dug in again. The back came into view, sliding out of his skin with a whispering noise like silk against satin and a feel like velvet. The dark gold fur shimmered.

Another pull and the top curve of the rump emerged, slow and steady, the top of its powerful hind legs, the tufted tail and last, the furred paws, with claws extended. His left arm twitched, empty inside. The griffin perched on his arm, as light as a robin, as heavy as an unavoidable truth.

This is not a dream, no matter how many times I close my eyes and wish it so. I smell it. It's alive and it was in me and now it's free.

Jason groaned and clenched his right hand into a fist. He shook his left arm. "Get off." The griffin did not budge; instead, it dug its talons and claws in even more. "Oh God, get off me," he shrieked, shaking his arm again. The talons ripped into his skin, sending fresh trails of blood down to his elbow. Only eight inches high, the griffin stretched out its wings, the span over twice the length of its body, and turned its beady, green eyes toward Jason. It gave a low hiss, its breath thick and fetid, and *grew*. A foot now. Jason's arm trembled under its changing weight; his knees pressed hard into the wood floor. The wings cast an uneven shadow on the wall. It pushed from his arm, using the muscular back legs to spring up and out, hovered over Jason, flapping its wings, and gave a low, reeking hiss. When it dropped down, it landed with a gentle thump and grew again.

Two feet.

No more, please. I can't...

The blood slid back into his skin. The little marks left by the talons disappeared. The outline of the tattoo remained, like a ghostly after-image, then it, too, vanished. The griffin expanded, the wings stretching far into the room. Three feet. Four. Six.

Stop.

The body thickened, the legs lengthened, the tail swelled. Seven feet. Jason's bed scraped across the floor, pushed out of the way. Tears spilled from his eyes.

Please just stop.

A hot, acrid smell spread out through the room—a strong, bitter reek of the wild. Its eyes screamed silent, green rage. The beak opened, and a sibilant hiss pierced the corners of the room. Jason covered his ears with his hands. He wanted it away. Out. Gone. It couldn't be real. It shouldn't be real.

It's a make-believe bird, not real. Not. Real.

And still it grew. Eight feet. Crouching down, wings half spread with feathered edges brushing the wall, its head inches away from the ceiling.

Go away. Just. Go. Away.

Ten. One wing swept across the wall. A framed picture fell to the floor, the glass shattering on impact. Another picture swayed from side to side, but held its place.

Dad, make it go away. I'm not doing okay right now. I'm really not.

"What do you want?" he said.

Laughter rippled through the room—Sailor's laughter. The griffin reached out a foreleg and swiped like a cat with its prey. Jason's cheek burned as blood, warm and wet, trailed down. He fell back, and everything changed to slow motion. The griffin opened its beak and hissed again, a low, triumphant sound. Too large to fly in the room, it folded it wings against its body and stalked over to the window with the stealthy grace of a cat, the muscles of its powerful legs flexing underneath the fur. It turned its head, gave another nightmarish hiss, then flattened its shape

Dad, please, help me. Not feeling so strong, inside or out.

into a paper doll horror and slipped out, under, the window, in between the jamb and the closed edge of the sash. Like a shadow slithering along a wall. The wings beat a dark curtain against the outside glass, once, twice, then it disappeared.

Jason's head hit the floor, and everything went black.

16

John S. Iblis walked through the streets of Fells Point with a smile on his face. This suit was more comfortable than some of his others, given the previous owner's size. He rather liked its imposing appearance—the perfect suit for an evening stroll in the city.

Jason looked right at him in the bar. He looked and did not believe. So much desperation in that glance, though. Soon enough, he would come with his questions, and in the end, he would beg. They always did.

He chose his canvases well.

Chapter Eight

Sailor's Delight

1

The shrill ring of a telephone pierced the inky darkness in Jason's head, and sunlight burned into his eyes when he raised his lids. He lifted his hands, blocking out the light, and winced when his palm skimmed his cheek. When he touched the skin with his fingertips, dried blood fell away in flakes onto the floor.

The floor?

He pushed himself up to a sitting position, bright spots of white dancing in front of his eyes. His head throbbed, and a foul taste like week-old Chinese food lingered on his tongue. A dull ache ran through his body, not just his arm. Why had he slept on the floor?

The phone rang again. Jason pulled himself all the way up. Something tugged at his memory, something dark and unpleasant, and he shoved it back, hard.

Not ready for that, yet.

Jason grabbed his cell phone from the nightstand just as it stopped ringing, then he saw the time—10:00 a.m., on a Friday.

"Shit."

His alarm hadn't gone off. Why not? Brian's voice mail was brief. Their boss had been pissed until he told him about Jason's illness the night before. The alarm didn't go off because he didn't turn it on, but he wasn't sick, he was—

Jason dialed his boss's number and frowned. The bed was out of place. He bent down, running his fingers over a long scratch in the floor. A picture frame lay in a mangled ruin at the base of one wall, surrounded by shards of broken glass. Another picture, several feet away, hung at a crooked angle. He pushed the bed back to where it should be, and sat down on the edge of the mattress just as his boss answered the phone with a clipped voice.

"I'm sorry," Jason said, eyeing the scratch. "I got sick again last night, and I just woke up."

"Brian told me. You sound terrible, I hope you're going to call the doctor."

"I am." Jason rotated his arm, stifling a groan at the stiffness.

That's what I get for sleeping on the floor.

"Well, get some rest and we'll see you on Monday."

You didn't sleep on the floor. Frank knocked you to the floor, remember?

He froze, and the memories rushed in. The smell of the fur, the angry hiss, the green, unblinking eyes. The bed pushed out of the way, the breaking glass. He moaned.

"Jason?"

The weight on his arm. The paper-thin griffin creeping out the window. No, not creeping out, sliding its way out. Through a very closed window. The shadow of its wings as it took flight. The night the tattoo wasn't there.

It wasn't there because it came out of my skin and flew away. Just like last night.

"Jason?"

"Okay, thank you. I, I need to go," he said, hanging up the phone before his boss could say goodbye. "No, I had a bad dream," he said to the room. "And I fell on the floor."

Liar. He threw the phone on the bed and held out his left arm. The lines of the tattoo were perfect. A masterpiece.

It came back home. Good old Frank.

A sound like shuffling footsteps slid from his lips, and his hands shook.

Last night was real. It's alive, somehow. Has it been alive the entire time? Since that first night? Yes, I think it has. My father saw it, too, in the hospital. He saw it come out of my arm and the shock killed him. His death is my fault. It's all my fault. Mac saw it, too, the night I spent at Brian's house, but it didn't come all the way out either time, because it knew it wasn't safe.

Jason clenched his hands into fists. Why? Why did Sailor do it? And how? He suspected the answers wouldn't be pleasant; they might be downright messy. A sinking feeling settled into the pit of his stomach. He had to know, no matter how much he didn't want to. He needed to know how to make it stop.

If he put it there, that son of a bitch can take it away. I remember. He said tattoo removal was one of his specialties.

2

After a quick shower, Jason went downstairs and grabbed his keys. If Sailor wasn't at the shop, he would wait. He'd wait all day if necessary. He opened his kitchen door, caught a whiff of something foul, then saw the hand on the doormat. A human hand.

It lay on its side, palm toward him, with the fingers curled in slightly, a ragged end where the wrist should be, the white of a bone (terribly white, as if washed clean) protruding beyond the torn flesh. The fingers were slim, delicate; the nails painted a pale pink. No maggots. Not much blood, only a few dried flecks of red. A raw, butcher-shop smell hovered over the grim offering.

Did the kid kill his mother? His sister? Jason rubbed the back of his neck. He should've talked to the kid's parents. He should've warned them. A slow trickle of guilt wormed its way inside. Maybe the kid had killed his entire family—farfetched, yet more than possible. There were plenty of news stories, plenty of kids with dark sides. No, this was not his problem. He'd call the police and let them take care of it, but he would *not* tell them about the animals. They'd want to know why he hadn't said anything before.

I think you're taking this too calmly. It's a human hand, for God's sake.

He let out a harsh, humorless laugh. Given the events of the previous evening, he *was* calm. Surprisingly so.

By the way, Officers, once you've taken care of the hand, I have this little problem. See this tattoo? It's real and I need you to kill it for me. You don't mind waiting around for the sun to set, do you?

Telling the truth would guarantee him a stay in a padded room, maybe a permanent one. A fly buzzed by his head, headed toward the hand. Jason waved it away, and the toe of his shoe caught the corner of the doormat. The hand wobbled. Something silver glinted in the sun. A *ring*. He prodded the mat with his foot, and the meaty smell flared stronger as the hand moved again.

Shouldn't touch that. It's evidence.

"Shut up."

I'll just say I did it accidentally. They won't be able to tell, I don't think.

He looked up and around, shifting his weight from foot to foot. He pushed the mat again, hard, and the hand flipped over. Sun glinted in rainbow arcs off the silver of the ring and the sapphire stone at its center.

It's not his mother or his sister.

The fly buzzed again, but Jason didn't wave it away. He couldn't move. A sick feeling wormed its way up into the back of his throat. The fly landed near the end of the ruined wrist. He remembered the ring from both the bookstore and the funeral home, worn by Shelley on her right hand, her *live* hand.

Maybe it's not her. Lots of people could have a ring like that.

It wasn't just the ring, though. There was a tiny dark mole near the little finger. A familiar mole. It would be a strange coincidence for someone else to have the same ring and the same mole.

It wouldn't be coincidence. It would be a miracle. And if it wasn't Shelley, why would the hand be on my *doormat?*

A soft breeze ruffled Jason's hair, breaking the spell. He had to get rid of it, but he couldn't wrap it up in the doormat, put it in a trash bag, and throw it in the garbage. A cat tail was one thing, a human hand another. But he did have to get it off his porch, just in case one of his neighbors decided to pay him a visit. Unlikely, but if they did, what would he do? Claim the hand was a Halloween prop, a practical joke? They'd only have to take one look, one good look, to know his words were a lie.

It's a real hand, all right. Mole and all.

He laughed again, and this time, there was humor. Not sane humor, not safe humor, but nonetheless, it was there.

The kid's caused all kind of problems this year. Yes, he has.

He rubbed the back of his neck again. Took a deep breath, grimacing at the stink. Okay. He could do this. He needed to wrap the hand in a heavy plastic bag and take it somewhere, then wrap the mat in a separate bag and take it somewhere else. That made sense. Water. He needed to dispose of the hand in water because it would wash away any evidence and fish would take care of the rest. He hoped.

Would a human hand float or sink? He had no idea, but it wasn't important. Not right now. He went back into the kitchen and grabbed several kitchen trash bags. They were a major brand and wouldn't be easy to trace, if found. Again, he hoped.

His cell phone rang, but he ignored it.

Sorry I can't take your call, I'm a little busy disposing of evidence right now, like a criminal.

Jason stood over the mat and swallowed hard. He dropped one bag over the hand, opened another and held it in his left hand. When sweat ran down his forehead into one eye, he brushed it away with his forearm. Holding his breath, he reached down, the bag slippery against his fingers.

It's nothing, nothing. Just picking up trash, that's all. Don't think about it too much. Don't breathe. Don't think about it.

He grabbed and

Shelley's

the fingers closed around his. He pulled his hand back with a groan.

No, just your imagination. Come on, come on.

More sweat ran down, burning as it trailed into his eye. He reached again and picked it up, grimacing at the cold, unyielding feel.

Can't do this. Can't do this.

A loose, liquid sensation turned in his stomach as he dropped the hand into the other bag. He tied a quick knot in the plastic and took a deep breath. His heart drummed a steady, heavy beat in his chest.

Not trash. It's not trash. It's Shelley. A piece of Shelley.

The thick, raw smell still lingered, and he left the bag on the porch and went into the kitchen. He'd just made it to the sink when his stomach let go in a rush of bile. He gripped the curved rim of the sink until his fingers hurt, and when the last dry heave passed, he turned and slid down to the floor, his back pressed up against the cabinet. How the hell did the kid even know where Shelley lived? How did he kill her? He was just a kid.

Another thought, a dark thought, tickled the back of his mind.

Maybe the kid didn't have anything to do with it. Maybe Frank did it.

3

The fly buzzed in the bag, bouncing against the plastic as it searched for freedom.

Because it ate its fill, like the griffin. It left behind what it didn't want.

He'd put the doormat into another bag, a flyless bag, and both sat on the back porch next to the railing. He didn't want them in the house. He needed to get rid of both bags but couldn't risk anything until after sunset.

It was a present. Frank left me a present. Like a cat with a half-eaten mouse.

The smell was a problem. He could still taste it in the back of his throat, and it would get worse. The day's warmth would make it even stronger, even through the plastic. He couldn't leave the hand on the porch, and he couldn't put it in his car, either; between the closed windows and the heat, he'd never get rid of the smell.

He walked back inside and paced in the kitchen, his shoes tapping a restrained rhythm on the tiles. His thoughts were no longer jumbled chaos. He felt removed, dispassionate, as if dealing with a problem device at work. He just needed to come up with the best solution.

He needed water with a current, and too many people, homeless and otherwise, lingered at the harbor to make it a viable option. Too many police on patrol as well. The Severn River, however, might work. Located about forty-five minutes away from his house, it had a decent current. Anything dumped would travel out to the bay (eventually), but this time of year, the Severn would be filled with boats, even at night, and the thought filled him with dread.

Hey Joe, there's a bag in the water. Give me a hand with this, will you?

That left the bay itself. Jason knew where he could go. Sandy Point beach was closed to the public at sundown, but he knew a secluded area where he could park his car and from that spot, it was a fairly short walk to the beach. Before they were married, he and Shelley once snuck in and walked the beach on a dark, moonless night. He could park, walk, throw in the hand and leave. Ten, fifteen minutes, tops. It would take longer to get there.

His biggest worry? Would it float? He thought it would, and a search on the Internet would give him the answer.

"Idiot," he said.

Once they found her, they'd come to see him. The husband was always the first suspect. And an *estranged* husband? Guilty before proven innocent. When they showed up, took his laptop away, and found the search in his history? It would scream guilty. Even if he wiped the hard drive clean, the evidence would still be there. He'd have to take out the drive and physically destroy it, and a missing hard drive would speak volumes in and of itself, none of them with a happy ending.

But if he froze the hand first, it would sink. A killer on a criminal investigation show had frozen a body, chopped it up, and tossed it into a river. Sure, he'd been caught, but not before he'd gotten away with it five or six times. Jason wasn't going to make it a habit.

He had a small cooler in the basement, the perfect size for a twelve-pack of beer or a small picnic lunch for two. Definitely large enough to hold a hand and one unfortunate fly. His father's voice piped up, too loud to ignore.

"What are you thinking, son? You've already tampered with evidence, but you didn't do anything wrong. Call the police."

See, Dad, I can't. Because I think my tattoo did it. Frank is not so good after all.

"Son, you should have read the fine print."

Yes, I know, Dad. You keep telling me that. I don't understand what you mean. Care to elaborate?

The voice fell silent.

Jason brought the cooler up to the kitchen and filled it halfway with ice, humming a tuneless song as he carried it out back. The fly still buzzed, tapping against his hand when he picked up the bag. He closed the lid of the cooler and frowned. Now what? It wouldn't take long for the ice to melt. Jason left the bagged doormat outside and brought the cooler in, leaving it next to the kitchen door. If the cops did show up, he'd honestly tell them where he found it and that he put it on ice to preserve the evidence.

And if they asked him why he didn't call? Shock. He'd blame it on shock. He thought they'd understand. In his opinion, a hand left on a doormat justified shock. He would deal with the hand, then he could tackle the other issue, the bigger one. Sailing ships and needle tips. He'd find a way; every problem had a solution.

Jason ignored his shaking hands as he sat down in the living room. He flipped open his laptop, opened the browser, and paused with his hands above the keyboard. A search for Shelley would be just as damning as a search for flotation properties of body parts. Maybe it wouldn't scream guilty, but it would whisper hard enough.

He closed his laptop, turned on the television and waited for the news.

4

The full moon sat low and heavy in the sky, dark gold with a pale halo. Jason drove into the Harbor Tunnel with his windows open, and air, heavy with exhaust, rushed in, blowing his hair into a porcupine mess. The woman in the tollbooth didn't even look at him when she took his money.

Good, she won't remember me because now I'm not just tampering with evidence.

His cell phone rang, shattering the silence in the car, and his fingers clenched on the steering wheel. He glanced at the display, his stomach twisting. Mitch. He wanted to talk to her, but he wasn't sure he could keep his voice steady. And what would he say? He was headed to the river with a part of his ex-wife? She was going out with the girls after work, and he'd told her to call when she got home, but he couldn't pick up the phone. Was he supposed to ask her to come over and meet Frank?

At least talk to her. You owe her that much.

He couldn't. It wasn't safe.

Coward. She believes in ghosts. You could tell her.

Ghosts were one thing. Tattoos another.

Maybe he should go over to her house. Maybe Frank wouldn't come out there. Jason pictured waking up in her bed, waking up to bloodstained sheets, a severed hand, and a well-fed griffin in the corner, gnawing on a bo—

"Stop," he said.

He would not take that risk. Even if it meant avoiding her call, even if it meant avoiding *her,* and even if it meant making her angry, at least she'd be *alive.*

The voices stayed quiet as he drove the rest of the way. He parked the car, and the moonglow guided his steps as he walked along the path to the beach. The cooler tapped against his thigh, but he didn't want to touch the bag until he had to. Soon enough, the slithery sound of melting ice blended into the gentle push of the waves against the shore. He stopped near the end of the path, concealed by trees and listened for voices or splashes of water, but the night air held only the song of the water and a few birds.

But no griffins. Frank wouldn't come out until after he went to sleep, and Jason wasn't planning to sleep anytime soon. He'd taken a nap after the news, the Shelleyless news, at noon but woke long before sunset. If he drove home quick enough after his

evidence disposal

errand, he'd make the eleven o'clock news. If no handless bodies were reported, he'd pay a midnight visit to 1303 Shakespeare Street.

After slipping off his shoes and socks, he paused to listen again. The sudden cry of a seagull close by made his fingers twitch. A soft wind caressed the back of his neck as he waited for the cry to drift farther out into the night.

His hands didn't shake when he pulled the bag out of the cooler. Melted ice dripped off the plastic onto the ground, a tiny whisper of sound in the night, but the fly didn't make a noise. Holding the bag out, away from his body, he walked onto the beach.

The water of the bay shimmered silver in the moonlight. His feet made a small, *whisk-whisk* noise and sand slipped between his toes, cool and dry at first, then cold and wet. It stuck to his feet and ankles, and a sour taste flooded his mouth. He'd never thought about the sand. The night he and Shelley went in the water, they woke up with sand everywhere, even though their clothes were almost dry and they'd brushed them off with towels before they got back in the car.

But you're not going in the water. The hand is, but you're not.

Jason sighed, and the wind swallowed it up and carried it away. When he reached the water's edge, he untied the knot in the bag with steady hands, grateful for the ice in his veins. He pulled on a thin leather glove, reached into the bag, and

just a block of ice, nothing else

took out the hand. It was rock hard, frigid even through the leather, the dead meat smell muted by the ice and the salt tang in the air. He pulled back his arm and threw it forward. The hand arced up and up, then a dark cloud passed in front of the moon, plunging the beach into darkness. The ice inside turned and pushed jagged points against his heart.

It's too long. It should have hit the water by now. Did I miss?

Then a soft splash broke the stillness. The clouds slipped away from the moon, something pale and small bobbed up twice in the water, then vanished beneath the dark. He gave a small nod and left the beach. He'd find a Dumpster on the way home for the plastic bags and the doormat.

5

Mitch's car sat in his driveway when he arrived home. His headlights flashed bright on the back of her car, and he fought the urge to throw his car into reverse and take off. If he'd been paying attention, he would have seen her car before he pulled in but he wasn't. He was thinking. Thinking maybe the hand wasn't real. Maybe it was a prank.

Sure and your dad is still alive. In fact, maybe he's inside, chatting with Mitch.

Jason left the cooler in his car.

Stay calm. Pretend nothing is wrong. Pretend you didn't just dispose of your ex-wife's hand and your tattoo is just a little bit of ink.

He walked into the kitchen, and she greeted him with a long hug. For several minutes, he pressed his body against hers. She smelled like the air after a summer storm, like daydreams and sanity and normal, good things. Jason bit the inside of his cheek. The back of his eyes burned, and the back of his heart twisted.

I love her so much. I have to keep her safe. I can't let Frank anywhere near her.

"I'm sorry I let myself in, but I tried to call you a couple times today, and I got worried. Are you okay?"

"No, it's okay. We had a problem at work. I've been dealing with it all day." He hated the easy way the lie rolled off his tongue, but he had no choice. He couldn't tell her the truth, and he couldn't let her stay at his house, not until it was done. He slipped out of her arms, crossed the kitchen, and grabbed the coffee pot.

"You're making coffee? This late?"

"I have to go back in at midnight. I'm probably going to be working all night."

He took his time measuring out the coffee, so he didn't have to see the concern in her eyes. He could tell her. He could tell her everything and watch her walk out the door. She'd probably think he was crazy, but then she would be safe. He opened his mouth, then clamped it shut. Maybe he was crazy. Maybe none of it was real. Maybe it was all just one big illusion, but if he said the words out loud, it might *make* them real.

Of course it was real. The bone, the blood, the flesh turned rock by way of rigor mortis, the thick, dead smell.

Stop it. Voices in your head, a griffin in your arm, and a severed hand. Do you know what this smells like, boy?

"I'm sorry," she said.

The feel of the skin, cold and hard. The heat of the griffin's skin. And its eyes...

It smells like psychosis. The big old "you are approaching certifiable". Lock you up for now and forever.

"Me too. I'd rather stay here with you," he said. "Unfortunately, if I do that, I'll probably lose my job."

The coffee pot started to hiss, and his hands shook. The noise was far too similar to the sound Frank had made before he went flat and out the window. Jason bit the knuckle of one finger.

Mitch came up behind him and rubbed his upper arms. "Are you sure that's all it is? Just work?"

Oh no. It's so much more. The last time I saw you I thought I was just sick. Sick and seeing things. Now I know.

"Yes." He forced it out. Behind the word, his voice shook.

She leaned her head on his back. "You seem different."

You have no idea. No idea at all.

"I'm fine. Just a little ragged because of work. I'm sorry."

What are you apologizing for? Maybe apologizing for going nuts?

"Shut up." The words came out in a tangled mumble.

"What?" she asked against his shirt.

He turned around, avoiding her eyes, and pulled her into his arms. "Nothing, just thinking about work. I'm not looking forward to pulling an all-nighter."

I'm not crazy. I'm not.

The news would be on soon. He needed to get her out of the house so he could watch for a special report, a breaking story about a missing hand or a strange bird flying in the night sky, then he needed to pay Sailor a visit.

Good old Sailor. Good old Frank.

"Maybe I should just stay here and wait for you to get home."

"No." It came out harsh, and he stepped back and raked his fingers through his hair. "I'm sorry, but I might end up working through tomorrow, too. I'd hate to think of you just waiting around. I'll probably just come home and crash when I'm done."

The coffee hissed and sputtered as it finished brewing. Mitch rubbed her palms on her thighs.

She knows I'm lying. She doesn't know why, but she knows something isn't quite right. I can only hope she won't hate me when this is all over. Because it will be over, somehow.

She brushed her hair off her forehead and looked down at the floor. Jason reached out and tipped her chin up. "I love you."

"I love you, too. Will you call me tomorrow, when you get home?"

"Yes, of course I will."

"Are you sure everything is okay? Did the kid do anything?"

No, it wasn't okay. Not really. Not okay at all. He'd had to get rid of his ex-wife's hand. Her *hand*. The ink on his arm came to life at night, and as an added bonus, it was responsible for his father's death. How was that for not okay?

"No, the kid didn't do anything. I haven't even seen him. I'm just tired, that's all."

He kissed her, and her lips tasted like a promise, a promise he didn't think he could keep. He wanted to take her upstairs and keep kissing her until he forgot about everything, but he couldn't. Forgetting wouldn't make it go away.

"Okay," she said when their lips parted.

You'll get through this. Remember your father's words. Strong on the inside, where it counts.

6

Jason caught the last ten minutes of the news, but saw no special reports. A phone call to Shelley would be the easiest way to find out, but if he called and she didn't answer, or worse, if she did answer, maybe with her left hand? He could ask her if she'd seen a griffin lately. Big critter with golden-brown wings, a lion's tail and wickedly sharp talons.

Jason laughed. Psychosis didn't run in the family, but there was always a first time for everything, even lunacy.

Call her.

"No, I don't think so."

That was what a guilty estranged husband would do. He had to do something, though. He couldn't sit around waiting for something to happen, not anymore.

7

Jason drove to Fells Point with a stone in his chest. He'd tell Sailor he saw the griffin and demand answers. Sailor might not even be at the shop, not this late, but Jason had a feeling he didn't keep banker's hours, and if Sailor *wasn't* there, he'd wait as long as he needed to. Sailor had to come back sometime.

He found a parking spot on the opposite side of the street directly across from the café and sat in the car, watching the dark windows, with only his travel mug of coffee for company. Neither the moon nor the pale glow of the streetlamps touched the shadows on Shakespeare Street. Noises from the bars, only a block away, should have been audible, but they weren't. A strange hush—the absence of sound—filled the spaces in the street. Even the wind was quiet; it reached into the car, touched his skin, then danced away. The silence tasted like tears and sorrow and dread.

The entrance to 1303 wavered in the darkness, a door-shaped suggestion, sometimes clear and sometimes not there at all. He laughed and the street swallowed up the sound. The street appeared abandoned, not deserted, the buildings standing like broken statues in a desert of gray, forgotten and neglected. The silent wind sent a twisted section of newspaper down the center of the street, but the paper made no sound as it bounced on the asphalt. The smell of exhaust and the water of the harbor should've kissed the air; instead, the street had no smell at all.

But it does. Underneath the silence, it smells of despair.

A fat fly, made lazy from the night's warmth, landed on his windshield and sat motionless, but nothing else moved. Not far away, a siren roared to life, loud enough to pierce the thick quiet, then the wail faded and vanished into nothing at all. Jason drummed his fingers on the steering wheel. An odd sensation buzzed in his ears, like soft, dangerous music.

After an hour passed, a group of people strolled down the street, their bright laughter odd and out of place, and stopped in front of a car parked in front of the café. One young woman with long dark hair turned to face the buildings, and she rubbed her upper arms, still staring as her friends climbed into the car. They didn't notice when her arms dropped down to her sides and her shoulders slumped. She looked directly at the door for 1303, and Jason wondered if she saw the door or brick.

It's stronger tonight. Whatever lingers here is somehow more.

Jason's fingers clenched on the steering wheel.

Look away. It's his magic. Sailor magic.

Another girl with copper-colored curls stepped back out of the car and shook the dark-haired girl's arm. When she turned with a face empty of all expression, the redhead backed up, talking to the others already in the car. Jason reached for the door handle as the girl shifted and flooded back into herself. The redhead got back into the car; the dark-haired girl started to follow. She paused to look over her shoulder, shuddered, and disappeared into the car. When the tail lights vanished around the corner, Jason gulped down the last of his cold coffee.

What am I doing here?

The answer, which seemed so clear earlier, was now hazy at the edges. When he reached for the key, the window above the door to 1303 filled with pale, bluish light. He shook his head, sure it was an illusion, but the image remained. The light appeared a little to the right the door, not directly above, which didn't make sense, since the door at the top of the narrow staircase had opened to the left.

Left. Right. Does it matter? Your tattoo is alive. You can't get more "doesn't make sense" than that.

High-pitched carnival music drifted past. Jason turned his head to catch the tune, but it faded away. An upbeat whistle began at the top of the street, growing louder as a darkness in the shadows moved closer. He slid low in the seat. A man-sized shape emerged, and the whistle slowed. Shifted to melancholy. A tune reminiscent of cigarette smoke, horned instruments, women with tight dresses and small waists and men with striped suits and dangerous smiles. The whistle shifted again, and the smell of the street became exotic perfume, hair oil and smoke hovering in a thick cloud overhead. Jason closed his eyes, sighing as the whistle slid inside his head, like a memory.

But someone else's. Not mine.

Notes shivered in the air as the musicians played in the crowded club, and even though the song held sadness in its words, laughter drifted under the haze of tobacco smoke. The women held cigarettes in red-lacquered nails and smiled in all the right places. They were window-dressing, beautiful, but curved to admire and bed and nothing more. A group of men with slicked-back hair leaned in over their table, their brows creased with the intensity of their conversation. They were the kind of men best to avoid; Jason moved away from their table as fast as he could.

Except I'm not here. Not really. I'm in his memories somehow, even though it feels real.

The smoke stung his eyes, and a woman bumped into him as she passed. She turned, smiling with full, pink-lipsticked lips in a way that said the bump wasn't accidental. Her lips matched the pink, satiny dress clinging to her swaying hips. He could follow her...

The music reached a crescendo, drowning out all the voices as it built and built, the notes climbing impossible heights. It hung, then with a clash of cymbals, stopped. Applause followed, some enthusiastic, some only polite. Perfunctory.

When the band members walked offstage, the drummer's skin shimmered like ebony in the lights, in sharp contrast to his crisp, white shirt. He wiped sweat off his brow and laughed, a big, booming laugh filled with genuine happiness, not caring if anyone in the room paid any attention at all; he played for the love of the music. His bald head bobbed through the crowd as he walked to the bar and stopped only once, when the pink-lipped woman touched his upper arm with an enviable familiarity and whispered something in his ear. As he laughed again, his eyes filled with naked hunger. She walked away, smiling.

I would stay away from her, buddy. I think she's more dangerous than the slick men.

The bartender slid a drink across the bar, nodding toward the end. Jason followed the nod. The man wore a dark, tailored suit, and his features struck a chord in Jason's own memory. The memories of the club

Max's

pushed it away. The suited man lifted his drink in a silent toast. The drummer did the same, then walked over to him. He sat down on the padded stool next to the man in the suit, their lips moving in

222

conversation.

It's when they met.

But how could I know that? This isn't real. It's some sort of illusion.

Jason stood too far away to hear their words, but they both wore smiles on their faces. The drummer turned to look at the woman in the pink dress several times, each time with the same expression. He wanted her. Maybe not for forever, but for more than an hour or two. He couldn't because she was married to a bastard with fast fists, and it wouldn't take much to push him over the edge. Her husband wasn't one of the slick men, but he was slick.

How do I know all this? Why is he showing this to me?

Eventually, another musician went over to the drummer and nudged his shoulder. He said his goodbyes to the man in the suit and walked back to the stage. The man left behind slid money onto the bar, and when he got up, his eyes—pale, watery green eyes—met Jason's. A razor-sharp jolt of fear sent his pulse racing. The man in the suit started to walk toward Jason, but he didn't walk. He *rolled*. Hips first, then legs, then hips again. A shipwalk. A sailor walk.

But he's never been on a ship. Not this man.

The music started again, and this time it wasn't sad. It was longing. The desire to possess the very thing you cannot touch. Whispered words and unrequited love. The green eyes moved closer, close enough for Jason to smell the oil in his hair and the smoke on his clothing. He rolled past Jason and smiled a terrible smile. It held dark promises, that smile.

A musician with a voice like warm honey sang with one hand pressed against his chest. "Had a girl and she sure was fine."

Jason shuddered.

"Don't worry. You'll have plenty of company," the suited man said in a husky, cigarette voice.

The memory disappeared in a flash.

It was a game. All of it. It wasn't real, even though I could hear their voices. And the music. The song...

Still whistling, the shape rolled out of the shadows, the orderly from the hospital, in a bright white dress shirt and black pinstriped pants, although not just the orderly, but also the man from the club. The bones of his face held a different shape, yet Jason knew it was the same man. The same man but with Sailor's walk.

The orderly stopped in front of the faded gray door and looked over at Jason with a smile on his dark face, his green eyes glowing in the darkness like a cat's, then he opened the door and slipped inside. Jason waited for five minutes.

With his heart racing, he got out of the car, darted across the street, and approached the door. It wavered in the shadows but held its shape. He raised his hand, reached out, and his fingers met brick instead of wood.

What the hell?

He stepped back. In several places, the faded paint peeled down in brittle strips with red underneath the gray, bright, vivid red, like streaks of blood under the paint. He moved forward and placed his palms on the door. Once again, his skin met rough brick. He slid his hands down the door

the brick

and paint peeled away. When he pulled his hands back and turned them up, a small, jagged piece of gray paint lay like an ashen tear in the center of his palm. It grew warm, then hot, hot enough to burn. Jason suppressed a shout, shaking his hand to dislodge the paint. A small pink circle of flesh appeared next to the line separating his thumb from the rest of his hand—his own personal stigmata.

The orderly had gone inside; the door had to be there. Jason put his hands back on the door and dragged them down, hissing through his teeth as the brick scraped the skin raw. More paint peeled, falling to the ground in flakes. Jason brought his hands back up, then down, pushing harder.

I can see the door. It's right here.

Heat bloomed against his skin again, and pieces of gray stuck to the bloody streaks on his skin. When he rubbed his hands on his jeans, the burn stopped. Blood streaked the surface of the door. Real blood, not paint.

He reached for the handle, and for one fleeting moment, his fingers curled around the cool curve of metal, then it vanished, leaving behind only brick. His eyes narrowed. He knew Sailor waited inside, just as he knew the door was real but hidden somehow, hidden by some dark magic.

Iblis magic.

Jason curled his hands into fist and pounded on the

brick the door the brick the

door. The skin on one of his knuckles split, leaving behind a long streak of blood on the gray. His shoulders hunched forward as he took his hands away. He knew he could stand there all night knocking; it wouldn't matter. If Sailor didn't want him to come in, he would never touch the door. It would always be the brick wall, because he—

Made a mistake, son.

"Go away, Dad. You're dead and you can't help me," he said.

But he had made a mistake, a grave one. Sailor wouldn't open the door because their business was done. The griffin belonged to him now.

"And I have to get rid of it."

The signs had all been there from the very start: the dogs' reactions, the tails left on his doormat, his father's words before dying, the strange heat in his arm when the minister touched him.

"Even my nieces knew."

All there, right in the open.

"And I ignored them all."

He'd been weak, spineless, and too afraid to accept the truth, so he'd turned away and tuned it out, the same thing he'd done for years and years.

"Brilliant, Jason. Just brilliant."

The last piece of the puzzle was why.

But right now, maybe the why—and the how—didn't matter. The time for sitting around and doing nothing had come and gone. He had a monster inside his skin, and he had to get rid of it.

8

When Jason got home, the first light of sunrise hung in the corners of the sky. He checked his watch three times, each time hoping the hands were wrong, but the sky didn't lie. Although it had only been a little after one when the girl stood staring at the door and only a little after that when the orderly's whistle filled the night, his watch read almost five-thirty. Five hours gone. But how?

And I wasn't standing at the door that long.

He dropped his keys twice, his hands shaking.

I was inside the other man's memory and time just slipped away.

Once inside, he turned on all the lights and opened all the curtains and blinds, banishing every shadow from every room, including the basement.

He did something to my mind, but was it Sailor or the drummer?

Jason paced in the living room until the purple faded from the sky. His head ached, not with a normal pain, but with a dark sensation of love and loss and futility. Fear, thick and unshakeable, gave his feet an unsteady rhythm. He wanted to forget his own name, his own face, close his eyes and sleep forever.

But more than that, he wanted it all to go away. He wanted his normal life back. He wanted to go to work, meet the guys for drinks and be with Mitch. He wanted his father to ask him how he was doing. He wanted to tell him he wasn't doing okay, because his father would know what to do. Jason didn't. He didn't know how to make it go away.

Dad, you were wrong. I'm not strong. Not on the inside. Not on the outside, and I don't know what to do.

He just wanted the nightmare to stop.

His father's voice whispered soft in his head. Soft and sad. *"Son, you already know it's not going to stop. Not until you stop it. The strange kid didn't kill Shelley. The griffin did. It came out of your arm and flew away and killed her. It left her hand as a souvenir. Just like a cat with a mouse."*

"I know all that, Dad."

His father spoke up again. *"It's not going to go away."*

"I know that, too." Jason could hope one night it would fly away and never come back, but that sort of hope was foolish. If he hadn't had his head in his ass, maybe he would've figured it out sooner. Maybe Shelley would still be alive, but how was he supposed to know?

Tattoos were just ink on the skin; every sane person knew that. But his tattoo was something more than just ink. Sailor didn't look like a magician, but it *was* some kind of magic. Horror movie magic.

Why would he give Jason a living tattoo? What was the point? To scare him? To terrorize his neighbors by giving the griffin a taste for pets? To cause a bit of madness, mayhem and murder?

"Jason, you didn't read the fine print."

"There wasn't any fine print."

"It is what it is, son."

"No it isn't, Dad, and I could use a little help. I'm not okay right now. I'm really not."

His father didn't answer.

9

Jason didn't remember falling asleep on the sofa, but when he woke up, the late afternoon sun streamed in bright through the open blinds. The acrid stink of his sweat rose up around him, and he stumbled into and out of the shower with slow, shambling steps.

He made coffee and drank two cups in rapid succession; as soon as he took the last swallow, the cramps struck. The mug crashed to the floor in ceramic shards, and he bent over the sink. From the living room, his cell phone rang out, the sound lost amid the groans he couldn't suppress. Fierce and alive, the cramps dug into his abdomen and *twisted*. Pain flared red in his eyes. His legs shook, sweat beaded on his forehead and the colors of the kitchen faded, then amplified. He held onto the sink; the drain pushed up the scent of old food and wet metal, and he fumbled for the faucet. Drops of cold water splashed up on his cheeks, chasing away the smell. His breath came in ragged gasps and moans and one harsh bark when his hand slipped on the edge of the sink, the fingernail on his pinkie bending back as he grabbed for purchase.

The coffee didn't make a second appearance. Jason slumped into a kitchen chair when the cramps faded, first to a slow burn, then a soft nudge of almost-pain. His cell phone chirped again, and he fought the urge to scream for silence. Small drops of blood welled up from underneath the nail of his little finger, a small, stupid hurt easy to ignore. The rush of feet running along the side of his house made him look up.

Son of a bitch.

Another index card, pale blue this time, hung on one of the windowpanes of the back door, secured to the glass with a wad of pink gum. The card wasn't there when he made coffee, nor when he finished the second cup. The kid had come to the door while he hunched over the sink, pressed his gum to the glass, pushed the card against the gum and left. Did he leave right away, or did he stay to watch Jason twist and groan at the sink?

I Know.

Jason left the card on the window and raced into the living room on shaky legs. Through the front window he saw the kid running across the street, back to his house.

The griffin. He's seen Frank. That's why he's been looking in the window. He thinks it's a pet or something. My pet Frank.

Jason laughed out loud. The answer was there the whole time, staring him in the face yet again. Maybe he should ask the kid to come over and help kill it. He laughed louder.

He had to catch the griffin before it got all the way out. Once out, it was too big. Its *talons* were too big. His laughter rose up and up. The sound—a little thin and high-pitched, a little crazy—held no happiness.

Maybe I am. Oh yes, maybe I am slip-sliding my way into lunacy. I should call the hospital and tell them to get my rubber room ready. But I'll need one with a window. For Frank.

The laughter bounced off the walls and the ceilings and he couldn't stop. It wasn't so bad. It was horrible.

They can bring all the doctors by to take a look. A man and his griffin. Maybe I should join the circus. The tattooed man. Come one, come all.

He laughed until he bent over, clutching his abdomen. Until tears spilled from his eyes. Until his breath emerged in little more than wheezing gasps of air in between.

Enough!

The laughter stopped, as if someone had sliced it in half with the edge of a finely honed blade. A trace echoed in the room, then echoed itself away.

His phone gave a muffled beep. He looked around the room, and it beeped again, somewhere near the sofa. He moved the pillows, checked between and under the cushions and finally found it underneath, keeping company with a small tuft of dust. Mitch had called twice; the thick, sorrowful sound of her voice in the first message made him sit down on the end of the sofa.

"Jason, my ex's mother died and because he's an ass, he didn't even bother to call me. His sister did. I'm flying out today at five. It was the only flight that had a seat available. I'm so sorry I couldn't say goodbye to you in person."

Her voice broke as the message ended, but remained calm on the second, ending with the words "I love you." He turned the cell phone over and over in his hand; the need to hear her voice tugged deep inside.

It was already after three. She was either on her way to the airport or there already, heading out, heading away. The silence in his house loomed large and empty. His fingers curled around the phone. But it was better this way, even if...

He sent a quick text message and ended it with "I love you, too." Her response came seconds later. "At Airport. Will call later."

He put his phone down with tears in his eyes. She'd be safe there, and maybe when she got back, it would all be over.

One way or another.

10

A heavy knock at the door left Jason breathless. When he looked out the window, his heart jumped in his chest at the shadowy figure standing on his porch. From the window he couldn't see the face. At least it wasn't dark enough for the griffin, and even if it was, it wouldn't come out yet, not until Jason slept.

There's the answer. Until I figure out how to kill it, I can't go to sleep.

He pressed his palms against the back of the door and lowered his eye to the peephole. An unfamiliar face stared back at him. His heart jumped again. Had they found Shelley's hand already? How? What would he say? He wiped all traces of the laughter and tears from his face and opened the door.

The years rested heavy on the face of the man standing on his porch. Mid-forties, perhaps, with dark, somber eyes and deep lines on his forehead. The purple shadows underneath his eyes spoke of late nights and early mornings.

"Jason Harford?"

"Yes."

"I'm Detective Collins. May I come in?"

The words hung in the air. No introduction, no explanation, just the question.

Give me a hand here, sir. What do you want?

He bit the inside of his cheek to hold in a smile. Put on a small frown instead, a frown he hoped was convincing. Concerned. "Sure."

The detective walked in, giving the living room more than a cursory glance before he sat down. Jason sat on the opposite end of the sofa, curling his fingers around the edge of the cushion, the edge away farthest from the detective's eyes.

"I'm here about your wife, Shelley Harford," he said, pulling out a small notepad and pen. "I'm sorry to have to tell you this, but there's been an accident."

Let me guess, Detective. She won't be able to clap her hands anymore.

Jason's heart sped up. "What kind of accident? Is she okay?"

The detective scanned the living room again. Tapped the pen on the pad. "Do you know a Nicole Darrin?"

"Yes, Shelley and I are separated, and Nicole is her, well, her girlfriend. She left me. Shelley, I mean, not Nicole. Is Shelley...okay?"

"No, I'm afraid she isn't. The bodies of both your wife and Ms. Darrin were found early this morning."

Jason looked down at the floor. A star-shaped clump of dust lay on the wood near his foot, and he nudged it away with the toe of his shoe. Dead, not just missing a hand. And both of them? Despite the air conditioning, a bead of sweat made its way down his spine.

I knew she was dead. I didn't love her. I didn't even like her much, but I didn't want her dead.

"I...I don't know what to say. What happened?"

You know exactly what happened.

"When was the last time you saw your wife, Mr. Harford?" The detective rolled the pen between nicotine-stained fingers.

When Jason looked up and met the detective's eyes, his mouth went dry.

Does he think I did it? Of course he does. The estranged husband is always guilty. Even if he's innocent. He's always guilty at first.

No, if they thought I did it, I would be on my way to the police station, but he thinks I might've been involved somehow.

Well, weren't you?

No. It wasn't my fault.

"Three weeks ago. My father died and she came to the viewing."

Detective Collins' pen scratched across the paper. "You sure about that?"

"Yes."

"Do you have a dog, Mr. Harford?"

"A dog? No. I don't have any pets."

Liar, you have Frank. Good old Frank. No pets, sir, just a griffin.

"Ever had a dog?"

"No, I haven't."

The detective ran his hand across the sofa cushion, turned his palm up, and ran his thumb across his fingers. "Do you have any questions?"

"What...what happened?"

"I'm not at liberty to discuss details of the case. I think I'm done here, for now. You're not planning any trips out of town, are you?"

"No, sir, I'm not."

"Good. If you do, make sure you let me know." He handed Jason a business card. "If I need anything else, I'll be in touch."

Jason walked the detective to the door. After he closed it behind him, he put his eye to the peephole again. Detective Collins walked with wide steps down to the curb to a large, dark blue sedan, and at the end of the sidewalk, he turned and looked back at the house. Jason froze. This far away, the peephole turned the detective's features to blurred, misshapen images. Finally, the detective got into the car and drove away. Jason stepped away from the door and ran his fingers through his hair.

At least he didn't have to watch the news anymore.

11

Jason watched it anyway. The weekend newscaster, a blonde woman with an artificial smile, had a shiny forehead and perfectly arched brows that remained still when she spoke. "The quiet suburb of Sandy Hills in Severna Park is reeling today from the suspicious deaths of two women. A cleaning woman found the bodies when she arrived for work. Details are sketchy at this time, but the police are not ruling out the possibility of foul play."

They switched to footage of the house. The newscaster droned on in her plastic, mock-sympathetic voice, but Jason tuned her out. Several uniformed officers stepped out of the front door; one looked directly at the camera, his face pale and his eyes shadowed.

Did Frank come in through the window? Did they even believe he was real?

Jason rested his elbows on his knees and his chin on his hands. They weren't providing any details because it was terrible. Unexpected tears burned in his eyes.

The camera remained fixed on the front door, and two men in jackets labeled *Coroner's Office* carried out a black body bag. The bag sagged in the middle, but each end remained flat. The tears caught in Jason's throat. It wasn't a body, not a whole one. It was missing a hell of a lot more than just a hand.

The blonde newscaster appeared again, her voice suggesting a frown, even though her face remained immobile. "Police are asking anyone who might have seen any suspicious activity in the last several days to please call the tip line."

Jason raised a trembling hand to wipe sweat from his brow as the phone number flashed on the screen. A twist of rage and fear bubbled inside him, growing like a vicious poison trying to eat him away from the inside out. "He didn't just kill them. He ripped them apart."

And didn't that make Jason an accessory to the fact?

He jumped up from the sofa and pulled off his T-shirt. The griffin stood out against his skin like an exquisite piece of art.

"I hate you, you son of a bitch."

He curled his hand into a fist and with a shriek, brought it down on top of the ink. Once, twice, three times. Pain ran down to his fingertips. It brought fresh tears to his eyes, but he didn't care.

"Go away and leave me alone. Just leave me alone. Get out of my life," he shouted as he punched his arm twice more. Underneath his skin, a soft fluttering sensation pushed up through the pain, and the feral scent of animal slid out. A warning? Frank didn't make an appearance, though. Jason couldn't make him come out. He couldn't do anything.

His shoulders shook, and his breath raced in and out of his chest. Bullshit. He would take care of it. He would kill the griffin before it killed anyone else, but first, he had some unfinished business with the kid across the street.

12

He kept his steps light as he crossed the street, passing through the empty driveway to the back of the house, and after he knocked on the back door, he stepped out of the line of sight. Sure enough, the door opened, and the kid half stepped out. Moving fast, Jason grabbed his upper arm and pulled him the rest of the way out onto the porch. The kid opened his mouth, and Jason shoved the note in his face. "Don't yell. Is your sister home?"

The kid shook his head. "What do you want?"

Jason laughed and shoved the note in his pocket. "Your name is Alex, right?"

The kid nodded, his dark eyes wide. Jason propelled him over to a lawn chair. "Sit down."

Alex didn't sit. He sank down, his eyes never leaving Jason's. It was almost too easy; Alex's bravado was merely a show. Jason's own heart raced in his chest, and he swallowed twice before speaking again. "What do you know?"

Alex looked down.

"What. Do. You. Know?"

No answer.

Jason pulled another lawn chair over and sat close enough so their knees almost touched. "Brave enough to leave notes, but not brave enough to talk to me in person?"

Alex looked up, his brow knitted together. "I know there's something weird in your house. That's what I know."

"Did you see it?"

"I don't know what I saw," Alex mumbled.

"Oh come on, yes you do. It sort of looked like this, didn't it?" Jason lifted his shirtsleeve, and all the color drained from Alex's face. "Bigger, of course."

"Not at first."

"Tell me."

"What is it?"

Jason grinned. "First, you tell me what you saw, then I'll tell you what it is."

"I thought it was a bird, okay, like an owl or a hawk. It was flying around one night when I was out riding, and I followed it. It disappeared for a while, then I saw it fly back to your house and go in the window. I don't know how because the window was closed but it went in anyway."

Jason leaned forward. "And?"

"I kept watching. I didn't see it the next night, but I fell asleep too early, maybe. The next time I saw it, it was bigger. That's why I was looking in your window."

"And hanging out in my backyard?"

"Yeah, and after I saw it a couple times, I left the note."

"Why didn't you just knock on my door and ask me about it?"

"Are you fucking kidding me? It looks like a bird, but it isn't. It ate a cat. I saw it. It ripped it apart. I think it killed that dog, too. The one that belongs to that old guy down the street."

"Yeah, I think it did, too," Jason said. "Listen to me, kid, Alex, you need to stay away from it. Stay far away."

"Where did it come from?"

"It doesn't matter. It won't be around much longer. I'm going to take care of it."

"Kill it, you mean."

"Yes."

Jason stood up, pushing the chair back with his legs, and stepped off the porch.

"Wait, what is it?" Alex got up and jumped down the steps. "You told me you'd tell me."

"I lied," Jason said as he walked away.

"That's bullshit," Alex said, following close at Jason's heels. "That's not fair. I told you what you wanted to know."

Jason spun around, and Alex stumbled back. "Stay the hell away from it. It's dangerous. That's all you need to know."

Alex grabbed his shirt. "I could help you kill it. I'm not afraid."

Jason brushed his arm away. "You should be. If you see it again, just stay inside. Remember that. Unless you want to end up like that cat."

236

13

John S. Iblis (not his real name, of course, but one of many) sat in the darkness. He wore no suit at all and enjoyed the private luxury of his true form. When he smiled, it revealed a million horrors, a million screams. Smoke rose from his fingertips and swirled around his head in thin, gray spirals.

The game was beginning to get interesting. His creation was a fierce hunter and had chosen well. The rules themselves were simple. So very simple. First, the tattoo. Second, the desperate pleas for removal. Third, the delicious pleasure of the removal itself. The look of terror on their faces as he traced his nail down the center of a spine or sternum, parting the flesh from the framework beneath, when they finally realized he was not simply taking the tattoo, but the entire canvas. And the screams—the more the better.

Perhaps when he finished with Jason, he would pay the stunning girlfriend a little visit. He did not think he could fool her too long, but to touch that beautiful flesh... Or perhaps he could offer his services as an artist of ink and skin. She would be an exquisite canvas, although a tight fit. To touch that skin at will, though, perhaps he would try. Unless Jason's griffin got to her first. That would be a shame. Would Jason wait that long? He hoped not.

When Jason had put pen to paper, he had sealed his fate. There were no cancellation policies and no hidden loopholes. John S. Iblis made sure of it. He was clever.

Always.

After all, he had had plenty of time to perfect his skill. Eons and eons of time.

Chapter Nine

Way Down in the Deep

1

Jason dug through the kitchen drawers and pulled out an old paring knife, a skewer, a wooden crab mallet and a corkscrew, unsure what good the latter would do, but it had a sharp, curving point that might come in handy. He lined the utensils up on the kitchen counter—a macabre battalion ready for the bloodletting to come.

Can I really do this?

He pulled out a glass from the cabinet, filled it with plain tap water, and leaned up against the counter as he drank. He emptied the glass, refilled it, drank again.

Do I have a choice?

He refilled the glass a third time, but drank only half before setting it back down on the counter. When he opened his arm, would he find the griffin coiled up neatly inside, sleeping away the daylight hours? If so, he'd yank it out, throw it in the sink, and start dissecting before it had a chance to breathe, let alone grow. Or he'd shove it down the drain and let the garbage disposal take care of the dissection. He picked up the paring knife and stopped with it in mid-air.

What if the griffin wasn't inside his arm, but in between the layers of his skin? He shook his head. It didn't matter. He'd find it no matter where it hid, even if he had to peel his skin back like the layers of an onion. He'd find it, kill it, dispose of the pieces, and everything would be right as rain.

Maybe I'll take the pieces and drop them off on Shakespeare Street. Here, have your tattoo back, buddy. I don't want it anymore.

His arm answered with a light thump, a mere suggestion of a nudge within. Gentle, even. Maybe the tip of a feathered wing. A loose, swimmy sensation gripped his abdomen.

No, you only come out at night.

The sensation passed and Jason grinned, triumphant. The daylight held the griffin prisoner. A second thump came, a little harder, and a small mound grew under the skin, then disappeared. Jason laughed. The next thump, not a small one at all, not even one thump but a succession of them, a jackhammer under the skin, determined to pound away until it met its goal, sent him scrambling back against the edge of the counter. Pain, red-hot pain, raced from his fingertips to shoulder. His arm shook, and the knife slipped from his hand, dropping back onto the counter.

"Shit."

You know what I'm going to do, don't you?

Another crazed set of thumps. Pushing up, pushing out.

He reached for the knife and knocked the glass off the counter instead. The water inside whirled as it spun down; when it shattered on the floor, shards of glass spread out like translucent, jagged teeth, and water splashed high enough to reach his forearms. His fingers jumped and shook. The small mound reappeared, blurring the ink. His skin stretched, while inside, the griffin shifted. Beneath his skin, in his skin, part of his skin. The top of the griffin's head emerged, slow but steady, all amber-gold and warm, displacing his flesh with its own without a discernible seam between the two. Attached, yet separate. Weightless on the in, weighted on the out. And still, deep inside, it moved, its tail curving around his bone, its feathers rustling against his muscle. The heavy scent of animal musk filled the room with a cloud of dark perfume.

No, you can't come out. Not now.

240

Jason reeled back against the counter, and his foot slipped in the water. His body spiraled down without a shred of grace. He plummeted to the floor, landing hard on his hip. Pain, new pain, flared in his ankle. A circle of blood appeared on the white of his sock, just above his anklebone, a long shard of glass sticking out in the center. The griffin hissed, exhaling a gust of foul air reeking of carrion, and turned its eyes toward Jason, eyes filled with rage and fiery purpose. Its scent pushed out fury.

Jason's hands slid in the pool of water. A sharp edge of glass sliced open the soft skin of his pinkie; the blood made a red ribbon in the water. The griffin hissed again, and one taloned limb emerged. The second followed, but the muscles in its limbs strained with the effort.

It's the daylight. It's easier for it to come out at night.

A horrible screech of madness emerged from its beak as it heaved its dark golden chest out of his arm. Its talons dug into his flesh with force. No pinpricks of blood this time, but small gashes, like raw, gaping mouths. Jason gagged, tasting the fur and fetid breath on his tongue. The griffin dug the talons in harder but paused. Its proud chest rose and fell. It lowered its head, and the talons ripped the gashes open wider. Jason hissed at the pain. The griffin hissed louder.

Mocking me?

Yes, its green eyes held a dark whimsy. Jason slid under the growing weight of the monstrous thing, and his hand pressed down on a long piece of glass. He yelled out as it cut deep into his palm.

The mocking hiss grew louder, its talons dug and ripped, and the edge of the wings appeared, vibrant and bronze. The griffin's eyes gleamed with triumph. Jason grabbed the glass, not caring that it bit back against his skin. The wings emerged, unfurled, and the beast heaved up.

Now. I have to do it now.

Jason shrieked and brought the glass down in a wide arc, slashing at one wing. A huge, stinging pain struck his right arm. The glass turned in his hand, slicing open another cut on his palm. The top of the griffin's wing split, and a horrific smell of rot and decay sprayed out into the room. A gash opened on Jason's right shoulder, a screaming mouth that vomited a great gout of blood. The griffin roared. Viscous, grayish-green fluid spilled down from its wing onto Jason's arm with a scalding heat. The metallic scent of his blood mixed with the foul stench of the griffin's. Bile burned the back of Jason's throat.

I will not get sick. I have to end this.

He struck out again with the glass, striking the griffin's furred foreleg, and another wound opened up on his own forearm. Fresh blood spilled down his arm in a crimson waterfall. The griffin roared again, and reached out one impossibly large talon. It grabbed the glass from Jason's hand and waved it back and forth, like a mother scolding a naughty child, then it slipped back into his skin, taking the glass with it, in a rush of wind and foulness. Jason's ears popped, and he fell flat on the floor. The smell of fur and blood and filth whipped around, and gray spots danced in front of his eyes as the light of his kitchen faded and dimmed. Jason had one last thought before he gave in to the gray.

I can't kill it.

2

Bright lights. Pain. Cold liquid under his cheek. Warmth on his leg and arm. Burning in his shoulder. Jason couldn't open his eyes. The lids were too heavy. He wanted to sleep, sleep and forget, way down deep in the darkness. The darkness wanted to take him in, wrap its arms around him, and fold him into its shadows. No talons existed there. No foul stench of matted fur. Only safety and warmth.

"You have to wake up."

His father's voice. Commanding. Strong.

Stronger than I am. Stronger inside and out.

"Now."

Jason sighed and opened his eyes. He pulled himself up to a sitting position, groaning aloud. Night had fallen. Blood, water, glass, and grayish-green

griffin blood, Frank blood

fluid colored the floor in a chaotic swirl of grim modern art. Jason shifted and pain seared his arm. Fresh blood trickled down his right shoulder. Shards of glass were stuck to his jeans. He tugged them out one by one, wincing when he removed the pieces pushed deep enough through the fabric to pierce his skin. He pulled the long shard out of his ankle with a grunt.

Jason stood up slowly, trying to keep his feet away from the glass. A wave of dizziness slipped in, and he leaned up against the sink until it passed. His left arm hurt, the tattoo hidden behind a dried film of blood and dark fluid. A vile, sickly stench hung in the air. He turned on the tap and closed his eyes, listening to the rush of water.

Once the water in the sink ran warm, he held his hands under the faucet, wincing at the sting. The water washed away the dried flecks of blood, revealing cuts on his palms and fingers, several already clotted shut, others leaking tiny, teardrops of blood. He soaked a handful of paper towels, wiped the blood away from his right arm, biting his lip to keep silent, and tossed the mess in the sink. Dark pink water ran down the drain. More paper towels, more warm water. The pile of paper towels turned into a mound, and watery trails of blood streaked the bottom of the sink.

When he'd used up all the paper towels on the roll, Jason turned off the water and grimaced. The wound on his shoulder gaped open, deep enough for stitches

not going to happen

but not deep enough to reveal muscle or fat. The ragged edges reminded him of the blade of a serrated knife, although neither knife nor glass made the cut. The inside of the four-inch gash gleamed pale pink with a line of dark at the center, oozed a snakelike trail of blood and burned like fire. The wound should not even be there at all. The cut on his forearm, not as deep

No, because I cut through fur and skin. The wings are more fragile.

243

seeped sticky, clear fluid and stung like a bad cat scratch. The edges appeared even more jagged, though, the shake of his hand apparent in its shape.

"What are you going to do now?"

His father's voice again.

"I don't know, Dad."

How many more would the griffin kill because of its monstrous rage? Its hunger? He couldn't let it live, but he couldn't kill it, not without killing himself.

Jason went upstairs and put bandages on his palm and fingers. When he put antiseptic ointment on his forearm, the wound cried out in protest; he ignored it. He covered it up and stared at his shoulder. More blood leaked out of the wound. He pulled the edges as close together as he could and slapped on a few butterfly bandages. With a shaking hand, he covered it with a gauze pad and wrapped tape around his arm, then used a washcloth to wipe away the gore on his left arm, the thick smell of the griffin's blood making his eyes water. Finally, clean skin emerged. The wounds from the griffin's talons were red around the edges, the only color on his arm. The rest of his skin was clean, pale and unmarked.

Frank was out again.

The dizziness rushed back in, and Jason stumbled toward his bed. He had one last thought before everything fell away—he hoped like hell the kid had listened and was safe and sound inside his house.

3

Jason dreamed of the white room, but it had changed. The heat in the air seared his lungs with every breath. Some strange perfume, dark and flowery and alive, kissed the air. Whispery voices drifted out from the walls, and when he looked behind him, he saw the outline of hands pushing from the inside. A song, sad and mournful, played only a little louder than the voices. A tall figure stood in one corner, hunched at the shoulders. A dark suit, crusted with dirt and other foul things Jason couldn't name.

"Dad?"

The figure turned with a wet, rattling noise. His father, but not. Decay had turned the skin gray and yellow, bony hands gleamed white below the jacket sleeves, and the cheeks were drawn, the lips pulled back from the teeth in a grimace. The not-father sighed, and the horrible smell of rot reached out across the room. The jaw moved, the mouth worked, but no sound emerged. When it found its voice, the words emerged thick and moist.

"You didn't read the fine print."

Then it raised its arm. The finger bones clattered together as it pointed. Jason turned his head. A black curtain hung in a doorway, swaying in a hidden breeze. Movement behind him. A creak of plaster. And hands pushed Jason's shoulders forward.

"What's in there?" he asked.

His father merely held out his arm in nightmarish silence. Jason took slow steps across the room. As he drew closer to the curtain, the heat grew. Beads of sweat burned in his eyes and trailed down his back. When he reached the curtain, he glanced over, but the not-Dad was no longer there. A dark suit lay puddled on the floor with a pool of yellow, viscous liquid seeping out beneath the fabric.

Jason pushed aside the curtain and stepped forward into chaos. A wave of scalding heat and roiling gray smoke washed over him, blurring his vision and filling his lungs. Screams, a dozen, a hundred, a thousand, filled the air. He tried to step back because he didn't want to see, didn't want to know, but the curtain no longer existed. A wall, a brick wall, stood in its place. The smoke swirled around him, long tendrils touching, tasting, his flesh, rising up from the chasm in front of him—a deep, horrible pit with moving walls.

Oh God, they're not walls.

Writhing, twisting figures lined the chasm. Bodies, raw and bleeding, with mouths open in grimaces of terror as dark flames of red and orange licked at what remained. The smell of smoke, ash and cinder filled his nostrils. He opened his mouth to scream; the sound disappeared into the voices.

So many of them.

They grew louder. Too many voices, blending together in sorrow, pain and bitterness.

"Please, help us."

"We didn't know."

"He tricked us."

"No way out."

"He lied."

"Father of lies."

"No way to undo it."

"Don't sign it."

A million faces stared up at him from the chasm. Screaming faces. *Skinless* faces. One face swam up to the top. A vile, inhuman face, smiling amid the horror. Sharp cheekbones, pitted flesh and a mocking smile.

"You'll be here soon enough, boy. Don't worry."

The mouth opened and laughter bubbled up, louder than the voices, louder than everything. The flames brightened and revealed walls rising impossibly high around the pit. And hanging on the walls, like empty shells, were faces and limbs and hair. Smoke swirled around them and sent them moving, swaying back and forth with a slippery, wet slither, hanging like coats in a closet.

But that's what they are. They are *coats. Human coats. Skin coats. No, this is not real, not real, not real.*

He turned and pounded the brick until his hands bled. His screams were nothing compared to the laughter. It wrapped around him and echoed in his ears. A voice, thick with foul humor, rose up over the others. "Had a girl and she sure was fine," it sang. "She was fine, fine, fine." The words dissolved into more laughter. Jason raised his hands and covered his ears but couldn't block out the sound.

Let me out. This isn't real.

The laughter went on. Tears coursed down his cheeks as he kicked and punched at the brick wall. He couldn't get out, and the laughter would not stop. It would never stop.

"Make it stop, make it stop, oh God, make it stop."

He sat up in bed with a lurch, instantly awake, whispering the words over and over again. Bright sunlight filled his bedroom, but it couldn't take away the memory of the faces. And their words. When his voice turned hoarse, the words slid away, and he wiped his eyes. The pain in his shoulder burned. He pulled his hands away from his face and froze. Streaks of gray, dark and oily, crisscrossed his palms. Jason looked down and scrambled from the bed, holding in a shout between clenched lips.

A fine layer of ash covered his chest.

4

Jason didn't go to work on Monday. His boss had called him three times. Brian, twice. The messages left by Brian held confusion and concern. Those left by his boss held irritation and outright anger. Jason turned his phone off. A jumble of images from the nightmare danced in his mind. He remembered voices and heat and smoke but what they said? Gone before he got in the shower. And something about coats...

"What was it, Dad? What were they trying to say?"

His father's voice did not reply.

The ash, though. Nightmare or not, he could not deny its existence.

Just like Frank, and he came back, oh yes he did.

The gray film did not wash off easily; it coated the bottom of his bathtub with an oily residue. After his shower, he rebandaged his wounds and grabbed his car keys with a cold, rock-hard knot in the center of his chest. An alien thing, like the griffin, but needful. He'd hold on to the knot as long and as hard as he could. That knot (his Alpha knot) was the only thing in between his sanity and darkness. The only thing keeping him from crawling into a corner and covering his eyes like a child.

He drove to Fells Point and when he turned on Shakespeare Street, the knot loosened and threatened to uncurl, but he thought of his father, and after several deep breaths, it coiled again. He'd failed his dad in the worst possible way. He could never make it right, but even if he had to fake it...

I have to be strong. I owe it to my dad. I owe it to myself.

Once again, he found a parking spot. In Fells Point, parking was always an issue, but not on Shakespeare Street. *Never* on Shakespeare Street. He stood outside his car, staring up at the row of buildings for a long time. In the bright sun, the crumbling brick appeared faded, a dull pink, chipped and worn. Dusty windows concealed the interior of the café, the window of 1305 had a long crack at one corner, the For Rent sign tattered and torn and in between, the door for 1303 did not meet the frame evenly on all sides. Paint hung in brittle strips. The last number on the sign beside the door hung askew. Even in the sunlight, it appeared vile and wrong. Jason stepped up to the door, his hands in fists. This close, the red underneath the faded paint was pale.

Not fresh blood at all. But I am. I'm the fresh blood. The orderly-musician? Old blood.

The musician wanted the girl. He couldn't have her, not for anything more than a stolen hour or two, so he got her tattooed on his arm. And then she...what? Came out and pressed those perfect pink lips on his skin? He probably thought he'd died and gone to heaven, until he saw the hand behind her back and the sharp steel it contained.

Jason grabbed the door handle and pushed. The door didn't move. He pushed it again. The wood creaked and groaned but didn't open.

The street was empty. Deserted. He turned and pressed his left shoulder on the door and *shoved*. The door quivered. He shoved again. Paint flakes rained down on his shirt.

Come on, come on, come on.

He shoved again. The gashes from the griffin's talons opened and warm blood ran down his skin. Jason swallowed the pain. The door moved, but the lock held. He stepped back from the door. Dark, wet streaks of blood gleamed against the paint. Jason wiped away a trail of blood seeping below his shirt, avoiding the tattoo.

Because it came back. Of course. Where else would it go?

The knot slipped, and Jason pulled it tight.

I'm not an Alpha, but I have an Alpha knot, so it's okay. An Alpha-knot for an Alpha-not.

He sighed and propelled his body toward the door. Fear stripped the moisture from his mouth.

It will be a brick wall this time. I'm going to break my shoulder.

His shoulder met the door, and the wood squealed, shuddering against his arm as it gave way and he fell into the building, onto his arm. He yelled aloud, scrambled to his feet, and pushed the door closed. His heart thudded in his chest, but the knot held.

Just me, my knot and I.

The staircase, a shadowy shape ascending into darkness, was just as narrow as he remembered. He stepped up onto the first step, and the wood bowed from the weight. Bowed, but held. He kept his hands close to his body as he walked up the stairs. His footfalls were loud, and his shoes left prints in the thick dust. The only prints. The design on the swirling wallpaper was faded and hung in long strips in several places. No moving faces, no tiny, grabbing hands. The combined stinks of mold, mildew and disuse clung to the air, worse than he remembered. Pain slid down his left arm and made his fingers tingle.

Jason counted the steps. An old, yellow newspaper lay across the fifth step. A laceless boot, the leather cracked and pitted, rested on the eighth. Small dark pebbles, possibly rat or mouse droppings, piled at one end of the tenth. The wood of the eleventh had splintered. Thirteen steps in total. A perfectly normal number. A *wrong* number. Jason peered over his shoulder, and the steps went on forever. No bottom landing. No door. He closed his eyes, and the smell grew even stronger.

This is crazy. Just leave. You don't need to be here.

Jason opened his eyes.

Yes, I do. I want answers.

The door at the top of the staircase stood open a few inches, revealing the black room beyond. Not gray and shadowy like the staircase but pitch black. Dread black. He pushed it open, ignoring the shake in his hands. It gave a loud creak, but only opened halfway. Some of the light from the hallway seeped into the room. Dust coated the floor. In a few spots, the warped wood showed through tiny swirls where small, inhuman feet had scurried around. He pushed the door all the way open and stepped inside. Pale light pushed through the grimy windows. Light enough to see the water-stained walls and wallpaper shreds in far worse condition than the paper in the hallway. A wet, noxious smell hovered in the air, almost thick enough to see. Cobwebs hung from the ceiling like old lace.

Jason sighed, and the sound echoed off the ruined walls. The last time he'd stood in the room, the bright light turned the walls gleaming white. A normal person would be shocked. That person would run away, unable to comprehend the truth before their eyes, but Jason wasn't surprised. A dark shape took up one corner of the room—a curtain. Inside his chest, the cold knot lost its shape.

My nightmare. The faces. All behind the curtain.

"Stop," he said. His voice broke the stillness, enough to take him above the panic. He padded across the dusty, warped floorboards to a spot on the floor not quite as unused as the rest, a spot with four odd, square shapes in the dust, as if from the legs of a chair.

The white room isn't here now, but it was. I think it comes back. Just like the door.

The curtain hung in tatters, a scrap of old, moth-eaten fabric. He had to look behind it. It didn't matter if the knot untied itself completely. His legs moved as if his feet were caught in quicksand, each step harder than the last. Finally, he stood only inches from the threadbare curtain. A small, skittering noise, quick and low, shattered the quiet. Beyond the curtain.

Something there.

He pushed the curtain aside, ignoring the dampness against his hand, and yelped when a small brown mouse raced out between his feet. A quick bark of laughter slipped from his lips. The hallway past the curtain loomed long and narrow with a tall window at the far end. More cobweb veils. The dust on the floor broken only by the mouse's trail. He stepped forward, his foot sending up a billow of gray. He sneezed twice, then walked down the hallway. The webs reached down, like ghostly arms, and brushed his cheeks.

Halfway down, a door stood open. He took two steps into the room, just enough to see a filthy sink, the porcelain chipped and stained brown, the mirror above cracked in a starburst pattern. No water remained in the toilet bowl, its interior stained darker than the sink, almost black. A large clump of paper towels where a bathtub once stood. Bloody paper towels. Old blood. Not his.

Jason left the bathroom and walked to the dust-caked window. He wiped at the surface with the side of his hand, and a small band of sunlight crept in. Dust motes swirled and twisted in the pale column of light. He went back down the hallway to the curtain. He'd wasted his time. Answers weren't hidden in the building, the room, buried under the dust. He should've gone to the hospital instead. How hard could it be to find an orderly, especially one with a pinup girl tattoo? The girl obviously didn't kill him. And that whistle? He didn't sound unhappy to be alive. Far from it. An image from the dream tugged at the back of his mind; when he tried to grab it, it slipped away with a small peal of laughter. Dark laughter. The front door leading out to the street slammed shut, and Jason bit his lip to keep a shout inside. The knot skittered away.

His mouth went dry, but sweat broke out of every pore on his body. It darkened his shirt and stung when it ran into his eyes and the cuts on his arms. His hands tightened into fists, reopening the cuts on his right hand. His chest tightened. A tiny drop of blood slid between his fingers and dropped to the floor. A tiny puff of dust rose around it.

Why did I come here? Trapped now. I'm trapped.

A smell grew in the room. Stronger than the mold and mildew. Ashes and smoke. The temperature rose. Fresh sweat dripped down his back. One footfall, then another, heavy and uneven.

He's here. He came back.

A soft, vile chuckle that held darkness and pain. A growl. A quick, animal squeak, then the smell of burned flesh and fur.

No way out.

A bead of hot sweat ran from under his scalp to his neck. Anger, hot and heavier than the footsteps, raced in and he shoved the curtain aside. "What the hell did you—"

The words dried up. Another drop of blood fell to the floor, spreading out in an oval, bright red amidst the gray. The door no longer stood open, but the room held nothing more than dust, hanging cobwebs and the charred corpse of one small mouse who had investigated the wrong room. The fiery heat left the room, slinked out like an overly dressed woman sneaking out of a house on a Sunday morning, all makeup smears and stiletto heels. A drop in temperature sent a chill down his spine.

Not here. Never here.

Bullshit.

The smell of ash lingered, though. A thin wisp of smoke hovered near the ceiling, gray and oily. It wrapped around the dangling end of a shredded web, rose up and out, then vanished. Jason took a step toward the door. The floorboards tilted like the deck of a ship on a stormy sea. He scrambled to keep his balance. Dust rose, filling the room with a cloud. He took another step and another, surrounded by the sour smell of his sweat. His fear.

It can't do this.

The floorboards heaved and sent him back two steps for every one. He reached out and his palm met the slick, slippery wall. A salt tang filled the air, sharp and biting. Voices, many of them, called out commands.

"Secure the rigging!"

The voices were rough, edged with excitement but not worry. Waves crashed onto the deck, but they'd seen worse than this storm. Their ship had seen worse. Men ran back and forth, securing lines and fighting to stay upright as the ship tossed on the sea like a child's toy.

"Batten down the hatches!"

A soft spray of water touched his face, and another roll of the floor pushed him down to his knees. The small body of the mouse rolled to the opposite end of the room. The floor shifted again. The mouse rolled closer. He struggled to stand, dizzy and confused.

"The storm's a nor'easter! Blowing in hard."

Another pitch and sway, and Jason fell back to his knees. The sea roared, lightning pierced the dark sky and men scrambled on the deck. Men with shirtsleeves pushed up and tattoos, some homemade, some from foreign ports, decorating their skin. One sailor, with a light in his eyes, laughed and climbed up the tallest mast, moving fast.

The first Sailor. The real one. A hard man who'd spent most of his life on the water, the ocean his only love. Ink lined his arms, some by men in ports with names he could not pronounce. The sailor climbed until he could go no farther and hung above the ocean with his head back, laughing at the sea. "Come and get me, you bitch!"

His laughter went on and on as the storm raged in chaos around him. Jason pressed his palms on the

deck

floor and pushed up. The floor rolled and pitched heavily to the right. The dust spun in mad circles. His foot landed on something small and soft that gave a quick crack, then a violent heave to the left sent him spinning. He struck the wall with his right shoulder, shrieking out loud as the wound split and pain shuddered down his arm.

I have to get out of here. Out of this room. Out of this storm.

The sailors, fearing neither the sea nor death, called out to each other. Words of encouragement and excitement, fueled by adrenaline. The floor pitched again and Jason stumbled, grabbing at the wall for safety. For anything. The wall flexed under his hands, flexed and softened and tried to pull him in. With a shout, he pushed off the wall and staggered toward the door. Another roll of the floor sent him back several feet. Laughter, Sailor's laughter or a sailor's laughter, echoed off the walls. He waved at the thick cloud of dust. It moved like a living thing, obscuring the door. It filled his nostrils. It traveled down his throat, burning. He coughed and breathed in another filthy mouthful. Tears streamed from his eyes.

"No," he shouted and thrust himself forward, toward the space where the door should be. The ocean roared. Angry, demanding waves crashed upon the deck. Jason reached out, and the floor gave way again. His fingertips brushed against the door. He spread his fingers and curled them around the doorframe. The floor lurched to the left. He gripped the frame tighter and rotted wood splintered under his fingers. Blood dripped down his arm, so much blood. The sharp smell of metal. The burning fire of his arm. The doorframe slipped from his hands. The floor rolled again, and his left shoulder met the center of the door. More pain.

Laughter and the sound of an ocean gone mad behind him. The dust burned in his eyes and lungs. He reached down again and grabbed the doorknob just as the floorboards rose again. His bloody fingers slipped, but he held on. The

deck

floor writhed under his feet. The dust clouded his sight, and a wave of heat, stinking of salt water and seaweed, pushed against his back. Jason twisted the doorknob. It didn't move. He tugged and twisted. The floor rose, pushing his body to the right, but he did not let go. He pulled again and groaned in frustration when the floor lifted once more.

The sailors laughed and called out to each other with sea-roughened voices. Jason took a deep breath and exhaled a mouthful of dust. The floor moved under his feet, the angle even more pitched. His hands slipped on the doorknob as his body lurched to the left. He grabbed the frame again with his right hand and the knob with his left.

Don't forget, the door opens in, not out.

With a shout, he twisted the doorknob and pulled. The sailor on the mast cursed the sea again and laughed, then he called out Jason's name.

"Come on, boy. A little swim will do you good."

Jason clenched his jaw and pulled the door. It gave one horrible squeal, then opened, crashing back against the wall. In front of him, a huge wave of dark water rose up, too high to be real. It climbed higher than the ceiling, higher than the building. He opened his mouth and the wave crashed down with a roar. Hot air rushed over him, filled with the stinking reek of dead and dying things. Jason reached out, grabbed the other side of the doorframe, and as the floor lifted again, pulled his body forward and out. His feet skipped a step, and he crashed into the wall above the stairs.

The sailor laughed one last time. The door slammed shut. Jason's knees gave out, and he sank down against the wall. His arms were streaked with dust and cobwebs and blood. His left arm burned; his right screamed in agony. The silence of the hallway wrapped him in its sanity. No ships, no ocean, no sailors. The back of his shirt stuck to his skin. He raked his fingers through his hair, dislodging a long cobweb strand, thick with dust. His Alpha knot gave a little tug.

Still with me?

A tiny hand touched his cheek—a wallpaper hand. The Alpha knot unraveled. Jason lurched to his feet with a sob behind his lips. He took the stairs down two at a time. When he stepped over the thirteenth stair, the door, the front door to the real world, was still far away. An ache grew in his chest.

Fifteen steps.

The sob broke free.

Nineteen.

The door receded farther away. His feet barely touched the steps. He rushed down, skipping two, skipping three.

Twenty-seven steps.

Not right, there are thirteen. I counted them.

Small voices whispered. Trapped in the walls, in the horrible paper. They pleaded with him, but Jason ignored their cries.

None of this is real. Just another one of Sailor's games.

Thirty-five.

Impossible.

The door receded, then faded into a brick wall. Far away.

Thirty-seven.

The brick faded and the edges of the door mocked him with its changing proximity.

Forty-three.

I'll never get out.

Forty-nine.

Jason ran. The door loomed up, suddenly there, and he skidded across the bottom landing. He reached for the handle

it won't be there, not now

and his fingers touched metal.

The door pulls in, don't forget.

His hands, desperate for the real, the safe, remembered. He stumbled onto the street, bending over with his hands on his thighs as he gasped for air. Tears, snot and sweat dropped onto the pavement, and he spat out a huge glob of gray phlegm that tasted like seawater. A knot tightened in his chest, but it wasn't the Alpha knot. The knot exploded into pain. Jason staggered across the street. He coughed up more phlegm, got in his car and locked the door behind him. A glance in the rear-view mirror revealed a stranger's face, streaked with dust and grime. Sticky, half-dry blood matted his arms. The sky was purple, not yet full dark, and he turned on the car and flipped on the headlights.

The sky had been clear and bright blue when he walked

broke

into 1303. Now twilight hovered at the horizon.

It can't be right. I wasn't there that long.

A low, ominous laugh drifted through his open window. The door to 1303 still hung open. Beyond the door—blackness, like a dark mouth. The laugh again, then a shape hovered in the open doorway. Taller than a man. Two eyes, pale green. One eye closed in a wink, and Jason shattered the speed limit as he fled Shakespeare Street.

5

John S. Iblis shut the door and ascended the steps to his room. Smoke trails curled up from his fingers, and his eyes blazed. He entered the room at the top of the stairs, and as he strode to the center, something small moved in the corner. One small mouse who'd come out to sniff the charred corpse of his cousin, perhaps. He held out one hand, and the mouse burst into orange-red flame. It burned brighter and brighter until it was nothing more than a small pile of smoldering ash.

"That is what happens when you go into places you have no business going into," he growled. "You burn."

Chapter Ten

The Center of the Whirlpool

1

Once home, Jason peeled off his shirt and the ruined bandages beneath. The gashes on his right arm oozed blood in a slow trail. Cobwebs and dust turned his hair and skin gray. His cheeks were gaunt, his eyes drawn and filth was caked in vertical lines across his forehead. He opened the medicine cabinet, not wanting to see his reflection anymore.

Could this get any worse?

On the top shelf of the medicine cabinet, propped up next to a tube of toothpaste and his deodorant, a white card answered his question.

Why, yes, of course it could.

He didn't put the card on the shelf. It most certainly was not there when he left this morning, but it sat there now. A white card with raised black lettering. The name. The phone number.

John S. Iblis, Tattoo Artist.

The answer had been there the entire time. Why didn't he see it before? The guy from the shop in Maine had said, "*Different religion and all, but whatever. It's still funny.*"

Because I thought it was just a joke.

His name. His fucking name.

John S. Iblis.

I didn't see it because it's not exactly there. It's like the door on Shakespeare Street. You don't know it's wrong right away.

A joke. A grim joke.

John S. Iblis.

The voices from the dream came flooding back.

Father of Lies.

I don't even believe in him. How can he be real? It's all made up. God, the devil, the Bible. Just stories to keep people in line. He can't exist.

Jason gripped the edge of the sink, tight enough to turn his knuckles white, almost tight enough to still the shaking of his fingers. "He can't. I don't believe in him."

His father's voice, paper-thin. *"I don't think he cares much about that, son."*

Jason stared at the card. "You don't exist."

Heat bloomed in his left arm, and the griffin twisted underneath his skin as if it stretched like a dog. *Oh yes I do*, that stretch said. *I am very real.*

What does he want from me?

But Jason knew. He knew exactly what Sailor wanted. The orderly-musician with the pinup tattoo. The sailor, laughing like a fiend at the ocean. Who else? The homeless man with his bottle of rum. The snarling bear tattoo. The old man at the bookstore.

"Had a girl and she sure was fine," Jason said.

The song. *Their* song. All the same man. Except he wasn't a man at all. How many others? How many times had Jason seen him and not known? All with the same walk. The roll. Not the end result of a life at sea at all, but the result of forcing limbs into ill-fitting flesh. Yes, Jason knew exactly what he wanted. He'd laugh at the absurdity, if he could, but the laughter would turn to screams.

The tattoo wasn't just magic. It was *Iblis* magic. The devil was all in the details. Sailor had even said it at the shop. When Jason had signed the consent form, he'd signed a contract. "Dad tried to tell me, and I didn't listen." The fine print—the spidery handwriting underneath the print he thought he'd imagined—was a trick, but it didn't matter; he'd willingly signed his name, and the hanging coats of human skin in his white room not-dream had belonged to all the other fools who'd done the same.

Jason lifted his hand and reached out for the card. His fingers weren't shaking. They were convulsing in a mad dance of flesh and bone.

Don't touch the card.

His father's voice? His own?

"He wants my skin." Jason said and slammed the medicine cabinet shut. His gray face peered back. "He. Wants. My. Skin."

He opened the cabinet and slammed it shut again. The bottles inside danced and shook against each other. His voice rose. "My skin." He opened and slammed it again. And again. The door shook. The hinges squealed.

"You can't have it. It's mine," he shouted, slamming it shut one last time. The mirror shattered, and the door bounced back open from the force. Jagged shards of glass spilled down into the sink. One long piece remained on the door, revealing half his face, and he recoiled from his own eyes. He reached out, pulled the piece from the frame and dropped it in the sink where it broke into a dozen, smaller pieces. The white business card fluttered down through the air, far too slow to be a normal business card. It tilted to the right, then to the left

like the ocean, like the floor

and Jason snatched it out of the air, hissing at the paper's heat. He dropped it into the sink, and as it fell down onto the

bad luck, seven years of bad luck

broken mirror, a smell, like ash and cinder, drifted up and wrapped around him. Like smoke.

Like skin.

And what exactly did Sailor look like underneath his human disguise?

Jason shuddered.

2

After a shower, Jason ordered a pizza (because that's what people, normal people, were supposed to do—things like order pizza, go to work, hang out with friends) and turned on the television. He checked his cell phone. Six messages. He listened to them with no expression on his face. The first from his mother, her voice thick with tears and anger. Why didn't he tell her about Shelley? Why did she have to find out from his brother? He pushed a button, and the automated voice told him the message was deleted. The next message from his brother, calling to yell at him for not telling their mother.

Click. Delete.

Mitch, calling to say hello and that she missed him.

Click. Delete.

From Brian, a quick "Sorry, man."

Click. Delete.

Another message from his mother. "Please call me, Jason. The minister asked about you again, and I really think you should talk to him. Especially now."

He laughed. Sure, talk to the minister. Maybe he could introduce him to Sailor, and they could discuss good and evil, souls and skin. He could come over, sprinkle Jason's arm with holy water, and say a few prayers. Maybe perform an exorcism. Except the devil wasn't inside him

not yet

just his unholy ink.

Click. Delete.

And the last, an apologetic call from his boss. Everyone knew about Shelley, then.

Click. Delete.

The white card, no longer hot to the touch, sat on his coffee table, lined up next to the edge. He liked it where he could see it. A hint of smoke lingered in the air.

Even though it was late, he dialed Mitch's number, hopeful her voice mail would pick up.

"Hey."

She sounded tired. *More than I do.* "Is everything okay?"

"It's been a long day. I'm looking forward to coming home."

"Me too," he lied.

Unless I can't take care of Frank. Then I can never see her again. For her sake.

"What's wrong?"

"What do you mean?"

"Your voice. There's something definitely wrong. I can hear it," she said.

Yes, there's something very definitely wrong.

Jason's hand tightened around the phone. "My ex. She was killed."

"Oh my God. I'm sorry."

"She and Nicole both."

"Both of them? What happened?"

Frank happened.

"They don't know anything yet."

"Jesus, that's horrible."

Silence.

"I don't know what to say," Mitch said.

"It's okay. It's all a little strange right now."

An understatement.

"Mitch? Do you believe in God?"

"What?"

"God. Do you believe in him?"

Another silence.

"I believe in something. I don't think there's a man with a flowing beard sitting on a gilded throne, watching over us, but I think there's something more, something bigger. Why? Do you?"

"I've been an atheist since I was thirteen," Jason said, even though he wasn't so sure about that now.

"My brother was an atheist, too, even at the end," Mitch said.

"And the, the devil?"

Mitch laughed, a quick little laugh, and he could see her so clearly in his mind, it hurt. "No. I think the devil was made up to make people think twice about doing the wrong thing."

To keep people in line.

Jason reached out and slid the card to the center of the table. The scent of ash and flame flared stronger.

Nope, he exists all right, and get this. He likes to wear human skin, and he wants mine next.

He pinched the bridge of his nose and shook his head.

I'm still not sure how I can keep that from happening.

"Jason? Are you okay?"

"No, I'm really not. I will be, though."

I hope.

"I'm flying in Wednesday night. I'll call you when I land, okay?"

"Okay."

"I love you, and I'm so sorry. I know she was your ex, but still."

"I love you, too."

Jason disconnected the call and turned the phone over in his hand. Her words rang in his head. "*Made up to make people think twice about doing the wrong thing."*

I wish you were right. I really do.

What the hell was he going to do? Laughter, reed-thin and shaky, rose up in his throat.

Funny choice of words there. What in the hell am *I going to do?*

Mitch was coming home Wednesday night. It was Monday night. He had one day to figure something out, because he couldn't risk seeing her until the griffin was gone.

Jason dialed the number on the white card. A hissing noise buzzed in his ear instead of a ring. A strange series of clicks, like a clearing throat, then a message for him to check the number and dial again. He did.

"Come on, you son of a bitch," he said.

The phone clicked then played the same message. He dialed the number a third time and hung up when the clicking started.

"The parents of fifteen-year-old Alex Marshall are asking anyone with information regarding the missing teen to please contact Baltimore County Police."

Jason dropped his phone and whipped his head around.

"At this point in time, police are not calling his disappearance suspicious. Alex suffers from depression and has run away several times over the past few years."

A photo of Alex replaced the newscaster's face. A school photo, featuring unsmiling lips and sullen eyes.

I warned him. Why didn't he listen to me?

"I could help you kill it," Alex had said.

Had he tried to kill it on his own?

Three hard knocks sounded at the front door and Jason froze. Had Alex been found? If so, maybe the police were back. Maybe they'd found parts and linked it to Shelley's death. It didn't take a lot of stretch to the imagination to realize the common denominator was Jason—ex-wife, neighbor, strange animal bites, and, "Mr. Harford, we'd like you to come down to the station."

The knocks came again and Jason edged over to the door, his heart thudding in his chest. When he looked through the peephole, he laughed. His pizza had arrived.

3

Jason's cell phone rang after he'd thrown out the pizza uneaten. The display read *Unknown Caller*, and he smiled.

"You rang," Sailor said.

"Yes, I did," Jason said. "I know what you want."

"Perhaps. Perhaps you do. You should come down to the shop so we can discuss it."

"How do I even know you'll be there?"

"I will be here. You have my word," Sailor said, then chuckled and the phone went dead.

4

The door to 1303 Shakespeare Street hung open; Jason took the stairs two at a time, ignoring the tiny wallpaper hands as they brushed against his arms. The door to Sailor's shop also stood open, revealing nothing but darkness. He took a deep breath, swallowing his fear (Sailor could simply kill him, he was sure of that, but he was also sure he wouldn't, not yet), then stepped inside.

The lights of the bar were low, and shadows lingered in the corners. The neon signs in the front window flashed primary colors in regular intervals. The faces of the patrons all wore the same vacant expression. Dull eyes. Slack jaws. Hopelessness and despair.

Jason sat down in the closest empty booth; the slick vinyl seat gave an almost human sigh. He wasn't surprised. He hadn't expected Sailor to play fair. Music played in the background. An unfamiliar tune. No fine women at all.

Right where we started.

The sad fates of the unwary mixed in with the stale smell of beer. It should have given him comfort to know he wasn't alone but it didn't. Anger bubbled up. Futile, perhaps, yet it burned deep. The knot inside the anger twisted even tighter. He needed it here.

Sailor rolled in the bar, wearing a bright blue Hawaiian shirt, with a smile on his lined face. On anyone else, the shirt would appear whimsical. On Sailor, it looked macabre. He rolled over to Jason, and the patrons he passed shied away with terror in their eyes. When he slid into the seat opposite Jason, his green eyes sparkled with good humor. A great deal of it.

"Bartender," he called out. "A round for everyone. On me."

A patron in the corner lowered his head, sobbing.

"Well, well, well," Sailor said in his gravelly voice. "So you know what I want."

"Yes. I do."

The bartender brought two bottles over to their table. He kept his face downturned, but not far enough to hide the fear in his eyes. Taking a step back, he ran his hands over his protruding belly. His round face gleamed with sweat, his nose reddened with broken veins. The edge of a tattoo—a cartoon cat—peeked out from underneath his sleeve, and Jason bit his lip to keep in a laugh.

Did it kill all the mice in his neighborhood? Or did it hunt down the dogs first?

"Anything else, sir?"

"Just make sure *everyone* gets a drink," Sailor growled.

The bartender scurried away, wringing his hands. Sailor lifted the bottle to his lips, drained half the bottle with one swallow, and set it down with a loud clink. He belched and a cloud of air, stinking of beer and ash, rolled across the table. "Enlighten me. What do you know?"

Jason lifted his hand. "I know this place isn't real. This room is whatever you want it to be."

And I know if I don't hold it together, I'll end up screaming in the corner, ready for an extended stay at Club Sedation. I need to hold on tight to that Alpha knot like I'm a five year old and it's my mother's hand.

Sailor laughed, and the other patrons cringed in their seats. Jason put his hand back down on the table and fought the urge to grab the edge.

"You came through the door, did you not? Several times, if I am not mistaken. I would say that is real," Sailor said. "But you did not ask me here to talk about my place of business, did you?"

The cultured professor voice in the worn face was wrong. Horribly wrong.

"I know what you want."

You are remarkably calm, all things considered. I mean, look around. Does anyone look happy to be here?

Sailor leaned over the table. "Do you really?"

"Yes. I want you to take it back."

Sailor threw back his head and roared. He slapped his hand down on the table, and the bottles skittered across the surface; when he stopped laughing, he pulled a handkerchief from his shirt pocket.

Lift. Dab.

"That is a good one. Take it back," he mocked.

"Why not? You have plenty of others. You don't need mine."

I am not going to grovel. I am not going to beg. But I am not giving up my skin.

"Perhaps not, but you signed your name. It was all there in the fine print. You are mine. Your skin is mine."

"The fine print was a trick."

"They all say that. Sometimes life is not fair."

"You never play fair."

Sailor chuckled. "True. Never have, never will, but I have your signature." He pulled a piece of paper out of his pocket and shook it open. "See?" He pointed to the bottom of the page, where Jason's signature was scrawled below a long column of spidery handwriting. Jason reached out his hand. Sailor shook his head and pulled the paper away.

One of the patrons, a man with thinning hair and an overbite, scrambled out of his seat and ran for the door. Sailor turned his head. "Sit back down."

The man turned and raised his hands. "You lied to me," he said. His voice quavered but he held his chin high.

"Sit down."

"No, I won't. You lied."

Sailor flicked his hand, and a thin trail of gray smoke snaked out from his fingertips. The man backed up.

"Please, no."

"I said, sit down," Sailor roared.

As the smoke wrapped around the man's shoulders, he shouted and tried to pull away, but it pulled him closer and closer. He screamed and struggled, but the smoke held him in a vise.

"Are you ready to beg?"

I won't beg. Not ever.

"No, I, no, no," the man stammered.

"Then sit," Sailor said. His words were calm, made all the more terrible by the rasp in his voice. He flicked his hand again. The smoke unwound and sent the man spinning into one of the tables. He landed with his legs splayed and his head against one of the legs. He did not get back up, just sat with a slack jaw and heavy-lidded eyes. Sailor turned back to Jason and pulled out his handkerchief again.

Lift. Dab.

"Now, where were we? Ah yes, we were discussing my methods."

"Take it back."

"No." He leaned over the table and patted Jason's left arm "Cheer up, boy. You will have plenty of company."

"You can't have it."

"Yes, I can and I will. Eventually."

"No," Jason said. The knot slipped, just a little.

Sailor took another swallow of beer. "We could sit here all night. The end result will be the same. Now, you look like you have discovered a few painful truths. You are going to have a hell of a scar on your arm. Just try not to damage it too much. Please."

Jason gripped the edge of the table.

Sailor tipped the bottle in Jason's direction and grinned. "I take it your griffin has not been quite what you expected. A shame. It really was my best piece."

"It's a monster," Jason said.

"You chose it. I just gave it something extra. With your permission, of course."

Jason laughed. "My permission?"

"Perhaps the griffin will take your mother next. Or your brothers. Or those cute little nieces. They will make a nice snack. It does have a healthy appetite." He leaned forward and gave a lecherous, wet laugh. "Or perhaps, just perhaps, it will take that pretty little blonde. That would be tragic. Tell me, is she as good in the sack as she looks?"

You son of a bitch.

"Leave her alone."

Sailor waved his hand. "I do what I want. I think you have figured that out. The griffin will consume everyone you care about until you beg me to take it away."

"I didn't care about Shelley. Your griffin got that wrong."

"It is your griffin, boy, not mine. Consider your ex-wife a warning. I could tell it who to take next, but I will let it make that choice. I wonder how long it will take. I wonder how many will die a terrible, painful death. Imagine their fear, their absolute terror." He smiled. "You *will*

270

beg. On your knees, preferably."

"I won't," Jason said.

"You will. I promise you. You will beg me to take the griffin away, and I will. Along with your skin, of course, but you know that already, yes?"

I won't.

Jason laced his fingers together to hide the shake in his hands. "Why skin?"

"Why? Why not?" Sailor grinned. "Humans like to wear fur. I like to wear human. Perhaps they are not Gucci, but some are quite nice. Yours, for instance, will come in quite handy. You have a face anyone would trust." He spread his arms wide. "'And thus I clothe my naked villainy with odd old ends stol'n out of holy writ, and seem a saint, when most I play the devil.' Shakespeare. Such a brilliant fellow. I do wish I had possession of *his* soul.

"Are you perhaps wondering about the whole soul thing? I have plenty of them, boy. More than enough for even my lifetime." He laughed and slapped his hands against his thighs. "They all sit around, moaning about my tricks and lies. Tiresome, boy, they are tiresome. And so easy. Everyone wants a million dollars or to be famous. Many people would give just about anything to make that happen. This is more fun. The same old, same old gets stale. When you have lived as long as I have, you have to come up with something new and exciting every few hundred years. I do think this is my favorite game so far. Much more inventive than convincing people I do not exist, and that in itself was sheer brilliance, if I do say so myself.

"And the best part of this game is that I get to walk around. It is far more pleasant topside, even for me. The weather in my own neck of the woods is so predictable. Hot one day, scorching the next. It is bad for the skin, no pun intended. I rather enjoy the chaos my artwork provides." Sailor smiled, then spoke with a British accent. "It is a good bit of sport, after all. Jolly good. Tell me, would you want to wear the same thing every day?"

He stood up and the bar shifted, walls melting into puddles of molten brick. The patrons screamed and shrieked as the center of the floor fell away, revealing a deep chasm. Heat, reeking of rotted flesh and burned hair, poured from the gaping hole. Jason scrambled out of the booth and stood as far away from the chasm as possible. The heat burned his lungs with every breath.

Sailor opened his arms. His laughter vibrated through the room, alive and cruel. Strands of smoke flew out from his fingertips, curling around the patrons and lifting them up. He dropped them into the chasm, one by one, and laughed as they fell. Flames roared up from the pit, but the sound could not muffle the screams.

When only he and Jason remained, he turned his back to the chasm and rubbed his hands together. "I believe it is time for your griffin to go hunting."

Jason clamped his fingers over his arm.

"Fool," Sailor said. He snapped his fingers together, and Jason staggered as the griffin exploded from Jason's arm in a golden-bronze blur. It flew in lazy circles, its wings making long, graceful arcs. The room filled with its musky smell.

"Leave us," Sailor said. "Enjoy your freedom. Enjoy your hunt."

The griffin flew over Jason's head, gave a lethal hiss, then disappeared through the space between the window and the frame.

"It is a beautiful creature. You chose well. Now, let me see your arm."

"What?"

Sailor sighed. "Your. Arm."

Jason shook his head and stepped back. Sailor cocked one eyebrow and reached forward. He grabbed Jason's right arm, just above the wrist; his fingers dug in, and heat burned all the way up Jason's arm. Fire ants, chewing at his flesh. Flames, charring his skin. Sailor laughed again and let go.

"Much better. No more of this nonsense, please. I prefer my skin unscarred."

"You will never have my skin. Never," Jason said.

"You are boring me with all of this. You have already discovered you cannot kill the griffin. What will you do? Kill yourself? Go ahead. Your skin will still be mine. Face it, boy, you have lost this game."

"I will find a way."

"Good luck with that. Are you really that naïve? That stupid? I think perhaps I should show you who you are dealing with."

His skin rippled. No, something rippled *underneath.* His real skin, not the sailor suit. Through the skin, scabrous flesh and an inhuman face shifted into view—a nightmare of scales and fissures. He shook his arms, and the human coat slipped off his shoulders.

No. Oh, no.

Jason couldn't help it. He screamed.

The face. Oh God, his face.

Sailor held out his hideous hand. "Give me some skin, boy." He roared with laughter.

No more.

Jason ran for the door. Sharp rocks dug into the soles of his bare feet. He slipped and staggered but didn't look back. The door wavered.

Just an illusion.

Sailor's laughter echoed, louder and louder.

The door swung open.

"You will be back. I promise you. Everyone comes back."

Jason ran through the door. Hot air turned cool and rocks turned to wood. The hallway. The door slammed shut behind him, but Sailor's laughter followed him down the stairs and out through the main door. When he got in his car and locked the doors, he covered his face with his hands and tried to forget Sailor's face. His real face.

His right arm burned. He took his hands away from his face and pushed up his sleeve. The bandages hung like strips of flesh, the open wounds gone, replaced with flat, pink scars. Fresh scars, the skin slick and shiny. The cuts on his hand were healed as well, with only thin, pale scars in their places.

He didn't do it for my benefit, though.

"I won't beg. No matter what. I will find a way." The knot in his chest tightened.

Please let me find a way.

5

Jason's bedroom filled with the gloom of an approaching storm, all shadows and gray. Appropriate weather, yet he wished for sun. Sunlight would make it a little more bearable. Jason flexed first his right arm, then his left. Of course Frank had returned while he slept, slinking back into his skin like a thief in the night.

"I'm going to find a way to kill you, you son of a bitch," he said.

I am not going to end up in that pit, screaming along with the rest of them. I'm not.

Jason checked his phone as he walked downstairs. His mother had called again, back to angry this time.

"Dad, I'm really not doing so well. If you wanted to give me a hand or something, I would appreciate it."

"Sorry, no more hands. You're on your own kid."

"Yeah, sure. I'm strong on the inside. Sure I am. Dad, I have to tell you, I'm not feeling so—"

He stopped just inside the kitchen. "Oh my God." The phone dropped from his hand and slid across the floor in a crack of metal and plastic. In the center of the kitchen table, atop the last index card the kid

Alex, his name was Alex

left on his window, sat an eye. A human eye, complete with the optic nerve intact. Even in the clouded light, the sclera appeared very white. It stared at him with silent accusation.

You knew and didn't do anything. Now look at me. All that's left is this. I'm dead and it's your fault, all your fault.

Jason held out his hands, fingers splayed. "Stop shaking," he said. "Stop, stop, stop." He couldn't panic. Not now. The eye could belong to anyone, anyone at all. He grabbed a trash bag, wincing at the loud slap of plastic as he shook it open. "Had a girl," he sang, his voice wavering. His heart beat a mad rhythm as he walked over to the table, dragging the bag behind him. "And she sure was fine. She was fine, fine, fine."

He reached out, then pulled his hand back. "I can't. She wasn't fine, she wasn't fine at all." He took a deep breath. A smell, high and rottensweet, filled his mouth and he gagged. "You're enjoying this, aren't you, you son of a bitch."

The bag at his side made a series of small, slithery sounds in his trembling hand. "Had a girl, had a girl, had a girl," he whispered as he walked back to the table and pushed the card to the edge of the table. The eye wobbled but stayed on the card.

Just a marble, that's all it is. Not an eye at all. Right, Dad?

"Okay, I can do this. I am fine, fine, fine." The foul stink in his mouth stuck to his tongue. After he shook the bag open wider, he slid the card over the edge, and it dropped into the bag with a wet plop. "I don't see you anymore. You don't see me."

6

The clerk at the home improvement store had a tic. Every few seconds, the corner of his mouth would lift up, revealing yellow-stained teeth, and the movement lifted his cheek in a one-sided grimace. He glanced at Jason, then lowered his eyes and rang up Jason's purchases.

A small thump, a nudge in his left arm gave Jason pause. A small *I am still here* message from the griffin, not painful, but a very clear reminder that something lived and moved inside him. Something not him at all, but a dark and terrible child using his arm for its womb, waiting to make its way through his skin in an obscene pantomime of birth.

The gardening spikes jingled when the clerk dropped them into a bag, but he was careful with the propane torch. The axe gave him pause. He looked up, his mouth lifted, and he shrugged. "You know how much it is? No price tag."

Jason swallowed hard, shaking his head. "No, I didn't look, sorry."

It doesn't matter. If one of these things doesn't work, I won't be around to worry about the bill anyway.

Another thump in his arm, but only a slight push. He rubbed his arm, and under his palm, the skin stretched up. The edge of a wing, or a leg, or the top of its head? Unless Jason took off his shirt, no one would notice. His fingers shook as he pressed his hand down. The small lump of skin pushed back. He pushed harder, and the griffin slipped back down even more.

The clerk's face twitched again as he called for a price check. While they waited, he picked at a scab on his arm.

Thump. A little harder. Insistent, but not painful.

Stop it.

"That's a big axe. You chopping down a tree or something?" the clerk asked. His face twitched.

Jason flexed his fingers as several quick thumps in his arm sent pins and needles all the way down. "Something like that."

Please call him back with the damn price. Frank isn't supposed to come out during the day, but I don't think he cares anymore.

"It's sharp, you better be careful. My uncle cut off part of his foot with one of them things."

Twitch.

"I will be."

"Something wrong with your arm, mister?"

Jason pressed down on his arm again. The griffin pushed back, the warmth from its body seeping through the thin veil of flesh joining them together. Keeping it in. "Just a muscle cramp, that's all."

"I hate those. I get cramps in my back. The pills my doc gave me make me tired, so I can only take them at night."

The griffin pushed hard, and Jason took a deep breath. "I'm sorry to hear that," he said between clenched teeth. He dug the heel of his hand in. His skin rippled as the griffin rolled out from under the touch. What if Frank decided to come out and have a snack?

"Looks like it's a pretty bad one."

Sailor's words echoed in his mind. *Your skin is mine.*

Jason shuddered. Pain raced down his arm as the griffin scraped talons on the inside of his skin in a gruesome caress. "It'll be fine," he said, forcing out the words.

The phone rang, the clerk listened, muttered, "Thank you," then hung up.

Twitch.

A steady rhythm of thumps this time, like a drummer pounding out the grand finale. His skin rippled again, faster, and beads of sweat ran down the back of his neck. He pulled his hand away, fighting not to shriek. After he paid, he lifted the axe over his shoulder, picked up the other bags, and headed for the exit. The griffin gave a huge push.

Patience, Frank. It's not time yet.

As he raced across the parking lot to his car, rain began to fall in a soft mist, but the sky, a dull gray filled with churning charcoal clouds, promised more.

7

Jason drank three cups of coffee, ignoring the griffin's random pushes. His skin rippled and rolled in a series of waves, visible even through his T-shirt. The griffin moved inside like a mythical sea monster floating beneath the surface of a dark lake. It didn't need to remain still or secretive any longer. It wanted him to feel it sliding beneath and stretching up against his skin, ready to emerge from the depths of sinew and bone. When it fluttered its wings, his arm quivered, a slithery, damp sensation that stripped the moisture from his mouth and left a sick feeling in the pit of his stomach.

The rain fell harder, crashing down on the roof with wild intensity. The sky darkened from dull gray to blue-black. Jason turned on every light on the first floor. Although it didn't banish all the shadows, it helped. Frank kept pushing away in his arm. He emptied the contents of the bags out onto his kitchen table and stared at everything for a long time.

He would not beg Sailor to take the griffin away. He would get rid of it himself, and his skin would be his own again. If nothing else, he had the axe. Even if he died in the process, it was worth the risk. He was not going to be a human coat hanging on the devil's coat hook.

The griffin thudded in his arm, pressing into the muscle. Jason could see it in his mind: green eyes flashing, chest raised, talons outstretched. It waited and hungered and soon enough, it would break free.

Jason opened a bottle of whiskey and took a quick drink. It burned like liquid fire, but if it worked for Civil War soldiers, it couldn't hurt. Of course, he couldn't drink enough to make himself truly numb, but it was better than nothing. He pulled out a bottle of rubbing alcohol and stopped with the bottle in mid-air. How many others had tried this? He knew he couldn't be the first. He had no idea how many people had Sailor's tattoos on their skin.

He remembered all the screaming, skinless faces he saw in the chasm. Hundreds? Thousands? Were there more? Thunder crashed, loud enough to send the bottle skittering out of his hand. He grabbed it just before it struck the floor.

Sailor didn't like the marks on his arm, but Jason was going to give him a few more. If Sailor didn't like it, he could show up and stop him.

"What the hell," Jason said, and drank another shot of whiskey.

When he wiped his arm down with alcohol, the griffin gave another sharp push. Jason picked up one of the gardening spikes. It had a knobby flat top and ended with a sharp point, like a giant ice pick. He gripped it in his fist, and his cell phone rang.

"Shit." He dropped the spike. It bounced off the floor with a metallic ring.

He took the phone out of his pocket with shaking hands. Mitch. She would leave a message. If he heard her voice, he might falter. It would be too easy to pretend this was all a bad dream or a horror movie. And if he did that... He pressed the ignore button and flipped the phone over. The battery came out easily, and he tossed both phone and battery on the table, a table that looked like it belonged in Dr. Frankenstein's lab. All he needed was some needle and thread and a few spare body parts.

"Coming up. Sorry, Frank."

Another crash of thunder, louder, and the rain danced chaos on the roof. The knot in his chest tightened. Jason took a deep breath, picked up the gardening spike, and shoved it in his arm, right in the middle of the tattoo. A strange heat spread out from the spike. Warm, tingling. Not pain. A runnel of blood, as thick as

a spike

his finger ran down his arm, a fat, lazy river of red.

No turning back, now. I'm changing the rules of the game.

The pain hit and Jason collapsed to his knees.

Oh God, oh God, oh God.

Fire in his arm. A burning pillar of fire. He clenched his teeth to keep the screams inside.

But oh God, it hurts.

The blood ran faster, spilling down his arm in a waterfall. The spike stuck out of his skin like a tombstone. His fingers twitched. A flash of lightning brightened the kitchen, turning his blood from deep to vivid scarlet. Muted hissing vibrated up from under the skin. Frank wasn't happy. No sir, Frank was not happy at all. The spike moved in his arm, moved up and out, wobbling as it rose, and the pain burst into a bloom of roses. A bouquet of thorn-tipped roses. The spike wiggled back and forth, back and forth, and the hissing grew louder. His fingers shook and shimmied. The spike leaned at a sharp angle, then clattered to the floor, followed by a spray of blood. A fountain of blood.

Jason pressed his palm to his arm. Red seeped out between his fingers, and the kitchen filled with a rich, metallic smell. Bright and sharp. Frank moved under his skin, a mad shift of position, the talons pressing against Jason's skin for one quick moment, sharp even under the layers of flesh binding them together and separating him from the outside. Pins and needles, spikes and razors, raced from under his palm down to his dancing fingers.

A huge chunk of concrete replaced the knot inside his chest. Jason pulled his hand back and slid down to sit on the floor, staring at the ragged, round hole in his arm. A gaping mouth of pain and gore. And on the inside—raw flesh, bands of pink muscle, yellow globs of fat, and a slight shimmer of bronze fur. A mere suggestion of shape, faint but there. Hiding within the tendons and bone.

Very slick, Frank. Good thinking.

Jason had pushed the spike into the center of the tattoo, but he hadn't injured Frank at all. Frank had moved out of the way, connected by flesh, but protected by the same. Spots of light danced in front of Jason's eyes as he pulled himself up to standing with his right arm. Blood flowed down his left and dropped to the floor in small, dark puddles. He pushed the gardening spikes out of the way.

Connected by flesh, but bound together by ink.

He picked up the propane torch.

I can do this. I will do this.

The Alpha knot wasn't his father. It was him. The new improved Jason Harford. The old Jason would have been crying in the corner, staring at the propane torch in horror. He might not be a real Alpha now, but he felt hard enough. Strong enough. Strong where it counted.

And mad. Don't forget that. A little dash of craziness sprinkled on top.

Maybe, but performing a little self-surgery in the kitchen was no worse than watching Frank climb out of his arm. No worse than tossing Shelley's hand in the Chesapeake Bay. A little more painful but no worse. He didn't care how much it would hurt. Sailor would not win.

"Do you hear that, Sailor? You will not win." He lit the torch and turned the knob until the flame glowed a small blue inch. "Here we go."

Jason brought the torch close to his skin. The fingers of his left hand kept their rhythmic tremble. Beads of sweat broke out on his forehead. The torch slipped a little in his hand, and he gripped it tighter. Destroy the ink and slay the griffin? He hoped. With his lips pressed together in a thin line, he touched the flame to his skin.

A thick, roasted stench filled the entire kitchen. Charred flesh and heated blood. Smoke rose in gray spirals. The Alpha knot shouted in pain, but it kept the pain locked inside and urged him on. He moved the torch along the edge of the inked wing.

Roasting meat. It's just roasting meat. Barbecued Jason with a side of griffin.

The skin sizzled and bubbled and turned black. Inside the hole, Frank shifted and hissed and retreated deep inside. The flesh of his arm rose and fell with the griffin's crazed path as it avoided the flame. Jason shoved the flame inside his skin.

"Got you now. Got you now. Got you now."

The Alpha knot slipped. Pain flooded in from his arm and his back, just below the shoulder blade. Jason shrieked and pulled the torch away. A tendril of dark smoke rose up from his ruined flesh. He turned off the torch and let it fall to the floor. The skin throbbed and ached and burned; underneath the char, it bubbled and melted. Jason collapsed onto the floor, his mouth and nose filled with the smell, the taste of it. He rolled onto his knees, scrambling to grab the torch.

Frank, not so good old Frank anymore, roared under his skin, and twisted. Tears, stupid, weak tears of pain raced hot trails down his cheek. He grabbed for the torch. His skin rose with an ink blur until it became a foreleg, and Frank shrieked in poisonous anger, the sound emerging with distorted amplification from the hole in his arm. The talons swiped across Jason's cheek, but he didn't stop. Blood ran down, warmer than his tears. A huge peal of thunder shook his house. He screamed in rage and frustration as his fingers slipped off the torch. The foreleg swelled and grew.

I have to get it before it comes out.

From kitten size to cat size to dog size and still, it kept growing.

Almost, almost, almost.

His fingers slipped and slid, then grabbed. And the foreleg, impossibly large now, reached out and up and swung. The torch spun away from his hands. A bolt of pain shook Jason from head to toe, brighter than the throbbing pain in his arm. Dark spots blurred his vision, gray specks of storm. The waves rushed up and pulled him down. Down into the dark. Down into nothing at all.

8

Swirls of gray. A distant voice. A hand shaking his right arm. The darkness gathered him back up, his eyelids fluttered, but the hand shook his arm again. "Jason, wake up."

He opened his eyes and blinked. Gray clouds, pale and ghostlike, moved overhead. The sky shimmered with a dull haze. Not blue but yellow. Sickly, sad yellow. Hospital yellow.

"It always was a pain in the ass to wake you up, son."

"Dad?" Jason whirled around. His father stood several feet away, draped half in shadow, half in the dingy light. A blue cooler sat open on the dry, brown grass, next to a grill with hot dogs sizzling on the grates. "Am I..."

His father shook his head. "Dead? No, you're not."

"Then where am I? What is this place?"

"It's nowhere. Just someplace you made up in your head."

"But you're here."

"Never mind that. We don't have much time. Things are pretty bad, but I'm sure you know that."

"What do you mean?"

"You'll remember soon enough. Just stay focused, okay? Stay strong."

"I'd rather stay here with you," Jason said. Because something horrible waited for him beyond this place. Something sharp and hurtful. And there would be blood. Lots of it.

His father sighed, and his breath smelled of old dirt. "I wish you could, Jason, but that's not how this works. You need to finish what you started."

"I don't know if I can."

"Of course you can. Just be careful with that arm."

Jason looked down. A thin tendril of smoke curled up from the blackened skin. Underneath the char, the flesh appeared pink-raw and oozing. A sick feeling climbed up to the back of his throat, and he looked away.

"I saw it, you know. I saw it come out of your arm. It looked right at me."

Jason put his head in his hands and remembered. "I know. It's all my fault. If I hadn't—"

His father held up one hand. "What's done is done. You need to forgive yourself. You didn't know. How could you? But now you need to go back and finish it. Don't give up. Don't let him win. Do whatever you have to do."

His father shimmered; his skin paled and turned gray, translucent, like smoke.

"Dad, wait." Jason took several steps forward, arms outstretched, closing the distance between them.

"Whatever you have to do, okay? And don't forget about the fine print."

Just as Jason reached, so close, his father's voice faded to a faint whisper. Then he slipped away, leaving behind a vague shape, like dust motes drifting in a patch of sun. Then that, too, vanished. Jason grabbed the empty air. "Dad, come back. Please," he said.

The hot dogs burned, pushing out a thick smell.

No, it's me. My flesh. My skin.

A cloud of smoke rose from the grill and moved toward him, alive and angry. Jason scrubbed the tears from his eyes as it whirled around him, tornado fast with a rushing noise like a scream.

"Son, go. Go

9

now."

Pain, like acid eating into the flesh of his arm, brought him out of the dark. A weight on his shoulder like a stone—his Alpha knot. No, it wasn't the knot. It moved and hissed and blew hot, stinking breath in his face. The griffin. Halfway out, halfway in, the space between the two a blur of ink and scorched flesh.

Jason opened his eyes, blinking away the tears, and rolled on his back, dislodging the griffin from his chest. Fresh pain exploded in his back, below his shoulder, and he rotated his body. He reached inside for his knot, but it didn't help. Too much pain.

He turned his head and laughed, harsh and brittle. "Good old Frank, not so good anymore, are you? You're not even supposed to be out yet."

The cat-sized griffin struggled to break free, too hurt to climb all the way out, too angry to hide back inside. The head, chest and forelegs pressed their weight on his arm. It hissed again. One of its ears was black and smoking. His skin stretched, the skin turning to feathers as the wings emerged, one whole and healthy, the other charred and ruined. As ruined as his arm. Black, stinking skin riddled with cracks. Clear fluid oozed out between the cracks, like tears. Pieces of his skin broke away under the griffin's talons. Ripped away.

Jason sat halfway up, and pain stabbed through his skull. A wave of dizziness poured over him like rain, teasing and threatening to pull him back down.

No.

He tried to flex the fingers of his left hand; they didn't move, but another bolt of pain shot from shoulder to wrist. The griffin glared at him with green eyes gone dark with pain. Its breath came in ragged gasps.

The propane torch rested at the base of the cabinet below the sink, a million miles away. He used his right arm and dragged himself across the floor, now slick with blood. Pain screamed in his back, and something warm and wet ran down his spine. His arm was a column of sharp, stinging pain.

The griffin shifted and grew, its weight tugging his shoulder down. Jason pulled himself another six inches, and the griffin hissed in his ear, its breathing labored. Another swipe of its talons sent fresh blood down Jason's neck. The torch, only four feet away, beckoned. He pulled again, and his palm slid in a small puddle of blood. His right shoulder bloomed with pain as he fell to the floor. The dizziness came again, stronger.

No. Can't pass out, can't pass out.

He rolled onto his hands and knees, dragging the griffin with him, like a hell-born tumor, small but malignant; his left arm buckled at the elbow and he pitched forward. His head met the tile with a loud thump. Stars doubled his vision—two cabinets, two torches, two Franks.

He raised himself up with his right arm. The griffin dug its talons, like small knives, into his left, and Jason shrieked. He pulled himself forward another few inches. The griffin grew again, heavier on his arm; it twisted the talons in his skin. Fire screamed in his arm. Hot and stinking. Pieces of charred flesh dropped to the floor, like black rain. His vision darkened, and he dropped down onto his right shoulder. More pain.

His eyes fluttered shut, then a loud crash of thunder filled the kitchen. He pushed himself back up and pulled. He dragged his burned, useless arm and the griffin behind him like a gruesome toy on a pull string. Everything turned to a blur in front of him, but it didn't matter. His elbow buckled again, but he stayed up. He dropped his head down, and the griffin stretched itself a little larger. Somewhere Sailor was laughing. He knew it. The griffin moved and shifted.

"Come on, Sailor. Don't you want to see what I've done?"

Frank hissed and shifted, then slid back into his ruined arm. Outside, the storm raged on. Jason struggled to his feet. He staggered to the table and sank down in the chair. He grabbed the bottle of whiskey, took a large swallow, and winced as it burned its way down. His stomach clenched and twisted.

Dutch courage. Just a little Dutch courage.

Another drink. The pain in his arm and back receded, turned from agony to dull throbs. A horrible smell seeped out of the burned flesh. Rot and ruin. He pushed the whiskey bottle out of the way, next to the blue propane canister, lifted the axe and balanced it on the edge of the table. He'd never chopped wood, but it couldn't be hard. He couldn't live with Frank forever. Their partnership had definitely crossed into hostile territory.

You're stuck with him unless you do this. Unless you want to go back to Sailor and beg.

Jason had the feeling Sailor would make him beg for a long, long time, and it wouldn't matter; he'd lose his skin in the end anyway. Sailor would put on the Jason suit and toss the rest of him in the pit. The smell of the room rushed over him, a horrible memory of screaming faces. Pain. Fire. No, he did not want that at all. The axe was razor sharp. It would take one swing. He hoped. Jason grabbed his left arm and stretched it out across the table. The pinkie finger

286

twitched. Once. Twice.

He sighed and lifted the axe as high as he could without moving his left arm. He couldn't swing it, so he'd have to let it drop on his arm and have faith it would hit hard enough. Hope again. Was it enough? The knot of ice in his chest thought so. His arm shook under the weight.

"Shit."

The handle. He'd bought it because it had the biggest blade, but the handle was too long. When it dropped, it would bury itself in the table, not his arm. He dropped his arm and the axe and shimmied his hand up. Too much of the handle stuck out at the end, throwing off the weight, and it shook in his hand.

Don't worry about the weight. Just let it fall. The weight will help.

He wasn't sure.

I should have tested it out. I should have tried it before.

He didn't raise the axe, just let it hang from his hand.

But you didn't. Suck it up. Stop this shit and drive on.

He lifted the axe, and a key turned in his kitchen door with a quick metallic snick. The axe slipped from his hand and dropped to the floor as he whirled to his feet. He stumbled, grabbing onto the edge of the table to stay upright. His left arm slapped down against his side, and a hot spike of agony pushed him down to his knees. The door opened. Mitch walked in and all the color drained from her face.

"Jason? Oh my God, what happened?" She raised her hands and took one faltering step forward.

He held up his right hand. "Don't come any closer, Mitch. You have to go. It's not safe."

"You're hurt." She reached into her pocket and pulled out her phone.

"No," he yelled. He lurched to his feet and swung his hand. Her phone went flying across the room and shattered against the counter. "You have to go."

She shook her head. "No, you're hurt."

Frank gave a soft little thump. Jason took a deep breath and tried not to think about the pain.

"I'm fine. You need to leave."

She looked down at the axe and back up to his face. "You are not okay. Are you drunk? What the hell's going on? What happened to your arm?"

Frank pushed again. The pain swept up and black flakes of burned skin fell down.

"I'm not drunk, but you have to leave. Right now. Go."

"Bullshit," she said crossed the distance between them. She touched the side of his face. "What happened to your arm?"

"There's no time to explain. You need to get the hell out of here."

"Not until you tell me what's going on."

He laughed and his words flowed out in a rush. "Fine. The devil lives in Baltimore. Not just a guy who thinks he's the devil, but the original badass himself. He likes to play games, see?"

Mitch staggered back against the counter. "Jason, stop—"

"And one of those games is with ink. His tattoos aren't just ink, though. They're real and they come out after dark and eat things. This one ate a few of my neighbors' pets. I thought it was the kid across the street, but—"

"Stop—"

"It wasn't. He told me tattoo removal was a specialty and it is, except I have to beg him to remove it. When he does, he takes my skin, too. He likes to wear them around. I mean, he can't exactly go outside as himself. He showed me what he looks like underneath. It's not pretty—"

She stepped forward, shaking her head. "This is crazy—"

"You wanted to know. I'm telling you. I'm not going to beg him to take this away. I'm going to do it myself. You really need to leave so I can finish it. Frank isn't going to stay inside much longer. I can feel him, underneath. Inside me."

But not just inside. A part of me, too. Twins born of darkness, trickery, and ink.

"Jason, I—"

His skin bubbled up, and the griffin exploded from his arm with a blur of ink, feathers, flesh and fur. It roared, the sound swallowing up Mitch's scream, and landed, cat-sized, with a heavy thump on the table.

"Get out!" Jason yelled.

She stood immobile, her hands raised. The griffin hissed as it jumped off the table; true to its nature, it landed with grace, its muscles rippling under the amber-gold fur. Jason grabbed the axe and moved in front of Mitch. If he had to kill the griffin and himself to protect Mitch, he would. The griffin lifted its head and roared again. It expanded and grew. The scent of its dark animal musk covered the smell of burned flesh completely. The size of a small dog, then larger. German Shepherd-sized. It flapped its good wing. Frustration flashed in its eyes as it lifted its chest.

It can't get any bigger. It's too hurt.

It moved forward, dragging its ruined wing and swung one taloned forelimb. It sent the axe spinning out of his hand and hissed in triumph. The good wing flapped and pushed air against Jason's face. The bad wing hung at an odd angle, the dark bronze a mess of black and char. It cocked its head and looked at Mitch with blazing eyes of green fire. It opened its beak and hissed again. It stalked closer, then away with hate in its eyes. Its back paws thudded on the floor.

It's playing with us. It can't kill me either, but it wants Mitch. I see it in its eyes.

The propane torch sat close to the edge of the table. Closer to them than to Fr—

the griffin.

It's not Frank anymore. It never was.

"Mitch, when I move, get the torch from the table and light it."

He moved toward the griffin. It raised one talon and growled. Mitch grabbed the torch and lit it, lightning fast.

"Hand it to me," he said.

He lifted the torch and turned the lever to adjust the flame. Mitch stiffened against his back as the griffin advanced with a hiss.

"Stop," he said.

The griffin turned its head and fixed one eye upon them. It took another step forward, flapping its good wing, and Jason lowered the flame close to his arm, close enough to feel the heat. The griffin growled but did not move closer.

"Can you reach the axe?"

She bent down behind him. The griffin moved closer. Too close. Its rancid, hot breath burned Jason's eyes.

"No, I can't reach it," she said.

"Shit."

"Okay, give me the torch back."

"What?"

"I'll distract it."

"No way."

The griffin moved away, flicking its tail. The ruined wing twitched.

"There isn't another way," Mitch said. She stepped around him, grabbed the torch with both hands and wrenched it away from him. "I don't know what you're going to do, just do it fast, okay?"

She took two steps forward. The griffin lifted its chest and hissed. It advanced. Jason turned, grabbed for the axe. It lay on the floor, half under the kitchen table and half out, close to the doorway between the kitchen and dining room. He bent under the table, pushed a gardening spike out of the way and reached out.

Mitch shrieked in anger, and pain flooded his left forearm. Huge blisters appeared on his skin. He reached out again. Too far away.

Mitch yelled again. Blisters broke out on the first two fingers of his hand. The axe was too far away.

No. Please, no.

Mitch cried out in surprise and stepped back into him. He banged his head on the edge of the table. The griffin was too close now; he couldn't reach the axe. Mitch bumped into him again, and he came down hard on his right palm, his thumb touching cool metal—the gardening spike.

Mitch cried out again, in pain. Jason picked up the spike. The griffin growled, and another bite of pain gripped his back. Deep pain accompanied by the thick smell of roasting meat.

Jason shoved the spike in his arm just above the elbow and dragged it across to the other side, using it like a knife. Blood poured down his arm and pain, brighter than sunlight, screamed in his skin. The rich stink of char and blood rose up and out of his arm.

"No, no," Mitch shouted.

Sailor will not have my skin. He will not wear my skin.

Jason moved the spike faster, tearing through skin and muscle like a knife through softened butter. All the way to the inner edge of his arm, then up, through the charred skin. Harsh grunts slid past his lips, dark, animal noises, but he didn't stop. Another flare of pain, on his leg. His hand shook, but he didn't let go of the spike. It tore through the skin. Almost to his shoulder. Over and then down. Down to the first cut. A rectangle.

Mitch sobbed. "Jason."

He threw the spike down with a shout and reached his fingers in the top cut. The skin slipped out of his grasp. He dug his fingers in hard and tugged. Pain like fire. A wet squelching noise. He pulled. The skin lifted. He ripped it down.

Tearing fabric. That's all. Just fabric.

All the way down to his elbow. Mitch shouted incoherencies. The griffin roared. The last bit of skin caught and held, and with a shriek of his own, he wrenched it free.

"You want my skin, you son of a bitch. Here, have it," he shouted.

The skin dangled from his hand like a wet glove. His arm screamed fire and razor blades and barbed wire. A wave of gray flickered across his eyes and he shook his head.

No, not yet. It's not done yet.

Jason turned and rose. Mitch held the torch out like a gun. "Give me the torch and get behind me," he said.

The griffin staggered from side to side. Its eyes rolled wildly back and forth, but it advanced. Its hiss held wild fury. Jason held out the dripping skin and lifted the torch. The griffin raised its head and opened its beak. No sound emerged. He held the flame close to the bottom of the skin. It blackened and charred, sizzling as it burned.

Jason dropped the skin on the floor but didn't take the torch away. The skin blistered and shriveled. A thick, noxious smell poured into the room. The smell of war. Of a thousand bodies trapped in a burning building. Jason gagged but didn't stop. Mitch covered her mouth and nose with her hands. The griffin writhed from side to side with its beak open. Its talons flailed, the tail whipped back and forth in frantic arcs and its eyes dulled to a green haze. The griffin shrank down smaller and smaller until it was the size of a kitten. It turned in on itself and flattened, quivering and shaking on the floor like a possessed playing card. The kitchen filled with the sound of rushing wind, a high-pitched scream that built up and out and ended with a loud tearing noise. Then silence.

The griffin was gone.

10

"Well, well, well. You have made quite a mess here."

Jason dropped the torch; he and Mitch whirled around in unison. Sailor stood in the doorway, dressed in his sailor skin, the doorknob a misshapen twist of metal with a trail of smoke rising up from the keyhole. "You do not mind that I dropped by without calling first, do you?" He shook his head. "Did you really think you would win this way? Others, many others, have tried the same. I like the torch, that was clever. Unfortunately, not clever enough."

"I don't need you to take it away anymore. The game is over."

Sailor held out a piece of paper. "I still own you, body and skin. You signed the contract of your own free will. Those are the rules."

"I don't think so."

"I might, however, consider a trade. Perhaps I could take this lovely woman in your place."

"No."

Sailor threw back his head. Mitch covered her ears as his laughter pealed out. Sailor crossed the room and grabbed Jason with both hands. "I told you I prefer my skin unscarred," he said. Heat pushed its way inside; Jason's arm burned as the skin knit itself back up. "Perhaps I should try it on for size." The sailor skin slipped off into a pile of fabric and flesh, Mitch screamed and Sailor drew one finger from the center of Jason's neck down to his groin. Jason collapsed to his knees as pain radiated out from his arm to every inch of his body— horrible, tearing pain. He looked up.

His own face looked back.

Two images—a whole Jason with wrong-colored eyes, a bleeding, raw Jason with right-colored eyes. Mitch backed away from both of them, her hands over her mouth, muffling her shrieks.

The wrong Jason, a Sailor-Jason, turned his head in her direction and grinned, then a gravelly voice emerged from his lips. "Nothing quite like the feel of a new suit. How do I look?"

The right Jason watched in horror; Mitch screamed again behind her hands. Sailor-Jason stepped to her side with short, awkward steps. "It will take a bit of time to break this one in," he said and stroked Mitch's cheek with a hand that rightfully belonged to Jason.

Sailor turned around. "Oh dear, that must be terribly painful.

Here, try this one. You cannot keep it forever, of course, but it will keep you warm." He flicked his hand, and the sailor skin flew up and over—around—the not-Jason.

Jason recoiled and fell back into the table. A stench poured over him in a wave—ashes, scorched earth, rotten flesh somehow still alive, and underneath it all, the salt tang of the ocean. He took a step forward and stumbled. The skin hung loose on his frame, an ill-fitting coat of horror.

"Be careful, boy," Sailor said. "That is one of my favorites. At least it was. I could get used to this one." He touched Mitch's cheek again.

Jason took another step. "You can't have her."

Sailor grinned, an expression turned macabre as the skin stretched across inhuman cheekbones. "Are you still clinging to a pretty fantasy that you have any control, boy? I will do what I want, when I want."

Jason stepped forward; the skin bunched at the ankles like a father's suit on a child's frame, and he fell. When he put out his hands to soften the impact, his raw flesh

no, not flesh, but what's underneath—unflesh

slid against the sailor skin. He moaned aloud behind lips that tasted of smoke and despair. As Sailor's laughter rang out again, Jason tried to pull off the terrible skin, but it wouldn't budge. Then his

no, not mine, his hands, Sailor's hands

met the rough edge of paper. The contract, the fine print, tucked away in the pocket of the sailor shirt and forgotten by the Sailor-Jason as he wrapped his arms around Mitch and pulled her close. Jason tried to grab the paper, but it slipped out of his grasp, sliding off the flesh dangling from the edge of his fingers. He grabbed a second time, pushing hard against the shifting skin as he pulled it from the pocket, angling his body away from Sailor and Mitch.

It fell from his hand, swaying back and forth to land on the floor by his feet. He dropped to his knees and pressed one palm against one half of the contract, holding it in place as he grabbed a free edge. Mitch

294

screamed, the sound cut off, and he ripped. A corner from the paper, a small, triangle-shaped piece, came loose. The skin around him shook and quivered. He tore another piece; the skin vibrated.

"What do you think you are doing?" Sailor roared.

Jason ignored him and lifted the paper to his mouth.

I'm taking care of the fine print, you son of a bitch.

Using his teeth, he bit off another piece and spit it out. The sailor suit slipped from his shoulders, his arms, his hands, taking the paper with it. "You will not win," he said, pawing through the rumpled clothing and skin, holding back a scream as the raw unflesh of his fingers burst into hot jolts of pain. He found the paper, lost it again as the scalp fell back, covering his hand, then found it again. "You will not win!"

Sailor stalked over with his rolling hips-before-legs walk and shoved him away. Jason's body exploded in agony, but he crawled over to the sailor skin. Sailor batted him away, a cat playing with a mouse, smiling a warped Jason-grin.

Jason pulled himself up, ignoring the pain. He ran forward, ducking an arm still wearing his real flesh. He stumbled, twisted around, righted himself and bent down. Sailor moved forward. Jason lifted the sailor skin with both hands and threw it in Sailor's direction. The paper remained behind on the floor, tattered and bloodstained. Jason grabbed it and turned to face his own image, still wrapped around the wrong body.

Sailor reached out. "You cannot do this," he hissed.

Despite the pain, Jason ripped another piece free from the contract. "Yes, I can." He shredded the rest of the paper; the pieces fell from his ruined hands and burst into tiny flames before they reached the floor, turning the fine print into nothing but ash. Sailor grabbed Jason's shoulders. Jason grabbed back and pulled at the flesh, *his* flesh. "Give me back my skin!" he yelled. He dug his fingers in tight. The skin unfolded, peeled back, revealing the nightmare hollows and planes of Sailor's true face. Hands ending with curved, sharp nails pierced his exposed tendons, but Jason did not let go. Sailor's eyes bored into his, his hot, reeking breath pushed into Jason's face and his nails dug deep. Jason curled his fingers and pulled the rest of the skin free. Sailor's nails flashed like knives in the air, but Jason threw the skin to the side and moved his body in between.

"It is mine," Jason said. "Our business is done."

The air sucked out of the room with a dull pop, replaced with a pulsing heat. Both skins rose in the air—a tornado blur of Jason-Sailor-Jason-Sailor-Jason-Sailor, flesh swirling into and around flesh, flapping like empty bags caught in a dry wind that reeked of pain and torment.

Jason stepped back until he pressed into the wall. Sailor roared again, the sound stretching out into a hideous carousel squeal of horror. He faded, first into a shadowy, monstrous figure, then to a vague, misshapen outline, then into insignificance—nothing—taking the sailor skin with him. Something wet and warm wrapped around Jason's limbs—his own flesh settling back over muscle, fat, tendons and bone. The searing pain and heat vanished; the floor shook, then the air rushed back in with a wet, sucking noise.

Jason sagged against the wall. The smell of spilled blood, charred paper and burned skin lingered in the room, but he didn't care. He ran his hands over his arms and legs and face. The stink of Sailor remained, but underneath, his own smell pushed up to the surface.

Mitch moved forward, stopped, then moved again. "Jason, is it you? Is it really you?" she sobbed.

He closed the distance between them, wrapped his arms

his real arms, his own arms

around her, and pulled her close, breathing in the scent of her hair. "I promise, it's me. It's really me."

She pulled back, ran her fingers over his face, through his hair, and down his back, laughing and crying at the same time, then folded into his arms, her head resting just above his heart.

And they stayed that way for a long time.

11

Inside his shadowed room of screams, John S. Iblis roared, and every bit of glass on Shakespeare Street, from light bulb to windowpane, shattered.

Chapter Eleven

Land Ho!

1

The warm spring day settled on Baltimore like a sheet shaken over a bed. Fluffy clouds dotted a sky so blue it was magical. Good magic, not dark. The sun hung high, half hidden in the cumulus. The kind of day that sent painters and poets outside, filled with the need to capture the perfection on canvas or paper. A day filled with promise and laughter.

The air, carrying a hint of flowers and freshly cut grass, pushed across the face of the man kneeling by the gravesite. A handsome man, but not movie-star handsome. The kind of man you would want your daughter to marry, until you saw the shadows in his eyes.

His face wore the burden of a man at war, although he did not look like a soldier. A private war, perhaps. If you met this man in a bar, you might notice, if his shirtsleeve rode up, scar tissue on his arm. He might tell you about the way the skin itched late at night while he lay in bed awake. He might tell you about his nightmares. He might tell you a story, a story so terrible it couldn't possibly be real.

Or he might just smile, a sad half smile, and tell you about his girlfriend and the way her eyes almost took the darkness away. The way her hand slipped into his at just the right times, how her hair always smelled of coconut. And when he lifted his glass to take a drink and the bar lights shined in his eyes and you saw, *really* saw, the shadows there, you would be glad he'd kept the dark things to himself.

Later, while walking your dog or tossing the ball to your son in the backyard, you'd remember the man and shudder, even on a fine, warm day. His eyes were haunted, you might say to yourself. Later still, in bed with the sleeping body of your wife warm against yours, you might hear a noise, a small little creak of the stairs and close your eyes, praying it was just house noise. Praying it wasn't that man's nightmare coming to visit.

The man knelt for a long time, not speaking, not moving. The air tousled his hair, and when he stood, he rubbed his left arm, and a quick wince of pain flashed across his face. Then he turned his face into the breeze. His mouth moved and the wind blew his words out into the air like tiny living things.

It is what it is.

2

The man at the end of the bar was thin but well muscled. His forearms bore the faded ink of old tattoos, his eyes rimmed with red. He raked his fingers through long hair in dire need of a shampoo. John S. Iblis tipped a nod in his direction before he waved the bartender over.

"Please give that man another drink. On me." He tipped another nod to the man at the end of the bar and grinned.

He had plenty of skins, but there was always room for one more.

About the Author

Damien Walters Grintalis lives in a Baltimore suburb with her husband. *Ink* is her first novel.

www.damienwaltersgrintalis.com

It's the dawn of a new era...the year of the zombie!

AZ: Anno Zombie
© *2012 Peter Mark May*

Fire rained from the sky over Tucson that day. A dust cloud settled over the city. And the dead rose from their graves. Tom Hollinger raced to his ex-wife's place to make sure she and his son were safe. They weren't. Tom was barely able to save the boy from his undead mother. Now, surrounded by a city in chaos, Tom, his son and a handful of friends are battling their way out of town, desperate to make it to safety while the army of the living dead grows in number every hour. The world no longer belongs to the living. A new era has dawned...Anno Zombie!

Enjoy the following excerpt from AZ: Anno Zombie...

Outside the world was silent. The sand storms of the night before had obviously blown themselves out. Tom was drinking some apple juice out of the cartoon, when a loud crash came from his backyard. Cursing and dribbling juice down his stumble covered chin, he slammed the carton down on the kitchen counter. Wiping his chin with his forearm, he walked over to the back kitchen windows and pulled up the blinds.

He thought it might he the Jacobson's dog from down the street, but to his surprise it was a large dark skinned guy in coveralls. The guy had his back to Tom and was routing through the garbage bins.

"What the hell?"

Tom jogged back to his bedroom and pulled on his pants and t-shirt from the previous day. He kicked on some shoes and made for the door that led into his garage. After picking up an old baseball ball that he and Tommy used sometimes on visits to the park, he opened the back door of his garage and raised the bat up beside his head.

"Hey, what the hell you doing, man?" he called. The man was rooting through his garbage, like a hobo who had been on hunger strike. The unkempt man seemed not to hear Tom and continued to root deeper down in the trash. Behind the intruder there seemed to be an orangey-brown mist covering the rear of his yard; probably a dusty remnant of the slept-through dust storm.

The smell of the guy wafted over, invading Tom's nostrils, which flared with disgust. The trashcan hobo stunk like had crapped his coveralls and then cleaned them with six week old rotted meat and vegetables.

"Hey, numb-nuts, I'm talking to you," Tom shouted and prodded the bat into the back of the man.

The guy jerked upwards like the bat was a 100 volt cattle prod and with spasmodic twitches of his elbows and broad shoulders turned to face Tom. Or he would have, if the man had a whole face. The left cheek was dark brown with a touch of grey to it, but the other was gone, with only cheek bones showing. His scalp on that side flapped slightly as he jerked and twitched and shuffled his large booted feet towards Tom.

"Jesus, you been in an accident or something?" Tom asked and stepped back.

The man raised his grubby hands and aiming them at Tom's throat, lumbered closer. Revulsion and years of army training took over and Tom swung and hit the guy on the exposed bone of his cranium before he realized he was doing it. The guy's lower jaw shattered, hung for a second and then fell to the dirt floor in two pieces. Something like brown snot shot out of the guy's remaining nostril and down his front. He staggered for a second, and then, fixing Tom with his remaining milky covered brown eye, raised his hands once more.

Tom took another step back, planted his feet and swung like he was hitting a home run out of Soldier Field. This time the force of the impact on the guy's head caused the bat to break, but not before knocking the guy's head onto his right shoulder with a sickening crack. Tom, hands numb with shock, let the bat fall, as the man tottered two steps to the left. The side of his face was cracked open into an oozing mess of broken bone and the left eye socket was shattered, exposing the grey inner workings of his brain.

To Tom's astonishment, the guy steadied himself in his big workman boots and advanced towards him again with silent menace. The guy's scalp was now flapping up and down with every jerky movement like he was wearing a badly fitted toupee. Weaponless, Tom retreat back into his garage and shut and bolted it.

Not once had the man spoken, cried out in pain, or even grunted.

Tom was thinking about what to do next when two hands came punching through the mesh covered window panes in the rear garage door. The glass gouged deep cuts into the grey fingers of the attacker, the hands flailing about after Tom, who ducked out of reach. Then the arms bent down as if the guy was trying to find the lock, unimpeded by the injuries his arms were taking in the effort.

Once again old army training kicked in. Tom ran over to his cluttered workbench and ran his eyes over every tool, screwdriver and socket wrench there. Even the two hammers he owned seem wrong for the job at hand. The man began to tug at the screen and the thin wooden frames of the six now broken window panes.

Gulping down some rising bile in his throat, Tom finally grabbed something from a cobweb covered shelf. He raced back to the door as his attacker pulled aside enough mesh to reach in and get a grip the doorknob.

Tom had to avoid the man's grayish lacerated hand as he plugged in the long unused power tool...

Available now in ebook and print from Samhain Publishing.

Four centuries ago witch hunters killed the seven Yardley sisters.
Now Department 18 must battle...the eighth witch!

The Eighth Witch
© 2012 Maynard Sims

Four hundred years ago six of the seven Yardley sisters—all witches—were hunted down and killed. The seventh lived long enough to give birth to a daughter. Now, centuries later, that daughter has resurfaced in the town of Ravensbridge, more powerful than her mother or aunts ever were. She has honed her powers, can change shape at will, and has only one ambition—to bring her family back from the dead to seek vengeance against the descendants of all who slaughtered them. Ravensbridge once lived in fear of the seven Yardley sisters, but they have yet to experience the terror of...the Eighth Witch.

Enjoy the following excerpt from The Eighth Witch...

The young woman held the dress up to her slender body and stared at the reflection in the full-length mirror attached to the wardrobe door. Her cold blue eyes narrowed critically and she shook her head, her shock of long, blond curls drifting over her shoulders like a yellow cloud. No, it wasn't right.

The evening dress was purple silk, long enough to touch the floor, with thin shoulder straps and a swooping neckline. It was much too old for her, too sophisticated. She closed her eyes and concentrated. When she opened her eyes again the person that stared back at her from the mirror was older. The blond curls had been replaced by an elegant, dark brown, chin-length bob that shone in the electric light.

The haircut framed an older face—haunting chestnut eyes and a thin, aquiline nose above a full-lipped mouth.

That was better.

The body in the reflection was different too. It fitted the dress perfectly. Maybe she'd take the dress with her when she left the house, after she'd done what she'd come here to do. Maybe not. She hadn't come here to steal.

As she pulled open the wardrobe again to replace the dress, her eye was drawn to a cashmere sweater folded neatly on the shelf above the hanging space. It was a rich shade of burgundy and would really enhance her new eye color. As she reached up to slide it from the shelf, her sleeve caught an empty wooden coat hanger and dislodged it, sending it clattering to the floor of the wardrobe. She froze in mid-stretch, listening hard, waiting to see if the noise had attracted the attention of the one other person in the house.

There was no sound of feet climbing the stairs, no sounds at all apart from the low rumble of Leonard Cohen's velvet-bass vocals issuing from the stereo speakers in the lounge.

It was as well because she wasn't ready yet. She still had another wardrobe to search through before the act, as she liked to call it. She thought briefly about what she was going to do and flicked a hungry tongue across her full lips.

There was a small, delicious knot of anticipation in the pit of her stomach that never changed, never varied, no matter how many times she performed the act, and in whatever form it took. The sense of anticipation and the accompanying excitement remained constant...and she loved it.

Sophie Gillespie lifted her head and stared at the ceiling. She was sure she'd heard something—a rattling sound of wood falling against wood, as if someone had dropped an armful of kindling on a parquet floor. She listened hard, her hand reaching for the remote and reducing Leonard Cohen to a low grumble.

Not for the first time she had the feeling she wasn't alone in the house, but there was never any evidence to show she was right. She thought maybe she should go upstairs and investigate, but the truth was the house frightened her, always had. From the moment she and Mark moved in two years ago she'd been beset by misgivings. Not that she ever voiced them to her husband. Much to her dismay, he'd set his heart on the place from the first moment he'd seen it.

In her opinion the house was much too old, too big, too dilapidated and too spooky. Too everything. He'd brought in a team of builders and decorators to completely gut and renovate the place, and while it was now a smart and elegant home Sophie held on to her reservations. It was still too old and too bloody spooky.

Location, location, location. It was her father's favorite phrase when he got onto the topic of houses and, more importantly, buying them. For him, where it was located was much more important than what the house actually was.

"Houses can be fixed, Sophie. They can be redesigned, renovated, extended. Damn it, if you don't like it that much you can always pull the bloody thing down and build it again. But where it is, where it sits...that's the crux, the nub, the heart of the matter. That's something you can't change."

She could still hear his voice in her mind. Her father had approved of the location of this house almost as much as he'd approved of Mark and their marriage.

"He's got a good head on his shoulders, that one. He'll be a millionaire by the time he's forty." His enthusiasm for Mark was palpable. "Snap him up, Sophie, before somebody else does."

So far her father had been proved right. Mark still had four years to go before he reached forty, but he was already over halfway towards his first million and Sophie was sure that her husband would justify her father's high opinion of him. As for the house, in many ways, her father was right again.

Set deep down in Yorkshire's Calder Valley in the north of

England, surrounded by lush, tree-clad hills, it was the grandest house in the town of Ravensbridge. The walls were Yorkshire stone, the color of clotted cream, and the tiled roof was a rich slate gray. It was a picture postcard type of house, the type that, as a teenager and through into her early twenties, she would stare at for hours in the pages of glossy magazines and dream of owning. It was a bitter pill to swallow knowing that her dreams and aspirations bore little resemblance to the reality of actually living in one.

She pressed another button on the remote and switched discs. Maybe it was Leonard Cohen that was making her feel so gloomy. Cohen's bass tones were replaced by the mellow soul crooning of Marvin Gaye. *Better,* she thought. She leaned back on the sumptuous leather cushions of the couch and closed her eyes, letting the music transport her back to happier times.

The idyll lasted no longer than thirty seconds before the splintering sound of crashing glass made her jerk her head and stare hard at the ceiling.

The blond curls were back. They were much more suited to the Armani suit she was holding against her. Taupe. That was the color. It was elegantly cut and she could imagine slipping into the expensive fabric and letting it hug her body. That would feel good.

With a sigh she put the suit back on the rail and went across to the bed.

It was nearly time.

There was a water carafe on the cabinet next to the bed. She picked it up and turned it over in her hands, letting it slip through her fingers and smash on the antique oak floor. "Whoops!" she said quietly, and then sat on the edge of the bed to wait.

Sophie switched off the stereo and listened to the crushing, pregnant silence. She felt sick. She tried hard to rationalize what she'd just heard, telling herself that maybe a cat had gotten into the house and knocked something from a shelf, but she knew that wasn't the case, and she knew she'd have to go upstairs and investigate. She glanced at her watch. Three hours before Mark was due home. She couldn't even wait it out.

She sat for a moment more in a quagmire of indecision and then suddenly sprung to her feet. "Right!" she said, her voice loud, steady with resolve. "Let's do this."

She took a heavy, wrought-iron poker from the hearth and started to climb the stairs. As she climbed she strained every sense, listening, watching, even sniffing the air, trying to detect anything that was in any way out of place.

Nothing.

She reached the landing and stopped, her breath coming in quick, startled-hare gasps. The noise of breaking glass had come from the room directly above the lounge. The master bedroom, the room she shared with Mark. If only he were here. As she'd climbed the stairs she'd felt her resolve draining away, slowly, like water down a blocked drain. Now she struggled to get it back, to reclaim it as her own. She hefted the poker in her hand and stared hard at the bedroom door.

Her fingers tightened around the brass doorknob and she twisted it gently, twisted it until it stopped turning, and then, taking a deep breath, she hurled the door open and stepped into the room with an incoherent cry, the poker raised above her head.

The young woman with the blond curls was sitting on the bed, staring at her impassively. Her gaze travelled from Sophie's face, to the poker and then back again, locking on Sophie's wild eyes. "Hello, Sophie," she said in a lilting, almost musical voice.

Sophie's gaze took in the broken carafe at the young woman's feet. Her arm was beginning to ache with tension and with the effort of holding the heavy poker aloft, but she kept it steady. "Who are you?" she said, immediately infuriated by the pitch of her voice. She sounded like a frightened schoolgirl. She made an effort to adjust it. "What are you doing in my house?" Better—deeper, more mature.

The blond woman's eyes widened slightly. "Your house? Well that's an interesting concept. Your house." She said the words again, seeming to mull them over, to digest them. Finally she said, "How long have you lived here, Sophie? Oh, and you'd better put the poker down. It's very hot."

Sophie glanced at the poker. She'd pulled it cold from the hearth and carried it up the stairs, comforted by the icy metal in her hand. So why was the tip now glowing red and the conducted heat from the poker scorching her palm? She cried out and dropped it, letting it clatter to the floor.

"You were saying," the young woman continued. "Something about this being your house?"

"It is my house. Mine and Mark's. We've lived here two years now."

"And the people before you, the people before them and before them. They all thought it was their house too." She looked about the room. "Strange, I remember this house being built and I remember hating it because it was my house they pulled down to make way for it. Oh, it wasn't much, my house. A hovel. We used to bring the animals inside in the winter to keep them warm...to keep us warm too." She laughed, a harsh, brittle sound. "Christ, it stank!" The laughter ceased abruptly. "But it was home. This land, the land now occupied by this...this monstrosity, was our land, me and my family's. We still have rights. We still belong here."

There was a fervent light in the young woman's eyes as she spoke.

Mad, Sophie thought. *Absolutely barking mad.* A small thrill of fear shuddered through her. How was she going to get the woman out of her house?

"Oh, I'll leave in my own sweet time," the woman said, reading her thoughts. "But first we're going to have some fun. Would you like that, Sophie, some fun?"

Sophie nodded slowly, deciding to humor her. "Yes," she said. "I'd like that."

The young woman's gaze swept the floor, alighting on a shard of glass from the carafe. It was about four inches long, curved and wickedly sharp. "Perfect," she said and picked it up.

In that second, when the young woman was distracted, Sophie could have run, turned and dashed down the stairs and out of the house. But the moment passed and instead she watched, captivated as the woman retrieved the shard of glass from the floor and held it to the light, making it glint and glisten.

"Now, Sophie, I want you to do something for me."

"What?" Sophie said.

"Take off your clothes. All of them."

"Don't be ridiculous," Sophie said, but at the same time her fingers were fumbling with the button on her jeans. She popped the button and slid the denims down over her thighs, letting them drop to the floor.

"Good girl." The young woman smiled encouragingly. "That's good. And now the rest of them."

As Sophie pulled her shirt over her head, her mind was crying, *I don't want to do this!* But there wasn't a damned thing she could do to stop herself.

The young woman moved towards her, the glass shard clasped tightly in her hand, so tightly it had sliced through her palm and fingers. She seemed oblivious to the blood that dribbled from her hand and dripped to the floor where the oak floorboards were sucking it in.

Once Sophie was completely naked and standing shivering, cold and vulnerable, the young woman moved closer still.

Sophie cried out at the first cut, but after that she was silent, unable to do anything but accept her fate.

Available now in ebook and print from Samhain Publishing.

PUBLISHING

It's all about the story...

Romance

HORROR

www.samhainpublishing.com

CPSIA information can be obtained at www.ICGtesting.com
Printed in the USA
LVOW081325010213

318245LV00003B/81/P